HOUSE OF WISHES

Dandelion House, 1974: Two teenage girls — strangers — make a pact never to tell their secret. Calingarry Crossing, 2014: For forty years, Beth and her mum have been everything to each other. But Beth is blindsided when her mother dies, and her last wish is to have her ashes spread in a small-town cemetery. Nearby is Dandelion House Retreat. With her stage career waning, and struggling to see a future without her mum, her marriage and her child, Beth hopes it's a place where she can begin to heal. It's not; but after a fateful encounter with a local landowner, Tom, Beth is intrigued by his stories of the cursed centuries-old house. Tom has the answers, but will the truth help Beth? Or should Dandelion House keep its last, long-held secret?

JENN J. McLEOD

◆

HOUSE OF
WISHES

Complete and Unabridged

AURORA
Leicester

First published in Australia in 2019

First Aurora Edition
published 2020

The moral right of the author has been asserted

A catalogue record for this book is available
from the British Library.

ISBN 978–1–78782–466–9

Published by
Ulverscroft Limited
Anstey, Leicestershire

Set by Words & Graphics Ltd.
Anstey, Leicestershire
Printed and bound in Great Britain by
T. J. International Ltd., Padstow, Cornwall

This book is printed on acid-free paper

DEDICATION

Dedicated to my dad, Don Lewis, who could do anything. Just give it go and 'Boom, boom!' Love you and Mum always. xx

Also, to every dad and mum, daughter and son — the loved, the forever lost, and the found.

And, as always, to Jeannette (The J) McAnderson. The person who is always 'home' no matter where we roam.

EPIGRAPH

'Bricks and mortar make a house, but the
laughter of children makes a home.'
Irish Proverb

DANDELION HOUSE, 1974

Scribbled in a child-like fashion across the bottom of both pages are two unsophisticated signatures as distinctive as their owners.

Above them, in increasingly crooked lines, are their wishes.

But how can she — a stranger — grant them?

She is a part of their lives for a mere blink in time.

The substitute mother they scream for at the height of their pain.

The friend they cry with at the depth of their despair.

Sometimes, in a forgotten part of the cemetery, she is the person who weeps for them.

But she cannot play God.

Can she?

1

Forget-Me-Not, Western Sydney

Having waited in the wings many times in the past twenty-four years, poised to step onstage and play her part, Beth wishes *this* scene were make-believe, because the blur of tears suggests she is far from ready to face reality.

'Hi, I'm Beth Fallone,' she tells the suited young woman behind the reception desk. 'I realise it's late in the day. I somehow missed your message.'

The woman — girl really — stands and smiles.

'No worries. I'm Katrina.' She points with pride at her name badge before presenting a pen and a typed form clipped to a board. 'You need to sign and date,' she says while drawing the 2014 desk calendar closer, should Beth need a prompt.

She doesn't. Today's date is already etched into a memory that has collected far too many painful reminders in recent years.

'Take a seat if you like, Mrs Fallone.' A stilted arm indicates the adjacent room filled with spongy sofas and perfectly placed cushions. Bowls of wrapped mints and tissue boxes decorate several small tables, and the excessive floral arrangements exacerbate Beth's queasy feeling. 'If you need water, there's filtered — '

'No, thanks,' Beth interjects. 'I want my

1

mother, that's all.' Her tolerance isn't what it used to be and her surroundings are not helping.

'Of course.' The employee walks away from the reception desk and calls back, 'I'll get them for you now.'

'Them?' The mumbled word stirs a sour taste. *My mother is not a 'them'*. For forty years she's been *everything*.

She wants to scream. Instead, she surrenders her sleep-deprived body to a sofa and stares down at the typed form on her knees. Still sick with grief, somehow she's managed to survive the destructive hate-the-world phase when, for the first time in her life, she had wanted to cause physical harm to another human being. She could, surely. Despair can make a person capable of almost anything. A month on, less angry, Beth's determined to get this next step done — hopefully without taking her bad mood out on an employee who's simply following a well-practised script for what must be a difficult job.

★ ★ ★

When the girl returns, Beth's head is bowed, both hands cupping her ears to mute the melancholy music seeping from hidden speakers.

'Mrs Fallone? Are you okay?'

Beth looks up but doesn't think to correct her marital status. Such detail is unimportant when hanging from the girl's right hand are two . . . *gift bags*? Arm outstretched, she's offering them with a shop-assistant smile as though Beth

2

has snaffled a bargain pair of shoes. A thank-you hangs on her lips as she stands, but Beth can't utter a word with the significance and unanticipated heaviness of the parcels punching a final, devastating blow to her badly bruised heart.

Beth's immediate thought is to examine the contents. Why? What does she expect to find? Something to tell her this is all a misunderstanding, a mistake, a nightmare — one Beth never imagined finding herself in so soon. Then again, nothing in her life has stayed the course: not marriage, not motherhood, and not her childhood dream of stardom. Beth's greatest fan, the one constant in her world, is — was — her mum. Best friends more than parent and child, the pair regularly joked about living to ripe old ages, together in the same over-fifty-fives village. 'We'll liven the old buggers up,' her mother would say.

A strange noise pierces the silence and Beth realises it's her. She's laughing and crying all at once while spewing an apology over the employee. 'I'm so sorry. I'll be fine in a minute.'

Or never! Beth tells herself. At that moment, holding her mother in a gift bag, Beth doesn't know how she'll ever be fine again.

'This is all very new,' she tells Katrina, whose expression has shifted from practised sympathy to uncertainty. 'What I mean is . . . I wasn't expecting *this*.' She raises the gift bags and watches what's left of the girl's smile disappear.

'I-I don't understand, Mrs Fallone.'

Should she explain? Did the young stranger need to know that Beth Fallone — consummate

3

performer — is more familiar with the Holly-wood version of death and dying? Like when the movie director shouts *action* and powdery ashes dance like dust motes in beams of sunlight. Drawn towards heaven, the scene is supposed to offer hope and strange comfort to those left behind to mourn.

Grow up, Beth! she silently chides. At half her age, Katrina of Forget-Me-Not Funerals is more equipped to deal with reality, and more acquainted with mortality and misery. *And it's all your fault, Mum. You equipped me so well for life. Why didn't you prepare me for the inevitability of your death, or tell me how much it would hurt?*

Glancing at the two bags, Beth knows one thing. Her mum and Anton should be together, because for ten years they were never apart. She's also wishing she hadn't volunteered to collect both lots of ashes because the burden seems twice as daunting, twice as sad. As lovely as Anton was, Beth doesn't want to share her grief. Saying goodbye to her mother is hard enough.

'Hold on a minute, Katrina.' Beth inspects the label with her mother's name printed in sparkly purple pen to match the bag. 'Why are there two smaller containers of ashes in *this* bag?'

'Mrs Fallone, I . . . um . . . ' A red blush explodes over the girl's neck and cheeks. 'I'll get Mum for you.'

Before Beth can finish mumbling, 'Your mum can't help me', the girl has disappeared into a back room.

She sighs and collects her handbag from the sofa with her spare hand, but as she turns sharply and bangs her shin on the corner of a coffee table, an intense pain shoots up her leg. When she bends down to rub the spot, stars whirl, forcing Beth to sit again.

'I'm so very, very sorry for the confusion,' a voice says.

Beth hears words reminiscent of her mother, a chronic apologiser raised by religious parents — but when she stands, she sees a woman whose voice is as ethereal as her appearance: skin ivory, hair ebony, eyes cerulean, but with lips blood red.

'Hello, I'm Jesamiah Huckenstead. This should've been with your mother's ashes.' The stranger, dressed entirely in mauve and smelling like a life-size lavender bag, holds out an envelope. 'As you'll see, her wishes are very specific.' The woman is talking while walking a bewildered Beth back through the reception area, opening the front door wide to let her pass. 'Should you need to contact me, however . . .'

Beth glanced at the proffered business card:

Madgick & Associates — Trust Managers
In Madgick we trust.

'Take care of yourself, dear,' the woman says, letting the stationery and the envelope fall into the gift bag with the ashes. 'Have a good and safe trip.'

'Trip?' Beth repeats.

With her head spinning from the somewhat

rushed exit, both her hands busy with bags, and her gaze intent on the contents, it takes her a few seconds to look up. When she does, the woman is gone, the door sign flipped to CLOSED, and Beth is on the footpath outside Forget-Me-Not Funerals alone — utterly and desperately alone.

★　★　★

Back in her car, Beth eases the envelope open as if whatever is inside needs to stay contained until she's ready. The truth is, Beth is nowhere near ready for more surprises — good or bad. She's already said goodbye to her mother too many times: at both the hospital and the funeral service. Beth's not sure she can manage another farewell. Not yet.

These last weeks have been the cruellest. She's not only lost the two people who were her world, but her mum lingered for two weeks. Long enough to give Beth hope. When the doctors eventually asked, and Beth understood her mum's beautiful heart could stay beating in someone, saving another family from pain — the most difficult decision had been made a little easier.

A tear lands on the two notepad pages she's slipped from the envelope, but with barely a few lines above the scrawled signature, there's little ink to smudge. The page is headed *MY WISH*, while the other sheet is reminiscent of a treasure map, a childlike diagram with squiggles and symbols surrounding a circle at the centre. The envelope's contents pose two simple questions in Beth's mind. When had her mother prepared for her death? And why was she wanting half her ashes placed with her partner in a lawn cemetery of his family's choosing, but insisting her grieving daughter spread the rest in a country town Beth has never heard of before now?

'Why, Mum?' She slumps in the car seat, slaps the letter on her knees, and opens the Maps app on her mobile phone. 'And where the hell is Calingarry Crossing?'

2

Two weeks later

Still some distance from her destination, according to the last signpost, a flash of grey and a thud force Beth to brake. The suddenness sends her hatchback into a slide and the rear wheels into a ditch. Although the car — along with her scream — stops dead, it takes a moment to realise what she's done.

When the red dust settles and she spots the lifeless kangaroo on the opposite side of the road, Beth eases herself slowly out of the driver's seat. She knows to approach with caution, like when a lorikeet strikes her loungeroom window. If left alone, a dazed bird will often recover. Hopefully the kangaroo is only stunned.

She inches closer. 'I'm so sorry.'

Why didn't she see the animal in time to react? Why was she not watching for wildlife? There'd been no shortage of victims, with carcasses in varying stages of decomposition dotting the country road for kilometres. She should have been more careful. If only she'd driven slower.

The ICU doctor's muttering to his nurse echoes in Beth's head: *Ten kilometres per hour can be the difference between life and death. If the idiots had slowed down and driven to the conditions, this woman might not be fighting for her life.*

Beth's mum had been a cautious woman. She would have insisted Anton drive slow in the wet that night, and she would have seen the warning signs for Beth today. It's what she did: watch out for the people she loved, protect her only child and patch her wounds — the real and the emotional.

'Oh, Mum, why am I here?'

Intruding on the roadside silence is the *woosh* of wings and the cawing of a lone crow circling the lifeless kangaroo.

'No! Shoo!' Beth's shrieking proves ineffective as more birds appear, wary of the strange now-sobbing human with the flailing arms and a vocabulary that would put a truckle on a two-way radio to shame. For every bird she shoos, another shiny black scavenger lands, eager to pick at the dead or dying.

'No more, please,' she cries as hopelessness folds her legs at her knees and she drops to a squat to catch the rush of tears in cupped hands.

Though desperate to stay strong, like her mum insisted women should be, Beth has locked too much inside these last few years. *No more.* As her gaze skims the creature she's killed, the endless plains and empty road, she realises no one can hear her weeping out here.

The pity party for one lasts long enough to bring the entire outback's population of flies to the kangaroo, and to have the murder of crows gain enough confidence to edge closer. But Beth's now conscious of the failing light, the precarious angle of her little hatchback, and the vastness and isolation of the landscape. The road running north and south is an undulant ribbon of black between flat, colourless fields stippled with small shrubs, ancient fence posts, and two wonky windmills as motionless as the poor creature. Closer to the road, gum trees with towering trunks and sprawling branches cast shadowy fingers over the plains. In their grey grasp is a mob of kangaroos standing erect and wary. *Are they family?*

Keen to feast in peace, the crows close in, no doubt drawn to the exposed soft part of the creature's belly. Glancing one more time through teary eyes and mumbling a heartfelt apology, Beth is startled when the animal moves. She gasps and clears the blur of tears with a swipe of a shirt sleeve. There it is again — a ripple under the skin.

'You have a baby in there? Oh, no, no, please, no!' Another mournful cry erupts so violently, the dozen crows take flight. Why couldn't she have run over a snake or a fox? Why a national icon — the one with a pouch and a family? She has to do something. But what?

The crows regroup on the ground, while overhead, the territorial call of the kookaburra starts out soft.

'Go ahead! Laugh, you stupid things.' They're watching her crouch over the animal, even though she has no clue what to do. Is it un-Australian to know so little about the national emblem, except that it's depicted proud and strong on the country's coat of arms?

She stands to change position before squatting again and trying a different approach. 'Just get it

10

over with, Beth.' Accessing the pouch is tricky and requires two hands — one to stretch the opening, while the other feels inside. 'Oh, good grief!' She's clamped her eyes closed and is making strange whimpering sounds when a warm *something* wiggles against her fingers. Frightened, Beth yelps and falls back on her butt. 'Ouch!'

While brushing the sharp stones from the soft flesh of her hands, Beth recalls that the part-time nail technician — and self-proclaimed fortune teller — had jabbed at the spongy base of her thumb and said, 'Hmm, your Mount of Venus is unusually hard and flat.' She'd explained it was a sign of a person lacking family connection.

Beth's response had been to laugh and tell the woman as loopy as her earrings, 'You wouldn't say that if you knew my mum.' Ten minutes later, hiding in a shopping centre toilet cubicle and inspecting her palms and their supposed lack of meatiness, Beth had told herself the woman was whacko. There was nothing abnormal about her hands. *Nothing at all!*

'What bloody bunkum!' her mother had said the next day while deliberately hiding her own meaty Mount of Venus. 'Ignore the silly woman. You have beautiful hands and we have a wonderful connection.'

Beth's inspecting her beautiful but smarting hands pitted with gravel and the odd speck of blood when another burst of Kookaburra cackles prompts her to try the pouch again.

'All right! All right!' she calls back. 'Give me a minute. I've never done this before.' And she'd

11

rather not, but she can't walk away when there's the possibility of a little life in need of saving.

With the sun trekking rapidly towards the horizon, however, she must do this fast and get on the road before the day turns dark and more wildlife is on the move.

'Need help?'

A male voice shocks Beth to her feet and she spins too quickly, almost losing her balance.

'Whoa there!' He grabs her by the elbow, stopping her from hitting the ground a second time. She's not about to pass out, but she is sweating and her mouth is thick from too many takeaway coffees and too little water.

'Where did you come from?' She didn't hear the car approaching over the raucous kookaburra chorus, but it's right there, door open and parked near her hatchback on the other side of the road.

'Are you okay?' he asks.

'A little light-headed, but I'll be fine in a minute.' A nearby log is the closest thing to a seat, but as she tries to sit, he tugs her straight.

'You won't be fine if you don't look first.' He huffs, like she's a child being told for the umpteenth time, and Beth detects a whiff of alcohol. 'We never sit in the bush without checking a *Joe Blake* isn't sharing the same bit of ground. Snakes are rather partial to long grasses and woodpiles.'

When the man's grip relaxes, she eases herself down, grateful for the copse of shade-giving gum trees.

'Now, let's check out those hands of yours,' he says.

12

Beth jerks her arm away. 'There's nothing to check. My hands are perfectly normal, thank you.'

His head cocks to one side. 'They're bleeding.'

'Yes, well, forget about me.' She folds her arms, tucking both hands out of sight. 'The kangaroo is in a worse state.'

'She's an Eastern Grey, and I reckon there's not much we can do,' he says. 'I'll take care of it.'

It's then Beth notices a rifle dangling in his other hand. Her shoulders fall, trapping a sob in her chest. 'I wasn't speeding. I didn't see it in the shadows, but . . . ' She almost chokes on the lump in her throat. 'I-I think there's a baby.'

'Not uncommon,' he calls over his shoulder. 'The female Eastern Grey is almost perpetually pregnant, except when giving birth. Imagine that!' His prattle continues as if this situation is an everyday occurrence for her. 'The female of the species can freeze the development of an embryo until the previous joey leaves the pouch. That makes them pretty awesome mothers, in my book.'

Beth's heart aches. She would've made an awesome mum.

'I'm guessing you're a city girl,' he calls over the noisy squawks of pink and grey galahs squabbling over tree limbs as they flit overhead. 'Most locals know that when a roo takes on a car, there's rarely a good outcome. We can only hope it's fast and painless.' His words fade away, as if not intended for anyone else. 'Unlike those left behind.'

Peeling his shirt away to expose a white

13

T-shirt-type singlet over a taut torso, the serious stranger drops to his haunches beside the animal.

'You will do something, won't you?' What's she expecting? Floral arrangements and a full service followed by tea, scones and sympathy? 'I mean, we can't just leave it there.'

He smiles — finally — and it is kind rather than condescending. 'There's no helping this one, but by moving the carcass away from the road we'll be protecting the birds and other animals that would otherwise loiter too close to traffic while feeding. As for this,' he says, returning to the log where Beth sits. 'This is why it's important to stop and check pouches.'

'Oh, my gosh!' She instinctively cradles her arms to accept the tiny hairless bundle of mostly ears, feet, and a tail swallowed up by the swath of navy-blue shirt. Unstoppable tears spill onto her cheeks as the joey's nose twitches and two heartbreaking brown eyes stare up at her. 'Please tell me this one will pull through.'

'Probably old enough to be viable.'

'Viable?' She immediately regrets the censure. The man doesn't seem to notice.

'Worth the resources,' he replies matter-of-factly. 'The odds are never good with the tiny ones. Volunteers do what they can, but these days, with so many animals needing help for different reasons, there's only so much a team of carers can do. Don't worry. What can't be saved is euthanised humanely.'

When he bends over to pick up the rifle he'd left next to her, Beth identifies the smell on his breath. It's the one she used to detect on Richard when he blamed his late arrival home on everything from bottlenecks caused by broken-down cars, to the broken-down actors he claimed were taking up space when they should bow out of the business gracefully. Her ex-husband was a producer and a director, so giving actors a hard time was in his DNA. Beth doesn't miss being married. She's glad to be clear of Richard and the whispered casting-couch references. What feeds her melancholy these days is missing out on motherhood, on feeling needed, and on the bonding experience that comes from nurturing a precious baby into a little person. Beth's heart breaks a little more when the joey in her arms wriggles. She is no substitute for a mother's warm pouch.

'He has to live,' she tells the stranger. 'He has to. You saved him. I'm not sure I was mastering the rescue technique very well.'

'You tried. Many drivers can't be bothered, while some farmers think the best roo is a dead one.'

A chill rattles Beth as the man heads for his car. With the air cooling, she fears for the joey's survival. When he returns with a spray can of fluoro pink paint, rather than the rifle, she's relieved but curious.

'What's that for?'

He shakes the can. 'To any wildlife warriors passing by, a marked animal means a checked pouch.'

'I see, well, thank you for being a wildlife warrior for us,' Beth says, still perched on the log. 'We're very glad, aren't we, little one?' She fusses with the navy fabric, tucking a portion of

15

the shirt under the joey's chin before glancing up at the man. 'Have we kept you from anything important?'

His shrug is small, the smile that follows barely there. 'You might've done me a favour.'

'Oh?' She studies him, but there isn't a lot of his face visible under the wide brim of the tatty tan-coloured cowboy hat. What Beth can see suggests the man's younger than she first thought, with brown skin on muscular forearms, and tan moleskins stretched over similarly solid thighs. He reminds her of the swoon-worthy young dancer she'd worked alongside one season, whose favoured form of core strength training was horse riding in Centennial Park. Cowboy, as he called himself, would turn up for rehearsals in his hat, singlet and worn jeans still smelling of horse. Although not Beth's type, the guy was an amazing dancer.

'Where are you headed?' The man is standing over her now, his body blocking the ball of dazzling tangerine, soon to be lost.

'Oh, um, a place called Calingarry Crossing,' she replies. 'I believe it's near here?'

'Good, because you'll need a tow. I'll drive you into town.'

Beth hesitates. With her phone in the car, she can't check if there is reception to call for the breakdown service — if such a thing exists in the middle of nowhere. But no way will she get in a vehicle with someone she doesn't know, especially if he's been drinking.

'It's not far,' he says, as if sensing her hesitation, 'and I'd suggest getting this little guy settled. A stable temperature is vital,' he adds. 'He needs

16

a pouch as soon as possible.'

'A pouch? Do I want to know how you manage that?'

His gaze shifts from her eyes to her blouse, briefly. 'If you'll forgive the suggestion, the most immediate solution is down your top.'

'I beg your pardon?'

He shrugs again as if she should know. 'Without warmth and the beat of his mother's heart, this little guy will be fretting. Keep your shirt tucked into your jeans and open the top few buttons to make a pouch. Easy! I'll take the joey while you — '

Beth flashes a palm. 'I can manage.' If not for the concept of having a small beating heart against her breast, Beth might have found a sliver of humour in a situation that has her fumbling with the covered buttons on her blouse while a stranger looks on. 'Okay, so you will need to help me,' she says. 'If you can hold my shirt open, I'll somehow tuck his legs in and, ah . . . Oh, there we go. He's in!'

'Perfect,' the man says. 'Now put one hand underneath for support, not that he's likely to fall through. What I mean is, um . . . ' His gaze darts around, looking everywhere but at Beth. 'No different to a human baby in one of those papoose thingamabobs, really, and you look like a natural.' He slaps his hands together. 'Now that the little guy is as snug as a buck's-night bachelor in a barmaid's breast, I'll check your car. You stay put.'

Beth watches him walk away, grateful for the time alone to settle into her bewildering role as kangaroo incubator, while at the same time shedding tears for the newborn she'd cradled too briefly. For twenty-four weeks, her baby girl's heart had beat inside Beth. If only the tiny organ had been stronger.

★   ★   ★

Now hatless, the brown-haired, brown-eyed stranger is back with Beth and brushing the dirt from his trousers and once-white singlet top.

'You've grazed your hands,' he says, looking down. 'What else hurts? Are you okay?'

For some reason, Beth's tempted to answer both questions honestly: *Everything hurts* and *no, actually, I'm not okay. Not at all. Not ever again.* Since her mum's accident, no one has asked Beth directly, unless she counts those perfunctory enquiries disguised as casseroles, cakes, and condolence cards.

She forces a smile. 'I'm grateful you stopped today. I'm Beth, by the way. You've already introduced yourself to my bra. And you are . . . ?'

'Tom.' His smile falls short of an actual laugh when another vehicle pulls onto the road shoulder, headlights ablaze.

The truck-like ute is big and dirty, with winches and a headboard heavy with chunky radio aerials resembling a spiny echidna with its black quills erect. An older fellow emerges and glances at the car in the ditch. Pausing at Tom's ute, like a policeman inspecting for defects, Beth worries he's an off-duty officer. She'll feel terrible if Tom loses demerit points, or if he's

18

nabbed for driving under the influence because he stopped to help. Then again, perhaps it's fate. What if he'd travelled a few more kilometres and ploughed into an innocent couple, killing the driver outright and fatally injuring a beautiful, caring woman who'd finally found love after dedicating forty years of her life to her daughter?

'G'day, Tom, mate.' The newcomer doffs his hat and introduces himself to Beth as Louis. 'As in King Louis of France, not Lewis — and not French neither. So, what 'ave we got 'ere?' he asks.

Tom brings the man up to date.

'Right-o, then,' Louis says. 'Let me transport the young lady into town. We'll have you settled in two shakes of a lamb's tail. Where ya stayin'?'

'I'm not sure,' she says. A look passes between the two men. 'My business is in Calingarry Crossing, but I booked a motel in Saddleton. Is my car really not okay to drive?'

'Nah, wouldn't risk five kilometres with that front panel. Could do more damage. Plus, to reach Saddleton, you'll have fifty-odd kilometres in the dark. My advice would be a room at the pub. Maggie'll look after you. Best if I can grab your luggage so we hit town with a few minutes of daylight to spare, and in time for the bistro special. And Tom, mate, you might want to hitch a ride and come back tomorrow for your car. My bro can collect both.' When Tom declines with a shake of his head, Louis says to Beth, 'Hugh's the town's towie and mechanic, and a roo repair specialist. You're in good hands.'

'Oh, I see, okay. Then I guess . . . ' Beth is

19

flustered. 'What about this little sweetie? What do I do?'

'Keep it warm until you get to town,' Tom says. 'Maggie's the fauna rescue coordinator. Best bloody nurturer I've ever seen. She can mother anything.'

Although unintentional, his words sting. Given the chance, Beth would've been a great nurturer. Motherhood was a role she'd wanted more than any other. If only she and Richard hadn't waited so long to try.

3

Calingarry Crossing's main street appears a charming mish-mash of old and new. It's late in the day and the shops are closed, but Beth itches to get out of the truck. A coffee would be good, as would some distance from her smelly chauffeur. Instead, the vehicle crawls along the empty street, passing a red telephone box with no telephone inside, and a barber's pole on the footpath without a barber's shop. Under ancient awnings, several tastefully decorated shopfronts displaying quaint country wares sit alongside businesses with windows spruiking in garish neon: *Free Wi-Fi* or *50% Off*. The rumbling ute completes a full circuit of the wide, tree-lined median to pull up directly outside a two-storey pub painted all white and occupying one corner.

'Thank you,' Beth says as Louis lifts the suitcase from the back tray. 'I can manage.' Three words she'd learned from her mother.

Only when on the footpath, with one hand holding her suitcase and the other supporting the joey bundle, does Beth's stomach hitch. Her mum's ashes remain on the back seat of her car, now waiting for the tow truck. She's on the verge of tears and wondering what else can go wrong when a woman sidles up and tugs at the opening of Beth's shirt.

'Hello there! We've been expecting you both,' she says, smiling wide. Around Beth's age, the

21

fit-looking woman with expressive eyes and a tangle of hair on top of her head strokes the little roo. 'Tom called me,' she explains. 'I have a room ready.'

Louis Ducker's description of Maggie's welcome was spot on. She's bubbly and chatty and everything Beth used to be. She's also determined to take the suitcase while Beth concentrates on transporting the precious cargo snuggling against her breast.

The hotel is typical of an old but cared for country pub, the windows still etched with big letters: LADIES' LOUNGE and PUBLIC BAR. The grand foyer, lit by art deco wall sconces and partially lined with polished wood panelling, features a picture gallery that will warrant further inspection. Beth's a sucker for sepia photographs. Her mum would say it's the storyteller in her. Right now, Beth needs to concentrate on navigating a curved carpeted staircase so narrow she and Maggie have to walk single file. Once at the top, they follow a hallway with scuffed boards before stopping at a street-facing room, the door already open. The small space is dark until Maggie turns on the overhead pendant and casts the heavy drapes aside to catch the day's dying light. She places the suitcase on a stand behind the door and tells Beth she'll be back in a jiffy.

The space is clean, but with the distinctive scent of a room rarely used. While modernised to a point, an original ceramic washbasin stands in one corner, an antique dressing table and mirror in the other, and a double bed has four puffy pillows and a floral quilt cover. Two narrow glass-panel doors on either side of a boarded-up fireplace open onto a veranda, and Beth can see iron lace through the sheer curtaining. After jiggling with her spare hand, she eventually realises the doors open outwards.

'Oh, hello!' Beth's surprised to find an elderly man tucked behind the open door. He's wearing worn denim jeans, a black shirt with a fraying clerical collar, and a wide smile. His chipped teeth are nicotine-brown, his spectacles black-rimmed and thick, and spiralling smoke from a cigarette wafts over a mop of bowl-cut black hair. 'Um, it's the doors . . . ' She feels the need to explain her raucous arrival. 'I wasn't expecting them to open outwards.'

'Life's full of surprises,' he says. 'Nice to meet you, neighbour.'

'I'm Beth,' she says, taking in several similar table settings along the narrow veranda.

'G'day, Beth. People call me The Rev. Mostly because I've never stopped listening, even after I switched from our Lord's Holy Spirits to serving the kind in a bottle.' When he grabs the whiskey glass from the table, the gold-brown liquid sloshes up the sides. 'As the publican in these parts for a long time, I've heard way too many bar-room confessions. Some habits are hard to break. But enough about me. Heard you had some bad luck on the road today.'

'Not as bad as this one's mum.' Beth realises she's bouncing the joey like mothers do when soothing a restless bub.

'The little guy looks to be in good hands now. Isn't that every mother's wish?'

Beth looks across at The Rev. 'I'm sorry?'

'A mother's wish is to know, once they've departed this life, their offspring will stay safe and loved. I happen to know the perfect person to care for one so small. They'll help each other,' he says. 'No better way to take your mind off your own troubles than to care for something with needs greater than your own. Don't you think?'

Footfall on the wooden boards gives Beth a reason to retreat inside. 'Yes, well, nice to meet you, Rev. Excuse me.'

Maggie arrives with a box crammed with knitted beanies and bags re-fashioned from old jumpers and pillowcases.

'What about this one?' The publican plucks out a striped blue and yellow bag. 'A good fit for this little guy? Let's take a closer look. May I?'

'Sure.' Beth's getting used to unbuttoning her blouse on command.

Maggie seems similarly unfazed, extricating the joey, unwrapping him, and dumping him unceremoniously headfirst into the makeshift pouch she's hooked on the door handle. Within seconds the joey completes a somersault and an inquisitive nose, two eyes, and big ears poke out the opening at the top.

'Good man,' the woman says. 'We'll get you into caring hands, eh?'

The hairs on the back of Beth's neck bristle at the thought of letting go. 'Maggie, if you don't mind,' she says, tickling the little joey's ears and contemplating how she could care for him in a tiny pub room, 'I think I might like to — '

24

'Yes, yes, of course! I should go. You must be worn out and I'm fiddling and fussing, as my son, Noah, often tells me.'

'Oh, no, Maggie, I didn't mean — '

'It's fine, it's fine. I'll let you rest,' she tells Beth, stopping at the dresser on her way out. Maggie fingers the lavender stems in a cut-glass vase before sliding the top drawer open. She extracts a plastic folder and drops it on the bed. 'Anything you need to know is in here. We serve dinner nightly between six and eight. Breakfast is help-yourself style. If you prefer a cooked brekkie, the cafe across the street does the best eggs Benedict, although with tomorrow's early meeting about the cemetery project, food service might be slow.' Maggie takes charge of the joey's pouch. 'You never know with our Will. He makes the best coffee, but he's somewhat *laissez-faire* when it comes to running a business. What do you do for a living, Beth?'

'I'm in the entertainment biz,' she says perfunctorily.

'Entertainment?' Maggie's ears seem to prick up along with the joey's, and Beth is quick to deflect.

'You said something about the cemetery?'

'Yes, it's a Poppy Project. Don't ask!' Maggie flashes that same wide smile. 'Poppy Hamilton is great at coming up with ideas and even better at delegating. At least this one is a good concept. An offshoot from 'Headstones for Servicemen'. Calingarry Crossing is doing their bit.' Maggie hooks the strap of the pouch around her neck and supports the bundle with one arm, gathering

25

the small box of beanies and bags with the other. 'As the old cemetery in town is on Presbyterian church land, and with my dad once the Presbyterian minister, the committee has roped me into helping.'

Beth's about to ask if her father is The Rev Mostly in the next room when Maggie says, 'Speaking of work, I'd better get into the kitchen or there won't be meals tonight. And we'll get this little guy collected.' She tickles the joey's head. 'Can I reserve a table for you? Noah's in town, which means he'll probably play a few sets. You might've heard of his band. Oh my, there I go chatting again. We do deliver snacks to the room. Whichever you prefer. Menu's in the folder and Ethne cooks up nightly specials. You can call or text or pop into the bar to order.'

Reserve a table? Beth muses as the woman leaves. How busy can a country pub be on a Monday night? Not that it matters. With exhaustion growing, she decides to pass on dinner.

After closing the drapes, Beth falls onto the bed trying to not think about the dead kangaroo, the motherless joey, or her mum alone overnight in the car at the mechanic's workshop.

4

Beth covers her head with a pillow to block out the morning sun. Hadn't she closed the drapes before falling into bed, knowing the last thing she would want was to wake early? Morning means attending to 'the task' and Beth isn't ready to leave her mum behind in a strange town. She'd barely coped knowing she had left her in the car overnight. Despite her grumbling tummy protesting its missed meal, she huffs, turns her back on the window, and closes her eyes.

A few minutes later, there's a tap-tap-tapping noise. She huffs again, louder this time while grabbing her phone, checking the time.

'Seven thirty? You've got to be kidding!'

Beth heaves her body out of the bed and flings the doors wide to find her neighbour, The Rev, attacking cobwebs in the corner of the veranda.

'Sorry, Beth, didn't mean to wake you. Can't seem to stay in bed too long these days. But as I figure God's keeping me here for a reason, I like to make the most of my time. Nicest part of the day, don't you reckon? He's done a good job this morning — weather-wise.'

'Yes.' Beth's tone is restrained, polite. 'I'll leave you to enjoy it.'

★　★　★

27

By eight o'clock, Beth's showered and back from the communal bathroom to dry her straight mop of brown hair without the pressure of someone knocking to hurry her. After braiding a single plait at the back, she pulls on the same denim jeans from yesterday, tucks in the tails of a fresh shirt in pastel pink, and buckles a brown leather belt over her small, persistent paunch. Told often enough regular workouts will tighten her tummy, the post-pregnancy podge remains Beth's one souvenir of a time when she'd been blissfully content. She has no desire to work off that reminder.

Filling both back pockets with the phone, her wallet, and the room key, she tiptoes down the creaking staircase and out the hotel's main door. The morning air is cool — too cool for the end of summer — but the temperature is invigorating and a welcome change from her city life where she moves between cars and cafes, dance studios and stages, shopping centres and office spaces, all with air-conditioned consistency. While the park-like median strip dividing the main street is home to three strikingly mature Morton Bay fig trees, underneath their sprawling limbs are bench seats and several garden beds newly planted with annuals and flowering orange clivia. A nearby patch of green is the breakfast of choice for a family of wallabies, with the mob standing alert and eyeing Beth as if the word is out about a reckless roo killer on the loose. Desperate for food, her thoughts shift to the little joey forced to rely on a synthetic substitute rather than his mother's essential milk. Hardly a good start to life. Hopefully he's survived the night and is doing okay, she thinks.

With the sun not yet high or strong enough to penetrate the fig trees' thick foliage, she stops to admire nature's unwavering tenacity in the jungle-like aerial roots, so determined to reach the earth. Beth is as determined to find coffee and she's grateful Will's Wheelie Good Cafe is open and serving.

'Take a seat,' a male voice calls from behind the coffee machine. 'Will be right with you! See what I did there?' The barista peers around the big red appliance and winks, then whistles the waitress wearing activewear and sneakers. She stops by Beth's outside table, order pad in hand.

Deciding eggs Benedict is the perfect protein hit, Beth adds a cafe latte to her order. 'Double shot. In a mug. As big as you've got.'

As the woman heads towards the kitchen, Maggie catches up, pausing long enough to wave and mouth hello to Beth.

Three taps on a glass bring the meeting to order, and the wheelchair-bound barista with the mischievous smile joins the table of six, announcing, 'You understand this town needs another community committee like I need a pair of thongs.'

'If it's okay with everyone,' Maggie says, 'I much prefer a late-afternoon time slot. Mornings and I are a bad fit.'

'Nothing Will's coffee won't fix.' This declaration comes from one of two people — a couple with matching red shirts and a dog each. 'Stay, Karma!' the woman says. Both panting dogs sit and wait for the sharp hand signal that sends

29

their noses diving into a giant water bowl.

'It's a coffee bucket morning for me,' Maggie says over the noisy lapping of dog tongues. 'I slept badly last night.'

'Hubby misbehaving?' Will winks.

'Saddleton Council want him to run next year. I'm praying he declines. Let's start, shall we?'

★ ★ ★

Having enjoyed her breakfast, Beth is contemplating more coffee when a greeting sounds behind her.

'Well, good morning!'

She gulps the last mouthful of egg, dabbing her smiling lips with a paper serviette. 'Hello.'

'Sorry, didn't mean to disturb,' Tom says. 'Saves me leaving a note at the pub. The mechanic is starting on your repairs. There appears to be nothing major.'

'Good news. Thanks!' She scrunches the serviette into a ball and looks up at Tom hovering awkwardly at her table.

He points at the empty chair opposite. 'Do you mind?'

'Sure! Coffee? My shout,' Beth adds. 'Another thanks for yesterday.'

'No need, and I'll take a coffee raincheck.' He leans closer to whisper, 'I'm supposed to be in there, but I saw you. Reckon I've missed anything interesting?'

Beth leans across to meet him halfway. 'I admit I have been eavesdropping. Something to do with the cemetery project.'

'Yes, Maggie and I talked a bit about it last night.'

'You did?' Beth's gaze instinctively drops to the fingers on Tom's left hand, which he immediately makes a point of wriggling.

'Yes, as friends she and I talk a lot,' he says with a grin. 'She was on her way to deliver the joey. We had a cuppa, and she went home. To her husband.' Tom's smile fades to serious. 'Beth, do I need to apologise for yesterday? I fear I wasn't my usual charming self. It was a tough day.'

'Everyone has bad days,' she says. 'Let's start fresh. You can tell me about the cemetery project sometime.'

'No time like the present.' Tom shifts to the adjacent seat so he can talk quietly without leaning across the table. 'Basically,' he starts, 'a simple idea has ballooned into a full-scale project requiring committees and minuted meetings, and all because Saddleton Council has gone consultation crazy. A working bee and a few emails would do, but no . . . ' Tom stretches his legs and sits back in the seat while rolling the cuffs of his navy work shirt to his elbows. 'If you ask me, the council's making up for dropping the paid caretaker position years ago. They've ignored the place for decades, but we owe it to our ancestors,' he says. With a history and headstones dating back to the late 1800s, so much of Calingarry Crossing's history lies within the borders of jacaranda, camphor laurel and flame trees. 'People have lobbied for funding over the years but we're a small town on the furthest edge of a big, greedy region,' he says. 'To be heard, we sometimes need to shout.'

31

Beth seems very interested, and Tom's happy to keep talking — no one is prouder of the town's growth — but he'd much prefer showing Beth around, letting her see the place the way he does: progressive, vibrant, charming. A lot like him, really, when he's not meeting a stranger on the side of the road and delivering inappropriate one-liners about bucks' nights and a barmaid's breasts. *Hardly an auspicious start!*

When the barista's booming voice stops Tom mid-sentence, Beth turns around to tune into the wrap-up.

'Right, then. A quick meeting is a good meeting,' he announces. 'You all have your worksheets. We'll reconvene next week, in the afternoon for Maggie. You ladies get a start on the paperwork, and if I can get me old mate over there to focus less on chatting up women and more on landscaping, Tom and I will organise the working bee.'

'Oh dear,' Beth whispers at Tom through her grin. 'Being volunteered happens when you miss a meeting.'

'Maggie and Caitlin,' Will continues, 'can locate old registers. Most should be in the council's safekeeping. Maggie is best placed to check church records. Tom, mate, I'll give you a few days.' The barista wheels his chair towards Beth's table. 'I know it's not the best time of the year for you.'

Beth detects Tom stiffen, even though he smiles. 'You know what they say? If you want something done, ask a busy person. Keeps them out of trouble.'

'As does a good woman.' Barista Will wheels his chair deliberately into Tom's legs. 'Get busy finding one of those. Got a date for the pub's big night?'

'Since when is a date essential?' Tom asks. 'It's not a bloody school prom. Speaking of the beach party . . . Last week I asked the council's new Environmental Protection Officer to supply the truckload of sand we'll need to create the beach in the beer garden. He's a good man, for a greenie.'

'Les Weeding?' Will seems beside himself with joy. 'Man-o-man, a moniker like that makes my job too easy.'

'The job of town clown?' Maggie chuckles, stopping to linger on the sidewalk with other committee members. 'See you later, Bozo.'

'See ya, Mags. And Tom, mate, I need your opinion on something. Men's business, you understand?' Will winks at Beth. 'Walk this way.'

When he propels his chair inside the cafe and Tom follows, Maggie slips into his seat and eyes Beth's empty breakfast plate. 'Told you the eggs Bennie is a good choice.'

'Yes, thank you, and Maggie,' Beth says, 'I might stay in town for a few days, if you have availability.'

'Sure, as long as you need. I have tourist information if you want things to do.'

'Oh, I'm not a tourist. I, um, well, I have my mother with me.'

'No problem.' Maggie scans the street as if expecting to see someone. 'Is she a local, or will she need a room?'

'I, um, don't mean she's with me as much as, um . . . ' Where is the confident Beth Fallone, the woman who can keep her cool before a theatre audience? 'What I'm trying to say is, I have Mum's ashes in the car.' When Maggie reaches across and pats Beth's hand, her touch and hum of understanding is almost her undoing. 'She's insisted I scatter them in a particular section of the cemetery.'

'You must mean Saddleton's new rose garden,' Maggie says. 'They've done a beautiful job.'

'No, it's definitely Calingarry Crossing Cemetery,' Beth states louder than she intended. 'She left me a map, of sorts.' The lingering committee turn their collective attention to the conversation. 'I'd never heard of this town until she died. I know Saddleton. My grandmother lives there. She's in a nursing home now, but I haven't visited for years.' Shame licks Beth's cheeks as she removes the folded sheet of paper from her wallet. 'Mum's note and this map both mention Calingarry Crossing Cemetery, and I assume there's paperwork or permission required before releasing ashes.'

'Condolences on your mum.' The man in the wheelchair has returned. 'And pardon my bluntness, but Saddleton Council will let you rot in their waiting area to ask a question. If you want to know more about our cemetery, you need only ask a local. Depending on what info you need, check with Tom. He'll be back in a sec. Maggie is another good source of information.'

'And the project you were discussing is to do with the local cemetery?' Beth asks.

34

'That's right. The project that gets headstones for old unmarked graves belonging to returned servicemen has taken a twist,' Maggie says.

Both the waitress and the woman in the red shirt, embroidered with the name *Cait* and *New-Age Veterinary Services*, look at each other with knowing grins and recite in unison: 'A Poppy Hamilton kind of twist.'

Beth smiles, too, despite the obvious inside joke. 'I only need to find a spot in the cemetery.'

'Then talk to Tom. Where is he?' Maggie cranes her neck to look through the assembly. 'I'll book a table in the bistro for tonight. You can chat over a meal. Let him know I've suggested dinner.'

Thank goodness Tom is not part of the conversation because Beth fully intends ignoring the idea. Socialising is not on her agenda.

'Can I get you another coffee, Beth?' Tom's back, standing at the table, wallet in hand.

'Thanks, but no.' She rises swiftly, keen to go before any more dinner suggestions pop up. 'I really need to check on my car.'

★ ★ ★

'She's good to go,' the mechanic says. 'Lucky it wasn't a big buck kangaroo you hit. You and your little car might not have fared so well.'

'Lucky?' Beth parrots absentmindedly, keen to check the backseat. 'Yes, I suppose.' She's relieved to find her mum still there, still waiting. 'I can take her now? The car, I mean,' she clarifies. 'You take credit card, I hope?'

'Sure thing,' the mechanic says, accepting the proffered card. 'But a good drive around town before heading on a long trip is wise. I find people are better attuned to their vehicle's sounds than me. If you hear something, or feel anything different in the steering, bring it straight back.'

In the car, Beth ponders Google Maps on her phone and considers her options. Is Saddleton considered a long trip? She could delay the dreaded ashes task by visiting Grandma Valerie today. Maybe she'll check out the new rose garden at the same time. The Saddleton location would be more convenient for Valerie, and Beth can only assume this bizarre ashes request is her mum's final attempt to reconnect the pair. Probably so Beth will have support doing a daughter's worst task ever.

5

On the mechanic's advice, Beth is driving the back blocks of town listening for unusual car sounds when she glimpses her smile in the rear-view mirror. It surprises her. The rowdy encounter over breakfast, and sense of community, have lifted her spirits. Maybe that's what happens around family and friends. Beth wouldn't know. Neither have played a big part in her life. Most friends are professional acquaintances, and while a film set or small theatre ensemble can seem like family — for a season — lately Beth hasn't felt part of anything. Husbandless (by choice), childless (not by choice), and with an ageing grandmother her only living relative, the cast in Beth's world is shrinking rather than growing. Connecting with her gran had been important at one time, until Valerie insisted occasional interactions worked best for her — even better when restricted to a Christmas catch-up once a year.

As a child, Beth was forced to endure the Fallone family annual get-together. Usually fraught with angst, the Christmas-in-the-country trip was deemed successful if the traditional argument about Beth and her mum not attending church was staved off until after the meal. The one time a curious Beth did accompany her grandmother, the pomp and procession — not to mention the exuberant priest whose spittle sprayed the first two pews — had made her giggle. When the services ended, the red welt from her gran's smack was still visible.

Rather than fostering relationships, the Christmas visits to the small fibro house on the outskirts of Saddleton forced festering issues to the surface, usually bursting on Boxing Day and turning toxic before the Sydney to Hobart's starting cannon set the yachts sailing. As a result, not one family get-together holds a special place in Beth's memory. She recalls little else about Saddleton, except their visits took the merry out of Christmas and the charm out of the phrase 'charming country town'.

What will Valerie make of her daughter's ashes ending up in an old Presbyterian cemetery? Beth might already know the answer if the woman had returned one of her multiple phone messages. Two weeks after doctors turned off her mum's life support, Beth had tried calling again, asking for the nursing home's administrator. If anyone knew the best and proper time to relay such sad news to a resident, they would.

'We can,' the woman had said without a whiff of sympathy, 'once you forward the death certificate to confirm the passing. A safeguard for our fragile residents, you understand.'

A stunned Beth had wanted to ask if many people telephoned with fake messages about devastating news.

As disappointed as she feels, and as distant as Beth and Valerie have been over the years, she can't be so close and not drop by. Maybe the shared loss will reunite them and Beth can plan another visit. That's *after* she gets her life back on track and resembling something close to promising, if only on a professional level.

'Damn!' She jerks the car to a stop in front of a padlocked farm gate and growls in frustration. 'Which way to bloody Saddleton?' She tries Google Maps on her phone. No reception. 'Great!'

After a few more wrong turns, the town with too few signposts suddenly throws up too many, putting Beth's idling car at a four-way inter-section with arrows pointing in every direction. There's a pot-holed strip of corrugated dirt named Sale Yard Road, an arrow pointing to Cedar Cutters Gorge, plus a third sign: 'The tip? Excellent!'

Beth's contemplating her choices when she sees a hand-painted sign staked low to the ground and displaying the words *Dandelion House Retreat*. Why hadn't the name come up as an option in her accommodation search last week? The place sounds lovely and only five kilometres down the road. A few days in a retreat — good food, a daily massage and fresh country air — was preferable to a country pub with the passive smoking threat from her nicotine-loving neighbour. A relaxing retreat might even tempt Beth to stay longer than a week.

Some five kilometres of dusty gravel later, how-ever, she's stopped at the end of a road leading nowhere. A well-preserved punt sits idle on the riverbank with various trespasser and warning signs suggesting Dandelion House Retreat might be an uber-private getaway for the rich and famous.

Her Google search is successful, but she's disappointed by the website description:

A retreat for children needing a break from the isolation of outback life. Dandelion House, through the founding members' trust — The Gypsy Foundation — offers fun out-of-school activities devised to promote a healthy lifestyle. The Department of Education, state health authorities, and charitable donations provide the staff required and pay for excursions and activities to establish friendships and increase self-esteem.

'Okay, so, not *that* kind of retreat. Shame.' She could do with a bit of those last two.

When a car pulls up behind, headlights flashing in her rear-view mirror, Beth realises she's blocking access to the single-vehicle punt. To her right is a small turning circle and an overgrown paddock with post and rail farm fencing rotting and on a lean. But before she can shift, the familiar bulk of a man grows larger in her side mirror.

'We must stop meeting like this,' Tom says as Beth emerges from her car. 'Are you lost?'

'Kind of,' she says, with the words *more than you know* sealed behind her return smile. 'I was taking a drive when I saw a signpost. To be honest, I hoped something called Dandelion House Retreat might be a healing place.'

'Opinions differ,' Tom says. 'Ask some in town and they'll tell you the isolation offered is therapeutic, while for many old-timers the place is cursed. You can't really see it from here,' he adds, pointing to the land mass on the far side of a watery expanse.

'All sounds very ominous.' And not something Beth needs any part of. 'Is that an island?'

'For eleven months of the year, yes, making a punt the only way over. Access from the opposite bank is seasonal, with the adjoining state forest four-wheel-drive country for the adventurous. Or the idiot. Come on over. I'll give you the free tour.'

'I don't want to intrude.'

'You won't be. We're dropping a load of pellets off for the donkeys.'

'We?'

Tom whistles and a black shape launches from the tray top, stirring a dust cloud before bounding towards them on four strong legs, a long tongue flying, and a skinny tail whipping in wild circles.

'Well, hello there.' Beth dangles the back of her hand at his nose while the back end of the dog wiggles, worm-like. 'He's friendly, then?'

'Wally adores people.'

Two sooky brown eyes stare up as she strokes the woolly coat of poodle-like black curls. 'And here I am thinking the kelpie or blue healer is the essential country ute accessory. What is Wally?'

He shrugs. 'No idea. Seven years ago, while working a boundary paddock, he limped out of the state forest and jumped on the back of my truck. Despite trying, I never found anyone missing a dog. As for his breed, my best guess is mongrel crossed with camel and with a disturbing taste for iconic Aussie fashion items, like my Akubra — as you can see.' Tom points to the nicks and bite marks in the brim of his felt hat.

41

'So, are we on? The tour, I mean. It's Tuesday,' he adds, as if sensing her reluctance. 'On excursion day, the kids go into Saddleton.'

Beth bites back a grin. 'Saddleton is an exciting excursion these days?'

'For School of the Air students it is,' Tom replies. 'Some kids have never experienced their own desk in a real classroom environment. They've never passed notes or flicked paper missiles to their mates. While in residence at the house, they spend a day each week at Saddleton Primary making friends, which means this place is deserted until dinner time. Come on over. You can park there.' He points to the section of flattened scrub where weeds seem to be the only thing holding up the fence.

★   ★   ★

The fact she's in a stranger's car, on a punt, headed to a deserted island in the middle of a river, is proof enough Beth is not her usual in-control self. What part of her brain considered getting on this contraption a smart thing to do? Hadn't Ted Bundy fooled everyone with his Mr Nice Guy act? Beth had made sure her car was safely parked in the lay-by and locked, but she'd given no thought to her own wellbeing. *Good work, girl. You've got your priorities right.* With Tom out of the car, she lifts her butt to retrieve the phone from her back pocket. No reception.

'Are you getting out, Beth?' Tom asks, as the motor-driven cable slowly pulls the punt across the wide expanse of water. 'Sorry, I should have allowed you more room.'

'I can manage,' she says, squeezing through the partially open door, careful not to let the duco rub against the punt's metal railing.

'I'm not used to passengers in the front,' Tom says, also out of the car, stopping at the rear of the ute to scratch one of Wally's floppy ears.

'And I'm not used to punts. Quite the novelty for a city girl,' she says. 'It's all very charming and peaceful.'

'Ah, yes, but looks can deceive,' Tom replies. 'Back in the 1930s, the original owner-builders of Dandelion House — Georgie and Jessie — drowned close to the spot we're passing over, their bodies never found.'

Her gaze instinctively sweeps the surface. 'Both of them? That's tragic.'

'Most great love stories are,' he says, 'and theirs is legendary, which is why it's better they went together. Neither would have wanted to live without the other, so the story goes.'

'What happened?' she asks.

'If a tale handed down over the generations can have any truth, no one would've drowned that day had they stuck to their tradition of skinny dipping.'

Beth's mouth drops open. 'Skinny dipping? Back then? Out here?' Then she laughs and leans back against the warm metal of the ute. 'Okay, I'm hooked,' she says. 'Tell me more. I love a good story.'

'Well, when Calingarry Crossing was nothing more than a dot on a map, but with a very big river, Georgie saw the abundant fresh water as vital to the travelling stock route of the day. He invested in infrastructure, starting with a pub, and the place grew. Basically, the hotel watered the drovers while the drovers rested their cattle. But Georgie was a Sydney businessman, so he built this homestead on the island as a summer residence for his wife, Jessie.' Tom scoots to the rear of the punt and the platform stalls, startling Beth. 'I want to show you something,' he says as if sensing her unease. 'You get the best view of the house from here if you know where to look — through those trees.' Moving behind her, he grasps Beth's shoulders, twisting them before leaning into her to point out the colossal Liqui-dambars festooned with green. Beyond them is a sprawling single-storey home perched proudly on a hill. 'On foggy mornings when a layer of mist sits low on the water, the place looks like it's floating on a cloud.'

'Were the owners deliberately going for the village-castle thing?' Beth quips, conscious of the man's hands sliding from her shoulders, and the cool breeze on her back when he shifts away to restart the punt. 'Were Georgie and Jessie vying for King and Queen of Calingarry Crossing and all they surveyed?' she calls over the motor.

'Quite the opposite,' Tom says, slipping back next to her. 'Generous Georgie and Jessie, as they were known, were entrepreneurial, but not bothered by rules. Polite locals thought them eccentric. Others called them bohemians. While in my uncle's era, kids made up stories about a resident witch who boiled bad children and used them for bait. But you know kids! Adults, on the other hand, claimed they were heathens and deserving of everything bad that happened.'

Beth is stuck on the 'disappearing bodies and boiled children' when the punt shudders to a stop on the opposite bank.

'Hop back in the car,' Tom says. 'We'll drive up.'

He's holding the passenger door open, seemingly unaware she's concocting *Psycho* scenarios in her 'Hitchcock head'. That's what her husband had called her over-active imagination.

'We can walk if you prefer,' he suggests. 'Although the hill *is* steeper than it looks.' When she doesn't budge, Tom smiles again. 'You really are a city girl, but wise to be cautious. I didn't stop to think. Stranger danger isn't such a big problem in a town the size of Calingarry Crossing.'

'You're lucky,' Beth says, feeling a tad silly.

'I've lived in the country all my life and we still don't lock our car doors. Any doors.' He holds both hands up. 'There's no ulterior motive, I promise, Beth. But if you want to go back to your car, hit the big red button over there — after Wally and I are safely ashore.'

She looks towards the button, up at the hill, and then back at the man with the cute grin. 'No, I'm being stupid,' she says. 'To be honest, I've been in a fog myself and it's clearly clouding my judgement. I'm usually a good decision-maker. Your story also has me intrigued. Let's drive up.' At least if she's forced to run for her life, she won't be breathless from climbing a hill.

After passing through the colourful tunnel of towering Liquidambars, the car circles a raised

45

garden bed, stopping near three veranda steps made from rough-cut stone. Annuals and perennial favourites sprout from amid well-trimmed groundcovers, and while grass is sparse, a generous covering of flowering weeds flows like a yellow carpet down the hill towards the riverbank and the distant punt. The homestead itself, with its wide wrap-around veranda and shady bullnose, seems typical, until Beth's gaze follows the trailing purple wisteria to the roof and to two brick chimneys at either end. She startles, the gulp loud in her ears.

'Gargoyles?'

* * *

Tom smiles at the sweet-smelling woman sitting next to him. He likes her. He likes that she's cautious, but with a feminine fierceness that won't let her be afraid. He likes confidence in a woman.

'Wait until you see the detail inside the house.' He turns off the ignition and opens his door. 'Renos have toned the place down. The previous resident was a tad eccentric, especially in her later years. There are old photos on the walls inside, in case you're interested.'

'And you're certain me being here is okay?' Beth asks while getting out of the car.

'Don't worry. People drop in all the time: history buffs, house lovers, curious tradesmen — you name it.' With a slap of the ute tray, the dog scarpers, nose pressed to the ground, tail erect. 'Public interest grew in Dandelion House a while back, after old Gypsy left everything to four out-of-towners — women,' Tom adds as they stroll towards the veranda. 'As for the gargoyles, my uncle reckons they were added decades ago to upset the gossips. Others say it's because Gypsy believed in the curse.'

When Tom retrieves a key from under a pot plant, Beth steps away. 'I thought your doors didn't have locks.'

'Like I said, this place has always been different. Attracting nosey parkers means taking extra precautions.' He turns serious. 'I'm not psycho or an axe murderer, Beth. There are no shackles in a secret basement with your name on them, or anyone else's. I have the odd bad day, like yesterday, but that's the only odd thing about me. At least no one's told me otherwise.' He winks. 'If nothing else, poke your head around the corner and check out the photo gallery in the entrance hall.' He steps inside, his arm fully extended to hold the screen door open for her. 'This is Georgie as a young Irish immigrant.'

* * *

Tom seems pleased when Beth steps inside and lets the screen door close behind her.

'The guy worked hard as a builder by day and dreamed of being a landowner,' he tells her. 'But Jessie was the clever one — and artistic,' he adds. 'Beauty and brains.'

The number of photographs is intoxicating, and Beth drinks in the details at such a rate she feels dizzy. 'These drawings are Jessie's?' Beth squints at the engraved plaque attached to the frame. 'Illustrations from *The Bulletin* magazine. Wow!'

'Indeed,' he says. 'And according to legend, she was the first female illustrator to work under her own name, rather than using her husband's.'

'Good on her!' Beth says. 'I like the lady already. Tell me more.'

Tom describes them as a couple with two incomes — also unusual for the period — who made their wealth early when Georgie became a builder in demand. The pair rubbed shoulders with Sydney's *Who's Who*, mingling with all walks of life, but mostly what he called 'thoroughly modern artistic types'.

'Jessie reminds me of a young Lauren Bacall,' Beth says. Tall and slender, with the same strong, angular features as Bacall, Jessie's untethered hair — parted low on one side and with a sweeping fringe — falls like velvet waves over her shoulders. Unlike Georgie's sterner portrait — chin stiff, gaze aloof — his wife stares hard, almost daring the lens to capture her true spirit. 'And she wore the pants, literally, from the looks,' Beth says. 'Bell-bottom trousers and tailored shirts would be unusual for the day.'

'I suppose you're right.' Tom points at another framed photo. 'Check this out.'

Beth's eyes widen. 'You mean . . . ? As in *the* Miles Franklin?'

'Same one.' Tom grins. 'In the early days of *The Bulletin*, Jessie illustrated her own stories and those of others, including Henry Lawson, so the story goes. A few years back, a box of her early works — newspaper clippings and the like — were discovered in a small annex off the kitchen you can see at the end of this hallway. The renovations have uncovered all kinds of fodder for the town's history buffs — and the gossips.'

'Does the signature on this photo say Banjo?' Beth struggles to keep the disbelief from her voice. 'Could he and Miles Franklin have walked this same hallway?'

'The timing fits,' Tom says with a shrug. 'I know Banjo liked his tennis and Georgie and Jessie installed a court right here on the island. While nothing would surprise me about them, Jessie was the powerhouse and part of the movement behind *The Dawn*. It's likely she was acquainted with all these people.'

Beth knew about the first women's magazine, which advocated for voting rights and divorce law reform. In her early twenties, she'd read a script called *The Dawn*, and immediately liked both the play and the fact a publication prepared and published *for* women, *by* women, existed so long ago. Beth had read for the role of Henry Lawson's mum, Louisa, who did *The Dawn's* editorials. Sadly, a lack of funding — and a lack of interest by the largely all-male industry at the time — meant the script never made it any further than concept stage.

'There are magazines stored away, if you're interested, Beth,' Tom says. 'One of the Historical Society members will know where.'

'Wow! Thank you so much for sharing the

story. I love Jessie. I'll be sure to google her later.'

'You'll be busy. Stories abound!' Tom grins. 'As you can see, everyone who was anyone visited Dandelion House. Rumour has it there was drug-taking — not by all, but some — and lots of drunken rowboat races.'

'Drugs?' Beth sounds prudish; she isn't. The entertainment industry was once rife with uppers and downers and everything in between.

'Opium,' Tom says, 'likely imported by Georgie himself back when drugs were legal, although subject to social disapproval, which I reckon didn't bother old Georgie.'

'I am seriously amazed,' Beth announces.

Tom puffs up in a clownish way. 'You're referring to my unrivalled wealth of minutiae, no doubt. You should see me in action at the pub's trivia night.'

She laughs, shakes her head. 'No, Georgie amazes me. He was a naughty boy for his time, but he looks so upstanding.' The serious-looking man with a goatee beard and eyebrows like hairy caterpillars stares back from the old photo.

'First appearances can mislead,' Tom says, sheepish again. 'They misunderstood Georgie. Like me, he had bad days, but there was never any disputing his good intentions.'

'Hmm, I see.' Beth grins and moves to the next picture of a small girl. 'Maeve, born 1908. Oh,' she says, 'they had a daughter?'

'Yes, and as you'd expect of their only child, she was headstrong and the reason the family eventually moved to the island permanently.

They'd hoped country life would rein the girl in, but she and her mother were too alike.'

'What happened to Maeve?' Beth asks.

'She met a young performer who came to the house one summer. They fell in love and she ran away with him to the circus.'

'Sounds like a movie script. Hopefully with a happy ever after.' Beth glances down the hallway to the open and sunny kitchen at the end. 'Do you mind if I grab a glass of water?'

'Help yourself. I'll store the pellets and check on the donkeys. Then I'll wash off whatever Wally has rolled in. Pull the door closed when you're done and I'll see you outside.'

In the kitchen, Beth strolls around the gigantic wooden table sitting centre stage, her fingers brushing over the surface etched with history. In the corners are names carved in what Beth assumes is the distinctive handwriting of each person, while at the centre, along with a fifth name, are five childlike stick figures holding hands. Although the house is eerily quiet, Beth's ears ring with the joyful sounds of the family saying grace, sharing stories, and later playing board games before hugging goodnight and being tucked into bed.

She sighs, long and loud, while filling a glass with tap water. Then she stares out the window towards the grove of willow trees at the bottom of the hill. There's a small tributary. Tom's there with Wally, the dog's blackness making him almost invisible in the shadows. Thirst quenched, Beth wanders back along the hallway, stopping before the door to glance down corridors to her left and right. It's tempting to take a peek, to envisage the place in its heyday, alive with trailblazing women and the amazing men happy to coexist with them.

On the veranda are signs of today's children, and lots of them, with scatterings of small shoes and sun-saver hats hanging from hooks. But some things never change. Chalk lines of a hopscotch grid cover a portion of the boards and Beth sneaks in a quick sequence: skipping, straddling, then bending to retrieve a leftover marker. She plays three pebbles before retiring the small flat stone to a wooden table where boxes overflow with sporting gear. Beth used to love school sports day, her long legs making her a team favourite, but a better dancer.

Those legs now carry her swiftly downhill towards the riverbank, where Tom's standing on a crooked jetty. She calls to him. 'That thing looks ready to fall into the river.'

'Solid as . . . ' he yells back, jumping on the spot to prove his point. 'Trust me.' He throws Wally a stick before sitting on the furthest edge, waiting for Beth to join him. 'And I thought my legs were long,' he quips as she slips off her shoes and dangles her toes. 'You might want to roll up your jeans.'

'Nah, I need to start getting my feet wet,' she says. 'Things change and I need to adapt. This, right here, right now, is certainly new for me.'

'How so?' Tom asks.

'For one, it's so quiet. I live in Sydney's west. A pretty part of Parramatta, but lots of cars, traffic lights, noise.' She casts a brief smile Tom's way. 'Secondly, I've never lived in a house and never enjoyed water views. Mum and I lived in rented flats in the suburbs. When I got my own place, I stayed close and an apartment made sense because I travelled for work. But this is peaceful and so beautiful. I could happily live with this view.'

'Mm, I've always loved coming over here.' Tom leans back on both arms, closes his eyes and tilts his face to the sky. 'And as much as I like kids, you can see why Tuesday is my favourite day. But as easy as it is to sit here and lose track of the time, I did hijack your day. I should get you back.'

'I'm in no rush, Tom.' Beth's toes send a spray of water skimming over the surface. The action seems as juvenile as her hopscotch game, but she's feeling childish and thinks it's because Tom is bringing out a side of her she's let slip. 'You and Wally, and this little detour, are a happy distraction from a task I'd like to avoid for a bit longer.'

'Not sure anyone's called me a happy distraction before, but I'm not complaining. What's the task?' Tom asks.

'Scattering my mother's ashes and saying a final goodbye. She's in my car, in a box in a purple gift bag.'

Tom's eyebrows ride up. 'Hmm, so that explains the wet feet remark, eh? Well, I reckon something stronger than water is called for, and old Georgie built a fine pub. It's changed over the years, but the beer is good and the atmosphere pretty awesome, especially with me at the same table. What do you say to dinner at the pub tonight? It'll just be me. Wally's table manners are not quite up to snuff. And in case you're thinking about saying no,' he says, 'I do have more house stories to tell, if I haven't already talked your ear off.'

6

Beth taps an impatient finger on the table for two and tries to ignore the ticking hands of the bistro's Jim Beam wall clock. She's no longer feeling positive about dinner tonight. She'd allowed the romanticism of the old house, combined with her eagerness to hear more tales, to sway her. But with the man twenty minutes late, Beth's patience is waning faster than her career, and tardiness is on the top of her Just Plain Rude list. In a profession that relies on tight production schedules and well-rehearsed cues, one ill-timed entrance can be the difference between a standing ovation and empty seats for the rest of the season. Lateness is simply unacceptable.

Five minutes, Beth tells herself while passing through the archway to buy a wine from the bar, only to find herself waiting for service and her foot tapping impatiently on the floor.

'Changing a keg over, love,' says a patron's voice from two stools down. 'Won't be long.'

'Thanks.' Not up to conversing with strangers, she focuses on the phone in her hand, before glancing towards the table in the bistro where she's stupidly left her handbag. *Dear, oh, dear, Beth! You'd lose your head if it wasn't screwed on.* How many times, while mid-daydream, had she heard her mother say those words? She's about to go fetch her bag from the bistro when the conversation along the bar catches her attention. A second voice, raspier than the first, mentions the name *Tom*. Beth tunes in.

'The poor bloke's not had it easy,' Man Number 1 says. 'Heard he stopped and helped a woman on the side of the road yesterday. When Louis arrived, he says there was a half-empty bottle of whiskey on the passenger seat of Tom's ute, along with a rifle.'

'Dangerous combination.' Man Number 2 sounds more concerned. 'Reckon the bloke's hitting the bottle? I'd hate to see him heading down the same sorry path.'

Number 1's grunt suggests he's in agreement. 'He wouldn't be the first farmer to take to the paddock with his gun. Tougher for some, but I've never considered Tom needs watching. The lad's seen his share, but he's solid, smart.'

'And soft,' Number 2 adds.

'You're right. Youngsters aren't built the same as us old bastards. Still,' Number 1 adds, 'next time I see him, I'll buy the bloke a beer and ask if he's okay.'

Silence hangs over the bar momentarily, broken only by multiple burps and the movement of metal stool legs over the tiled section of floor.

'I'll tell you who won't be okay if he doesn't pull his finger out and get home to the missus. A bloke could die of thirst first.'

No longer desperate for a drink, Beth grabs a cardboard coaster from the bar and returns to the bistro where she searches her bag for a pen, planning to write a note.

'Hey, Beth, I'm so sorry.' Tom's puffing when

he slips into the seat opposite her. 'I look after my uncle and, well, sometimes my schedule goes out the window. He takes on more than he can manage and each time it's *muggins*, here, left to pick up the pieces.' Tom's gaze seems to stop on Beth's pen poised over the drink coaster and the word *Tom*. He grimaces. 'I should've planned for something to go wrong tonight, but to be honest it's been ages since I've had anyone relying on me to be punctual.'

It's obvious to Beth he's put effort into his appearance. The lightly bearded face from earlier is now squeaky clean, and in the pale blue shirt, both dust and wrinkle-free, he looks different, younger. He looks impressive — and a little cute.

'Your uncle's okay?' she asks.

'The usual dramas,' he says.

Tom taps his finger on the table and looks around the room, one knee jigging under the thick vinyl tablecloth patterned to resemble red gingham.

After the discussion at the bar, Beth can't help herself. 'Are you *okay*, Tom?'

His head cocks to one side and he grins. 'Now I'm here I am, except for dying of thirst and wondering what's keeping Ethne.'

On cue, the kitchen doors swing open and a woman heads their way, her ample girth corseted by a black apron, wet in places and smelling strongly of ale. 'Sorry, folks, bloody beer line exploded. What'll it be? And you'd better not say beer, Tom.'

'Ha! You know me better. My usual lemon squash, thanks, Ethne.'

The barmaid looks to Beth, who is completely thrown by Tom's order. 'Um, ah, a white wine — anything dry, but not wooded chardonnay.'

When the barmaid's eyes twinkle, a blush warms Beth's city-girl cheeks.

'Right-o. Check out the meal specials.' A chubby thumb directs their attention to a chalkboard.

The pair look briefly before speaking in unison: 'The pasta, please.'

'Done,' the waitress says. 'You know the drill, Tommy-boy.'

★ ★ ★

'Thanks for the tour today,' Beth says when Tom returns with a water jug, two glasses, and wrapped cutlery for them both. 'I've been mulling over Georgie and Jessie and the curse you mentioned. Do you believe in curses, Tom?'

He shrugs. 'For me, the jury's still out, but bringing kids back into the place and filling rooms with positive noise and energy was a good step forward. If you listen to the gossip, however, mysterious forces were behind the house's positive resurgence a few years back.'

'Glad you didn't tell me that while on the punt.' Beth grins while mouthing a thank-you to the young waitress delivering their drinks. 'What sort of mysterious forces?'

'I mentioned that the unconventional woman who lived there, Gypsy, bequeathed Dandelion House to four estranged school friends. Well, there were conditions, however, which required they each stay a season in the place. They did, but that's a whole other story for another time.' He raises his glass to Beth's. 'Here's to small towns where everybody knows too much about everything and everyone. And here's to me,' Tom adds, 'a truly terrible blatherer.' He leans closer to whisper, 'I gossip about dead people — and their houses. I can't help myself.'

Beth's laugh is unexpected, and loud enough to turn the heads of another couple seated by the windows. She's glad she stayed.

'I'm fascinated someone would build a house on an island so long ago,' she says. 'They must've had their choice of building blocks at the time.'

'Georgie and Jessie were Calingarry Crossing's greatest conundrum,' Tom tells her. 'They liked their privacy and yet, to venture into town, they kept a horse and buggy for Jessie and Maeve, while Georgie rode alongside, strutting his stuff on his attention-seeking velocipede.'

'His what?'

'They had the new-fangled bicycle shipped to Sydney direct from a Melbourne factory. No one in Calingarry Crossing had ever seen the two-wheeled contraption before Georgie wobbled along the main street. The historical society is currently restoring the bike, with help from the same Melbourne-based company claiming it's one of the first to have come off the line.' Tom stops to glug the lemon squash. 'Two years ago, local history buffs searched through National Library archives to check the facts with the fiction. As well as their eccentricities, the pair was mostly famous for the guests who stayed. In addition to the painters, sculptors and writers,

59

they invited flashy theatre people.'

'Flashy?' Beth hopes she's doesn't sound offended.

'Pretentious entertainers,' Tom says unwittingly. 'The type who expect constant amusement. They ended up being partly responsible for the outcome that tragic day.'

'How so?'

'Well, when Georgie got into trouble and Jessie threw herself into the river, clothes and all, spectators had initially thought it was some kind of pantomime, even cheering Jessie's fearlessness. By the time they realised, it was too late. Both Jessie and Georgie had disappeared, lost to the murky depths of the Calingarry River.'

Beth gasps. 'No trace — ever?'

Tom shakes his head. 'A dry season did uncover some clothing remnants snagged on submerged branches. Rivers can be dangerous places.'

'But beautiful,' Beth says, preferring to recall the river's hypnotic pull. Like the hypnotic pull of her dinner companion's eyes now fixed on her from across the table.

'And tempting,' Tom adds. 'Which is why the town warns visitors and kids — as well as the odd bucks-party reveller — to consider hidden hazards, particularly before wading into the river fully clothed. The greatest irony is, had Georgie gone for a swim in the nude, as usual, they might've avoided trouble.'

Beth toys with the stem of her wineglass, wanting to shift the conversation to something lighter, something more whimsical, more romantic.

'What happened to the daughter and her circus beau?' she asks Tom.

60

'All I know is, Maeve eventually walked away from circus life and came home, but without her husband. She returned with her young daughter, Gypsy, and an unmarried woman in the family way. You can imagine the welcome from the town's busybodies. It surprised no one when Gypsy grew up and went back to the circus for a time.'

'Was she following her heart, like her mum?'

Tom shrugs. 'I'd be guessing. Gypsy's a mystery, but her passing a few years back was a catalyst for change. Dandelion House is what it is for kids today because of her. And that's ironic because, like I said, in the seventies the kids at school called her the 'Spooky Lady'. She lived in a cursed house, boiled little children, and her mother was once a crystal-ball-brandishing fortune-teller in a travelling carnival.' Tom drains his glass. 'Sadly, the colourful bike-riding granddaughter of Georgie and Jessie died alone. Gypsy never rid herself of the crazy title.'

'No friends and no summer soirees?' Beth asks.

'Not at all. Those who took the time to know her, like my uncle, say Gypsy had a good heart and loads of love to give. But with no bloke stepping up to the plate, she gave everything to caring for young girls in need, and later in life, her daughter.'

'And you were born and bred in this town, Tom?'

He nods. 'The fourth of five generations on the one property. We've downsized our land, leasing half to the State Forestry department, and we have three houses, all in varying states of

61

restoration. My uncle lives in the same small cottage, even though I've offered to fix up the larger family homestead. The other place is mine, which I tinker with in my spare time. It's me and my uncle these days, and at last count, one thousand and fifty-nine Angus Brahman cattle. Which reminds me, I have to see a fella regarding a feed contract and I've spotted him at the bar. Excuse me for a minute?'

On his way, Tom stops at several tables for a quick g'day. The pub is surprisingly busy, and Beth assumes the young guitarist setting up an amplifier on the small podium is the drawcard. There is, however, a sense of being watched, and when Beth looks around, faces smile back. Some people nod and raise a hand as if they are already acquainted. As a group drags tables together, Beth lets her thoughts drift back to the kitchen at Dandelion House. She imagines sitting at the table, surrounded by friends and family, all with a history and shared roots running deep. The home pulses, alive with happy banter and laughter, like the pub dining room is starting to do. What a shame Beth doesn't identify with the word *home* because her mum had moved them both too regularly.

'A new beginning,' she'd say with each relocation announcement.

'As long as it's not back to Gran's,' Beth would grumble.

Her earliest memory of Granny Valerie had been around the age of five. Beth remembers the year because she should've started school and didn't. For reasons unknown, she'd blamed

Gran. The sullen woman who shushed Beth every five minutes — who'd made her attend Sunday-school lessons where kids picked on her for not knowing the Lord's Prayer by heart — overshadowed all other childhood recollections Beth might otherwise have retained. Even now as she pictures Gran's contorted face pressed against the window of their overloaded little car, and hears her screaming, Beth winces.

'You'll rue the day, you stupid girl. You've ruined your life and disgraced the family's name for the last time. I should never have taken you in. You are no daughter of mine. Go and don't come back.'

Beth remembers crying on that occasion, but they'd been tears of relief; she'd been certain her mum would comply and they'd never return. Not long after, Beth came to understand that the packing of bags and car boots was to be a regular thing, with each move meant to better themselves. No sooner was Beth settled into a different school — initiated into a new clique — than her mother would start boxing their meagre belongings to take up a better-paying job in a fancier suburb. Then, at Christmas, a visit to Saddleton became her mum's way of rubbing Gran's nose in the fact they were far from ruined or *rueing* their days.

Constant moving had meant no lasting friendships for Beth. Only when she finished year ten of school did mother and daughter settle into a concrete villa on the outskirts of Parramatta, west of Sydney. Beth recalls silently cheering the day they bought furniture that didn't need folding to fit on roof racks. That was the year Beth took up drama and joined a community theatre group. She made friends, while her mum fell in love. He was a house painter — an Italian man who'd dropped an advertising brochure on the front porch. It took him four weeks to paint the interior of the two-bedroom villa while enjoying conversation and coffee breaks. Beth would come home from her part-time job, or from rehearsals, to find fresh cake on the kitchen counter and flushed cheeks on her mother. As it turned out, the painter owned commercial properties in Sydney and painting was something he did on the side because, in his words: 'Keep busy and keep breathing.' At last, her mother was letting a man share the heart she'd kept solely for her daughter. Coincidental or not, with the responsibility of her mother's happiness lifted, Beth and Richard hooked up soon after.

'You look sad,' Tom says as he drops onto the dining chair opposite Beth. 'Anything in particular?'

'Tired.' She smiles and raises the glass to her lips. 'And terrible company.'

'You mean me?'

She almost gags on the water. 'No! I meant *I'm* terrible company.'

'I don't agree,' he says. 'To prove it, I was about to ask if you'd like to do something tomorrow. We could visit the little joey.'

' 'I'm afraid tomorrow I'm off to Saddleton, Tom.'

The waitress delivers their meals and Tom asks if Beth would like more wine.

'We could share a bottle,' she suggests.

'Thanks, but I don't drink much.'

'Really?' Beth sounds more surprised than she intended. 'I thought you might enjoy a whiskey.'

Tom flinches. 'Not normally, no, although I admit I did recently.' He says nothing further as he starts on his meal.

The pasta smells delicious, the guitarist is crooning a favourite tune, and there's a charming man sitting opposite Beth. If only she hadn't dropped a giant elephant in the middle of their dinner table.

'I'm sorry if I said something wrong, Tom. The whiskey comment, I mean,' she clarifies. 'I overheard some men at the bar earlier. You were the subject. They seemed . . . concerned.'

'Let me guess. At least one of them was a Ducker triplet. Drew, I imagine.' Tom huffs. 'Hugh, Drew and Louis — A.K.A. Huey, Dewie and Louie. You've now met all three.' Tom's laugh sounds different, restrained. 'I saw the way Louis Ducker stopped to check out my car at your accident scene.' His smile fades and he speaks to his glass, rather than to Beth. 'They're good blokes to be concerned. Yesterday tested me. Always has, always will. I know what he saw in the car and I can't be mad.' He raises his face to hers again. 'I did have a quick shot yesterday. The whiskey is a ritual and a way of honouring my dad who died. I drop into my uncle's place with a bottle of fine malt and we throw back a glass each. Then I take the bottle away, and into the cupboard it goes until next year. You happened to meet me on the anniversary of the saddest day of my life, Beth.' Tom raises his fork in lieu of a drink. 'How about we toast to sob stories?'

Beth returns the smile and the gesture, clinking her fork with his. 'Don't think you're alone in the sob-story department, mister. I may have mentioned my mother is in a small plastic box in the back seat of my car, and I've driven almost a thousand kilometres to bring her here for reasons I'm yet to understand. We make a sorry pair,' she adds.

They laugh again when Tom tells her about his introduction to the big smoke as a nineteen-year-old. He was to be a groomsman for an ex-classmate and the buck's night had ended with all four men enjoying the hospitality at Kings Cross police station.

'Not sure which was worse,' he says, grinning, 'sharing a cell for three hours with those guys, or the tattoo infection that lasted three weeks. I decided then the city was not for me.'

'You've figured out there's more to Sydney than Kings Cross, I hope?'

'Yeah, and I've been back several times, briefly. Met my ex-wife there, in fact. Always glad to come home to the country, though. Surely you have a worst-ever bridesmaid story?'

At that, Beth suggests they should each come up with a *worst-ever list* and deliver the results fast, as if contestants in a warped quiz.

* ★ ★ ★

'I'm game if you are,' Tom tells her, happy to agree with any idea that keeps her from saying goodnight too soon. 'Ask away.'

'Right!' Beth taps a finger to her lips. 'Worst song ever written?' she asks.

''Achy Breaky Heart',' he announces.

'Ooh, harsh!' She laughs. Tom likes the sound. 'Worst ever movie?'

Tom's raised eyebrow suggests that's a no-brainer. 'Anything starring Tom Cruise. He doesn't do the name *Tom* justice.'

'Agreed!' Beth hoots. 'What about worst ever *faux pas*?'

'Way too many to choose from — and that's only since meeting you.' Tom winks. 'Next question?'

'Worst kiss?' she asks.

'Ah, well . . . ' There's only one answer he can give with Beth looking so cheeky. 'I never kiss and tell. What about you?'

'Hey, I'm asking the questions,' she says. 'You'll get your turn after you've shared your worst decision ever.'

Tom rolls his eyes. 'Way too easy! Marrying too young. What was *your* worst decision, Beth?'

She doesn't falter. 'Marrying too late.'

It's a sad and cryptic reply begging for clarification, but the game feels over, Beth's laughter fading. Should he give her an opportunity to call the night?

The guitarist is packing up, the bistro emptying, the rabble of diners replaced by the clanking of glass as bar staff stack empties in the crooks of their elbows. Tom can't remember a time he's felt so comfortable or chatted so freely with a woman — a stranger. Though there *is*

67

something familiar about Beth, he can't put his finger on what it is exactly. He likes her glossy mane — hair super thick, straight and pulled back from her face to leave a heavy fringe of dark brown to mingle with her eyelashes each time she blinks. And she has the most expressive eyes that seem to change with her mood. She could be a model or an actress. Then again, she seems sporty and what Tom calls coltish — tall and slender, but with an exaggerated poise, confident shoulders, and badass biceps. He can't imagine Beth is the type to quaff boutique wines and nibble croissants in bed while browsing Facebook — and that's reassuring after his last relationship.

'Shall we have a hot drink to finish?' he asks Beth.

'Tea,' they say, and laugh in unison.

Tom agrees to a pot of chamomile he doesn't want, but at this point in the evening, having enjoyed her company, he'll gladly down muddy river water if it keeps Beth sitting on the opposite side of the table.

★　★　★

Beth doesn't want the evening to end. She and Tom might've talked and laughed themselves hoarse, and it's late, but it's been too long since she's enjoyed conversation without the stiffness of two people trying too hard to impress each other. It helps he's easy on the eye, with that not-too-soft, not-too-rugged look certain to get a second or third pass with a producer seeking a quintessential country guy.

68

'I'm sorry about your mum, Beth. Losing someone you love is hard, whatever the circumstances.'

'A drunk driver T-boned the car she and her fiancé were in,' she says. 'An induced coma meant her death was agonisingly slow for me, but I'm grateful Mum never knew what happened and she didn't have to mourn the man she loved. I can't imagine watching the love of your life slip away and there's nothing you can do. If only those drunken teenagers had decided to walk home.'

'Beth.' Her name is a whisper on his lips. 'I'm so sorry. I can't imagine what you must've been thinking yesterday. Then hearing Drew Ducker talk about me tonight . . . I can't believe you stuck around to have dinner.'

'I'm a big girl, Tom, who makes her own judgements. But after hearing the conversation at the bar, I am keen to know . . . ' She pauses. 'Are you sure you're okay?'

He settles against the back of his chair, smiling. 'I'm all good, and I credit my uncle for that. He's taught me how to stay strong and be grateful, even when the going gets tough. So, yes, life's good. Thanks for asking.'

'What about your dad, Tom? How did he die?'

Tom narrows his eyes. 'You mean Drew Ducker didn't include that titbit?'

'Forget I asked. It's none of my business.' Beth retrieves her handbag from the floor. 'I'm tired and not thinking straight.'

'Hang on,' Tom says. 'I don't mind sharing with you. I only hesitate because I've enjoyed tonight and I'd rather end on a happier note.

69

There's always tomorrow, and a smart bloke leaves a snippet of information about himself for a second date.'

Beth looks up from the bag, room key in hand. 'The thing is, Tom, I'm not sure how much time I'll spend with Gran tomorrow. But thanks. A fun evening was not what I'd been expecting.'

An awkward few seconds follow as she extends a business-like hand. Tom stands with her, his handshake lingering and firm. Strong enough to lean on.

'I had a great time too,' he says. 'And I'm sorry, again, for your loss.'

Beth's heard that line so many times in the last month. Not once, however — not even when spoken by the sympathetic funeral celebrant with the sing-song voice — had the words sounded sincere. Dozens more people had shaken her hand at the funeral, but none had felt as soothing as this sweet stranger's hand tonight. She and Tom shared more than a sad story each. There's a connection, and something in the way he's looking at her suggests she's not alone in feeling it.

'Thank you, again,' she tells him while peeling her hand away. Tom's been a lovely distraction, and he could be a dangerous one if she's not careful. 'Good night.'

★ ★ ★

Back in her room, Beth dumps her bag on the bed and throws wide the narrow doors to step onto the veranda. Tom is standing on the far side

70

of the street, holding the open ute door and looking up as if anticipating her appearance. She returns his wave before he climbs into the car and pulls away.

'He's a good kid,' a voice in the dark says.

Beth grabs at her chest, too late to stop a little yelp escaping.

'Could do worse than that one,' The Rev says.

'Believe me.' Beth scoffs, 'I did a lot worse already, years ago.'

'Pull up a pew. Pardon the pun!' The man has a smoker's laugh.

'I won't, thanks,' she says. 'I have a full day tomorrow and then I head home.'

'Can I ask why the rush? What's so important it can't wait a few days?' A red dot in the semi-dark brightens, his sucking on the cigarette as audible as the crackle of burning carcinogens. 'You have choices, Beth. Consider yours carefully.'

She could say the same. Choosing to smoke is surely choosing a shortened lifespan. Then again, the man seems to be fit and doing fine.

Beth takes hold of both doors, preparing to close them. 'I will, Rev. Good night.'

Her day is ending on a positive note, and therefore very unexpected. Beth's showered now, humming a song from earlier tonight as she walks the hallway back to her room. She's happy her mind is busy with something other than misery for a change. Visiting Dandelion House, putting real faces to Tom's tales of fanciful summer soirees, has stirred something in Beth. She sits on the bed, slipping her shoes off one

71

after the other as she tries to recall the name of *The Dawn* scriptwriter. Did the woman get her funding, or is the script, twenty years on, languishing in a writer's bottom drawer? Beth has lots of contacts, and tracking the author down with a view to resurrecting the concept is the sort of project she needs to sink her teeth into. A storyline about strong Australian women — movers and shakers of an earlier era making their way in the man's world of publishing — would get snapped up by a film company today. A place called Dandelion House and a century-old curse is perfect for *Netflix*. At least the place *was* cursed until the mid-1970s, when Tom said something changed.

With that thought, Beth switches off the bedside lamp with The Rev's voice echoing in her ears. *What do you have to rush home to, Beth?*

7

Dandelion House, Winter 1974

Even before Don reached the opposite riverbank, the blaring beat of pop music was setting the rhythm for his hands. He worked the punt's towline, his forward foot tapping in time with Johnny O'Keefe's *Shout*, but he didn't sing. Don Dawson could do most things he put his mind to, except hold a tune. The family joked he sang like a strangled canary, but in case a miracle had changed his voice overnight, and with the young woman responsible for the music at the forefront of his mind, Don dared a few lines out loud of the catchy chorus. At the same time he attempted the twist, but Don couldn't dance well either, which he blamed on his flipper-sized feet on the end of lanky legs that were constantly tripping him up. He had good traits, but less than average looks meant he could never impress the girls. That quality made Don Dawson the only man at the end of every bachelor and spinster dance sober enough to dismantle the makeshift bar and tackle the tidying up under harsh lights. Meanwhile, the good-looking blokes took their dates into dark corners to tackle tight dresses, stubborn buttons and bra clips.

'No shame in being a late bloomer,' his mother, Barbara, had said about her son's unusual voice.

In his teens, the doctor mentioned *puber-phonia* and recommended a specialist to figure out why Don was failing to transition into the lower-pitched voice of adulthood. But cash-strapped farming people avoided costly medical consultations, which meant Don had been teased in high school, despite Michael threatening to beat the crap out of anyone who dared bully his young brother.

Don loved his brother, but the two were very different.

'Chalk and bloody cheese,' their father would say.

Michael was popular with the girls, and in the looks department he took after their dad, Bruce. Both men were stocky, with thick mops of hair and big personalities. Don, on the other hand, was considered compliant and scrawny, and with a ridiculous receding hairline which he made up for by growing Elvis sideburns and letting his hair sit well over his collar at the back. Despite the constant physical work, Don's arms and legs remained toned rather than Herculean, while Michael had a bravado to match his stature. According to his mother, Don was 'the sensitive one' out of the pair because he was kind and respectful. But, for some reason, when spoken by Barbara, the traits never sounded desirable or flattering.

There were worse qualities, Don reminded himself as the old punt glided towards Dandelion House. And worse places to be. Many of Don's mates were opting for a life in the city, attracted like bugs to the glitter and the opportunities. Many gladly said goodbye to their inheritances because working the land was too hard and came with no guarantees, and often no regular income. Don occasionally heard of mates adapting well to city life, marrying the perfect girl and buying the perfect picket-fenced house on a quarter-acre block in Sydney's outer suburbs. But surrounded by hundreds of houses was not his idea of home. Country dust coated Don's world, the perfect colour, and he'd found the right girl right here at Dandelion House. Finally, he was back to thinking positively about his future and, should he get his wish and finally know what it was like to get the girl, Don looked forward to telling the family. Naturally, he'd break the news gently. Lissy wasn't what parents expected their sons to bring home.

The girl with wavy hair the colour of straw, and big animated eyes, arrived at the house over a month ago. They met officially a week later, when Gypsy invited Don to stop on the veranda for morning tea. Before his second cup, he'd fallen for her. Even more amazing, ever since that first day, Lissy always seemed just as rapt to see him. While desperate to know her true feelings, he understood he had to be patient. No worries, he told himself while preparing to disembark. By his calculation, he had at least four months to make Lissy fall in love with him. Then he'd never again have to worry about being alone.

The sound of music hurried him, knowing Lissy could not be too far away. He slapped the weather-beaten stockman's hat on his head and braced as the punt groaned and nudged the riverbank. After pushing the sleeves of his home-made turtleneck jumper to his elbows, Don heaved a bag of cement onto one shoulder and looped his khaki duffle bag on the other. Then he traipsed uphill along the track lined with Liquidambar trees that would one day stand strong and afford privacy for the sprawling single-storey homestead. For now, the immature saplings swayed, like somewhere atop the hill Lissy would be swaying to the beat, her feet dirt-stained from dancing on dewy grass.

The impish, highly spirited almost-eighteen-year-old seemed unfazed by her predicament. Nothing bothered Lissy: not being pregnant to a transient grape-picker; not being banished from her parents' vineyard to have her baby in a century-old house on an island in the middle of Calingarry River; and not Don's gangly appearance and odd voice. Every day he saw Lissy, he fell deeper in love, and after every awkward goodbye at the punt, she would dawdle back up the hill, stopping at the top to wave as he set foot on the far side. The first time a kiss had accompanied her goodbye, Don could have floated across the river.

The most notable difference to every other girl Don knew was Lissy's self-confidence. She seemed mature beyond her young years and forthright, often speaking out, sometimes without thinking first, although never anything hurtful. Don preferred honesty to the way town girls would lead him on and tell him to his face he was funny and cute, before whispering and

76

giggling among themselves, 'Shame about the weirdo voice.'

No wonder he felt comfortable at Dandelion House. Neither Gypsy nor the girls who came to stay judged him, and he never passed judgement on them. During his time as handyman, there'd been numerous 'special' boarders at the house, but what made Lissy stand out — apart from piercing eyes framed by bright blue mascara — was that she didn't shy away from Don like the quiet one named Irene, who'd arrived two weeks after Lissy.

By the time Don had hiked up the hill, Johnny O'Keefe was a memory and two lissom bodies, hidden under shapeless outfits and wrapped in warm woollen cardigans, pranced across the ground. The Seekers' 'Georgie Girl' rang out from tinny speakers and mingled with the sound of multiple cheap metal bangles jangling on Lissy's arms. Both dancers had long knitted scarves around their necks to combat the chilly July air, but Lissy had unravelled her bright red one, snaking it around one arm and incorporating it into her routine. Don stopped to observe, hoping the tree trunks would be cover enough, but they were far from fully developed, much like the two gyrating houseguests oblivious to his approach.

'Hey there, Georgie girls!' he called over the music. 'What are we up to, ladies?'

As usual, the girl who wore misery in the way other women wore too much makeup skulked away and dissolved into the grey shade of the veranda. When Irene stopped the music, Don winced at the jarring scratch of a needle on vinyl. Despite the silence that followed, and as if the song still played inside her head, Lissy shimmied in Don's direction while coiling a lock of long blonde hair around one finger. The pouty smile and provocative moves as she drew closer roused Don in unspeakable ways. He was, after all, a man.

'Well, well, Don Dawson . . . ' When she raised her face to his and purposely huffed into the cool air, Don imagined the mist of warm breath was a kiss settling on his lips. 'You need only look at our bellies to know what we've been up to.' Then she turned around to shimmy towards the veranda where the quiet one sat, now with a book open on her lap.

Gosh! Don said to himself as he followed behind. Lissy was so pretty and waggish. Every smile gave him hope, despite the almost five-year age gap being enough to wag tongues, even without her *situation*.

Situation was the term townsfolk favoured when gossiping about the girls who had been coming and going from the old house since Gypsy's mum, Maeve, first established the facility for unmarried mothers. The Dawsons were not gossips, and the family farm was a good twenty miles from town, but they heard the stories, including the earlier scuttlebutt about Gypsy's bohemian grandparents. News of Maeve returning with a child had stirred a town in need of a scandal, while the young mother-to-be she'd brought with her had whipped the moralistic mob into a frenzy. The unmarried woman had been surrendered to a maternity home where they'd stripped her of any rights and stamped her medical file *BFA: Baby for Adoption*. Once the girl and her child moved on from Dandelion House, the doors stayed open and more single girls arrived to be nurtured and supported by Maeve until her untimely and tragic death ten years ago. When young Gypsy left her circus family to come home and carry on her mother's work, the biddies and nosey blokes in Calingarry Crossing continued to tut-tut and cluck so hard Don wondered why those busy tongues never snapped in two from overuse. Only last Sunday in church, Reverend Lindeman's resounding sermon had reached the gardens where Don was weeding. The minister reminded his flock that a wise person has long ears and a short tongue, while the devil finds work for idle hands.

Don's mind had been entertaining devilish thoughts since Lissy's arrival, her warm smile brightening a chilly Calingarry Crossing winter. To battle the devil, Don kept his hands and mind busy with the mowing and general maintenance tasks Gypsy set, meant to take a few hours over two days each week. But to see more of Lissy, he was inventing new projects to volunteer his time to, like motorising the punt to make it less reliant on muscle power. After decades of service, the contraption appeared adequate enough, but with the extra-precious cargo it now carried, Don was never keener to make the crossing easier and safer. If council wouldn't do it, he would.

He didn't mind doing extra things for Gypsy. He felt a synergy with the woman who refused to

79

allow the whispered disdain of townsfolk worry her. After his first day of work at Dandelion House, he'd found Gypsy hunched over the old concrete tub in the outhouse. She was tie-dying fabric for a new kaftan.

'Nice!' Don had commented.

'Yes, I think so,' she said, 'even though some shy away from colour. There are people who prefer a black and white world, Don, not realising both are still colours. Black is simply the result of an object absorbing all the hues of the visible spectrum while reflecting none of them. It's like this fabric.' She draped the wrung-out material over the edge of the tub and proceeded to pluck at her pink rubber gloves finger by finger. 'Nothing wrong with mixing things up or being a bit of every colour. And there's nothing wrong with what we do out here at Dandelion House,' she added. 'We're good people doing good things differently, Don. Good things made better by nobody knowing the details. Do you understand?'

He did. He understood even more now one of those good things was dancing her way back across the grass towards him with mischievousness written all over her pretty sun-kissed face.

* * *

Lissy tugged the cardigan tighter to cover the nightdress she hadn't bothered to change out of yet. The sun had woken her early, and she'd leapt out of bed prepared to make the most of the day. At twenty weeks pregnant, she'd long since come to terms with her predicament and no longer sat around lamenting the punishment imposed by her parents. Lissy would greet each day with defiance until she got to go home and restart her life: different, wiser, and a little sadder.

Seeing the handyman so early was a nice surprise. She enjoyed his company more than she let on. He was both endearing and terrible at hiding the fact he fancied her, but he wasn't her type. Not that Lissy was old enough to have a type, other than the love-comic heroes she and Ella Armitage, her best friend, devoured. There wasn't much about Don that warranted the words *handsome* or *hero*, except for his nose. Like a crooked line splitting a long face in two, Lissy preferred to think it had been broken defending a woman's honour.

'You're early today, Don,' Lissy said. 'Can I help?'

'No! Cementing is heavy work and Gypsy will kill me if you hurt yourself trying.' As if to prove his point, Don let the bag slide from his shoulder. It landed with a thud.

'I'm pregnant,' she snapped. 'Not a fragile flibbertigibbet. I don't intend sitting around afraid to say boo, like some.' She flicked her head in Irene's direction. 'Besides, Gypsy's not here. She's taken little Willow with her to collect a new girl.'

'Oh yeah?' Don flinched. 'Ouch! What did you poke me for?'

'Don't you go all googly-eyed at the prospect of another female in the house, Don Dawson. I can only hope that whoever she is, she'll be more fun than Irene.'

'Won't matter to me,' he said. 'In case you

81

haven't noticed, I only have eyes for you, Miss Lis.'

'Well then, Don Dawson.' She rammed both hands on her hips and cocked an eyebrow. 'I suggest you use them to see I am no shrinking violet. Anything you can do I can do better,' she sang. 'Besides, constantly talking about babies is not only a total waste of time, it's boring me brainless.'

'Aren't you cold without shoes, Lissy?' he asked.

'No, Don, dancing warms me up and I love the earth beneath my feet. Don't you?' She pirouetted and plied, her hands reaching towards the sky, drawing her hair with them before letting the mass of blonde tumble back over her shoulders. 'At home I crush grapes with my bare feet for harvest. It's staged, but the tourists really go for that stuff.' Her arms fell back to her side and she sighed. 'I am missing home. There's so much more for me to do there.'

'I thought you kept busy with the soldier care packages,' Don said. 'I cart enough of them to the post office every month.'

'I suppose.' Lissy sighed. 'Although dispensing coffee, Kool-Aid, and sherbet powder is not exactly riveting work.'

Goodness knew how many hours of her life she and Irene had already lost to apportioning coffee from the giant International Roast tin into small white bags. Sometimes they dispensed jelly crystals and icing sugar. Anything sweet and soluble was valued.

Lissy appreciated the care package concept.

Soldiers in Vietnam were fighting in terrible conditions and forced to drink putrid water from their canteens. Flavourings helped and sweet stuff was a treat, while basics like Bic pens, notepaper and razors were apparently in short supply. Anything Gypsy could get her hands on went into the packages, like toothbrushes, because soldiers were using the same one to clean both their guns and their teeth. Irene was handy with knitting needles, and at the rate she was going there'd be a mountain of scarves and beanies. Yes, the care packages were a nice idea, but creating them was monotonous and the chore had Lissy longing for textbooks and homework.

She missed school and her best friend terribly. A few months ago, before Lissy made the biggest mistake ever, the pair had been ready to sit their final exams and follow their dreams. Now she was trapped on an island, in an old house, with her only company a girl whose crying at night kept her awake. For that reason, she supposed a new person might be a good thing, because Lissy had nothing in common with Irene, except that neither was here by choice.

'Cheryl's supposed to help with the packages,' she told Don. 'But she's never around.'

'As well as helping Gypsy with you girls, Cheryl works part-time at Doc Wynter's,' Don said, sounding defensive. 'Plus she has little Amber to care for, and babies her age demand attention and constant entertainment.'

Lissy smiled. 'As do almost-eighteen-year-old girls.'

83

'Yeah, well, Lis, I'd better get stuck into this job.' Don hoisted the cement onto his shoulder. 'I have to be back at the farm by lunchtime. And while you can't help me, I'd enjoy your company.'

Within seconds, his face resembled the beetroots Lissy had dug up yesterday, her hands still tinged pink from Gypsy's pickling lesson. Though there was little she didn't know about pickling, the activity had filled in time. Hanging out with Don could also be fun — she did enjoy making him blush — but then Lissy would finish her care packages. She quite liked the idea of a soldier somewhere in Vietnam chewing on the dried apple she'd sliced, soaked and baked, or biting into a batch of her Anzac biscuits, if they made it to their destination in one piece. Other bits and bobs went into the boxes, with popped corn an edible addition to fill remaining nooks and crannies. According to Cheryl, the soldiers weren't fussy about what arrived. Often the parcels were simply a sign they hadn't been forgotten, and encouragement to be strong and to come home safe.

Gypsy set tasks to keep the girls physically active, and in their free time she would remind Lissy and Irene to use their solitude wisely.

'Explore your feelings and write things down,' she'd tell them. 'Lists help.'

When Irene had asked what sort of lists, Gypsy had said to jot down how they felt about life, what was important to them now, and how they saw themselves in five, ten, twenty years. All Lissy discovered from such activities was an

84

aversion to lists. But because she enjoyed writing, she penned the *Dear Soldier* notes that went into each box.

Lissy was a better doer than she was a thinker, mostly because activity helped her sleep at night. Back on the family property she had her regular chores, like wrangling the sheep daily, working them through the vineyard section by section, and helping her dad with the necessary drenching and crutching. After harvest and before budburst in spring, the lawnmowers on legs — as her dad referred to the flock of about fifteen — were as effective at weed control around the vines as slashing and spraying. The sheep also had a taste for vegetation other than grass, and readily ate grapevine leaves, helping with the laborious leaf-plucking. 'Without all the complaining,' her dad reckoned.

Though there were too many in the mob to name, Lissy had her favourites. Unsurprisingly, she'd formed an attachment to the black sheep, naming it Baa Baa. On weekends when the tour buses called in, Lissy worked the cellar door with her dad and sister. Then each day after school she helped her mother prepare meals for the pickers. With her older sister now in Italy and a new hubby on her arm, Lissy had stepped up and taken on more responsibilities with the harvesting contractors. What a shame she'd acted grown up in all the wrong ways.

As she rubbed her twenty-weeks-and-growing bump, still not really believing she was here to have a baby and give it away to strangers, a sharp gust of wind blew up the hill from the river to permeate the thin nightdress and prickle her limbs.

'You're cold,' Don said.

'Because I've stopped moving, and that's all your fault,' she chirruped. 'I'll boil the kettle for tea.'

'I should start work, although . . . ' Don grinned. 'If you make a cup for yourself and you happen to, oh, I dunno, find me over in the shed sharpening tools, then . . . '

'Gotcha!' She giggled and ran towards the house. Lissy got a kick out of being a little bit bad.

Her smile was still firmly in place when she reached the veranda, where Irene had wrapped herself tight in the pink Chenille dressing gown she wore ninety-nine percent of the time. Asking if she wanted a hot drink was on the tip of Lissy's tongue. If only the girl hadn't kept her head bowed, her nose in a book, and one big toe propelling the swing seat with maddening monotony. Sitting around like a sick person, wishing the days away and bemoaning one dumb decision, was not how Lissy planned to get through the next few months.

'What's done is done,' she muttered over the boiling kettle.

They were the same words she uttered every morning after opening her eyes to the wallpaper-less bedroom assigned to her upon arrival. The single metal spring bed with its foam mattress, a study chair, and a desk built into the corner, plus a no-frills dressing table, were all practical and suitably punitive, she thought, but the room had no home comforts and no favourite bits and bobs. For the term of her confinement, Lissy had only the things she'd found through tear-filled eyes and slammed into a suitcase before leaving the family vineyard. She was missing television, her Partridge Family posters, the chock-a-block jewellery box, and her clips and ribbons and electric hair curlers. Worst of all was not having access to her makeup — two entire drawers with every colour of nail polish and her new green mascara. Instead, she'd stupidly packed favourite clothes, none of which were practical for a changing body, and scattered handfuls of this and that into the suitcase's crevices. The floppy sunhat still fitted, and her bikini briefs sort of fitted. Everything else, including the hot-pants outfit she'd got last birthday, and the shirred midriff tops that squished her boobs firm, were almost stretched to their limit.

Before dressing each morning, Lissy would stand side-on to the mirror and pull up her nightie, imagining herself at forty weeks. She'd tuck the hem under her chin, pinning it there while both hands emphasised her belly. Scared and homesick at first, she'd blamed everyone but herself for her predicament. Why didn't the school vaccination program vaccinate stupid girls to stop them getting pregnant? Even God got a mouthful for making pregnancy possible in someone so young. Irene's arrival was possibly the best thing to happen, with Lissy scarcely shedding a tear since the sooky girl moved into the room next door.

If there was one positive thing about being

sent away, it was no longer witnessing her family's shame-filled faces, although the memory of her mother's anguish the day she'd confronted Lissy remained vivid.

★ ★ ★

She'd watched her mum's face turn as white at the bedsheets Lissy had been hiding under for three weeks, refusing to get up, or to eat, and claiming she had a virus that would go away if everyone left her alone and let her sleep. How she'd wished there was a pill or a shot of penicillin to make her better. Instead, she'd stayed bedridden after school each day, depressed and bad-tempered, her blinds permanently drawn. The only time Lissy ventured into the hallway was to use the bathroom and pray she got her periods.

When no amount of mollycoddling worked, her mum had barged in one morning and demanded to know what was going on. Lissy responded by lashing out over the lack of privacy, and mother and daughter were soon arguing over every mundane and irrelevant topic until, finally, Lissy's anger gave way to tears.

'I assume this is to do with a boy?' Her mother waited. 'Did you sleep with this boy?'

Lissy had prayed she wouldn't ask because saying the word aloud would make the situation real.

Her mother said it for her. 'Are you pregnant?'

'What do you reckon?' Lissy snapped. But rather than watch her mum's disappointment,

Lissy suffocated her sobs in the pillow she pressed to her face.

'I see.' The bed shifted as her mother rose. 'This person, I assume, is the new picker? And I thought you were smarter.'

'I'm so sorry, Mum,' Lissy cried, her words muffled. 'What am I going to do?' When she dared drag the pillow away, her mother was looking everywhere but at her. 'Help me.'

The only response was to retrieve a white handkerchief from the cuff of her cardigan as shame and sadness showed in the shape of fat tears on flushed cheeks. 'Your father's waiting for me outside.'

For the next four weeks, Lissy refused to cry a single drop, not even as she stared out the back window of the car at her mother's white handkerchief flapping farewell. She was never without at least one multi-purpose cotton square, which Lissy had grown to understand was more than a symbol of her mother's sadness. Like a ceasefire flag, one appeared each time she succumbed to her husband's demands.

The priest's visit had required several handkerchiefs, especially when he suggested that a place south of the Queensland border would provide 'a solution for an awkward situation'. When he'd insisted Lissy register under a different name, she'd stood tall and stuck out a defiant chin.

'Why should I?' Her eyes were already aching from holding back tears when a terrible thought sneaked through. Was the mistake so bad that her family would disown her? 'I like my name.

I'm keeping it,' she announced to all in the room.

While her mother stood at the loungeroom window, whimpering into her handkerchief, her father, unyielding, fumed in the wingback chair.

'You'll sit down, listen, and do as you're told for once,' he said while grinding the stub of his cigarette onto the spinning ashtray before plunging the knob — cigarette gone.

Soon she would disappear — problem solved.

The priest stood and laid a firm hand on Lissy's shoulder. 'Sit down, dear,' he said, squatting before her, his eyes wise and compassionate. 'Imagine yourself years from now. Imagine you were to meet someone — socially or in the street, a friend of a friend, a colleague — and they were to recognise your real name from your period of confinement in Calingarry Crossing. All the family is doing for you now will have been for nothing and your secret, your shame and your good name will be fodder for the gossips in town for years to come. So, listen to your parents.' The priest stood again, collected his satchel from the sideboard and looked to Lissy's father. 'As a temporary name, I suggest a girl takes on that of a saint. There's a lesson in there.'

There'd been no argument, no discussion, and no choice for Lissy. She'd considered pleading with her father to change his mind, but the thought had been brief while obediently packing her bags and tossing up between white lace-up boots and her favourite cork wedges with the ankle strap. Impossible decisions! She hadn't been able to choose a nail polish colour, so she'd packed two. How was she ready to be a mother if she couldn't make the simple choice between Wicked Blue or Watermelon Pink?

At the last minute, with her father waiting in the car, she'd crammed more just-in-case clothes into a small airline bag. Banished to the back seat of the family sedan, Lissy had sat, staring at the St Christopher medal swaying from the rear-view mirror, and muttering a prayer to the patron saint of travellers to see her home soon. Clenched in her fist was the St Monica pendant and rosary her mother had placed in her hand when they'd hugged. Was Lissy to be known as Monica from now on? Why St Monica — patron saint of wives, difficult marriages, mothers, and disappointing or wayward children — was her mother's spiritual guide, Lissy didn't understand. Perhaps it was because good ol' St Monica was also married to a quick-tempered man.

* * *

Don Dawson could not be more different from Lissy's father. Considerate and earnest, regularly questioning what she was thinking and what she needed, the handyman was a nice distraction on long days when there was little to do besides household chores, keep up with schoolwork under Cheryl's guidance, or waste time studying mothercraft. As if she'd get the chance to be a mother, even though the quirky woman who ran the place, Gypsy, was of the opinion every girl who came to Dandelion House had a choice. Not Lissy. She was, according to her parents, too young and irresponsible to make her own decisions. Between now and the birth, Lissy needed only to be a good daughter and deliver an adoptable baby by staying healthy and getting through each day without turning into an Irene. At no time, however, did her parents tell Lissy to avoid the attentions of a happy handyman — one who was becoming a regular at the house and who liked drinking tea.

★ ★ ★

'Whoops! Sorry.' Lissy had walked in on Don as he was changing into a work shirt. She turned away, but not before glimpsing his lean frame ordinarily hidden under a jumper or shirt. With his fair and weirdly hair-free body, Don was nothing like the olive-skinned picker whose chest hair had started as a thin stem at his belt buckle before branching out over his upper torso and curling over the collar of his T-shirts.

She scanned the dingy shed for a place to rest her tray. A nearby stack of old rubber tyres looked sturdy enough, but as the tray tilted and Lissy tried righting the steaming mugs of tea, liquid scolded her left hand and splashed over her thigh.

'Ow! Ow! It hurts!'

★ ★ ★

Don rushed her to the water tank outside the shed.

'I'm sorry if it stings,' he said, feeling the resistance in her hand as water from the tap splashed the reddening patch, and tears spurted from her eyes. 'Cold water and lots of it is best for burns.'

'What the hell's happened?' Irene stood six feet away, cocooned in pink Chenille and calling out over the thrum of the water pump. 'I heard your scream from the house.'

'The tea . . . I-I got distracted and it spilled.'

'I guess that's what you get for sneaking around with the hired help,' Irene scoffed. She turned to leave, pausing briefly. 'Oh, and so you know, I saw the punt picking up on the other side just now. Cheryl's with Gypsy, and I don't reckon you'll want either of them to find you both in such a state.'

Don knew there was nothing wrong with sharing a cuppa with Lissy — Gypsy often invited him to join them all on the veranda on his way home — but he had no desire to get on his boss's bad side. Don had originally taken on the general maintenance role because Cheryl Bailey asked him and he liked her, too, despite her marrying the biggest moron in town. Why she'd married Jack in a rush two years ago had got people speculating, until soon after, when Gypsy became a mother in her forties, those tongues found a new gear. While the woman became further maligned, Cheryl remained a firm friend, as did Don, who knew all too well what it was like to be the butt of jokes and picked on for being different. For that reason, he'd hate Gypsy to get the wrong impression.

'Irene's right,' Don said. 'You need to go with her, Lissy.'

'But why?' she said, her voice whiney. 'We're not doing anything wrong.'

'I agree.' He was no itinerant grape-picker delivering empty promises and taking advantage of a gullible young woman. 'But look at us.' His gaze took in Lissy, shivering in the nightdress, now tea-stained and water-soaked from squatting at the tap. 'Look at *you!*' With the lightweight fabric transparent against her skin, the extent of her growing belly was obvious to Don for the first time. 'Please, go back to the house. Ice will stop the blistering. And use a clean cloth, Irene,' he called out.

The girl huffed as if to say, *I'm not an idiot*, and strode away.

'What about you, Don?' Lissy stopped to ask, clutching the cardigan to her body.

'What about me?'

She reached towards him, her thumb hooking the tail of Don's unbuttoned shirt to peel it open. Until her fingers traced the red skin above his belt, Don hadn't realised the severity of his own burn. With her touch like a switch, deflecting the throbbing elsewhere in his body, he stepped away, dragged the damp shirt off and covered his crotch. 'Thank you for worrying, Lis. I'll be fine. Go, quick.'

With the girls on their way, Don returned to the shed. He didn't enjoy sneaking around with Lissy. Such behaviour only cheapened what was

94

a genuine desire to get to know the girl with the teasing eyes and an opinion about everything. While Irene would roll her eyes, Don admired Lissy's openness and enjoyed every spirited debate. Honesty always sat better with Don, and yet here he was still beating around the bush when he should tell Lissy straight up she was the prettiest girl he'd ever met and he'd like to get serious. Well, as serious as her condition allowed. It was obvious they enjoyed being in each other's company, and while Lissy was reluctant to discuss anything family related because it made her cross or sad, the pair was never short of conversation. Don was more than happy to talk about himself and the dreams he hoped to share with a wife one day. Dreams that required a paying job. Every cent earned from every extra hour of paid work added to his bank balance and to the rainy-day money he was setting aside.

While packing his duffle bag and waiting for the coast to clear, Don questioned the irony of rainy-day money for a farmer, given such savings were needed the most when there was no rain. The Dawsons were not alone in their struggles. Decades of drought were testing farmers across the state, driving many to the brink financially and emotionally when their cattle turned into walking bags of bones.

'Dry enough to fart dust,' his dad would famously say season after season, when the same paddocks didn't get enough rain.

Then they'd get too much, with water saturating crops and washing their half-finished hard work away. While everyone suffered, the wives seemed to take Mother Nature's fickleness hardest of all, their smiles never quite reaching their eyes as Don doffed his hat when passing them by in town. Then again, country women were often difficult to read and their resilience mistaken for harshness and inflexibility. His mother was no exception. As families went, the Dawsons were not overly demonstrative, nor the sort to be in each other's pockets. Though once fit and capable, Barb and Bruce Dawson had hit hard times. With too many homebrews and ciggies between them, and too few sons to carry the load, they aged prematurely and cared less. With their joints and their patience turned as brittle as the baked paddocks, passion was the next thing to leach out of his parents. Handing the property down should have been a new and happy chapter. Instead, with Michael constantly needing advice, the pair had resigned themselves to being farmers until they died. Their remaining days would be spent on the farm rather than on board a P&O liner enjoying Captain's Club status with their city counterparts. Don didn't doubt his parents' love of family. What he saw in them was two people too tired to bother or to notice their sons' needs.

That was never more apparent than the day Don learned about his inheritance. Despite his admirable traits and talents, and his affinity with the land, documents had established Michael as the official third-generation Dawson. He'd inherited the family property in its entirety because he'd been first born, and that was how things happened in the country. Disappointment made Don even more determined to buy a place of his own and prove that while lacking his brother's brawn, the youngest Dawson had brains and was neither weak nor soft.

Besides the handyman job putting money in his pocket and providing personal satisfaction, all occupants at Dandelion House appreciated Don's efforts. They respected his abilities. He wasn't taken for granted and, best of all, he was doing the sort of stuff he was good at: creating, building, fixing. Don loved breathing new life into broken-down things, and he was particularly proud of his motorised punt plans. He couldn't wait to start. Some tasks took priority, though, like the mowing, pruning, pump repairs, woodcutting, and general maintenance. In addition, he kept the generator running and topped up with fuel during the cooler months, like now. With less yard work in winter, Don delivered the feed for Ruby — the pony who stayed in a yard on the mainland with two rescued baby donkeys, a jack and a jenny. Besides the copious chickens and other kept animals on the island, wild rabbits usually found their way over, with the visiting foxes keeping their numbers in check. When river levels were low enough, and the small tributary at the back became passable on foot for a few weeks each year, kangaroos and other native fauna found their way over. If a sudden rise in water volume occurred, they'd be trapped until the next dry season allowed them to leave the same way. There were worse places to be stuck, Don reckoned. All its surprises and many nooks and crannies made the island unpredictable and infinitely more interesting.

As did Lissy.

* * *

Don didn't stop by the main house on his way home, instead hurrying down the hill, his head abuzz with the punt upgrade plans. A motorised underwater pulley system would make the crossing easy enough for a child to manage, and safer during storm season when the current increased in speed and strength. One day he'd like to see something capable of transporting the donkeys to the island, or even a vehicle. Not that Gypsy needed a car. She used to own one — a Morris Mini Traveller. With its wood trim long gone, the tiny station wagon remained on the mainland, slowly rusting away under a eucalyptus tree with a sapling rooted and growing out of the front windscreen. Leaning against the abandoned vehicle was Gypsy's preferred mode of transport — a Dragster bicycle, which she rode into town at speed with her daughter strapped in the cart behind.

'Hold tight, Willow,' she'd call as they bumped over ruts and corrugations.

She looked ridiculous on the two-sizes-too-small pushbike, faded handlebar streamers fluttering in the breeze, her capacious kaftan billowing like colourful sails. Sometimes Gypsy used the gig with Ruby the pony in harness — *if* the coaxing carrots worked. Once harnessed and with her precious cargo on board, the little pony seemed to fluff up and take pride in her job. Don got a kick out of seeing the outfit on Calingarry Crossing's main street, tied to the only remaining hitching rail adjacent to the red and white helix of the barber's pole — although never on a Sunday. Gypsy steered clear of town on a church day.

8

Don tended the same spot in the cemetery gardens each Sunday so he could listen to the congregation singing inside the church — one of only two in town: Presbyterian and Methodist. While not close enough to make out the words, he enjoyed the majestic organ music that spilled through a side door. If not for the strangled-canary sound of his own voice, he might have joined the choir officially. Instead, he hummed while he pruned, as he'd done for the last seven years as cemetery caretaker. The maintenance job had initially provided sixteen-year-old Don with pocket money — and his schoolmates with more reasons to rib him and call him weird. Although not how he saw his future, the job offer had come the week after he'd learned his place in the Dawson hierarchy.

Don knew how things were done in the country. The phrase was used often enough by both his parents. But never did he imagine his father would strip Don's inheritance away in favour of Michael. He'd announced it so casually over breakfast one morning, as if the decision was nothing more than choosing which brother got the crust from the fresh-baked bread loaf. Had Don known his dad's intentions in advance, he might have sat him down and shared out loud the million ideas he'd been nurturing since he was a boy, storing them away until handed

Dawson's Run in an even split. He might have pointed out that he was the cautious one, unlike his brother who worked hard but without prudence. Instead, their parents chose Michael as the sole recipient of the living inheritance arrangement, and any attempt by Don to change his father's mind was futile.

Ten days later, after his sixteenth birthday came and went without a fuss, Don developed plans of his own. At some stage, Michael would have his kids and, as long as there was a male in the mix, a new generation of Dawsons would grow up on the land and take over. The oldest male would pass the property down, and so it would go with every generation. Don was welcome to the small worker's cottage, but he had no interest in staying on as his brother's lackey, dependent on a salary from a business he had no say in. Especially one reliant on fluctuating prices, fickle government policy, and the changing weather. With his brother's choices dubious more often than not, Don saw no future relying on Michael and his children for the rest of his days. But he'd need more than a little rainy-day money to get ahead.

Six months after his father's announcement, after hearing pallbearers chatting about old Gus Moore's need for someone to teach, Don took up a trade to save more money, faster. Monumental stonemasonry would not have been his first choice. Staying local, however, meant he could stay involved at Dawson's Run for the duration of his apprenticeship, if only to keep an eye on his brother's farm management practices.

'I thought you'd prefer me to stay close to home,' seventeen-year-old Don had said after revealing his plans to the family over Sunday lunch. 'Both Gus's boys left town ages ago, and he's keen to pass on his knowledge.'

'Can't blame them for nicking off. Bit of a *dead-end* job.' Michael enjoyed snorting at his own jokes.

'Don't be an idiot.' His brother's wife-to-be, Wendy, nudged so hard the fork flew out of his hand, scattering peas as the somersaulting utensil stabbed the bowl of stodgy mashed potato to stand as straight as a yard post. 'Your brother is at least making money. All you do is whine about working hard and everything going wrong.'

'Not my fault,' Michael said in his defence. 'It's the damn drought.'

'Oh, I know!' Wendy snorted. 'And if it doesn't break soon, Don's headstones will be in so much demand he'll end up richer than all of us.'

At the head of the table his mother sighed long and loud, the crack of her knife on china cutting the air.

'I agree.' Barbara Dawson offered the opinion through a mouthful of potato as she stacked empty plates in front of her and licked gravy off her finger before standing. 'You'll never run out of clients in this town, Donny-boy. Apple pie, anyone?'

The family's observations, while depressing, had not been far off the mark. How many times over those first four years had Don waited with Gus by a newly dug grave, while inside the church the congregation sang 'The Lord is My

Shepherd'? Working with Gus had exposed Don to many sad stories of tough men who'd buckled to the demands of heartless banks. Most farmers fought back by shouting endless and futile obscenities at the sky. They were the ones willing to try anything to stay on the land they loved. A despairing few succumbed to desperate measures in distant paddocks, finally at peace, their souls seeping into the land they couldn't leave but couldn't keep. Don's father was one of those blokes who too easily got lost in the past, lamenting the good old days rather than looking forward and embracing new ways. Michael appeared to be taking after him, while Barbara and Wendy remained *wallowers*, their constant negativity yet another reason Don found himself drawn to Lissy.

Despite the hardship and the pessimism, the dream to own his own place never changed. If anything, the need to nurture and grow things increased, evidenced by his handiwork in the cemetery's native nectar-heavy garden, purposely planned to attract birds and bees. While birth had dictated Don's future, making him feel like a squatter — still, six years later — he continued to work for his brother and save hard. What he needed now was to find the right place and the right woman to share his life. The size of a farming property wouldn't matter as much as deciding how he used the space. Like getting the bread crust before anyone else, it was what one chose to do with it that made the difference: fresh or toasted, Vegemite or peanut butter, triangles or soldiers? No matter how trivial or how significant the issue, there was no dignity in having your ability to choose and take control of your life stripped away. His father's decision had taught Don that much.

If anyone understood the importance of choice, Gypsy did. Age or family circumstances didn't factor into her stance that every woman — married or not — needed to decide on her own future and that of her baby's.

Gypsy had said to Don, 'Being told you're not old enough or good enough to do something is not productive.'

At that, Don had nodded.

'I've seen young women defy their parents and make rash decisions to prove a point,' she'd added. 'Regrets often follow.'

Those last remarks were playing on Don's mind now as the hymn finished and the sound of a congregation collectively closing song books reached him at the scented garden he'd established two years ago. The mass rows of annuals and perennial favourites were doing well, with the jasmine vine covering the arbour budding early. Everything was enjoying the break from a harsh outback summer.

As soon as the church service was over, Don would clean up and head over to Dandelion House, hoping God and Reverend Lindeman don't notice a few yellow daisies and stalks of lavender missing.

'Oops! Sprung!' He doffed his hat but didn't bother hiding the small posy from the woman walking purposefully along the stone path, her little girl hoisted high on one hip.

'Say hello to the flower bandit, Amber,' she said.

'Good morning to you, sweetie.' Don's finger-tickle forced a giggle. 'And you, Cheryl. How's things? Lovely day!'

'A day of rest, Don, but you're here working every Sunday. Or are you simply nicking flowers?'

'You know what they say about no rest for the wicked!' He smiled. 'I'll be heading over to Gypsy's later to chop wood, and I thought these would look nice on the kitchen table.'

'Did you?' She grinned. 'And chopping wood again so soon? *Would* there be another reason for the visit?'

Don felt comfortable in Cheryl's company. She wasn't much older than the girls she helped at the house, but she was smarter than some women twice her age. Her father-in-law was an important man around town — her husband Jack, a suck-up — and while neither liked her friendship with Gypsy, Cheryl seemed to have a way around their disapproval, as if she held something over both men. Her work with Doc Wynter might have contributed. No one wanted to get on the wrong side of the only physician in town. Cheryl reckoned Doc was a good teacher and she'd learned a lot, but the small-town job was a far cry from her dream of being a qualified nurse and midwife. An unplanned pregnancy had forced her to change plans and settle for the part-time job with Doc, while volunteering to assist mothers-to-be at Dandelion House.

Don looked up from the contraband bouquet

and over Cheryl's shoulder to glimpse Jack Bailey: legs spread-eagled and arms crooked like wings to make himself appear larger.

'Cheryl! Let's go!' he called across the church grounds in a voice so commanding, the pealing of bells seemed small by comparison.

'Look at him.' Cheryl nodded towards the man clinging like a parasite to chatty parishioners. 'So full of himself, while brave men his age, even younger, are in Vietnam fighting a war we shouldn't be fighting.'

The sadness in her eyes caused a flicker of self-consciousness in Don. He was also one of the lucky bastards who'd avoided conscription, which was why, at Cheryl's request on the first of every month, he willingly lugged those soldier care packages from Dandelion House to the post office.

'Jack only worries about himself,' she added. 'And getting into God's good books, obviously.'

Despite his unpleasant qualities, Jack Bailey — now standing shoulder-to-shoulder with Reverend Lindeman — had a presence. People stood to attention when he spoke. These were not traits Don would ever know, and he envied the bloke in a way. Jack was not short of a quid, nor purpose, but watch out if you got in his way. Even now and from a distance, menacing eyes drilled his wife.

Don lifted his hat and with the same arm swiped a shirt sleeve across his forehead. 'You need to take care of yourself, Cheryl,' he said.

She pecked his cheek. 'Thank you for worrying. Your beautiful heart needs looking after, too.' She turned to walk away, pausing briefly. 'Actually, can I ask . . . ? Do you think it's wise? You and Lissy, I mean.'

Don cocked his head, his gaze trained on his friend, his choice of words deliberate. 'You can't help who you fall in love with. Can you, Cheryl?'

When the woman lowered her eyes, Don needed no more confirmation of a certain bit of scuttlebutt.

'I don't want you to get hurt,' she said. 'There are other girls in town. Ones with less complicated family situations.'

Don's body deflated. 'Are you letting me down gently? Has Lissy said something?'

Cheryl sighed. 'No, Lissy likes you, but she changes her mind every day about what she wants. Gypsy's noticing how much attention you're paying to the place, and to Lissy, and she worries. I can assure you, Gypsy's rules and her methods are in the girls' best interests. Pregnancy is difficult enough. Lissy's around twenty-one weeks. There are still lots of changes and big decisions looming.'

'I understand, Cheryl, and I'm trying to learn,' Don said. 'I got a book from Saddleton library.' He sounded ridiculous, like the goody-two-shoes in class. Cheryl's smile made him feel smaller still.

'You've gone all the way to Saddleton for a pregnancy book? You're so sweet, Don. But it's different for the girls who come to Dandelion House. They're young and easily confused and with no textbook to help. Their bodies are telling them they're all grown up, and at their young age, nine months seems like a long time to make up their minds. But those months fly by, Don, and as quick as a flash there's a baby. Or babies,' Cheryl added while bouncing Amber on her hip. 'Suddenly everything's different. Lives are changed irrevocably, and whatever decisions they make about their future, believe me there will always, *always* be doubts.' Cheryl caught her breath, her eyes glistening in the sunlight. 'Not straightaway, mind you, but the regret will be there, for years. A grief so overwhelming it will last forever.'

Don nodded. 'I know what you mean, Cheryl.'

'Do you?' she challenged. 'I don't think so, and I pray you never have to understand, my friend. Books don't tell you choosing motherhood means packing away your dreams and suffering a stigma that casts a woman as a stain on society. Single mothers are being forced into choices out of fear and desperation.' Cheryl's angst seemed to ease a little as she stroked the tight coils of ginger-coloured hair that added to Amber's adorable dishevelment. 'Adoption might allow these girls to go home and pursue opportunities, but as strong as they appear, and no matter how many times they hear their parents' words — 'It was the right thing to do, darling' — any success they enjoy will be forever spoiled by the memory of what they'd had to give up.' Cheryl placed a hand on his shoulder. 'Gypsy never coerces the mothers or forces them into giving up their children. Despite what parents believe when they leave daughters in our care, the girls get all the information they need. They get to choose. Not an easy decision for anyone at any age, but that one small act of making one's own decision can help as they move forward in life. Gypsy's role is to support them until they're ready. You might make it harder for Lissy in the end.'

Don wanted to reassure Cheryl, but Jack Bailey's booming voice gagged him. 'Come on, wife of mine, time to go.'

'We can talk more later, Don, and I can tell you anything you want to know about what happens to a woman's body during pregnancy.'

Don must have blushed because Cheryl's voice softened, her hand squeezing his shoulder. 'I have a book, too.' She smiled. 'A proper textbook. I'll leave it in the shed at Dandelion House. With Lissy, though, take things slow, Don. While she's a born actress, behind the big, brave performance is a scared young woman. The news from her mother isn't helping.'

Don stiffened. 'News? What news?' Had Lissy deliberately not told him? 'Is it bad?' he asked.

'Now, Cheryl!'

She flinched at the sound of Jack's command. 'I'm sorry, Don, I thought you would've known. Best ask her yourself.' Cheryl jiggled the now squirming child on her hip. 'Okay, someone will start whining if I don't get Sunday lunch on the table.'

Don tapped little Amber's nose. 'I'm guessing you don't mean this sweetie?'

Cheryl plucked a small cap from the tote bag and plonked it on Amber's head, despite the child's protests. 'Bye for now, Don.'

'Cheryl, wait!' He walked with her. 'What

happened to the third girl due to arrive at the house? She never showed.'

'That's right. Her family had a change of heart. Nice when it happens. Best for everyone. She's a lucky girl. I have to go, Don.'

9

Before leaving the farm early, keen to finish his chores and get to Dandelion House, Don hid Cheryl's 624-page textbook. He couldn't afford for a member of the family to drop by the cottage in his absence, and to a Dawson, any door in any of the three houses on the property was an open one. Don considered the largely text-driven and line-illustrated explanations about reproduction informative, but he wasn't a total dummy. He'd helped cattle calve, witnessed pigs pop out one after the other, and assisted old Bess, the kelpie, with her litter: six pups, two stillborn, one successfully resuscitated. Then there was Henrietta. As a boy, Don had helped hatch her chickens by prematurely cracking the eggshell. When the chicks didn't move, he'd peeled more membrane away and tried poking the baby birds awake.

'A good lesson to learn,' his dad had said after hurling the eggs one by one over the fence before dragging his youngest son into the laundry. 'Never interfere with a mother and her babies.'

'But, *Daaaad*,' he'd whined. 'It's Henrietta; her chicks weren't hatching.' Don had winced as the peroxide seeped into his skin and the open wound on the back of his hand fizzed and turned white.

'You think everything smaller than you needs help,' his father had added. 'Or because they are young, they can't possibly manage on their own. Nature has a way of giving strength to the smallest creature, son. You need to trust a mother knows what to do and let them. Be patient and extra careful around a brooding mother.'

Now, whenever an increasingly temperamental Lissy baulked at something Don said or did, an image of his docile Henrietta flashed in his mind, along with the sting of her beak that had pierced the young flesh on the back of his hand enough to leave a scar fifteen years later.

Pregnancy did change women. Chapter One in Cheryl's book, *The Mother's Body*, confirmed as much. The Lissy he'd met two months ago had been so positive, and with every passing week she'd continued to wear her belly with a kind of defiance and pride. The quiet one, Irene, remained shy, usually cowering whenever Don was around.

As he neared the circular garden, noting the wilting flower heads, he could see Irene. She was alone and hovering nervously in the veranda's shadow, silently eyeing him as if he wasn't to be trusted.

'G'day, Irene,' he called. 'Lissy around?'

She pointed towards the vegetable garden, located between the house and the big shed, where Lissy was crouched.

'Oh, goody, company at last!' She dropped her trowel and sashayed towards him while stuffing the dirty garden gloves in the bib pocket of her overalls. She looked so darn cute; Don immediately felt the devil in his pants.

'Are you doing my job?' Don nodded towards

the vegetable patch where she'd left the wheel-barrow piled high with pulled weeds. 'Should you be doing such hard yakka?'

'I'm twenty-four weeks pregnant, I'm not dying. And I'm not precious, like some,' she added in a whisper. 'But I like that you worry, Don.'

Recently, Lissy's affections had shifted from coquettish pecks on Don's cheek to lingering kisses that grazed the corner of his mouth long enough for her sweet-smelling breath to infiltrate his nostrils. The scent, combined with her lips' warmth and velvety softness, could send that devil into overdrive and, like now, force Don to remove his hat and dangle it strategically in front of him.

'Yeah, well, I'd better get a move on. I've got chores,' he said, turning on his heel.

'Wait on!' Lissy caught up and hooked a hand around his elbow. Her other hand shifted to her growing bump.

The way she cupped her belly, often rubbing in circles as she chatted, was new and a sign of her growing confidence. In the oversized overalls, the trouser legs rolled up to expose skinny ankles, she could easily be a farmer's wife — his wife.

Irene was the complete opposite. The girl constantly fiddled with the favoured maternity smocks, concerned with the way the fabric fell and caught on her body. With her build heavier than Lissy's, Irene's hips and bustline were ballooning, and the latter seemed to bother the girl more than anything. Don could tell she

113

dressed to disguise her womanly shape. Even now she was fussing with the smock's floral fabric while eavesdropping from the veranda, eyes shooting daggers in Don's direction to make him even more self-conscious about the placement of his hat.

'What are your plans today, Don?' Lissy asked.

'I'm building seats,' he said loud enough for Irene to hear.

'What kind? Where?' she asked excitedly. 'Down the back by the willows, I hope.'

The wooded section of the riverbank was a favourite spot. From the old jetty and the sandy beach downstream, to the waterhole and the shallows with its curious curves and riffles, there was always something going on, something moving or feeding — something to watch. Even when there was nothing, Don enjoyed the stillness. Since catching Lissy dancing under the willows one day, he loved the location even more.

'Yes,' he replied. 'By the willows and other places. You ladies will be able to rest your growing behinds. No more sitting on damp ground.'

'Did you hear, Irene?' Lissy raced ahead to the veranda. 'Don Dawson has been sneaking a peek at our growing bottoms.'

Irene looked up. With the day bright and warm for spring, the sun had added colour to her pasty complexion, making her appear less dreary. Still, Don had no desire to get to know her. He knew only what Irene wasn't: not tall, not short, not fat, not thin, not pretty, not unattractive. Irene was simply the quiet one who lacked Lissy's brightness.

'What do you think, Irene? We'll be needing somewhere comfortable to sit in a month or two.' Lissy had squatted behind the girl, knees either side as she gathered Irene's hair into a ponytail. 'The rate we're eating Cheryl's scones, we'll need to do lots of strolling. Have you ever tasted them, Don?' Lissy asked while slotting stems of yellow dandelion flowers along Irene's thin brown braid. 'I swear they're the best. If she opened a bakery in town, I'd work there for free as chief taste tester.'

Irene barked a rare guffaw, barely lifting her nose from the book on her lap. 'Yeah, you'd be good at that.'

'Well then, I'd be a regular customer,' Don said. 'I'd be in every day to see you and we'd both get as big as this house.'

Lissy rose, securing her own hair into a ponytail and letting it hang over one shoulder. Wedging the stem of a leftover flower under the elastic band, she sauntered down the stairs and over to the raised circular bed where Don had stopped to pull weeds. 'Then me and you, Don Dawson, would stroll together.'

'Would you like to go for a walk now, Lissy?' He brushed his hands against his pants. 'You can tell me where you'd like the seats.'

'Well, how very audacious of you, Mr Don Dawson,' she said, taking the crook of his arm. 'I'd be delighted to take company with *ya'll* on such a *fine* day.'

Back on the steps, Irene pretended to barf. 'And I'd be delighted if you both nicked off and let me throw up in peace.'

115

'Or,' Don called, 'come with us, Irene.'

When she didn't respond, Lissy tugged his arm. 'Let's go. I'm feeling so trapped hanging around this place. I could just scream.' She opened her mouth to pretend.

'Okay, okay!' Don said, laughing. 'You'll scare the wildlife.'

Once out of Irene's sight, Lissy stopped walking, threw her arms around Don's neck, and kissed him noisily on the lips. 'Mwah!'

'What's that for?' he asked.

'Well, if you must know, I'm so glad you turned up today. I was going bonkers. Gypsy forbids us to walk too far on our own, but getting Irene to do anything physical is impossible.'

He'd read about pregnant women having a radiance. Lissy not only had bucket-loads of the stuff, it was contagious. Being with her made him puff up and stand tall, proud and confident. She made him a better person. Don couldn't say Irene radiated much, and he'd seen no glow in his brother's wife while pregnant. It was likely Wendy's booze intake doused her spark, or she was the exception to the rule. A book couldn't cover every woman's experience. Not even the 624-page text Don tackled each night before turning off the light.

Last night's chapter on human reproduction had been rather enlightening. While familiar with breeding processes on the farm, Don's interest in human pregnancy had been, until now, limited to the important stuff most young blokes needed to know, like how to avoid it happening. The more he learned about the miracle of human conception and development, and the more time he spent listening to Lissy interact with the baby growing inside her, even the doleful mooing of a cow separated from its calf was affecting Don in new ways.

'Is Wendy still in Sydney?' Lissy asked.

'Yeah, she is.'

It was hard witnessing his brother's distress after doctors transferred his wife and baby to a big city hospital. Wendy wasn't coping as a new mother — no doubt missing her daily dose of wine — and the infant wasn't taking to the breast, which was probably a good thing. Both mother and baby had since been discharged but, rather than return home to Dawson's Run, they'd moved into her parents' house in Sydney.

The longer Wendy stayed away, and the more unsociable and uncommunicative his brother became, the more Don worried she'd never return. Unlike Lissy, pregnancy and motherhood had dulled Wendy. Gone was the spirited hitch-hiker Michael had driven to Saddleton seven years earlier, proposing marriage not long after, despite Barbara's suggestion the girl was 'hardly cut out for farm life'. Don suspected Wendy knew her mother-in-law's opinion, because from day one as Mrs Michael Dawson she'd met every expectation — except one. The woman had stuck around when Barb had predicted she'd walk away before their first anniversary. The unexpected announcement of a fourth-generation Dawson — a boy — finally silenced the critics and had everyone at Dawson's Run dying to see the little fella home

117

where he belonged.

'What are you thinking, Don Dawson?' Lissy was squinting up at him from the log where she'd stopped to rest by the river's edge, legs outstretched, feet flexing.

'About being an uncle,' he said. 'I can't wait to hold my nephew. It'll be good practice for when I'm a dad.'

She cast a cheeky sideways glance, tugging at Don's hand until he sat beside her. 'And when are you planning on being one of those?' she asked, not appearing to care her canvas shoes were developing a muddy tide mark from the lapping waves.

'I guess after a girl tells me 'yes'.'

'A girl would have to be asked first, wouldn't she?' Lissy teased. 'And there's the ring and the minister and the church to organise. Oh, and the dress! A wedding is *all* about the dress. In fact, there's an *awful* lot a bride has to consider. You guys get the easy bit. You only have to pop the question and turn up on the day.'

Don liked how Lissy made him laugh, which was good because none of the people at his other jobs were much fun. Working alongside a brother on a slow simmer from sunrise to sunset was downright unpleasant, while grieving families arguing over headstones and epitaphs came with no joy. Only Lissy and her baby glow brightened Don's days.

'Then, once married,' Lissy was saying, 'you'll have at least nine months to wait for a baby.' She sighed and rubbed tiny circles over her belly. 'And I can tell you, Don Dawson, those nine months can seem like for-ever.'

'Or a bloke could get lucky,' he said with a wink and an elbow nudge.

'What do you mean by lucky?'

'Well, I mean, a fortunate fellow might find himself a package deal with the baby-waiting part already done.'

When the light disappeared from Lissy's eyes, Don feared he'd assumed too much, too soon. What he hadn't expected at that moment was a kiss, or the veil of early tears in Lissy's eyes when she pulled away. 'Don't joke about such things, Don.'

'I-I wasn't joking, Lis.'

She stood and stepped away, not looking at him or caring the current was now lapping at her ankles. 'You'd really marry me?' Lissy asked. She was still staring across the water into the distance. 'I'm awfully fat and frumpy. What if I stay this way?'

Don had to admit it was an odd feeling to watch the woman he loved blossom with another man's baby. Lissy's shape was changing, her belly expanding, her next-to-no boobs burgeoning. Even the proud angles in her chin and cheekbones were softening as her face filled out. But no way was he about to share such ruminations. Standing with her back to Don, she looked like any other young woman. Not until after the birth would he discover the regular-sized Lissy, and whatever that ended up being, he looked forward to the opportunity very much.

'I meant what I said, Lissy. We're both learning. We can get our feet wet together.' He'd moved in behind and wrapped his arms around her belly, his chin dipping to settle on her shoulder. 'We can be a family.'

'You're seriously asking me to be a farmer's wife, Don Dawson? Like, this is a proposal for real?'

'What do *you* reckon?' he said.

She turned in the circle of his arms and pulled one of those scrunched faces he was still learning to read. 'I reckon it's time you showed me your farm. Come on.'

'What? Now? Like this?'

'Once I've change clothes. I want to make a good first impression. Come on,' she called over her shoulder, already on the move.

Don met her stride for stride, but all the way back to the house he was wishing she'd change her mind. How was he supposed to explain Lissy to his parents?

'It's too late to go today,' he said, dread rising. 'Gypsy and Cheryl could come back from Saddleton any time.'

'Yeah, back with crying babies.' Lissy was puffing as they made a small rise. 'Oh, look, Don. How cute is that family?' She pointed to a pair of mallard ducks with six fluffy chicks in tow. 'Is that what people mean by having all your ducks in a row?'

'It means being well prepared,' he explained. And Don wasn't. Unleashing Lissy on his parents at this point would not work in their favour. 'I really think we should slow down.' He took her hand so she didn't slip or trip, but she shook him loose and leapt onto another log, balancing like a gymnast, toes pointing, arms raised and extended.

'I'm not going to break and I'm so over being told to be careful and being shushed when in the house,' Lissy said. 'When they aren't sleeping, Amber and Willow are screaming their little lungs out.'

'No doubt we all did,' Don said, walking alongside, prepared to steady her if needed.

'Not me. Reckon it's because I'm Italian. I had no choice but to get used to loud noises, louder relatives, and crowded family gatherings. Did you hear me in there, kiddo?' She prodded her belly. 'Yeah, you in there. Learn to love noise.'

'Get down, Lis, or you will break something.' He tried helping her off the log, but she smacked his hand away and jumped.

'See?' she announced. 'I'm unbreakable and so is bub. He just needs to get used to noise. Come on, Don, scream and shout with me.' Hips twisting and gyrating, she broke into a chorus of O'Keefe's *Shout*.

'Lissy!' Don's warning came too late. She'd slipped on the spot where too much fancy footwork had turned damp dirt into a muddy slick. 'Are you hurt?' He dropped to one knee and waited. 'Talk to me.' Her mouth and eyes, shocked wide, had Don fearing the worst, until a giggle grew, low and unsure at first. 'You frightened me, Lis.'

When she tugged playfully at his shirt and he fell onto his bottom beside her, both dropped onto their backs and laughed hysterically, while holding their stomachs and begging each other to stop.

★ ★ ★

'Imagine that,' Lissy said, composed again and staring up dreamily at the bluest sky. 'Mrs Don Dawson. Do you think we'll be allowed? I mean, I'll be eighteen soon so I can do what I want, but well, I'm already a big disappointment to my parents.'

Don rolled his head sideways to look at her but said nothing.

'Do you reckon Gypsy will help me tell my parents?' Lissy asked. 'Is Gypsy even her real name?'

'I don't know,' Don said, answering both questions.

She sat up and crossed her legs, but the change in position did little to alleviate the discomfort in her back. 'I can't imagine someone like Gypsy doing something as crazy as joining a circus.'

'Her mum did that,' Don clarified. 'But an apple never falls far from the tree. Her grandparents were legendary around town.'

'What's *apples* got to do with anything?' Lissy asked.

'It's a saying,' Don explained. 'It suggests we inherit our parents' traits and beliefs.'

Lissy harrumphed. 'Not all of us and definitely not me. I'm no apple and *nothing* like my parents. I certainly would never punish my child for one silly mistake. My dad's nothing but a bully who nags Mum until she gives in. I can't be like him. I hate him.'

'We all lock horns with our parents,' Don said. 'Dads can think they're doing right by their kids. They're a bit blind, or too busy, or they don't get being young. He's still your father, and he's doing what he thinks is best.'

Lissy pouted and studied her lap while stroking the ponytail straight where it tipped her left boob. 'Gypsy says the same, but I don't want to talk about him. Tell me a happy story,' she said. 'Like how Gypsy's mum ran away with the circus. How unreal. How awfully romantic!'

'If you say so,' Don said. 'Would you have run away with the picker?'

Lissy shrugged. 'I thought he liked me enough. I really, seriously did or else I would've never . . . It's just, well, he was such fun and always making me laugh. I used to take supplies down to the workers' lodge each night and he'd sneak me a drink. We mucked around a bit and when he talked about getting a permanent job on a nearby winery, I thought it was for me. I thought he loved me, but like Dad said, I was stupid. No one falls in love that fast, do they?'

'Time is irrelevant,' Don said. 'I absolutely know it's possible to meet a complete stranger and know they're *the one*.'

Lissy's hands and her gaze dropped to her belly. 'What do you suppose I have growing in here? Apple? Orange, maybe?'

Don's eyebrows arched. 'From where I'm sitting it looks more watermelon.'

She smacked his hand away. 'Ha, ha, very funny! I'm so much smaller than Irene, though.

123

Just my luck it'll be a grape.' Lissy leaned back on her arms and forked her legs straight out in front. 'Not that it matters. I'll never know what my baby grows up to be if my father gets his way.'

She put a hand to her cheek. If the sharp slap to her face that day hadn't driven his message home, Aldo's final words had as she'd slid across the backseat of the family car in Calingarry Crossing's main street: 'Stupid, stupid girl. There'll be no bastards in our family.'

'I'm *stupider* than stupid,' Lissy muttered as she yanked long brown blades from a clump of weeds and tied them in knots. If only she could go back to the last night of summer when she'd sneaked out of her bedroom and across the vineyard to meet the cute picker.

★ ★ ★

With his tight jeans, tanned skin, and the whitest smile, the new picker had been the subject of Lissy's girlish infatuation last harvest, causing lots of giggles on sleepovers when Ella's Ouija board thingy had spelled out his name. By the following harvest, Lissy's body was changing. Things were different. She was different, and not only physically. Curiosity had taken her crush to a new and serious level, so when the picker flirted, her body responded in new and exciting ways. Their first tongue-kiss had been a shock, but she'd got the hang of it. He liked her. She could tell.

They kissed heaps, almost right under her

124

parents' noses, and when he begged Lissy to meet him after work, somewhere they could be alone, her tummy tingled for the rest of the day. That afternoon, she plucked her eyebrows for the first time, took extra care styling her hair, and rubbed moisturiser on newly shaved legs. As she blew hot breath on a final coat of fingernail polish, Lissy imagined the scene in her head. She would run in slow motion through the moonlit vineyard, the cheesecloth peasant top she'd borrowed from her sister's wardrobe swirling around her bare midriff. He would be waiting on a soft blanket, stretched out and smelling of Blue Stratos, his shirt unbuttoned and the belt on his jeans unbuckled in anticipation.

So uptight about the date, Lissy feigned an upset tummy to avoid dinner, because no way would she be able to eat at the dining table with her parents at six o'clock knowing she'd be in the vineyard necking with a boy at eight. But by 7.30 pm, Lissy was dreadfully hungry and nervously flicking though a *Dolly* magazine. According to Dolly Doctor, losing her virginity would be *a milestone moment* and *one to remember*. Come 8 pm, Lissy tiptoed out of the house.

When she found the cute picker, he was still in grubby work gear and guzzling beer with his mates behind the workers' quarters. The moon had clouded over; there was no music, no warm blanket waiting, no candles, and no tingles along her spine. Hours of preparation had all been for nothing. When the men whistled and sniggered, shame trembled Lissy's chin, and her eyes, heavy with mascara, blinked into the spotlight she

125

didn't want to be in.

She ran. Like a rabbit she sprinted as fast as she could, until the picker caught up with her, pleading for forgiveness and kissing away her pout. Lissy had been so, so close to the house and to the safety of her room with its posters of pretend boyfriend David Cassidy stuck to the walls. If she hadn't heard her father yelling at that moment, followed by her mum's cries and the banging of doors, Lissy would have kept running. Instead, with an urgent need to know not every man was harsh and heartless, like her father, she let the picker lead her between the vines and show her true love.

Within seconds, his bulge was pressed against her tummy, his open mouth muzzling hers, his stinky slobber sliming her face. It all happened so fast, and he seemed so wrapped around her, Lissy couldn't breathe. They must've looked like the brown snakes she'd come across having sex last spring. So entangled, the reptiles had resembled plaited rope, magically erect and thrashing about. Now here she was between the vines writhing with the cute picker, wondering if her boobs were big enough, her tummy flat enough, and unsure if she wanted to go all the way. When she laughed nervously and pulled back to catch her breath, he tugged her onto the ground and kissed her child-ish giggles and all caution away.

'Far out! You're friggin' gorgeous!' The words were like a growl, his mouth suffocating her, his tongue tacky and lips like sandpaper. After manhandling one boob out of her bra, his mouth made its way to her nipple, and a hand, hot and heavy, gripped her thigh. Good Lissy wanted to push him off her and run home to her mother. The rebellious, curious, and ripe-for-the-picking Lissy wanted to know what a man's love felt like — just once. In that moment, as he sat back on his haunches and slid her shorts off, his hands had felt right and his wanting her so real.

With the cold, hard earth pressed into her bare back, and with the full weight of his thrusting body forcing unladylike grunts, Lissy began to question if this was how sex was meant to be. When she shoved him off, telling him it hurt, he rolled onto his back and told her to get on top. He said it would be better, easier.

It wasn't. Lissy's memorable moment had been so rushed and unromantic she was left wondering what all the fuss was about.

As he dragged his pants on and yanked up his fly, he seemed surprised she was a virgin.

Did he think she met all the boys between the vines?

★ ★ ★

'Hey, hey, what's up? What's with the tears, Lis?' Don's lips were gentle and warm where they brushed her ear. 'You're not stupid. Your dad's the dummy for saying so, and that picker took advantage of you. If I could get my hands on him . . .'

Aldo had spoken the same words after finding out his youngest daughter had sinned, and the whole family would suffer as a result. Her dad had yelled for weeks. Her mother had cried.

127

'My beautiful baby girl,' she'd said, wailing while stroking Lissy's hair. 'This is not how I imagined your life would turn out. I remember being pregnant with you, and with your sister, and both times the experience was wonderful and exciting. I have wished the same for you, so when it is your time to have a baby, you, too, will be surrounded by people who will support you and feel the excitement *with* you. Your father is right, darling. You are too young for this experience and so we have decided for you. There will be more babies when you are older and when you have found a wonderful husband. That is when God will say you are ready to keep a child. There is an order. Anything different goes against the church. It will never be right.'

★ ★ ★

If this wasn't right, why was Lissy's last thought each night and first thought each morning about how amazing her baby would feel in her arms? What if Lissy's *un-ordered* life was God's special plan, and being sent away by an angry father was fate letting her meet the wonderful and supportive husband her mother said she would find? Don Dawson could be her husband. If only she could see her future on a farm with him.

'What a big sigh, Lis.' Don pulled back, his gaze searching the depth of her eyes before wiping a teardrop clinging to her chin.

She sat straight-backed. 'I was thinking about

those apples. A child *can* be different to their parents. They can be whatever they choose: apple, orange, watermelon, grape. I don't care. Maybe I'll have one of each and end up with fruit salad.'

Don chuckled. 'I love the idea of fruit salad.'

Lissy leaned in and pecked his cheek. 'Thank you, Don, and I'm sorry for being dull. As if you don't get enough grief from your brother about Wendy. It's probably too late to go to the farm today. Besides, Irene's bound to make a fuss and dob on us.'

Don stood first to lend Lissy a hand. Then, while helping brush leaf debris from her clothes, he asked, 'Would you run away from your family, Lis?'

'To join the circus like Gypsy's mum? Sure would!' She took Don's hand as they walked the rest of the way up the hill towards the rear of the house. 'If I joined a circus, I'd be a trapeze artist *flyyyyyyying* through the air. But you'd have to come. I'd need someone to catch me. You would catch me, wouldn't you, Don?'

'Every time, Lis, although I'm not so good with heights.'

'Really?' She tapped a finger to her lips. 'Well, what are you good with, besides kissing?'

'Horses,' he said.

'Well, that's perfect! I can be one of those ballerinas with a pink tutu and a tiara who dances on horseback. I wonder how you keep a tiara on while dangling upside-down on a horse?'

Don laughed. 'I wouldn't know, but I think you mean a trick rider. I saw a show at the rodeo last year. The riders were amazing.'

'A rodeo? In town? Are you serious? When?'

'It was part of the annual agricultural fair. First weekend in September.'

'Annual? As in next month?' Lissy almost tripped, she was so eager. 'Do they have fairy floss and Ferris wheels and Sideshow Alley?'

'And pluto pups,' Don added. 'And show bags, and dodgem cars — the works. Not sure about trick riders. They might've been a one-off.'

'I don't care,' Lissy said with renewed excitement. 'I'm going. Take me, Don.'

'Not sure you'll be allowed, Lis.'

'Allowed?' She groaned. 'I'm tied to this place every day. Punished every day because of one stupid mistake. I'm tired of being told what I can and can't do. I'm doing everything that's expected of me, but I need variety. I need to be entertained. I need to go to the fair.'

'You can stomp your feet all you like,' Don said. 'Gypsy won't be keen on me taking you.'

'She'll surely let me go if I tell her it's for my birthday. We can meet up in secret. Hey, Irene!' she called, hurrying towards the veranda. 'Guess what?'

★ ★ ★

Irene was curled up on the yellow and white striped swing seat, but rather than the usual book on her lap, Don saw some kind of letter.

'Have you got news from home?' he asked.

'No, Don,' Lissy answered. 'That's Irene's letter to me. I wrote mine to her already. Gypsy makes us write stuff all the time. The letter is

130

about us and our wishes for the future.'

'I don't get it,' Don said as he perched his butt on the step. 'Why write to each other when you're both here? Why not tell each other?'

'Aw, der! It's part of our pact.' Lissy walked over to flick through the selection of LP records stacked in a blue plastic milk crate under the table where the portable player sat. 'Gypsy's encouraging Irene and me to be part of each other's lives. She says writing what we want for our futures, and making a kind of contract with ourselves is the first step to having our wishes come true. Our parents don't care about anything except their reputations. To them we're an embarrassment and always will be. We'll keep our dirty little secret, but we'll never feel shame, will we, Irene?'

Irene said nothing, the pen stalled in her hand.

'They expect we'll go home and forget, or be happy to pretend none of this happened,' Lissy continued. 'But it did, and our pregnancies won't have to remain a shameful secret and never be spoken about again *if* we have someone to share stuff with. The two of us have a special connection now, and we'll understand the importance of birthdays when no one else does.' Lissy had placed the record's hole over the central pin and was positioning the stylus on the first track when she added, 'Don't forget to put your name at the bottom, Irene. A pact needs a signature.'

Don squinted up at the quiet one, and trying for a smile, said, 'You can be grateful she's not insisting you sign in blood.'

The dulcet tones of Diana Ross and the Supremes singing *Baby Love* not only drowned out his chuckle, the voices muted Irene's response, which looked an awful lot like *Drop dead, Don*. When the girl sprung to her feet, setting the swing-seat into action as she stormed inside, Don waited until the screen door slammed shut.

'Not going to Dawson's Run was the right decision, Lis.'

'Good to know I can at least make one.' Lissy huffed and walked back to the record player, turning up the volume so she had to yell. 'We've got plenty of time, I suppose. It's not like I'm going anywhere in a hurry. Except to the show.' She grinned. 'Gypsy won't say no. I won't let her.'

10

'No. Definitely not. I'm sorry.'

'But why not, Cheryl?' Lissy whined. 'You said we shouldn't hide ourselves away or feel ashamed and pretend our babies don't exist. We don't even go into town once a week like we used to do.'

'We missed two Sundays,' Cheryl clarified. 'Only because Irene no longer phones home and you were in a bad mood. If, however, you want to talk to your parents for your birthday . . . '

'Yeah, right,' Lissy said. 'And hear Mum deliver the same lines over and over on behalf of Dad? No thanks. I want to do something exciting, like go to the annual show. I asked Gypsy. She said to check with you.'

Cheryl raised an eyebrow. 'I'm sure that's not true.'

'Well, I do plan to ask once you agree to take us. Please, pretty please?' Lissy pleaded. 'A couple of measly hours can't hurt. Long enough to stuff ourselves full of pluto pups and cheese-on-a-stick. Irene reckons it'll stop her morning sickness.'

'Cure you or kill you,' Cheryl said. 'But I'll ask Gypsy. You two might bring me luck. I'm entering my scones in the Bread and Bakery section, but I have to be bright and early with my entry.'

'No problem, and you're bound to win,

Cheryl,' Lissy gushed. 'They're the best scones ever, and it'll be so cool to see them draped in a blue ribbon.'

★   ★   ★

Too early for crowds, the amusement rides were warming up, making Lissy dizzy from the whizzing and flashes of colour and lights. Carnival music blared out of big-mouthed metallic speakers mounted on tall poles, and the smell of buttery popcorn clashed with sickly, sugary floss. There'd been rain overnight. Not much. Enough to make Lissy watch where she walked. Irene, on the other hand, was looking everywhere but the ground. She was the liveliest Lissy had seen her, making her glad she'd pushed Gypsy into agreeing.

'Cool! Pluto pups,' Irene enthused. 'Who else wants one?'

'I'll pass,' replied Lissy. As tempting as a crunchy batter-covered hot dog dunked in sauce might be, she was too eager to rendezvous with Don in Sideshow Alley, as arranged.

Cheryl consulted her wristwatch. 'I need to drop my scones into the hall for judging. Where will you girls be waiting?'

'Do the displays include handicrafts?' asked Irene. 'I'd enjoy that.'

'Not me,' Lissy declared. 'I'm off to spend my telephone money on the laughing clowns. I want a Kewpie doll with a pink tutu.'

'Seriously?' Irene scoffed. 'They totally rig those games, you know.'

'How?' Lissy challenged. 'You put a ping-pong ball in a mouth and it rolls down a chute. Where's the rigging?'

'Why not just buy a Kewpie doll?'

Lissy's hands settled on her hips and she smiled. 'One day, Irene, I'll sit you down and explain the concept of fun, and the thrill of working for what you want.'

'That's rich coming from you. Getting what you want must be such a struggle, Lissy.'

'Okay, girls, that's enough,' Cheryl said, looking preoccupied and a little nervous. 'Let's meet back here in half an hour.'

Lissy agreed and headed off on her own. The morning was sunny and warm, but not too hot for the jeans she had miraculously squeezed into, despite being twenty-eight weeks. While the zipper didn't zip all the way, several nappy pins had done the trick, with the loose-hanging shirt ample cover for her belly and the temporary fastenings. Tie-dyed or not, Lissy wouldn't be seen dead in the old-lady kaftans and the unfashionable maternity gear Gypsy provided. Empire-line tops, elastic waistbands, and granny-print smocks were like giant billboards shouting the words: *Look at me and my mistake.*

At the start of Sideshow Alley, the laughing clowns looked lonely without a crowd, their astonished expressions turning one way and then the other as if wondering, *Where is everyone?* The prize wall didn't impress Lissy — there were no Kewpie dolls on offer — but she felt sorry for the clowns and determined to prove Irene wrong.

135

She counted off the required number of twenty-cent pieces and had a go. The prize? A plastic keyring with a red and black ladybug on a chain. It wasn't much, but the win filled Lissy with a smug sense of achievement. She couldn't wait to tell Irene. Adjacent to the laughing clowns was a quoits game involving round rubber rings and floating targets. Again, the prize wall held no Kewpie dolls.

'Try your luck, little lady?' The Shoot 'em Up attendant thrust an air rifle towards Lissy.

'I want the pink doll on a stick. Can't I just buy one?'

'Take down three yellow ducks in a row and it's yours,' he said.

'You want me to shoot three ducks in a row?'

Lissy was about to walk away when he added, 'Unless you don't think you can. I don't want to waste your money. I'm not a man to take advantage of a young lady.'

Lissy huffed and dropped the keyring into her breast pocket. Then she slapped two coins on the counter, selected a rifle and took aim. 'They're going awfully fast,' she said. 'Will one do?'

'Three ducks, three shots and the Kewpie doll is yours,' the operator explained. 'Come on, little lady, give it a crack and show us what else you're good at. I bet your daddy wishes he was a better shot.'

Lissy had no interest in the man's chatter. Her focus was on the prize, on the rifle's unreliable crosshairs, and on her twitching trigger finger.

Bang! She squealed as the duck fell back flat. 'I got it! I got it!'

'You got *one*.' The cocky attendant leaned against the side wall of the trailer. 'Bang, bang,' he said while he jiggled the leather money pouch hanging over his groin. 'Want another *duck*? Give it your best shot, girlie.'

A small crowd, mostly bored carnival staff, gathered. Some cheered her, while others deliberately distracted Lissy's next two attempts.

'Aw, shucks! Bad luck, little lady,' he said. 'Only you're not so little, are you?'

Frustrated, Lissy was about to give the guy a mouthful when arms wrapped around her from behind, almost lifting her off the ground. She squealed.

'Found you,' Don whispered, hugging her tight.

'Quit that. You frightened me. Put me down.'

'Hey, mate!' The attendant moved swiftly, took the rifle Lissy was waving around, and winked at Don.

'You look like a bloke who should know better than to sneak up on a lady with a loaded gun. Or maybe not.'

Lissy tugged at Don's shirt to shift his attention. 'I already won this on the laughing clowns.' She held out the keyring in one hand while pointing with the other. 'But what I really want to win is one of those dolls.'

Don dug deep into his pocket as he approached the counter. He smacked the coins down and took up a rifle. *Bang! Bang! Bang!*

'Yay!' Lissy squealed. 'You did it! You won! Come on, mate, hand it over. What are you waiting for?' She wiggled her fingers at the prize

137

on the back wall. 'No, not a blue one,' she said as the man reached up reluctantly. 'I said the *pink* tutu. And hurry. We've got more prizes to win in the campdrafting arena.'

The attendant called out as they walked away. 'There goes one lucky little lady, folks, and a bloke who doesn't fire blanks. Roll up! Roll up!'

When Don tensed into defensive mode, Lissy tightened her grip around his arm.

'Let me.' She marched back to the amusement, hurling the bamboo stick — prized Kewpie doll still attached. 'You can shove that you-know-where.'

'Whadaya know, ladies and gentlemen? One minute a girl wants it, and the next she's changing her mind. What's a poor bloke to do?' The attendant was enjoying the groundswell of curious onlookers, his cronies egging him on. 'Step up and shoot with confidence, gentlemen. Unlike my friend, these rifles only fire blanks.'

Within seconds, Don had run back to the trailer and leapt the counter, pinning the attendant against the flimsy prize wall. Cardboard cowboy hats, Kewpie dolls and stuffed animals rained down as fellow stallholders joined the melee.

'You're all thugs,' Lissy cried as Don landed with a thud in front of the stand. 'If you've hurt him . . .'

A burly man wearing a uniform rushed towards them and squatted beside Don, followed by two St John's first-aiders. Don tried shaking the lot off, but something hurt. His grimace was

138

tight, face flushed, eyes watering.

'Settle down, mate, and we'll look at the shoulder you're hanging onto,' the first-aider said. 'What's your name?'

'Dawson. Don Dawson.'

The security officer had got up again and was busy lambasting the carnival workers, urging onlookers to clear the scene, when Lissy saw that her ladybug had been ground into the dirt by someone's boot. So much for being lucky. She was brushing the keyring clean when she saw Cheryl's horrified expression.

'What on earth happened?'

'Can we get out of here, please?' Lissy asked. 'We have to take Don home.'

The first-aider stood and shook his head. 'I'm suggesting a shoulder X-ray in Saddleton. Are you and your baby all right?' He glanced at Lissy's belly. 'Can you drive your husband, Mrs Dawson?'

'I beg your pardon?'

'Can you get your husband to the hospital?' the man clarified. 'We can arrange transportation, if you'd prefer.'

'Oh, my husband? Right, um . . . '

Don was sitting now, adjusting his torn shirt with his good arm. 'Listen, fellas, I appreciate your concern, but I'm good. My brother's over by the cattle yards. He'll take me. As for you . . . ' Don squinted at Lissy. 'I'll see you at the house later, *wifey*.' He winked and kissed Lissy on the mouth before shooting Cheryl a silent apology.

Lissy might have been regretful as well, except

for a short while she had been Mrs Don Dawson, and she liked the sound of that very much.

11

Saddleton, 2014

'Your grandmother's door is easy to spot,' the nurse behind the desk tells Beth. 'Look for the one *not* covered with family pictures. On the right, before the TV room.'

Guilt nips at Beth's heels as she passes a dozen doors plastered with curious art projects, kiddy photos, and stick-figure families. The same self-reproach bites deeper when she passes an open door and sees a young woman settling a baby swaddled in blue into the arms of a wheel-chair-bound woman. All Beth's arms cradle is a ridiculously large bouquet of Australian natives wrapped in blue tissue paper.

'Hi, Gran!'

'Well, well, do my old eyes deceive me?'

Looking frail and less intimidating than the version in Beth's memory, her grandmother's swollen and slippered feet keep the recliner rocking in short, sharp movements. She's grey and wrinkled, but with the same hard-boiled scowl and inquiring eyes. They fix on Beth. Is she pleased about the visit? Beth's never been able to tell. Not even after those few Christmas holidays when, laden with tins of fruitcake and shortbread they couldn't afford, she and her mum would arrive at the front door. In Beth's young mind, the deathly boring drives had been

141

a big effort to maintain a relationship no one seemed to want. However tenuous, though, family connection had always been important to her mum.

Sadly, Gran is yet to reach out to Beth for a hug. Instead, she grunts. It may have been a cough.

'Best open the blinds. I need a good look, Bethy. Been so long, I hardly recognise you. You always were scrawny as a kid, like you could do with a good feed.'

Gran had several signature snipes which she dragged out at Christmas along with the fake tree and tinsel. Some lines her mum would repeat on the trip home and the pair would laugh them off. Others had hurt, Beth noticed, especially the judgmental slurs.

'Sorry, Gran,' Beth says. 'I've had a lot on. Loose ends to tidy and Mum's place to organise. My job can make getting away tricky.' When the lie forces Beth to look anywhere but at her gran, she notices the bouquet's cheap wrapping has stained one sweaty hand blue. 'I brought flowers.'

She searches the room that's been her grandmother's home for half a decade. She feels remiss for not visiting earlier, but this was the last place Beth had thought to come for sympathy. On opposing ends of the antique lowboy, she spies two separate but identical displays of artificial roses. She busies herself ramming both bunches of yellow into one cut-glass vase.

'I brought the service card from Mum's

142

funeral.' Beth might have added how lovely the send-off had been or mentioned the generosity of Anton's relatives. Even while dealing with their own grief, Angela's family had been mindful of Beth having no family support. 'There was a huge crowd, Gran,' she says pointedly while transporting the dry vase to the en suite.

'I see your ex-husband's show is up for a Logie award.' Gran shouts over the running water. 'Do they hand those out to adulterers these days?'

Beth manages an unnatural sing-song reply. 'I guess they do, Gran.' She glances up from the washbasin hoping to see the *joie de vivre* from last night's dinner with Tom in her reflection. Nothing. She's looking as faded as her jeans.

Beth prefers not to think about Richard still raking in work while she faces ever-diminishing opportunities. Skill seems no longer an essential attribute for those with creative aspirations. Everyone is after the big name to draw big box-office figures. A huge social media following helps. Why pay for genuine talent when a human headline or a celebrity can recoup ten times the investment? After every unsuccessful audition, Beth tells herself it's time to quit, to diversify, to reinvent herself and begin again somewhere new, like her mum had done with each relocation. Had Beth's life gone to plan, by now she'd have a house with a backyard swing-set and a hole-digging dog. She would've taken that final on-stage curtain call while still on top of her game, confident the person waiting in the wings

— her writer/producer-husband — was ready to be the greatest dad, and motherhood Beth's greatest and most rewarding role.

'Hurry with those blasted flowers and help me up, will you, dear?' Her gran is staring at Beth from her chair, one arm flapping. 'Running that water has made me want to pee.'

'Sorry,' Beth says, before sliding the bathroom door shut and flopping on the bed, cursing her gran for mentioning Richard.

The pair met ten years ago, both ambitious thirty-year-old thespians, moving into an apartment not long after to give her mum and Anton space. Richard had also wanted to start a family, although at that time, Beth had been in a great place career-wise, so she'd stalled. They could afford to wait a few years, or so she'd thought. When they did start trying, three prime child-bearing years passed Beth by in a flash. Next, the stress of fitting IVF schedules around two busy lives wasted three more, until the news came a few weeks after Beth's thirty-seventh birthday. Impatient and excited, she'd telephoned Richard from the doctor's office and for twenty-four glorious, mind-blowing, amazing weeks her baby girl's heart had beat inside her. Soon after burying their daughter, her writer/ producer husband wrote himself out of Beth's life, and her happy ending was cut and discarded on the editing-room floor.

When the bathroom door slides open and bangs, the sour-looking woman with wide hips and swollen ankles shuffles back to the padded armchair.

144

'So, do you want a hug?' Her arms flapping wildly suggest the offer has an expiry. The embrace ends with Beth supporting her aging grandmother back onto the chair.

There had been times, Beth recalls, when her mum's cuddles had felt just as perfunctory and in response to a need rather than spontaneous and genuine affection. Although there had been no shortage of them, some hugs had lacked substance, much like the sixteen-year-old drama students Beth had started teaching six months ago — all brash, brawn and bravado until directed to express emotion. Other times, the mother-daughter embrace seemed too eager, too desperate.

'Have the police made any arrests?' Gran's asking. 'If I could get my hands on those drunken idiots who killed Andrew and your mother . . .'

Beth doesn't correct Anton's name. 'I'm sure they'll see their day in court, for all the good a slap on the wrist and a fine will do. They weren't eighteen, Gran. Kids with no idea of right and wrong.'

The woman huffs. 'Old enough to be accountable. Same age as your mother when she got herself pregnant.' The clunk of uneven trolley casters and a rattle of crockery becomes the focus. 'Oh, good, time for tea.' Valerie's smile welcomes the young woman wearing blue food-safety gloves and an unattractive hair net. 'Good morning, Verity. One for my granddaughter, please, darling. Any bickies?'

'Oui! Oui!' the worker says over the sound of

crinkling cellophane wrapping. 'Verity has Iced VoVos. Valerie's favourite variety!' The tea-lady's titter suggests she gets a kick out of the alliteration.

After Beth passes on a biscuit and Verity disappears with her noisy trolley, an awkward silence fills the space, while coconut crumbs fill the rumples in her gran's cardigan.

'Anton's sister, Angela, helped me sort Mum's things,' Beth says. 'She admired a few pieces. I let her have them.'

A harrumph sends Iced VoVo spraying from Val's lips. 'No sense hoarding,' she says before blowing coconut specks on the tea's surface, impatient for it to cool, her scowl set in place once more. 'When I could no longer stay in my home without a family member around to help care for *me*, I let go of the lot.'

With little nostalgia, I bet, Beth muses.

'Do you know, Gran, Mum and *Anton* racked up a pile of photo albums. I packed some in a box with other bits for you to sift through.'

'Humph! All those travels around the world and not a single road trip to Saddleton in the last five years. I chose here for your mother's convenience. Didn't matter to me where I died, although Queensland might've been warmer.'

'The room's lovely — and big,' Beth says, desperate to change the subject.

When another harrumph and a flick of both hands sends crumbs raining over carpet designed to disguise, Beth stands, peels the elastic band off her wrist, and tugs her hair into a ponytail, as if constraining her hair will help clip her tongue.

'I'll get the box from the car.'

If Beth could ask her mother one thing, it would be what happened with Valerie to make her so indifferent, especially as Beth and her mum were so close. The pair did everything together: shopping, cooking, crying through every Nicholas Sparks movie. Her mum had been Beth's best friend and biggest fan. They would celebrate auditions that ended with a 'Yes' by starting a new scrapbook for the playbills, the pictures and the performance critiques. Her mum loved scrapbooks. The good reviews called for a special dinner, when they'd pop the spumante and pretend it was expensive Champagne.

At her car, Beth pops the hatchback's boot, immediately questioning the smallness of the box waiting inside. Should she have brought more of the personal effects and favourite ornaments? Given the choice, Beth would've kept everything in its place, maintaining the villa as a manifestation of the happiest time of her mum's life. But hoarding can't make up for a loss any more than the contents of a box can magically bring a loved one back. Practicalities, and Anton's family, had required consideration, and both had helped Beth decide on the fate of each object. If not for Anton's niece, Beth didn't know how she would have managed sorting through the remnants of two lifetimes.

★　★　★

She'd arrived at the villa before Angela and slipped the key into the lock, hearing the click

147

and the squeak of hinges but nothing else. No 'Hello! Who's there?', or 'Sweet-pea, is that you?' Greeting Beth instead was the familiar scent of her mother's life. It permeated the carpets, the curtaining, and cupboards crammed with clothes. The smell was so precious, Beth wished she could bottle it, put a lid on it, and eke it out for the rest of her days.

When Angela arrived, the pair immediately raided Anton's wine collection, indifferent to the age or value of the bottle. Getting through this task would require degrees of indifference. Why not start with a 1994 Henschke Hill of Grace and not give a damn how much it was worth? With every sip of the shiraz to pass over Beth's lips, she reminded herself the villa was no longer a home, but a museum of memories and a collection of material items classified as ruthlessly as: keep, bin, donate.

When the oddest of trinkets turned on tears, the pair sought comfort by hugging and sipping more wine. Music helped soothe — it always had — and Beth was grateful she wasn't on her own doing the cruellest duty a daughter can be dealt. When the opening few bars of The Carpenters' *Close to You* started, Angela tugged Beth's hand.

'Let's tackle the bookshelves,' she suggested. 'You can't cry over those, unless we find that dreadful novel that should never have made the bestseller list. Then I'll cry with you.'

While admiring Anton's personal trove, Beth acknowledged that the Fallone family's contribution was a few children's classics. Her mum had loved books, but she always seemed too busy to read, while constant relocations — combined with little spare cash — meant borrowing from a library had made more sense to Beth than buying books to keep.

'This lot will definitely take more wine,' Beth said as the pair ogled the collection of cookbooks, biographies, photo albums, and treasured Australian fiction. Though her mum had encouraged reading from a young age, Beth preferred inventing stories and putting on her one-woman shows. Had she been into books like her mum, rather than taking up acting as a career, Beth might have been a fiction writer. Would she have found greater success, made more money, written her own happily ever after? *Maybe*.

After emptying the bookshelves into the boxes branded *keep, bin, donate*, Beth helped Angela attack the glass display cabinet chock full of mementoes, each miniature trinket a prop for an epic Anton travel story. While Beth never tired of those welcome-home reunion dinners, or the souvenir tea towel she was presented with each time, more precious than any material gift was seeing her mother's world unfurling to become more than just about Beth. The woman had given so much of herself and her life to being a mum.

The very perceptive and patient Anton had once explained their long courtship to Beth by saying, 'Your mother is like a tiny bud. One with its protective sheath too tightly wrapped, too afraid to let go, to let the beauty show for fear someone will pick her and take her away from all she knows.'

Who wouldn't fall for a guy who spoke like a poet and made the most mundane tourist anecdote a journey for his audience? Anton had so many places to see. How sad and ironic that a run-of-the-mill car ride home on a local road had ended the exciting itinerary he'd planned for his betrothed.

When Angela prepared snacks and hot drinks to soak up the wine, Beth started on the walls dotted with favourite holiday happy snaps, all in Anton's beautifully crafted frames. Such a clever man.

'Good with his hands,' her mum had said with a wink one day. Beth didn't share that titbit with Angela about her uncle, not even when they took their coffee into the bedroom her mum had shared with Handyman Anton.

The caffeine added a short-lived buzz to the tranquillising power of alcohol, but neither tonic could mask the sorrow of packing up someone else's life. With crockery, casserole dishes, lounge chairs and side tables easy choices for the op shop, where did she start on those personal items and precious possessions accumulated over decades? What did her mother truly treasure and what would be meaningful to Beth in the future? Precious or not, was there any point in preserving belongings when Beth had no child and no family to pass them on to when she died? That sad fact had made the sorting process even more painful.

Angela was crouched in front of a camphor chest at the foot of the bed where Beth had removed two musty blankets, checked they were free of moth holes, and dropped both into the charity box. After returning for the third, she saw Angela holding a wooden container.

'This is spectacular workmanship, Beth. Do you suppose Uncle Anton made it?'

'Your uncle *was* handy and clever with his hands,' Beth said, hesitating when Angela proffered the box. 'Why don't you take it?'

'Because what he's carved suggests it's your mum's. Look here.'

Beth shrugged. 'Probably.' Her fingers traced the elaborate etching in one corner. 'But to be honest, Ange, when I look at those letters I think of Mum and I think 'If only . . . '. Two words she said so often, and two words I'd rather not. Take it with you. Seriously. Such an object needs handing down. It needs a family. The box is your uncle's handiwork. I'd check the contents, but it's locked and goodness knows where the key might be.'

'If you're sure,' Ange said. 'I'd love for Leticia to have it. As for the lock, my husband is very handy when it comes to getting into things.' If Angela wondered why Beth tittered, she didn't let on. 'I'll return the contents to you, of course.'

Beth shrugs. 'Could be anything. I've accounted for Mum's personal papers. After so many relocations, my mother was a gold medallist in packing and organising. Some boxes she never emptied. 'Easy to grab and go,' she'd tell me, because 'A wise person has an exit plan in case of fire or catastrophe.' She was one of a kind.' Beth smiled. 'There were cartons we folded flat and reinstated as required — same cartons, same contents, new

151

apartment. We had quite the relocation routine until Anton. Bless him.'

'Your mum's grab-and-go catastrophe boxes are probably the ones in the garage,' Angela said. 'Although I saw one labelled *Christmas*. Decorations, I assume?'

'Speaking of catastrophes!' Beth snorted. 'Our family's festive celebrations were certainly that. You're welcome to open the carton and use whatever. If not, give it to the Salvos and spread some cheer.'

'How would you feel about Cameron transporting all those boxes when he packs up Uncle Anton's man cave?' Angela asked. 'We have a container behind our garage to store them. There's no rule about having to deal with all this at once.'

'You're right. But I will take the smaller carton over there when I visit my grandmother.' Beth pointed.

'Let me know how hubby goes with the locked box. If it is Mum's stuff, I can drop by your house when I head to Saddleton next week.'

'You plan on visiting Valerie so soon?'

'Not soon enough, really.' Beth grimaced guiltily. 'Wish me luck.'

★ ★ ★

The contents of Anton's carved box, now crammed into Angela's big yellow envelope, are with the original owner — Beth's beautiful, strong, courageous mum in the purple gift bag. Sighing long and loud as she lifts the packing carton marked *Gran* from the back of the car,

Beth harnesses her mother's courage and retraces her steps to Valerie's room.

When she arrives, no Valerie in sight, Beth tucks the box safely in a corner and continues along the corridor to find the TV room. Nursing staff are shuffling residents in various states of cognisance into chairs. They form rows of old people, each one planted in front of the big screen like the wilting flowers they are — at the end of their bloom and biding their time. Beth shivers at the thought of ending up the same, deciding then to visit more often. In between seeing Gran, she could volunteer at an aged-care home in Parramatta. Or perhaps get a Labrador or a Groodle and join the Delta Dog Therapy program. Dementia studies have shown two hours of dog patting is preferable to two hours of TV time.

'Movie matinee day,' says the carer, pointing a TV remote with fierce determination. 'Arnold Schwarzenegger's *Total Recall*.'

An interesting choice, Beth wants to reply, considering the dementia-affected residents would have very little. Perched in a corner of the room, on a throne-like armchair, Valerie looks the fittest of the bunch.

Beth scans the area for a spare seat to drag over. 'I've left the box in your room, Gran.'

'Going now, are you? Short and sweet, like your mother's Christmas visits. Good-o.' Valerie turns her cheek in readiness for a goodbye kiss.

'Oh, okay, I guess.' She bends down obediently. 'Well, as Schwarzenegger says, 'I'll be back.''

The joke falls flat. So does Beth's mood.

At the Calingarry Crossing Hotel, fully prepared to buy a bottle of wine to drown her sorrows in private, Beth bumps into Maggie.

'Someone's trying to track you down,' the publican says, smiling. 'Thought you might want to visit the joey. You'll find Tom in the beer garden.'

12

Calingarry Crossing, 2014

One glimpse of the tatty tan cowboy hat, and all traces of Beth's bad mood fade.

'Well, hello! You are exactly what I need, Tom.'

'Oh yeah? That's the nicest thing I've heard in a while.' He stands until Beth sits.

How sweet! Who does that anymore?

Straddling the wooden bench, Beth is grateful for the shade of a market umbrella. Maybe she needs to buy a hat. Not that many people wear them where she lives. Peak caps, maybe. *Why is that?* she wonders. Same sun. Same risk of cancer.

'Hello there?' Tom questions, peering hard. 'I asked how your grandmother is.'

'Oh, sorry. I swear, the devil has nothing on that woman. And no . . . ' Beth thrusts a palm in his direction as she gulps a mouthful of the lemon squash she'd bought on her way to the beer garden. 'I don't want to talk about her.'

'What would you like to do?' he asks. 'Any plans? Want to see the joey?'

'The thing is, Tom,' she says, 'these ashes will not spread themselves, more's the pity. As much as I'd like to put the task off forever, I should tackle the cemetery.' She takes the notepaper from her bag, noticing the yellowing foolscap-sized sheet getting flimsy along the folds.

'May I?' Tom reaches out and takes the map, rotating several times. 'Might be easier if I take you. I'm familiar with the place.'

'You are?' Beth's intrigued. 'How familiar, exactly?'

He barks a laugh. 'There goes that imagination. You're thinking graveyards, full moons, and howling wolves, I suppose?'

His ghostly wail draws amused chuckles from nearby pub patrons, but Tom isn't bothered.

'Admit it,' Beth says, 'a person saying they're familiar with an old cemetery is unusual. On the other hand, some company might be nice.'

Your company, she might have clarified. He really is exactly what she needs — a dash of exuberance after her nursing home visit. There's a youthfulness about Tom, even though his face shows signs of age, like the splayed white smile lines noticeable only when he's not smiling, which isn't often, she's learning.

He's staring at her from under the well-worn Akubra hat, two brown eyes questioning. 'Want to go now, Beth?'

'Sure, my car's out front. Unless you have Wally somewhere.' She grimaces. 'Don't get me wrong. I love dogs, but not enormous mutts with a penchant for rolling in animal poo.'

Tom chuckles. 'Nah, he's at home. Besides, you can walk to the cemetery from town. There's a path we can pick up behind the old church. Rough, but a decent shortcut on a nice day — if you're up for it.'

'You mean the old church in the main street?' Beth might have noticed a walking trail, had her

156

focus not been on the *For Tender* sign and wondering what sort of person buys such a building in a small town.

'That's the one,' Tom says. 'Been on the market a while. Unfortunately, real estate moves slow in country towns. Maggie knows all about that. The church has a lot of land. Goes all the way back,' Tom tells her. 'Behind the church is the cemetery and beyond that is mostly state forest, which is why driving takes longer. We have to go around. If we follow the walking path, it's only about two kilometres. Shall we?'

★ ★ ★

Tom's right about the nice weather. Noticing the blue of the sky and the white of the clouds is not something Beth does at home. The sprawling fig-tree canopy creates patterns of sunlight over the main street, and leaf debris litters the sidewalk to add a shabby charm to the rows of imperfect storefronts. Under each awning is a hanging shop sign with decorative metal trims and brackets to keep the quintessential country-town feel.

When did her mum come here? Did she walk this street? The place is not ringing any bells for Beth. Surely she would remember visiting. It's not as if she and her mother had lived separate lives, either. They didn't do much without the other knowing where they were going or when they'd be home. Even when Beth travelled for work, voice or text messages were a nightly ritual.

She instinctively feels for her phone in the pocket of her jeans, remembering the day she'd let her mum choose her own custom notification tone. How Beth misses hearing that over-the-top bugle fanfare. Then, when Anton came onto the scene, her mum asked Beth to help her assign a cheerful chime to announce his texts. Not long after, Beth became Richard's official leading lady and moved into his high-rise apartment. Seven years later, the much-anticipated *Beth Has A Baby Show* folded. What she'd expected would screen for a lifetime — every milestone recorded, edited and filed — had ended when her baby's tiny heart failed. A precious life over before it had begun. In the months that had followed, her mother was a constant support and a clear head when decisions were required. She took charge. She was there for Beth every minute of every devastating day. Now she's gone, too.

'Good heavens! What's the matter, Beth?'

She's stopped in the middle of the roadway, hunched over and cupping cheeks tacky with tears she didn't know she was crying.

'Come over and sit down.' With his hand supporting her elbow, Tom guides a dazed Beth towards the grassy median.

At a park bench, she sits somewhat robotically and curls her fingers around the folded handkerchief he's pushed into her palm. To her right, the cafe is pumping out music and caffeine-fired conversation, while on her left, Tom sits silently rubbing between her shoulder blades as Beth tortures the cotton corners of the hanky.

She forces a smile and straightens to look at him. 'A man offering a fresh handkerchief, folded and pressed? You don't find that in the city.'

'And I bet you don't find too many people stopping in the middle of the road.'

He grins back and Beth can't work out what it is about him she likes the most. With her initial roadside appraisal unduly influenced by her mood and the gravity of the situation, she's seeing Tom with fresh eyes today. He's definitely good-looking, charming, and refreshingly unhurried. But what's more impressive — having made Tom her last conscious thought as she'd hopped into bed after dinner — is how relaxed he makes her feel. The easy-going grazier seems sensitive to the moods of others, his concern genuine, like he's got all the time in the world for someone else's problems.

Probably too good to be true! That was another of her mum's cautionary life lessons. What would she make of Tom and his pressed hanky? Beth had guided a few men through the front door for the dreaded meet-the-parent session. Afterwards, they all said they didn't get a good vibe. But Mum would like Tom, Beth decides.

She's dabbing her eyes when a green figbird lands nearby, drawn to the glut of fallen berries. It's close enough for her to see the bare red-coloured skin around both eyes. With hers probably appearing much the same, she's almost embarrassed to look at the man sitting patiently beside her.

'I'm sorry to be such a city girl,' she finally says. 'But I have to ask. What does a woman do after snivelling over a man's clean hanky? Give it back?'

Tom chuckles. 'No. She agrees to have dinner with him.'

'Really?'

'Yup!'

'Okay.' Beth says without missing a beat. There'll be ample time for misery when she returns home. 'But as I've cried my quota for one day, I say let's give the cemetery a miss. I'd love to visit the little joey and have dinner with you tonight.'

★ ★ ★

Taking up most of the twenty-minute drive is Tom's chatter about his farm: what he grows, the breed of cattle, and how he learned everything from his awesome uncle. Beth is surprised to discover Tom's Uncle Don is also the person charged with bottle-feeding the joey.

'Does your uncle care for all kinds of injured animals?'

'Only what he can manage,' Tom says. 'The bloke's a born carer. Always has been. Raised me after Dad died and Mum took off. Did a remarkable job, don't you reckon?' He smiles before slipping somewhere serious.

Tom has stopped the ute at a cattle grid beside a cut-down tree trunk with the property name burned into it in big letters. Although nestled between swathes of long grass, she can make out

160

the name: *Dawson's Run*. On the opposite side of the entrance is a sign standing tall and proud: *A Future Farmers' Education & Research Facility. Don & Tom Dawson — Award-winning Brangus Beef*.

'Shall we?' she asks, but Tom seems distracted all of a sudden, his stare fixed straight ahead.

'Before you meet my uncle, Beth,' he says, 'I need to prepare you.'

'O-kay,' she replies dubiously.

The jab of his thumb draws her attention to a paddock — on the right, beyond the gates. 'Years ago, Uncle Don was working on a fence over there when he tangled with some machinery. The result wasn't good.'

'Machinery?'

'An auger,' he clarifies. 'Digs fence post holes, among other things. A tractor powers the device through the PTO shaft and the thing you can't do when using one is get distracted or get too close to a moving part.' He pauses to clear his throat. 'Doctors said his survival was miraculous, but surgeons could only do so much. The reason I'm telling you, Beth, is because Uncle Don is . . . Well, he's so much more than what you'll see. Like *Phantom of the Opera*,' Tom says. 'Behind the mask of scars is a beautiful man. And like I said, he raised me, so I should know.'

As quick as a flash, Beth responds. 'Then he must be amazing.' Having played Esmeralda twice in two separate stage productions of *Phantom*, she appreciates the analogy. Now to reassure Tom he can trust her to mask any reaction. After all, her job is about manipulating

161

emotions — hers and her audience. She touches his hand where it rests on the steering wheel, the knuckles white. 'Thanks for the heads-up, Tom.'

'I'm not used to warning people and I don't drop by Don's with many women. I've only reached the *let-me-take-you-home-and-freak-you-out* stage in one relationship since my wife.' He doesn't smile.

'Poker face, I promise,' Beth says, keen to know one thing. 'You said your uncle raised you. From what age? How old were you when your dad died?'

'I turned seven the day after he took himself and his rifle for a long drive into a distant paddock.' Tom is still staring straight ahead, his hands gripping the steering wheel at ten and two, arms stiff. 'Trauma and my age at the time has let a lot of the detail slip, but I recall Dad not coming home for dinner, which wasn't unusual. He was going to the pub a lot around that time. On those nights, I'd walk from the main house to Uncle Don's cottage because, unlike our place, there was always food in his fridge. Plus he had a computer game that helped with his hand-eye coordination rehab. For a long time he couldn't speak or write. Using the joystick helped him communicate. He let me muck around with the equipment.

'Anyway, that night I stayed with Uncle Don, and the next day, when I went home to unwrap my presents, there was still no Dad. Only a gift on the kitchen table. I still have that stuffed toy horse and his note: *I'm sorry, son,* he wrote. *I wanted you to have a real horse, but I couldn't*

162

do that right either. Don't be a failure like me. Make something of yourself. I love you.'

Beth doesn't know what to say, and she resists the urge to physically comfort Tom because he's trying so hard to keep it together, as men do.

'Mum and I searched everywhere. We looked for him in every room, every shed, every car on the property. We ended up at my uncle's, and the sound Don made after mum thrust the birthday note at him was like nothing I'd heard before.' Tom stops to breathe in, exhaling heavily as both hands drop to his knees. 'If anything good was to come out of Dad's death, it was my resolve to make him proud, and Don's determination to reclaim his independence.' He swivels in his seat to look at Beth. 'Being confined to a wheelchair, unable to join the search for Dad, was a real turning point. During his initial recovery years, Don had been like a kelpie taken away from the paddock and put in a backyard. He was restless and without a purpose. After Dad died, there was no stopping him.' Tom huffs, shakes his head. 'Geez, Beth, I'm sorry. I haven't done that for a while.' He drags the back of one hand over both eyes. 'Next time I promise a meltdown-imminent warning.'

'No need. Let's call it even,' she says. 'And I do understand the pain of losing someone special.'

Tom nods and stares straight ahead again. 'It sucks that Dad's struggle was about living up to Granddad's expectations and an inheritance he would've been better off without. To think his fear of failing me terrified him more than a bullet. It's ironic,' Tom says. 'The man was afraid

163

if he stuck around I'd grow up to be like him. But what he did actually pushed me to prove I could be both Michael Dawson's son *and* a successful farmer.'

'Which you've done, obviously.' Beth nods towards the billboard.

'Bloody shame Dad missed it all.'

Beth looks beyond the cobbled stone pillars to the tree-lined strip of gravel and the distant buildings. There's nothing striking about the entrance, although a few mature but out-of-place Tuscan-type pencil pines suggest someone might have had grand plans for the long driveway many years ago. Instead, flowering natives and the odd gum tree clutter the edges. To the left and right of the driveway, the landscape stretches towards the horizon, while bunched at the fence closest to them is a dozen cows with inquiring eyes.

Beth turns her attention back to Tom, his gaze still glassy. 'I think we're being watched.'

'My audience,' he tells her. 'They like to watch. They can be good listeners, too, and the best company when all you want is a pity-party for one.'

Beth nods. 'I understand, Tom, truly. In the last few years, I've heard the word 'sorry' way too often, along with other perfunctory phrases like 'you'll be fine'. Drove me nuts at Mum's funeral. One woman I didn't recognise told me I'd get over '*it*' soon enough, as if my only ailment was the flu. I miss my mum so much, but at least I have forty years of memories. You were a child, Tom.'

'And the circumstances confusing,' he says, 'even with Uncle Don sheltering me from town talk.' He pushes back against his car seat, both hands gripping his neck as if stretching the tension away. 'Like I said, my memories are hazy. Doctors told Uncle Don our brains deliberately block traumatic events so we don't have to relive them. That doesn't mean the pain leaves us, of course. Grief simply changes shape and we push it down to dilute it with everyday stuff. I guess that's how we keep functioning. Then there are those emotions burrowing so deep inside we don't know they're slowly building, waiting for a crack to form on the surface, because misery knows if it waits long enough we'll weaken. My dad knew all about that.' Tom fossicks in his pockets, then in the centre console and glove box, eventually finding an unused fast-food serviette to blow his nose on. 'Uncle Don was still relearning to walk and talk when he lost his brother. Two years later, he buried his dad and mum. But the worst thing was losing the one person who meant more to him than anything else.'

Beth says nothing when Tom's gaze shifts to the empty paddock. She's barely keeping it together herself.

'He was besotted,' Tom says, answering Beth's unspoken question. 'I remember a woman. It was a long time ago. She drove away, out this very gate, but she might as well have died. His grief seemed the same. There's not been anyone else to love him since. Only me, and I'm a poor bloody substitute.' Tom snorts, his smile brief. 'To be honest, Beth, that kind of loneliness terrifies me.'

Beth is about to say 'me too' when Tom shifts the ute into gear.

'Bloody hell! I'm a ball of fun. Bet you're glad you said yes to visiting Dawson's Run. Home to too many generations of sorry bastards!' He plants a foot on the accelerator. 'Lucky I got dinner in last night because no way will you be showing up tonight.'

'Stop the car, Tom!' Beth tugs on his arm and he yanks on the handbrake, his head snapping around to face her.

'What? What's wrong?'

'You said your dad died the day before your birthday, and the anniversary was the day I arrived in town, which means . . . Yesterday was your birthday?'

'Ah, look, movement at the station. Don is no doubt wondering what I'm doing down here all this time.'

'Then we'd better carry on,' Beth says. 'I'd like to meet your lovely uncle. We can discuss the matter of missed birthdays later. And we will, Tom Dawson.'

As the car approaches the small cottage, Beth glances out the passenger window towards a large shed and an abandoned tractor swallowed up by long grass. It looks sad compared to the more modern machinery taking pride of place under-cover. Up ahead is a small house with fencing draped in a flowering clematis creeper. Smack-bang in the middle of the yard is a straight concrete strip stretching between a closed-in veranda and a Hills hoist. A woman trying to keep her yellow hat in place while battling flapping sheets manages a wave as Tom toots but keeps driving.

'Ah, there's a sight to warm my heart.'

'Seriously?' Beth queries. 'A woman doing the laundry warms your heart, Tom?'

'Not just any woman. That one — a beautiful soul, once married to the biggest moron in town, and one of the few people who has always been there for Uncle Don. The pair go way back. While Don insists he doesn't need her help, Cheryl wins any arguments and finds reasons to drop by for tea. Her friendship makes a world of difference to him, and me. So, yeah, I love the sight of *that* woman doing laundry — doing anything at Dawson's Run.'

As Tom steers left and brings the car to a stop, a second vehicle pulls alongside and a young man gets out, pausing to tether Wally on the back tray as Tom and Beth alight.

'Are you checking up on me?' the driver calls to Tom over the *thump-thump-thump* of the dog's tail on metal. 'Thought you had important *stuff* to do. G'day!'

Even with his hair curlier, his build stockier, and his teeth set straight — likely at great expense — there is no missing the family resemblance.

'We came to check on the joey. This is Beth,' Tom says on his way to the back of the ute.

'Aw, the joey lady! Nice one, Dad.'

A playful flick of Tom's hand sends his son's hat flying. 'Did you get around to refitting those gate latches?'

'Under control.' Matt collects the cap and slaps it against a thigh as he returns to his car. 'I'll let you know if I need help. Check ya later.'

167

'Sorry.' Tom's face creases guiltily as the exuberant and dusty departure forces Beth to turn away. 'That's Matt, the fifth-generation Dawson and the only good thing to come out of my brief marriage.'

'You did mention a fifth generation over dinner. He lives here?' Beth asks.

'Sadly, no. Let's walk over to the house and I'll get you a drink to wash the dust down.' Tom leads the way while explaining Matt is a full-time college student, and the Dawson's Run operation highly regarded by career advisors keen to encourage kids into agriculture. 'We mostly accept high school students who are still undecided about a career on the land, but we could hardly say no to a certain university student looking for field work. He happens to be very impressive and extremely persuasive, like his old man.'

Tom tells Beth they offer hands-on experience for city-based kids who might be needing a shove in a country direction.

'Textbooks and YouTube can only do so much,' he explains. 'Here, they experience the real thing, with Don's knowledge of past farming practises a bonus. Our industry's future will depend on a balance of old and new, with technology and tradition complementing each other, rather than competing. The kids who visit Dawson's Run not only see two generations working as a team, in Don they see a man who never gave up.'

'A good lesson for anyone,' Beth says. 'But often difficult to do when life keeps knocking you down.'

'The difference is passion,' Tom says. 'I'm not sure Dad loved the land. He saw Dawson's Run as work, whereas Don saw an opportunity in everything. Long before any Calingarry Crossing farmer knew how to spell the word 'permaculture', Uncle Don was spruiking the benefits.' Tom grimaces at Beth. 'I'm getting carried away again. My pet topics are sustainability and diversification, while Don starts by showing students how revisiting past processes can actually be a way forward. Let me show you something quickly. This way.' They turn back towards the paddocks.

Beth keeps pace with Tom until they reach the metal maze of yard fencing, where he instinctively climbs the rails to perch on top. He notices her follow suit unwaveringly, swinging her legs high to sit beside him. He's ridiculously impressed. He's sat on fences all his life, but never with an attractive, intelligent woman — musically gifted, according to Maggie — and with two very long and delightfully flexible pins.

Beth nudges him and grins as if she can read his mind. 'Do you plan on telling me what we're doing up here, or is this about perving at my legs?'

'Yes, um, right, well . . . I wanted to explain how Don starts his lesson in this yard with these beauties, telling students how Australia's national herd — currently some twenty-five million head — started when the 1788 First Fleet landed. When they got to Sydney Harbour, they off-loaded seven beasts, just like these.'

'Only seven?' Beth grins. 'They were very busy.'

'Yes, and only two boys. Being the bull back then was not a bad gig. They done good!'

'Hold on, cowboy.' Beth jabs Tom in the ribs. 'The girls did all the work to grow your national herd. The boys got the easy job.'

Tom laughs. 'You have a point. In fact, I recall a fiery young female student last year putting me in my place over a similar wisecrack. I did tell you over dinner there were way too many *faux pas* for me to pick a 'worst ever'. But I'm learning. Last year, females made up seventy per cent of our intake. We're also seeing computer geeks and programmers opt for field experience to better understand the land and the processes they'll be developing robots for in the future. Starting with the history lets them see how far farming has come and, therefore, where it can go. Kids know drones and robotics are already being used or trialled, and they're not daunted by the possibilities of artificial intelligence in agriculture. Early automation processes might have once been about supporting farmers with physical difficulties, like Don, but the application and advances in A.I and automation can be for anyone's benefit. We show students the Dawson's Run Command Cockpit, as we call it, and the computer-driven processes being designed to allow producers to run aspects of their business without leaving the house.'

'Wow! I'd like to see that myself. Is that what the Farmer's Future thing on the sign out front is about?' Beth asks.

Tom nods. 'Don's involvement began ten years ago after a scientific research engineer contacted him about testing robots capable of on-farm crop analysis and other basic tasks. Dawson's Run has been involved in the testing ever since, making Don well placed to let students see anything's possible. He's not only living proof, he's also a lesson in acceptance — and in potential for those kids who think they have none.'

'Your uncle puts a new perspective on 'Those who can, do. Those who can't, teach'. He clearly does both well.'

'Whoever invented that saying has never taught,' Tom says. 'Teaching is simply sharing what you know, so others get to enjoy the same. What's wrong with that?'

'I had a recent teaching stint,' Beth says. 'And a colleague dangled an opportunity to start a dance school. A kind of exclusive performance clinic.'

'You weren't interested?'

'I'm considering it,' Beth tells him. 'But the timing is all wrong and I'm kind of struggling to find my passion for theatre work. Mum could always knock sense into me whenever I doubted myself. I miss her. I miss the way she always looked out for me — always her little girl and being reminded to eat properly, to be careful, to put on sunblock. You know mums!'

'Not really,' he says. 'But I reckon yours wouldn't want you getting sunburned. Here.'

He transfers his hat to Beth's head, slapping the oversized Akubra low on her forehead. When she strikes a pose, her cute factor skyrockets, but the cheeky pout can't take away the dark circles under sad eyes. She's hurting and putting on a brave face while Tom bores her stupid with a history lesson. Maybe he needs a lecture from Matt on how to be cool. Ordinarily a good listener, for some reason this woman has Tom blathering like a schoolboy. If he gets to dinner after today, he'll make a point of shutting up in the hope she might open up. Talking about grief can be half the battle, according to his uncle. Tom might even tell Beth about Wendy — the woman who wasn't interested in being his mother.

'Come on.' After he throws his legs over and jumps to the ground, he purposely clamps both hands on his hips to stop reaching up to help Beth down. Being overly chivalrous is one more trait Tom is having to unlearn around women. 'Let's go see that joey.'

13

They approach the small dwelling to find a man sitting under the shade of a huge veranda awning. His head is bowed and a single ray of sun spotlights the chair as though he's starring in the opening scene of a stage production and waiting for his cue to look up. That cue turns out to be the listless yap of a lounging dog, lazily soaking up the same sunrays.

As Tom stops to pick up a stick, there's the unmistakable sound of claws long overdue for a cut and struggling to find purchase on the timber boards.

'Come 'ere, Lazy Bones. Have you forgotten how to be a guard dog?' The three-legged animal, the colour of copper, charges in the direction of Tom's throw. 'Hey, Unc, I've brought someone to meet you.'

When Tom pauses at the base of the stairs, perhaps allowing Don time to gather himself, Beth returns his hat and quickly frees her hair from the elastic band. For some reason, she's fidgeting more than on opening night with a full house to please. Beth is madly finger-combing her fringe, pinning the rest behind her ears, when Tom presses his hand to the small of her back. It takes every scrap of acting ability to tread the boards, her practised red-carpet smile fixed, arm extended.

'Hello, Don!' She calls him Don because she

feels too old to be calling him Mr Dawson, but hesitation on the man's part adds an awkward silence.

He leans forward in the chair, and his eyes — one obviously a prosthetic — bore into Beth. 'Lissy?'

'No, Unc, this is Beth. Remember I told you I'd resorted to picking up women from the side of the road?' Tom is the only one amused. 'I messaged you about us coming over.'

'Hope you don't mind the intrusion,' Beth says apologetically. 'I was keen to see the little joey.'

She'd imagined his uncle would be an older version of Tom, but he's far from the chatty, easy-going nephew he's raised. She's about to suggest they return another day, when Tom drags a chair away from the wooden table and pats the cushion. Dust eddies, landing on the highly lacquered table dominating the veranda.

'What a lovely cool spot,' she says, accepting the silent offer to sit.

There's a masculine feel to the weatherboard place painted gum-leaf grey, and an organised chaos about the generous hardwood veranda littered with trestle tables, furniture and equipment. Rows of tube stock cover one trestle top, something green and leafy sprouting profusely. Butted up against the wall is an outdoor kitchen with blackened pots and pans hanging overhead on 'S' hooks, and an old Companion camping stove, gas bottle and microwave oven occupying a second trestle table. An assortment of old bakers' shelves holds plastic tubs — dust-proof lids sealed tight — while a full-sized refrigerator, box freezer and

174

bar fridge huddle together, their combined hum audible in the awkward silence.

'I'll get us all a drink,' Tom says. 'A coffee to wake Uncle Don, who seems to have forgotten how to welcome a visitor. What would you like, Beth?'

'Um, a bit more of a look around your lovely property. I've not been on a farm before and I need to rattle my insides back into place after that drive. Road corrugations must take some getting used to.'

She's grateful Tom takes the hint, and for his reassuring wink. 'You don't need to ask twice for a Tom Dawson tour. We'll be back soon, Unc. Come on, Lazy Bones. You really do live up to your name. Exercise time.'

* * *

'I'm sorry, Beth,' Tom says as they stroll the wraparound veranda to the back of the cottage. 'I'm not sure what's come over him. I've never seen Uncle Don go so quiet.'

'Who's Lissy?' she asks as they head down the stairs and back along the entrance road they'd driven up.

'I don't know why he used her name. Lissy is — or was, to quote the man himself — the love of his life. I knew her by name only, because for years Don would cry it out in his sleep. That's after the surgeons put his jaw back together. He had to re-learn how to speak. Then he learned to walk and to write with his other hand. By then I was being picked on in class for being a lefty. So,

175

together, Don and I retrained our brains. We taught each other lots of things during his recovery. About Lissy, I learned very little.'

'It's an unusual name,' Beth says. 'Is it short for something? Alissa, Larissa?'

Tom shrugs. 'When I was old enough to ask about her, I saw the hurt in his face and in his voice, and I watched him go somewhere in his head while staring off into the distance. I swear, whenever he spoke that name, his one real eye cried the tears of two. I never asked about her again.'

'I gather she was a local girl?'

'No.' Tom raises his hand at the tooting sedan driving past. The laundry lady in the yellow hat waves back. 'Lissy stayed at Dandelion House when Uncle Don was working as handyman. Reckoned he was lovestruck the second he set eyes on her. He first saw her among the willows, at the bottom of the property where she was pretending the dangling limbs were dance partners. He said he watched for a long time until he got the nerve to approach, and when he did, he bowed and addressed the tree directly. 'Do you mind if I *cut in*?' he said. 'Refuse, my good man, and I'll cut you down to size.''

Beth laughs. 'That's pretty adorable.'

'Yeah, and now you know where I get my sense of humour.'

Yes, Beth thinks, but equating the stiff man she's just met with the charming one from Tom's tale is another matter.

'You mentioned Don was the handyman at Dandelion House. If Lissy was staying there, then she was . . .'

"'Unmarried, pregnant, and captivating,'" Tom finishes the sentence for her. 'Don's words, not mine. They were planning a life together. He extended the veranda so his herd of little Dawsons would have a shady place to play. He started planting Italian pencil pines to make her feel at home. And he painted the nursery, thinking she'd move in when the baby came.'

'Why didn't she?'

'In his mind she did. She's always been in this house. I think he still dreams of her turning up, offering her hand, and dancing in the willows with him. Poor bugger,' Tom mutters. 'I moved out of Don's and into the house over there a long time ago, but it wouldn't surprise me if he still calls out her name in his sleep. I can only guess, when he saw you today, he was waking up from a dream. He did have the sun in his eyes.'

'Makes sense,' Beth says. 'Sad he never got to marry or have his herd.'

'But he got a nephew and we make a pretty good team.'

Beth sighs. 'Yes, Mum and I were a team. It makes the loss so much harder.'

'Reckon you might be right. Not sure how I'll cope when Don goes, but I don't dwell on the thought.'

★ ★ ★

Having completed a huge loop on foot, taking in distant views of all three houses, and with a commentary from Tom on his childhood, they are back on the entry road into the property and within sight of Don's cottage. Some time ago, as if knowing not to stray too far, the three-legged dog with the bushy tail and yellow eyes had turned around and trotted off. From where Beth stands, it looks like he's back to being a small smudge on the veranda, asleep under his master's empty chair.

At the large sheds, Beth stops to examine the heap of unwanted and unworkable equipment tightly bound with cobwebs and weeds, and all in various stages of decomposition.

'That's the monster responsible for Don's accident.' Tom points out the old tractor.

Machinery graveyards are common in rural landscapes, but seeing one up close makes Beth wonder how long it takes for something neglected and unloved to perish. If left alone long enough, does everything rust away and turn to dust, its contribution and importance forgotten? Will Beth be forgotten one day?

She shakes the gloomy notion from her mind as they start walking again.

'There, under the old coral tree.' Tom points to a spot in the distance, down a small slope to a shady section of yard. 'That's my treehouse.'

'Really? And here's me thinking a treehouse needs a tree.'

'Ah, yes, but I'm told I insisted on wheelchair access, as it was my doctor's office.'

Beth laughs so hard she surprises herself. 'You played doctors and nurses?'

'Only doctors,' he replies. 'I wanted to fix my uncle.'

'Tom Dawson!' she says, stopping to look at

him. 'That is *very* cool and very cute. What a sweet boy. Tell me more.' She hooks a hand around the crook of his arm and they start walking again.

'Dumb more than sweet,' he admits sheepishly. 'By the time I'd figured out the benefits of having a nurse friend, I'd outgrown the cubbyhouse. Why are you laughing?' he asks, straight-faced. 'What was your pretend game as a kid?'

'Without a yard to play in, my playground was my bedroom. While you were going through your playing-doctors stage, I wanted to be National Velvet.'

'Who?'

'Never mind.' She laughs. 'I suspect every city girl has dreams of owning a pony at some stage. I had a rocking horse when I was young. At least I think I did.' She taps her lips with a finger as she tries downloading more detail from her memory. 'Weird how the image just came to me. Must be the country air. No idea what happened to the horse. Probably got left at Gran's because we moved a lot. Why Mum bought me something so impractical is also kind of weird. Guess I really wanted a pony. All I remember is, someone had to hold me because my legs weren't long enough to reach the stirrups.'

'No problem in that department these days.'

The teasing twinkle in Tom's eyes is a look Beth is beginning to recognise. 'Thank you, I think.'

'I've got an idea,' Tom says. 'Let's head down and hitch up my old rocking horse.'

Beth is about to agree when his phone sounds.

'Hello?' He looks towards the cottage. 'Ah-huh! Yep! Yep! Yep! I'll definitely ask my friend if she'd like to stay for tea and cake. Yep, I'll tell her that as well.' Tom slides the phone into his back pocket. 'Uncle Don said he didn't mean to be rude. He hadn't been awake long, but he's ready to break out the welcoming fruitcake. No pressure,' Tom adds. 'I'm happy to tell him you had to go. I understand.'

'So you can have the fruitcake to yourself?' Beth elbows his ribs. 'Nice try, buck-o! Come on.'

As they head back to the house, she can't help taking one more look towards the shed and the monster tractor.

* * *

'If you want the bathroom, it's at the end of the hall,' Tom says as he stops at the outside kitchen to help his uncle with the tea and cake. 'And you can stick your head inside the room next door. Dawson's Run Command Cockpit is where it all happens. Take your time. I have the fruitcake under control.'

The living area she passes through is outdated but well-maintained, and with a woman's touch in the drapes, the crocheted throw rugs, and in the dust-free display cabinet with its treasury of fine china heirlooms, a sprinkling of novelty trinkets, and a seriously impressive blue-ribbon display courtesy of — she reads: 'The Calingarry Crossing Agricultural Society'. Without a lot of big windows, and with the veranda keeping out any direct sunlight, there's a welcome coolness about the place. Even the tight confines of the little bathroom with its pedestal washbasin and clean guest towel is charming.

Before heading back to the men on the veranda, Beth pokes her nose inside the door on the right. Crammed with monitors, keyboards, CCTV screens and a wall of filing drawers, the Command Cockpit is intimidating and a complete contrast to the mint-green walls and faded bunny-patterned borders. There's the unmistakable smell of country wafting through the window, and lace curtains trap decades of dust in a thin horizontal brown stain. Ready to pull the door closed, Beth notices a frame hanging on the wall. She examines the intricate cross-stitch featuring a loveliness of ladybugs and reads the verse, pausing as the memory of her mother's night-time voice whispers the same words:

I had a little girl once, a bond that will never sever.
I knew the moment I saw her she'd be a part
of me forever.
A teeny tiny wonder, as cute as a bug was she,
exploring with all her ladybug friends under the
lovely linden tree.

'Found you,' Tom says from the doorway. 'I thought you might have gotten lost — or fallen in, as Uncle Don used to say to me.' When Beth doesn't smile back, he asks what's wrong.

She points at the framed verse. 'This was my mum's poem. I always thought she made it up for me. Of course, I'm being silly.' She shakes her head clear of the crazy. 'Who wrote the words shouldn't matter. It's the sentiment, right?'

Tom pats down the two breast pockets of his shirt and checks his trousers. 'Do I need to rustle up a clean handkerchief?'

'You must be running out of them by now.' She tries smiling. 'And you must think I'm a total fruitcake.'

'Nope, just a fruitcake lover, like me. Come on, before my uncle eats it all.'

★　★　★

With Don less stiff and more talkative after tea, Beth assumes she's passed some kind of shock test. Understandable, she muses. The scarring *is* hideous, with the most significant damage to his right side. Visible from under the cuff of baggy trousers is a plastic brace supporting what Beth assumes is a drop foot. A limp arm hangs from where there should be shoulder muscle, and the hand on the end is tucked awkwardly in a side pocket on his pants. He's missing his right ear, where there was once hair is now red scar tissue, and the one working eye — the left — is watching Beth watch him over the rim of her teacup. Softly spoken, and with the odd word difficult to decipher, she needs to concentrate when he speaks, which is easier said than done.

Beth used to be a good listener, until she'd learned to *not* listen to chatty colleagues as they waited in the wings for their cue. Even more annoying are those in the biz whose idea of a deep and meaningful conversation is limited to disingenuous praise or annoying self-admiration. While not everything in her world is superficial, lately Beth is having trouble seeing the industry any other way. Is it possible the universe is telling her something and she hasn't been listening? She's listening now, to Don and Tom discussing life on Dawson's Run. And yet, for some reason, she's still under the old man's scrutiny.

14

Dandelion House, 1974

For the past fortnight, following his altercation with the moron Shoot 'em Up attendant at the show, Don had juggled his responsibilities while nursing a badly bruised shoulder. Despite the family's dire prediction he would never run out of stonemasonry work, headstone orders had slowed, with the downturn partly due to a new business a few towns away offering cheaper factory-made products. Unable to compete on price, Don had chosen to specialise in detailed work and restoration jobs, and word was getting around about the quality workmanship.

The Dawson's Run herd was also calving unexpectedly, with the influx due to one gate Michael should have closed and one bull wreaking havoc among the ladies. Every mistake Mike made added to the workload, forcing Don to rise earlier each morning and fall into his bed later at night. Overwhelmed by a lazy and indifferent wife, Mike was making lots of mistakes, but even more annoying was that his brother remained unsympathetic towards Don's needs and his desire to see Lissy. The pressures of parenthood also had Michael taking out his troubles on others, including their father. Even now he was yelling orders from across the yards. Rather than arguing back — stressing the cattle

184

in the process — Don did as instructed, knowing the sooner he finished, the sooner he'd see Lissy.

By now, Don was hopelessly in love with her and falling deeper every day, but with the thirty-week mark looming, he was running out of time. Both Gypsy and Cheryl had warned him to take things slow, for Lissy's sake, and had the circumstances been different Don would happily do so. If the situation was *normal*, he would court Lissy with flowers, ask her out on dates, and send her Valentine's Day cards. If the situation was *normal*, they'd both take time every day to share their feelings and cover the important subjects like kids: Would you like them? How many? How soon? If the situation was *normal*, he'd regularly shower her with spontaneous gifts. He'd drive all the way into Saddleton to have dinner somewhere swish or to see a movie, and every month they'd celebrate the anniversary of their first date with another date. On one of those nights he'd pop the question — if the situation was normal.

But Lissy's situation was far from normal, and while it was affecting Don's approach, it didn't alter his feelings. That's why he had to make sure Lissy understood he was serious. Should she genuinely feel the same affection for him, he had to let her see he was more than willing to make her family his family. Like Gypsy, his priority was to help Lissy understand she had choices — and he was one. To delay telling her until after she'd decided about the baby would be like trying to change his dad's mind about the inheritance.

185

'Time to take the bull by the horns,' Don mumbled while freeing the last of the day's mob from the crush.

With a half day spare, he showered, put on clean jeans and a shirt, and headed to Dandelion House with two jobs in mind. First, he'd get stuck into cementing the rock supports for the four promised bench seats because hard yakka was the best way to expel the nervous energy building around the second job: to sit Lissy down, be up front about his feelings, and hopefully discover she felt the same.

★ ★ ★

After sorting the rock stockpile by size, Don worked the cement mix in the wheelbarrow until he achieved the stodgy consistency needed to form a strong bond. He couldn't remember where he'd learned that *cement* in Latin is *caedere* and means *to cut or chop*. All he knew was the therapeutic benefits of cutting and chopping a moist mix. Since meeting Lissy, he was even more intrigued by the possibility of two entirely different elements coming together to remake themselves into a lasting bond. Cement might be the least complex combination — simply calcined limestone and clay mixed with water — but the medium was versatile, like Don. Whatever the need — a firm mix for moulding into shapes, or a loose slurry capable of filling gaps and bonding fractures — cement could do the job. Like the paste he now plied to cobbled-together stones, Don would one day be the glue, and his love the rock-solid framework necessary to support a family. Lissy might be carrying another man's baby, but nurture rather than nature would see the child grow up to be like him in the ways that mattered most. With luck, when he finally introduced Lissy to his parents, he hoped the Dawson's shambolic lives might come together, strengthen, and have something to celebrate.

With the rocky supports for two seats fixed and drying, Don returned to the shed. He was washing the wheelbarrow with a hose when he looked across the yard to the main house. Ordinarily, Lissy would be calling out and suggesting he stop for tea on his way home. On this occasion, the veranda remained unoccupied, as did the work area where the girls sat to wrap care parcels.

Disappointed the surprise he'd brought from home would go to waste, Don was about to head off when he noticed colour and movement down by the willows.

'I should have known!' His mood lifted.

He grabbed a blanket and the esky he'd packed before leaving Dawson's Run and strode down the hill to the sloshing sound of melting ice and swimming soft-drink cans.

'What are you doing down here on your own, Lis?'

'Nothing,' she said, her voice flat. She wove between the willow's branches, watching while he spread the picnic rug on the ground. 'What's in the esky?'

'A surprise.' He opened the lid, took out the

187

strawberries he'd picked and packed into his mum's Tupperware, and then plucked two of the three bobbing Solo soft drink cans. He always packed for Irene, in case.

After shutting the esky, he tapped the lid, inviting Lissy to sit. Then he opened a bag of chicken Twisties.

'Wish I was having your baby,' she mumbled, ignoring the open packet he placed on her lap.

Wishing the same, but unwilling to confess as much, Don rose and wandered to the water's edge where he collected a half-dozen pebbles from the shallows. He adopted his well-practised stone-skipping stance and slowly drew his arm back. The secret was not trying too hard. Overthinking things never got the best results. Instead, Don found solace in the activity, as if each stone he threw was one less worry. At Dawson's Run, after too much Michael, he'd saddle his horse, ride out to the boundary and spend an hour on another part of the same river. He could pretty much empty his mind skipping stones, and with Lissy in one of her morbid moods he didn't know what else to do.

'Don?' she finally called.

'Yes, Lissy?'

'I'm wishing for a boy as sweet as you.'

He stopped pitching, smiling inside and out. 'Then I'll teach him to skip stones,' he called back.

Don would enjoy teaching a girl, too. Truth was, gender didn't matter to him any more than the order his children came into the world. Neither factor would determine their future or sway his decisions as a father.

Between stone tosses, he glimpsed Lissy twirling a sweet-scented freesia she'd plucked, brushing the petals over the cupid's bow on her top lip.

'Are you going to cheer up, Lis? Why so quiet?'

'I feel a bit off. My insides felt weird when I woke up today, like I had bubbles bouncing and bursting inside. Now it's like corn is popping in my belly. It's happening again — harder. Come feel.'

Brushing his hands against his pants, Don hurried back to the blanket and squatted in front of her. He flattened a palm to her belly and the pair waited.

'There!' Lissy startled. 'Feel it? Popcorn.'

'Popcorn?' Don grinned before leaning in to peck her on the nose. 'More likely it's your baby kicking.'

The notion seemed to flick a switch, bending Lissy's downcast mouth into a girlish grin, her eyes wide. 'Do you think?'

'Reckon, and maybe he's already skipping stones with his old man.'

Cross-legged, the pair sat together in excited silence, poised to cheer and chuckle over each subsequent kick. If Don had needed any more convincing that he wanted to be a father, this moment with Lissy was it. He desperately wanted to be still cheering his son's kicks from the sidelines in ten, fifteen, twenty years from now.

When it seemed the baby was sleeping, and Lissy fell quiet again, Don untangled his legs, grimacing as the muscles straightened out.

'Talk to me, Lis,' he said, peering at the top of her bowed head. 'What's wrong?'

'I'm scared,' she told him without looking up. 'The priest had made it sound so easy. Go away. Have the baby. Come home. Problem fixed. But what if I no longer want it fixed?' Her eyes found his. They were red and raw-looking. 'Before all this, I could picture my future. I knew what my life would look like, Don. First, I'd finish school. Then Ella and I were going to secretarial college in Brisbane. After that we planned a Contiki tour of Europe so we could drink heaps, muck around, come home, and eventually marry twin brothers — Italian, of course — and let our babies grow up best friends. That's what good girls do, and in the proper order to make their parents proud.' A rush of new tears streaked her face, the blue trails of mascara pooling at the corners of her mouth in a clownish way. 'My dad used to call me his little girl. These days I can't even get him to talk on the phone. So, you see, Don, any way I look at it, choosing means losing: him, the baby, my future. Because of one stupid mistake, I no longer get to have it all.'

Don had never seen tears flow the way Lissy's rained down, falling from her chin to form two wet patches on her belly.

'What do I do?' She was searching his eyes as if they had the answer. 'This is getting so real. Keeping the baby isn't possible, is it? No!' She answered before he could speak. 'I know I said it was before, but I can't be a mother. Even though you'd be an awesome dad. I'm only eighteen and

190

I'd be going against everything my parents want for me. But now he's growing, adoption doesn't seem right either. This is *my* baby. Why is this happening to me, Don? I'm so confused.'

As uncomfortable and awkward as it was while she was perched on the esky, Don rose on one knee to hold her close and let her sob on his shoulder.

'I don't want my family to disown me, like Irene's,' she spluttered. 'I can't live without Mum, and yet they expect me to live without my baby.' She jerked straight, breaking their embrace. 'How is that fair?'

Anger sparked inside Don. A rare thing for him. Rather than guiding and loving their children, both Lissy and Irene had families happy to wipe their hands of the problem by sending them away. It wasn't right. Every daughter deserved respect, in the same way every son deserved to be heard. But it wasn't fair of Don to speak about his family woes while Lissy was so upset.

Still on one knee, he collected both her hands, pinning them to where his heart hammered inside his chest. 'Whatever you decide won't be an easy choice, Lis, and I can't stop you feeling scared. It kills me to think there's no way I can help, other than tell you this. If you keep the baby, I won't ever let you be alone. I see you in my future as clear as I see you here. Both of you.' He waited for those downcast eyes still drowning in tears to meet his. 'I'm in love with you, Lissy, and I reckon if you can stop feeling frightened, you'll figure out it's okay to love me back. But

191

for the time being, you need to concentrate on staying healthy and happy. I've read that a baby in the womb can hear your tears. You don't want him learning how to cry.' Don breathed when he saw the hint of her grin. 'All the other stuff is detail, Lis, to be worked out when the time's right.' He hugged her again, and she rested her cheek on his shoulder, arms locked tight around his neck.

'You really love me, and the order of things won't matter?'

'The order?' Don pulls back to inspect her at arm's length. 'No way. Who needs order? I can't wait to live a crazy, muddled, disorderly, upside-down and inside-out life with you, Lissy . . . ' Maybe he should have included surreal, because it was. Don was yet to go all the way with a girl, and yet here he was preparing for fatherhood. ' . . . if you'll agree to marry me, that is.'

He told himself her answer came in the taste of her lips lingering on his mouth. Then, hidden by the curtain of weeping willow limbs, Don lowered Lissy to the ground and returned her kisses with a recklessness and intimacy that until then he'd only dreamed of in his bed at night.

★ ★ ★

Don pulled away so fast, Lissy gasped. She sat up and scanned the immediate vicinity beyond the willows, fearing Irene — or worse, Gypsy — had caught them necking.

'I-I'm sorry, Lis. It's not because I don't want

to. I really, really do and I can't wait until we can, but . . . But we need to cool it.'

'Cool it?' she repeated.

'Yes, as in we can't. Not now, not yet, not like this.'

Don collected his hat from the ground and perched on the esky, leaving her on the blanket to adjust the swathes of smock fabric and wish she'd chosen something else to wear. She must look hideous, but it was impossible to tolerate tight clothing while feeling so unwell in the tummy.

'I'm guessing bub would kick me from here to kingdom come if I tried anything with you now,' he added.

Part of Lissy was relieved. The rest of her craved more — although not the sex bit. What she craved was the way Don made her feel wanted and special and safe. He'd actually asked her to marry him, but she was different now. No way would she recklessly accept and rush into another situation she couldn't undo without hurting the people she loved, and who loved her.

She reached out both arms. 'Help me up, would you? Maybe we do need to cool down.' The hat covering Don's crotch suggested as much. 'And I know the perfect way. Come on.'

Lissy wandered downriver to the small stretch of light-coloured soil she and Irene called The Beach, where the smaller tributary's confluence with the Calingarry River commenced. She stood on the sandy patch and waited for the duck mother to gain control of her six chicks struggling in the strong current.

'You're not seriously going in,' Don called.

'You said to cool off and I'm tired of being this big hippo person.'

'You're not a hippo,' he said. 'Come back.'

'I am,' she said, looking down at legs too swollen for the ankle strap on her sandals. 'I'm wearing scuffs, Don,' she shouted. 'Old people shuffle around the house in scuffs and stupid smocks. Look at me!'

'You make scuffs sexy, Lis,' he called back while bent over the esky.

'As if,' she grumbled. Not even Jane Fonda could make flip-flopping footwear sexy.

Lissy high-kicked her feet one after the other, sending both the scuffs and sand soaring. Then she gathered up the knee-length fabric and took two steps backwards. At least in the water she'd feel like the old Lissy, the fun-loving Lissy who would go swimming in Ella's above-ground pool.

The last time she'd visited, she'd been wearing a brand-new bikini. What a waste of money! No way would her body ever shrink back to bikini size. She looked down at the water swilling around ankles, once slender, and saw the web of purple lines. Cheryl had assured her they were nothing to worry about, except Lissy's favourite knee-high boots would never lace up properly over gross elephant ankles.

'Come on, Don,' she called again. 'Don't be a chicken.'

'Not now and not in clothes, Lis,' he shouted back. 'And you shouldn't, either. Come here and help me pack up.'

'Come get me. I dare you.' As Lissy took two

more backward steps, water rose high enough to seep through the thigh-high gathering of fabric.

'Lis, come on, I'm serious.'

'So am I,' she muttered, freeing the smock to let a defiant mass of tiny blue and red flowers from the granny-print pattern float over the surface. 'It's beautiful once you get used to the temperature.'

'Rivers can be dangerous, Lis, especially in those clothes you're wearing.'

She liked that he worried. She liked teasing him. 'Are you trying to get me naked, Don Dawson?'

'No! I'm trying to get you out.'

By now, the urge to feel free and weightless was too great. Two more backward steps put the swirling material waist-high, and when Lissy fell backwards, cool water trickled into her ears and lapped at her neck and cheeks. She shivered, but she hadn't felt this good since last summer when, slick with baby oil, she and Ella had baked themselves to a crisp in the backyard and floated around the pool on blow-up beds.

When something grabbed Lissy's skirt, she opened her eyes, expecting to find Don mucking about, but he was further upstream, his back to her, focused on rinsing the esky. Finding no foothold when she tried to stand, fear became the overriding emotion and murky water rushed into her mouth, choking her cry for help. She kicked her legs, tugging at the smock, but the entanglement only worsened and dragged her under, lungs bursting.

★ ★ ★

195

'Now do you believe me about swimming in a river fully clothed?' Don didn't know whether to cuddle her or be cross, but with Lissy still on all fours spluttering dirty river water onto the ground, and with Gypsy's signature kaftan billowing like a distant warning, there was no time for lectures. The quiet, caring, and generous woman he knew would not hesitate to kick Don from here to Christmas if she'd caught him and Lissy doing more than kissing. What would she do if he'd let Lissy drown in the same river responsible for taking her grandparents' lives?

'Sure you're okay, Lis?'

Panting and sobbing all at once, she sat back with her legs folded under her. 'I got a fright.'

'You and me both, but that won't be as scary as Gypsy if she finds out what happened. Go, quickly, and tell her you accidently fell in so she calls Doc to check you over. But first . . . ' He squatted before her, hands gripping both shoulders, his head stooped to look her in the eye. 'Tell me you understand what I was saying earlier about you and the baby.'

'Y-y-yes, I-I do, D-Don.'

'Whatever the next few months brings, Lis, you need to know I can be your future — you and the baby.'

He let go of her arms to pick at the river debris caught in her curls. 'We'll get our own place in the country so both families can still be a part of our lives. And they will be. I promise.'

'Lissy!' Gypsy called. 'Back in the house — now.'

Don unfurled the blanket and wrapped her in

it. 'Once they meet the baby, your parents will come around, and they'll love me the same way my family will love you.'

'Do you really believe they will, Don?'

'We won't give them a choice.' He grinned. 'Besides, there's a cute little Dawson boy who'll adore having a cousin to play cowboys with.'

Gypsy called again.

Knowing he might well be banned from the island for the remainder of Lissy's confinement, Don told her one more time, 'I love you. Remember that.'

15

For seven days, while staying clear of Gypsy, Don caught up on a headstone restoration and picked up the slack around Dawson's Run. Only on the eighth day, when he could no longer stay away, did he put on his best shirt and corduroy pants to head across to the house.

* * *

How can one week make such a difference?

Wrapped in a dressing gown, the toe of her slipper making a metronome of the squeaking swing seat, Lissy had turned into Irene. Her face was fatter, breasts fuller, her belly bulging, and when she grumbled about being too tired to sleep, Don sat beside her and held her, expecting to hear Irene blamed for keeping her awake. Instead, Lissy cried, pushing him away. The next thing she was hugging him tight and demanding he stay.

'I missed you, and I miss my mum and my room and all my stuff. I don't belong here, Don,' she whined. 'But I don't want to leave. Why do I have to choose? I want everything: you, the baby, my family.'

'I know.' Don peeled her arms away and let them fall to her lap before he stood to survey the area. 'Where's everyone else?'

'Gone,' Lissy mumbled at the hands now

clenching and unclenching in her lap.

'They left you here alone?'

Her exasperated huff was like a switch, turning off her tears and turning on the temper. The swing seat lurched as she heaved herself onto slippered and swollen feet, putting her eye to eye with Don. 'I'm not a child. I'm having a baby. I can manage a few hours without supervision. In fact, you don't need to be here either. Just go!' The shove to Don's chest almost winded him. 'I want to be alone.'

When he reached out to comfort her, she knocked his hand away. When he said goodbye, she snapped a teary command. 'Stay!'

They sat together a while longer, mostly in silence while Don's mind compiled a list of all the jobs he could be doing back on the farm, including checking in on young Tom. When Lissy eventually grumbled about being 'too tired and terrible to be around', telling Don he should go, he didn't disagree.

★ ★ ★

As the punt began its slow journey away from Dandelion House, Don thought about Irene and his sister-in-law. Had they been his only reference for *Nesting Mothers-to-Be* — Chapter 8 in Cheryl's book — he would have thought all pregnant women hid inside the house and indulged on snacks while simultaneously complaining about putting on weight. A post-natal Wendy still complained, but at least she'd returned to Dawson's Run, quashing yet another of Barbara's expectations. Since coming home, however, Wendy had resumed her favourite time-wasting, television-watching habits, and Michael was regularly dumping his concerns on Don about his wife's poor mothering skills.

'Unless I·take him outdoors myself, the little bugger rarely sees the sun. I'm expected to be everywhere and do everything, like Dad. But I'm not him,' Michael mumbled, 'and I'll never be like him — or good enough for him.'

One day, Don offered to drop by the homestead to check on his nephew and the afternoon visits had turned into a happy habit. Don would let himself into his brother's house and find Tom in the usual place on the lounge room floor — strapped into a baby bouncer. Don hated that thing. All he saw was a convenient contraption designed to constrain and curtail an adventurous child. Upon seeing Don, Tom's eyes would light up and he'd reach out grippy fists, eager to be plucked from his little prison. When Tom chuckled, Wendy shushed him, but her eyes never drifted from *Days of our Lives*. While the woman seemed content to let the sands of her life trickle through an hourglass, Don worried more about the speed with which she drained her wineglass.

With a child needing the earth beneath their feet and for the sun to brown their limbs, Don made sure he was the parent Mike and Wendy seemed incapable of being. He sought advice about Tom from Gypsy, who suggested the little rascal visit and meet Willow. Don liked the idea. No one was ever too young to enjoy a punt ride.

Different sights and smells were certain to delight and, over time, Don would make sure the boy learned all about the Calingarry River. He'd grow to appreciate how easily it could take away, but also how much it gave to the town. If no one else was interested, Uncle Don would ensure a love of the country seeped into the boy's blood.

If Wendy told her husband about Don's fussing, Mike never let on, probably because he rarely admitted to needing help, and never from his little brother. When Don had aired his concerns about Wendy to Bruce and Barb, all his father had said was, 'Your brother makes his own bed, son. Hopefully you'll do better. For your mother's sake, find a nice girl soon and settle down.'

Watching Lissy from the punt, back to being herself and waving wildly to Don from her usual spot at the top of the hill, he was tempted to tell his parents he'd already found a nice one. At the same time, he wondered if pinning someone as young as Lissy to the land, and to him, would only create another Wendy, who constantly complained about the isolation. Don didn't understand how anyone could feel trapped on a property as sprawling as Dawson's Run. His idea of trapped was doing what his schoolmates had done — leaving their home in the country to have a city boss tell them what to do and when. Don's needs could be easily satisfied with his own slice of land, worked his way, and with the adorable, crazy Lissy by his side.

16

An unsettling quiet at Dandelion House told Don something wasn't right. He hadn't expected to see Gypsy. She and her daughter had been away a lot over the last few weeks, with sweet little Willow undergoing painful treatments for a hip problem and a foot refusing to point in the right direction. Not yet toddler age, she was incredibly brave, and a constant reminder not every birth goes to plan. With no sign of Lissy or Irene at the house, however, he walked around to the back and spotted two figures down by the river, perched on the edge of the small jetty — another job on Don's to-do list. The wonky structure served no purpose other than to provide a place to catch the breezes whipping over the water's surface. Gypsy had agreed the girls should stay clear of it, but as usual, Lissy wouldn't be told.

Nearing the jetty, Don noticed Irene sitting stiffly on the greying boards, protecting her modesty by pinning her frock between her knees, while Lissy's exposed legs dangled freely, her toes tipping the water's surface. One shoulder of the frilly top had slid down her arm to expose a beige-coloured bra, and she sported a white floppy-brimmed hat and huge sunglasses with thick frames.

'Gee,' Irene exclaimed as Don approached. 'Look who's sneaking around and perving, Lissy.

And surprise, surprise, more flowers.'

How was it some women could so easily make a bloke feel foolish? Don had brought yellow daisies — Lissy's favourites — from the church garden. Now he was wishing the fistful of flowers would vanish — and Irene right along with them.

'What are you doing here, Don?' Lissy asked. 'Not destroying our jetty, I hope.'

'No, but Gypsy does want the old tennis court dismantled and the wire put to good use on a chook house extension. I thought you might want to watch me work, Lis.'

'Ooh, how romantic!' Irene chimed. '*Don Dawson on the tennis court. The sky is blue above. Lissy on the other side. Of course the score is love.* Aw, you're so sweet I think I want to puke.'

'Shut up, Irene.'

'No, you shut up, Lissy.'

Don hadn't witnessed the two girls bicker before. They got frustrated with each other and took the occasional verbal swipe, but this was unusual behaviour. Perhaps their moodiness was the result of the same hormones responsible for Lissy loving him one minute and condemning him and every bloke to hell the next.

According to Cheryl's book, those hormones somehow helped. They didn't do Don any good. Not one bit. Lissy's growing baby meant the simple task of preparing her tea in the wrong-coloured cup, or with too much milk — or too little — came with a heaped spoon of those hormones, plus a generous side order of tantrum. Telling her she looked beautiful could end in tears, as did suggesting she should rest because she looked tired. The truth was, those dreaded hormones of Lissy's had made coming over to the house a game of potluck. Making matters worse, Don had two moody females to contend with, and the quiet one was a constant challenge. Cheryl's suggestion that Irene might be jealous of Lissy had made things clearer, but not easier. All Don knew — all he cared about — was that the calendar on the back of his dunny door showed two months to go, or thereabouts. In the meantime, he had to meet Gypsy's various requests while finding opportunities to start on his cottage extensions. The plans now included a bigger veranda and fancy wallpaper trim for the nursery room, in the hope Lissy made him the happiest man in Calingarry Crossing.

'Are you making wishes, Lissy?' Don asked, noticing the collection of spent dandelion stalks wedged in the rotting jetty boards.

Her shoulders rose and fell, forcing out a huge sigh. 'I no longer believe in wishes, Don.'

'Then what are you doing with those?' he dared.

'Setting the seeds free.' She folded the brim of her hat back. 'Dandelions are more than pretty things we admire — or mow down.'

He braced. 'Oh?'

'Yes! Everything that lives has a purpose,' she said matter-of-factly. 'Even this dandelion has a destiny to fulfil before it rots away.' She raised the last fuzzy seed ball in a hand as if sacrificing it to the gods. 'Just because it's here, doesn't mean it has to be here forever.'

Lissy was obviously having one of her 'dramatic moments', as Cheryl had referred to her moods one day. 'Indulge her,' she'd advised Don.

'What is the dandelion's destiny, Lissy?' he asked gingerly.

'They're meant to fly,' she replied without hesitation. 'To float on the wind until they discover a new place to put down roots. We're all born for a reason, and we have to find the place we'll grow best. There's purpose in death and dying. These seeds are the circle of life, Don.'

'Hmm, I see.' He couldn't disguise the disappointment in his voice any more than he could ignore the thud of his high spirits. 'Are you deciding where you'll grow best?'

Irene scoffed. 'Gawd, you're so full of crap, Lissy. Right now all I'm deciding is where I'm going to puke.'

'Why don't you go throw up some place else?' Lissy shoved Irene's shoulder. 'I'm so sick of you constantly being sick.'

The usually compliant Irene shoved back and at the same time snatched an envelope from the boards under Lissy's bottom.

'Give it back, Irene, or I'll — '

'Or you'll what?' Irene demanded. 'Stop stalling. The guy deserves to know.' She waved the envelope at Don, urging him to take it. When he did, she flapped her hand in the air. 'Now, help me up, would you?' Grunting and groaning, but without a word of thanks, she worked her feet into her slippers, stomped over the daises Don had inadvertently let fall to the jetty before helping her up, and trudged uphill towards the house.

When Lissy didn't react — her gaze fixed on the foam-lipped eddies forming along the riverbank — Don slowly unfolded the letter.

Good news!

I am hoping your father will come around to my way of thinking soon and understand the blood running through that little baby's veins is our family's. We all want to watch your baby grow up. And we can. When your sister and her new husband return from Italy, they will take over the vineyard and raise the next generation, and I can tell you they are both beyond excited about raising your baby as their own. Once it is arranged, we will share our 'good news from abroad' with friends and they, too, will welcome the newest family member.

Your father is desperate to have you back home, as am I, and if I can get him to accept the baby in this way, it could be the best outcome for all. As a family, we will celebrate your sister and hold our heads high, while your reputation will remain untarnished. Best of all, you will be unencumbered, able to find a man to love you, and my wish for you will come true. You will have your big wedding and babies, in the proper order, but before then all you dreamed of becoming is back within your reach. In the meantime, I will arrange for you to stay on at Dandelion House and have your sister join you there. Both you and the baby will need time to adapt. Then, when everyone is ready, we will make the proper announcements and bring you all home.

Please, Lissy, be a good girl and do not make a fuss. Your father will agree, but on his terms. You are in the best place for now. Stay well, my darling girl, and know we love you and cannot wait to hug you both.

The letter was poison to Don and potent enough to kill every drop of optimism. Had the news been in liquid form, he might have downed the deadly shot on the spot to avoid the misery losing Lissy would bring.

'You've had this for how long, Lis?'

★ ★ ★

Lissy didn't know what to say, like she hadn't known what to do when the mail arrived. Initially, she'd said nothing to Irene, or Gypsy, blaming hormones when Cheryl asked why she wasn't her usual self. Not that Lissy knew what her *usual* was these days. Not only was her body changing, she was different. No longer the flirtatious and foolish young winemaker's daughter, she understood the implications of a wrong choice. She wasn't one of *those* girls — the type her father had said got what they deserved. Lissy was a good girl but scared: about the birth, about motherhood, and about making more

207

mistakes. If she'd learned anything, it was that her choices no longer impacted her alone.

Choosing motherhood and marriage to Don would mean that who she was now, she would always be: a wife, a mother, a nobody in a small town. Could this really be her destiny? One alternative — becoming Aunt Lissy to her own child — would lock a huge lie inside her and she wouldn't stay a third wheel at home. But would the pursuit of frivolous dreams make her family proud? Could she do enough to redeem the sins of a stupid seventeen-year-old? Should she try?

'I'm sorry, Don.' Lissy kept her head bowed, the hat brim turned back down to hide her face.

She hadn't expected to factor him into her decision-making. At first, she'd thought her attraction an infatuation and a rebellious response to her parents. What better way to upset her mother during the weekly phone call than by repeatedly referring to a cute handyman? If Lissy mentioned him enough, her parents might regret sending her away and insist on bringing her home to have the baby. But with her affections for Don growing every day, making him a thorn in her parents' side had definitely been a dumb move.

If only she could think straight and be certain of anything other than her increasing reluctance to give up the baby, even to her sister. Her parents had already welcomed one son-in-law — a man from the other side of the world, known only to them through correspondence. While Don was not of her father's choosing, and not as familiar with grapes as Marco Morelli of

Italy's Morelli Wines, he was smart and a hard worker, and he loved to learn and build and grow things.

She hoped a man who believed in silver linings would see the positive in her proposal. He'd tried to explain the concept one day. They'd been sitting in this exact spot when Don had suggested Lissy needed to look for them.

★ ★ ★

'And where do I find a cloud with a lining?' she'd asked him.

Don had laughed. 'It's a saying, silly. An old one meaning something negative can lead to something positive. Take you falling pregnant, for example.'

Lissy had huffed and poked at her belly. 'As if there's anything positive about this.'

'You're sitting with me, aren't you?' he'd said. 'If you'd made a different choice with the picker that night, you wouldn't have fallen pregnant, your parents would not have sent you here, and there would be no *us*. Getting pregnant is the silver lining, Lis. Tells me we were meant to meet. So ... ' Don had paused, his smile waning. 'You need to decide if we have a future together, Lis. I know I'm totally committed, and if I had to prove how much by letting you go, because it was the best thing for you and bub, I would. Love is letting someone make their own choices.'

★ ★ ★

'Hey, you, under there,' Don said. He'd sat in Irene's place on the jetty and was now peering under Lissy's ridiculously large hat brim while she stared at her feet swinging back and forth, skimming the water's surface.

'I won't blame you if you never speak to me again,' she mumbled.

'Of course I'm going to speak to you, Lis,' Don said. 'But only if you come out from under that hat and let me see your face.'

The air was cooling, the afternoon breeze tugging on the letter he'd since returned to Lissy without another word. She thought about releasing her grip on the paper to let the wind decide her fate. If, like the dandelion seeds, the letter was carried away, it would be a sign she, too, was destined to soar. But if the letter blew back to the land, what then? Was she prepared to stay with Don and let her life take root in this little town?

Her fingers curled, pinning the paper to her palms. 'I'm so sorry, Don, but I don't think I can stay.'

★ ★ ★

Although Cheryl had warned him Lissy would change her mind a million times, Don had not fully appreciated the tug on his heart each time.

'You can stay, Lis. You can do anything you put your mind to. It's what scares me about you. But you have to tell me what's going on in here.' He tapped his knuckles against her skull.

'It's what's in *here*, Don.' Lissy hugged her

belly. 'When the doctor let me listen to the heart beating, all I could do was cry out for my mother. Surely that means I'm not ready to be one myself. So you see, I have to go home, Don. Mum's relying on me and I've let her down.' Lissy lifted the bottom of her top to wipe her nose.

'Relying on you for what?' He turned her face towards him and saw her eyes were raw from too many tears. 'I can't help you if I don't understand.'

Lissy breathed deep, letting the lungful out in a long sigh. 'Mum said, when my sister married in Italy, she'd felt more like a guest than mother of the bride. She came home with a bee in her bonnet about my wedding being bigger and better. But it won't be now because, as Mum says, I don't get to be a mother *and* have the big white wedding. I know I've disappointed her, but I've realised what's more important is this baby. This little heartbeat inside is depending on me to choose its future. Me! How, when I can't decide what to put on my toast for breakfast? I've tried, Don, but I can't find a silver lining to this. I can't!' She snatched up the remaining dandelion stems in her fist and chucked them into the fast-flowing water.

Don tugged her close. 'The people who love you will support your choices, Lis, whatever they are. And I do love you and want to marry you. If you choose to go, I'll ache for you every day, and I'll never love you less for choosing the best life for you and bub, but at least give us a go.'

★ ★ ★

Lissy nuzzled Don, feeling the weight of expectation floating away with the dandelions. He was absolutely, one hundred per cent correct. Her mother's solution was not about love and choice; it was about convenience and control and customs, like white wedding dresses. Don was right about her, too. Lissy wasn't stupid. She could do anything, including be a mother and make her own silver lining.

17

The following week, with both Gypsy and Cheryl occupied with their respective children, Don volunteered to drive Lissy and Irene into town so they could call home. On the way in, Irene had announced she would rather spend her collection of twenty-cent pieces on the pinball machine in the milk bar, and she asked Don to drop her at the door because the day had turned grey and windy. Lissy, on the other hand, announced she had something important to discuss with her mother, which left Don sitting in the car parked outside the telephone box and listening to coins dropping with the same regularity as Lissy's whine. 'But why, Mum?'

After slamming the handset into the cradle, she stormed towards the car, huffed into the passenger seat, and reefed the door shut.

'You okay?' Don asked while winding his window closed. The wind was whipping up, but it wasn't as wild as the look in Lissy's eyes.

'No,' she snapped, folding her arms over the top of her belly with a petulant huff. 'I want to go.'

'Okay.' When Don tooted the horn to hurry Irene from the milk bar, Lissy whacked him on the arm.

'We can wait. Let her have some fun. Things aren't good for Irene.'

'Can I do anything?' he asked, while a hand

soothed the spot on his arm.

When Lissy swivelled in the seat to grin at him, Don grinned back. He'd finally figured out that the best way to survive her mood swings was to follow her lead. If she fell quiet, he fell quiet. If she laughed, he laughed. When she cried, he followed the push-pull directives: hug me, leave me, hug me.

'Dear Don,' Lissy said. 'Don't you tire of rescuing damsels in distress? And why are you smiling at me like a goofball?' She went on before he could answer. 'It's hard for Irene, you know? My parents love me. They want me and the baby to come home. Even though I let this happen, they'll always love me.' She looked away towards the milk bar with its wind-blown rainbow of plastic ribbons in the doorway. 'As stupid as I was, doing it with the picker was my choice. But not poor Irene. Her creepy uncle just did it.'

'Her uncle?' Don tried to swallow the lump of disgust that surged up his throat.

'He's been fiddling with her for years. He'd come to her room while her family was in the backyard having a barbecue with the neighbours. One day he reckoned she was old enough to go all the way.'

A whistle escaped through the small gap in Don's teeth.

'Irene told him no, but he did it anyway, dirty old bastard. Then her mum didn't believe her or help get rid of it.'

'Irene's distrust of me makes sense now,' Don said.

'Sorry I didn't tell you before.' Lissy reached out a hand, squeezing Don's hand briefly. 'She made me promise, but I knew you'd understand. Poor Irene's so torn. The baby is half her. You know what I mean?'

Don nodded. 'How was your phone call?'

'Mum wanted to know if I got the letter.' Lissy bit into the quick of her little finger, peeling a skin sliver away. 'I told her I wasn't ready to decide. I told her the baby is half me and she said she understood and that's why being Aunt Lissy was better than nothing.'

As she attacked another finger, causing the quick to bleed, Don looked towards the milk bar down the street, wishing Irene would appear so he could start the engine and drown the sickening silence that had filled the car's interior to overflowing.

'Don?' Lissy said, not looking up from her picking. 'Do you think I'd make a good aunty to my baby?'

He shrugged as though he didn't care, when the truth was he cared too much. 'I guess you would. The same as I'm a good uncle,' he told her. 'But uncles don't get to have a say. I couldn't stop Wendy if she one day saw fit to leave Michael and take Tom, no matter how much I've grown to love the little guy. Not that I'd change anything or spend less time with him while I have the chance. But Uncle and Aunty are titles without a voice, Lissy.' Don reached over and flattened his hand to her belly. 'You are this baby's mother and you'd be great.'

'You'd be a good dad, too, but . . . ' When she

215

paused, every second of silence added another stone to Don's already heavy heart. 'I admitted I was wrong about the picker, but Mum's insisting I'm still not old enough to know what real love is. I told her the way I feel when I'm with you makes me want to figure it out, and for that reason . . . ' she said, looking at Don, 'I believe we should be together. We should try, and we can — at the vineyard.'

Don stared at her, blinking in disbelief. 'Your family vineyard?'

'Of course,' she said, her eyes coming alive. 'What do you think?'

All Don's hopes plummeted. He had no idea about grapes, no interest in making something he didn't enjoy drinking, and he saw no benefit or personal satisfaction working for someone else. He could do that by staying on at Dawson's Run. At least on the farm he would remain a cattleman where he was content with a good steak — plain and simple — and an occasional beer at the pub.

'But, Lis, I thought you were excited about our own place out at Cedar Cutters Gorge,' he said.

She appeared to mull over his words until a sob escaped. The sound was so sad it broke his heart.

'I-I did. And I d-do want to marry you, Don, but you have to understand . . . I *need* my mum. Please, don't you make me choose. Say you'll try. Say yes.'

Unable to look at Lissy, he focused on the other young mother-to-be walking towards the car, head down as usual as if no eye contact might make her invisible. At least now Don knew why Irene never drew attention to herself. He probably should feel sorry for her, but he was too busy feeling sorry for himself.

Both Gypsy and Cheryl had warned him about getting involved. Most girls who came to stay at Dandelion House brought emotional baggage, which often got packed up and taken straight back home — and he knew most of them went home alone. If he loved Lissy, he could give the vineyard a go. She was, after all, being asked to make all the choices. It was only fair Don make one. Wasn't it?

18

Dawson's Run, 2014

Don Dawson is tiring from the constant chatting and the unspoken memories, still painful and exhausting four decades on. He sits back, silent, and observes his nephew sharing his love of Dawson's Run. The lad is trying to impress the girl and all the indicators suggest he's on track. The fact she stayed after Don's woeful welcome is proof enough. Then there's the way Tom's eyes follow the slightest move she makes, the mirroring of her posture, and how he smiles when she smiles.

Don might be in his mid-sixties and never married, but he understands body language and can read a woman's expression well enough. He's particularly familiar with their unspoken displays of shock, and worst of all pity, because Don Dawson's appearance has been successfully frightening the females and small children of Calingarry Crossing since 1979.

★   ★   ★

Unsure how long he'd waited in the dusty paddock for someone to find him that day, or even which way was up as the merciless sun baked his shredded and bloodied body dry, Don remembers wishing he'd die and that Michael, and not his parents, would find him. Little had he realised at the time that his brother had been the most fragile of them all.

Doctors had done their best putting Don back together, but compartment syndrome had been quick to set in, limiting the blood supply responsible for muscle health. Debriding his right leg, arm and shoulder of muscle had been the most painful procedure — one repeated over and over, bit by agonising bit. After months of rehabilitation, including more operations to wire his jaw and graft skin around what was left of his right ear, Don returned to Dawson's Run half a man. Frustrated he had to rely on his mother to mash his meals, and unable to do his share around the farm, reading became Don's saviour, with Cheryl supplying books and magazines regularly from Saddleton Library.

The accident had been the beginning of the end for Don's overwrought parents. Constant trips to city hospitals, months of rehabilitation, and referrals to reconstruction specialists — only to hear there was nothing viable to reconstruct — had put their farm under financial pressure. With so much focus on Don, Michael managed alone, ignored his wife, and struggled to meet the requests of his curious six-year-old boy. He made mistakes, repeatedly, and his decisions at one point were bad enough to force their ailing father to take back the reins. According to Bruce, his eldest son had achieved one good thing — he'd produced an heir. A boy to carry on the Dawson bloodline. Sadly, he'd married a woman who didn't know how to raise a child.

Over a weekend roast dinner, to which young Tom had insisted on wearing his brand-new uniform, Bruce had announced to all, 'Look at my clever grandson, so keen to start school. Good, cos we'll be needing another Dawson as smart as a whip, like his uncle. Our Tom will top kindergarten class for sure.' Bruce had raised his schooner glass with such enthusiasm, white froth had oozed over the sides. 'But I suppose, give our Michael time and he'll be sure to bugger that up, too. Hip. Hip. Hooray.'

Days later, Michael Raymond Dawson walked into the paddock and shot himself. A man of few words, he left Don a letter:

We all know I'll bugger Tom's life up if I stick around. You'll do right by him, Don. You're a better dad than me and the old man put together. A scallywag like Tom can't replace all you've lost, but you do now have loads of love to give. Hug my boy for me every day, mate. I love you, brother, and I'm sorry a million times over for what I'm about to do.

Some locals will call me a coward, but they'll be the same ones who see you as half a man, when the truth is you are more than I could ever be. Wendy won't stick around for long once I'm gone. This way gives her an out. She doesn't love me or Tom nearly enough, and she sure as hell never wanted this life. She's been itching to go for years, so tell her 'bugger off' for me, would you?

My boy deserves more. He needs to grow

up and make his own choices and you'll make sure he knows how. One day I hope he understands I tried. I get up every morning determined, but at the same time I feel like I'm dying. Nothing stops the blackness. I could try sticking around and drink myself to death like the old man's doing, or hope the smokes do me in, like poor old Mum's discovered. Instead, mate, I'm opting for fast and painless, and far enough away so no one will find me.

I can't give you back all that was taken away from you, but I can return Dawson's Run and ask you to give all that love to my boy. He deserves that much.

Michael.

When Bruce and Barbara eventually passed away within months of each other, Don was left to live for them all, and to fight with the authorities so he could raise the next-generation Dawson. Not only live, but show a devastated and confused young boy that anything is possible. Tom became Don's reason for everything, and the silver lining to come out of the dark cloud that had hovered over the property for too long.

Sensitive, thoughtful and curious, the young lad questioned a lot. He needed a strong role model. If Don was going to be the best father, he couldn't hide himself away. He needed workers to help re-establish the property, regular trips into town for the food required to sustain a growing boy, and there were sports days, special assemblies, and school concerts to attend.

With his clothes and hat concealing much, townsfolk eventually got used to Don's appearance, which made visitors and newcomers easy for him to spot. They were the folk who steered clear of him in the street, avoiding him, his lumbering gait, and his uncontrollable arm. Doctors hadn't been able to get his right leg, arm, or eye working, but with a glue-like compound to strengthen his skull, they'd saved his brain from falling out. What a shame the slurry of bone cement turned out so strong it locked in every memory.

★ ★ ★

One of those memories is sitting opposite him now. It has to be her. Or is Don so desperate for closure he'll clutch at any straw? He's certain of one thing. He's tired. So tired and overwhelmed that, for the first time in forty years, Don feels closer to understanding Michael's motivations. There was a period in his life, after the accident, when Don had waited for the black dog to bite him, rather than constantly nipping at his heel. If seeing himself in the mirror every day hadn't been enough to push him over the edge, he'd buried three family members, one after the other. Making Don strong had been the young boy who'd stood silently by his side through every eulogy.

When his nephew's first question about his father's death had been 'Why?', Don had explained the best way he knew how. But nobody really understood Michael's internal grief, even those closest to him. The depression he'd suffered was like death daily. His parents' tough love — their stepping away — was meant to snap him out of his melancholia; their father had said as much. But once again, Bruce had expected too much from his eldest son. Instead, Don discovered the hard way how, every day, a tiny piece of the thing keeping his brother out of the dark had died inside Mike. He was like a crop that has borne its fruit, in the process exhausting itself of the good nutrients required to keep it strong. It's when a plant dies back that something new is sown, to grow and bloom in its place.

'Nothing could grow inside your dad because there was no light,' he'd told Tom that day. 'There was goodness — lots — in him all along. He simply couldn't find it in the dark.'

Don should have died a long time ago, too. If not on the day of the accident, then during one of his many medical procedures. But each anaesthesia brought his brother's image to Don, and his words in those final moments of consciousness were always Michael telling him to pull through and to live for Tom.

★ ★ ★

For every one of those occasions, there was another reason for Don to stay alive, and she's sitting next to his nephew.

He interrupts Tom's lecture on the economic benefits of barley sprouts to enquire, 'Do you have family living close by, Beth?'

223

'Ooh, Unc!' Tom grimaces. 'Not the best timing.'

Beth puts a reassuring hand on Tom's leg and looks across at Don. 'It's okay. I'm happy to shout from the rooftops forever that I had a wonderful mother who I loved dearly. But she did pass away recently and I'm in town to scatter her ashes.'

'I'm sorry,' Don says clumsily. 'Seems I've put my one working foot firmly in my mouth. She's the reason you're in Calingarry Crossing?'

'The truth is, Don, I'm not sure. Mum never mentioned this place or came here as far as I know. And I should. We were close. Even if she'd visited when we lived in Saddleton — briefly when I was first born, although I'm remembering less about that these days — I'm not sure why this place is so special.'

'That's a bit harsh, Beth,' Tom says with a wink, keen to lighten the mood and move on. 'The locals are special, in my humble opinion, and very friendly.'

'Eventually! After they've woken up,' Don remarks. 'I apologise for my sullen greeting earlier, Beth. I wasn't expecting to meet anyone so, ah, familiar.'

'Do you recognise her, Unc? Beth *is* famous. We're sharing fruitcake with a star of the stage. She sings, she dances. Maggie tells me she's very talented.'

'And beautiful. I see it now,' Don mumbles. He's been studying Beth, wondering what it is about her appearance that warranted his earlier reaction. With her dark mane smooth, her complexion tanned, it's like comparing night

224

with day, but look deeper — at how she fusses with her hair, her expressiveness, and her tidy nose and full lips that bunch up when she tries to wink at Tom — and there's no doubt in Don's mind. 'You take after your mother,' he says.

★ ★ ★

'Thanks, but no.' Beth smiles. 'Mum couldn't hold a tune. I'm guessing one of my dad's many talents was singing, as well as being swift on his feet once he found out about me. I didn't know him, but we were fine without a man in the family. Mum was the perfect blend of both parents. I never went without.'

'A child needs a father figure though. Did she not give *any* bloke a chance?'

While Beth maintains her composure, if only to further demonstrate what a good job her mother had done, Tom doesn't hold back.

'Uncle Don! What's got into you? You've always championed people's choice to have kids any way they can: straight, gay, single. You had to fight to keep me, and we did okay.'

'You're right, Tom. I apologise, Beth,' Don says. 'Let me get the joey. You came to check on him, not on me.'

'Please, don't disturb the little guy on my account.' Beth's already standing and tucking her phone into the back pocket of her jeans. 'I should make a move. Thanks for the tea.' *And sympathy*, she adds silently, sarcastically. Only when a tear drops from the man's eye does Beth falter. 'It really was nice to meet you, Don.'

Tom takes her hand in both his as they stop by the car door. 'I'm sorry again. I'm not sure what got into him. Tell me how I can make it up to you?'

'Cake,' Beth says without missing a beat. She opens the car door and drops onto the seat. 'As lovely as the tea and fruitcake was, we're going to the cafe and I'm buying me a real coffee and you a belated birthday treat. Something decadent, full of calories and guilt, and I won't be taking no for an answer.'

19

'That's the saddest cake face I've seen in a long time,' Tom says when Beth clutches her stomach and leans back. 'You're quiet. My uncle upset you more than you're letting on.'

'No, it's fine, really. I can't imagine I'd be the life of the party all the time if I was him. And we interrupted his nap,' she says, pushing the plate to one side. 'I'm like a bear if anyone wakes me before I'm ready.'

Tom fashions an imaginary pen and a notepad on his palm. 'Let me jot that titbit down for future reference.'

'Ha! Very funny.' Beth returns the smile, albeit briefly. 'At least Don's snappishness is justified, unlike my grandmother's this morning. Oh, look!' She points to a moving spot at the centre of the cafe table.

'You don't like ladybugs?' Tom asks.

'I loved them as a kid, but I haven't seen one in I don't know how long. Finding the cross-stitch poem at your uncle's made me think about the imaginary ladybug friend who used to keep me company while Mum was at work.' Beth blocks the insect's path with her finger, redirecting it to the centre of the table. 'I can't say why I chose a ladybug friend. All I know is after school each day I'd catch the bus to whichever hair salon Mum was working at. Mostly I sat in the pokey back room with nothing to do, so I made up a friend for company, and to help me with my homework. Buggy-boo was very smart.'

Tom's smile takes over his face. 'Bug poo?'

'No! I said Buggy-*boo*, and I was obsessed for years, which resulted in ladybug-themed birthday cards and presents.'

When the frustrated bug finally flies away, releasing its fragile wings from beneath the spotted shields, Beth recalls the plastic vanity mirror with the glass protected by moveable ladybug wings. Yet another long-gone victim of too many house moves.

'Do you and your friend still chat?' Tom asks.

'No, not for a long time. I gave the ladybug thing away after an embarrassing twenty-fifth birthday celebration.'

'Why? What happened?'

Beth sighs and sits back. 'The date coincided with a final show at the Belvoir St. Theatre, and the cast presented me with a coffee mug and a pair of ladybug slippers before heading out to the pub. One minute I'm celebrating with colleagues, chugging beer in my ladybug mug, and the next I'm crying over lost slippers.'

'You lost your slippers, Cinderella?'

'I put them on that night, to be funny,' she says. 'But as the evening wore on, I drank too much, and my ladybug slippers and I found our way to the dance floor. A male dancer scooped me up and spun me around, and the next thing my slippers are flying off my feet, and I'm screaming hysterically and crawling over the dance floor crying *Buggy-boo! Buggy-boo!* It's not funny,' she tells Tom, who can't keep the smile from his face. 'So, there I was, weeping as if lost slippers were the worst thing that could happen. I was twenty-five, with the world at my *slipperless* feet, and no idea about real loss.'

The levity is lost, and Beth is left to focus on the fact her little finger is within brushing distance of Tom's where his hand rests on the table. Both their fingers twitch with the desire to touch, but Beth is not interested in a pity hold from this man. Her feelings for Tom are changing, moving fast, and she burns to make that connection — the one that comes with a promise of something more than sympathy. As if reading her mind, his hand engulfs hers and there is a sudden, staggering jolt of something between them. It's a sensation better than sex. *Almost!*

'I'm forty,' she says, as if divulging a life-changing secret. The ridiculous announcement, combined with the warmth of his hand on hers, makes her chuckle. 'Soon to be forty-one, and still not sure what I'm doing or feeling most of the time. I'm so lost without my mum.'

Tom doesn't squeeze her hand in sympathy. Instead, a finger moves over her skin and along her wrist as if signwriting a message. One she might say yes to under different circumstances.

'Grieving doesn't come with a handbook, Beth,' he says. 'No one can tell you what to feel or when you're supposed to feel it. Finding your own way in your own time is okay.'

Beth lifts her gaze to his. 'Turns out this ashes thing with Mum is not as simple as driving here.

229

The fact I've not yet made a serious attempt to find the spot marked on her map tells me I'm not ready to say goodbye. And to be honest, I think Calingarry Crossing is an odd choice. With absolutely no connection to the town, the idea makes no sense. I don't want this to be the place I leave her.'

'Then don't.' His finger stills on her hand. She wishes it hadn't.

'But it's Mum's wish. She left a bloody diagram! Besides, what choice do I have? Buy a fancy um for the mantelpiece?'

'A common enough practice,' he says. 'Although you would need a mantelpiece.'

She smiles. It's hard not to around Tom. 'I live in a small high-rise apartment because it's easier when I travel for work. No fireplaces allowed. Then again, not too many interstate work offers lately, either.'

'You have a fan in Maggie. She is seriously impressed to have you staying at the pub.' When Beth doesn't react, Tom asks, 'So, what do you love about your work, Beth? Personally, I can't imagine a career in the spotlight. Putting yourself up there, being scrutinised and criticised, is surely only for the strong.'

'Such thoughts rarely come into play,' she tells him. 'When I'm on stage, I'm representing the writer, telling their story, taking the audience on a journey and moving them emotionally. That's if I've done my job well.'

Tom pats her hand and sits back, smiling. 'Whereas my audience demands very little,' he says. 'Food, fresh water, and a kind word. No

230

critiquing, just curious looks.'

'I do miss the sense of achievement and the validation if a critic reviews my performance well,' she says. 'Other times require a tough hide.'

'Hmm!' Tom cocks his head to one side. 'It's probably inappropriate to say I checked out your hide at the yards today, and it didn't look too tough.'

'Ha!' Beth hoots. 'Some women would definitely slap a label on you for that comment, Mr Dawson. Not me, which is further proof about that hide of mine.'

'Surely critics aren't the be-all and end-all,' Tom says. 'I imagine applause is the best and most immediate feedback, although you don't get that in films.'

'No, and the screen is less forgiving as you get older. Too many close-ups,' she says. 'Theatre is kinder. Mind you, the last role I auditioned for went to a twenty-two-year-old who was prettier, perkier, and enjoyed showing the director how *passionate* she could be. Speaking of drama queens . . . ' Beth straightens. 'I'm overreacting and over-thinking this ashes thing. I'll feel better once I've worked out Mum's map and found the spot.'

'You want to go there now?' Tom looks towards the street. 'Could be rain in those clouds. At least, I hope there is. I'll drive you.' He raises both his palms. 'And before you decline the offer, I know you're a smart, confident, independent woman. You are also female.'

Beth widens her eyes in disbelief, before narrowing them to ask, 'What did you just say?'

'The truth can be hard to swallow,' Tom replies, 'but despite what women think, map reading *is* a man's job.' He immediately cowers, holding a protective arm to his head and standing so abruptly his chair tips and crashes onto the hard floor.

Beth erupts into a fit of the giggles and the relief of unrestrained laughter, after months and months of misery, has her falling into Tom, her arm holding his waist, hugging the line of his leather belt. He does the same and the pair stagger away from the cafe like a couple of drunks, roaring louder still when two grey-haired women sitting al fresco scowl their disapproval.

★ ★ ★

When they hit an unsealed section of road, Beth looks sideways at Tom, sitting relaxed behind the wheel of his ute, both index fingers tapping to a silent tune.

'Are you sure this is right?' she asks. 'Do you need to consult a map?'

'Ha! You're almost as funny as me,' he says. 'We're basically circumnavigating the old grave-yard and the adjoining state forest — which, if you drove through it, would get you to Dawson's Run. That makes driving definitely the longer option, especially now council has stopped maintaining this section of road.'

Goat track, Beth muses, as Tom steers around ruts and pot-holes.

'The cemetery is bigger than I imagined,' she says, staring out the passenger window. 'Finding the right spot could take time. Are you sure you don't have other things to do?'

'On a property the size of Dawson's Run? Sure, but while I love nothing more than an early-morning natter with the mob, having human company that talks back is a nice change. Plus,' he says, 'I'm unashamedly taking advantage of having my son in town for work experience. With anyone else I'd need to set up and supervise tasks. Matt knows what he's doing, and Don is the best reminder to be careful and safety-conscious.' Tom slows the car to a stop and cranes his neck to peer skyward. 'That said, I'd understand if you'd rather some alone time.' He yanks on the handbrake. 'I can drop you here and you can take your chances with those clouds.'

'No, please, Tom.' She pins his forearm where it rests on the steering wheel. 'Don't go. I beg you. I need a big, strong leading man to help me find my way.'

Tom's still laughing as he opens her car door. She hadn't been waiting. At forty, Beth is more than capable of doing most things unaided. So far she's opened all her own doors and successfully negotiated streets, steps, and crowded dining rooms without the gentle guidance of a masculine hand on her back. Then again, Tom's chivalry comes so naturally it's kind of adorable — and the seatbelt clip seems stuck.

'Thanks,' Beth says when he leans across to release her, the closeness triggering a twitch in her tummy.

'There you go,' he says. 'Told you I rarely have passengers.'

Beth climbs out of the car, checks her pocket for her phone, then pulls her hair back into a ponytail with the black elastic band that routinely adorns her wrist. She follows Tom to a crooked wire gate hanging by one hinge, where he stops to yank on a vine, freeing the weed's entanglement with a flowering bush.

'The working bee can't come soon enough,' he says. 'No moth vines survived in Uncle Don's caretaking days. Even after his accident, once he could get around on a crutch, he'd insist on coming here regularly. What he couldn't do in those days, like drive a regular car, I managed. Luckily, the back roads between here and Dawson's Run allowed an unlicensed teen to evade the law. Or have the law turn a blind eye, I suspect.

'One day a week,' he continues, 'while my mates sat in church, Uncle Don took to these grounds with his modified gardening tools and educated me on what was and what wasn't a weed. Take this one, for example.' Tom bends over to pluck a yellow dandelion flower. 'What do you see? A weed, or a wish in the making?'

'Maybe wishes are only for children.' The blissful bubble encasing Beth on the drive pops. 'Sorry, that's morose of me. I think it's being here.' With a sweep of her arm she tries encompassing the massive expanse of concrete and marble. 'Cemeteries are such sad places.'

'Not always,' Tom says. 'Some people feel sorrow. Others come to celebrate a life lived.

They bury bodies here, Beth, not hopes and not futures. Uncle Don made sure I understood that. But I realise it's early days for you, and I can understand your discomfort, Beth. I, on the other hand, am Tombstone Tom. Nice to meet you.' He extends a hand, smiling at Beth's wide-eyed reaction. 'My schoolmates gave me the moniker. Not that I told Don. He would've stopped coming, and I didn't want that to happen. So ... ' He snaps impatient fingers. 'Come on. Let's get this map-reading show on the road. Hand it over.'

With Beth's hand hovering over her back pocket, she says, 'You know what, Tom? I think I would like some of that solitude and time to work it out myself. Do you mind?'

'I get it,' he says. 'I've done nothing but talk your ear off.'

'No, it's not you,' Beth insists. 'Thanks for dropping me.'

'There is one more thing, and I'll go,' Tom says, pointing to his left. 'See the red dome in the distance? It's the highest point in the cemetery. From there you'll be able to make out the tip of the old church spire. Head for it and you'll pick up the path to lead you back into town.' He rests both hands on Beth's shoulders and dips his head to peer into her eyes. 'As long as you understand I'm dropping you *here*, not dropping you completely. I'm enjoying the company way too much. Do you reckon we can do dinner tomorrow night? You'll still be here?'

'Hopefully not here.' She delivers the line deadpan and Tom's expression does not disappoint. 'Depending on my map reading and your directions, Tom, by dinner tomorrow I'll either be in Timbuktu or I will have found my way back to town.'

20

Dandelion House, Spring, 1974

When Don found the quiet one, she was sitting stiffly in a straight-backed chair on the veranda.

'G'day, Irene, how are you? Good book?'

'You can cut the nicey-nice crap, Don. I know you know. You have for a while. No wonder I can't wait to get away from this place. Can't I trust anyone?'

Don made no comment while dragging a chair closer. He'd sought the young woman out to say one thing. After he'd said it, the rest was up to her.

'You can trust *me*, Irene.'

'Trust!' The book snapped shut. 'You know what, Don? The first words Uncle Pete said every time were 'Trust me, Irene'. And they were the last thing my mother told me as she packed my bags. 'Trust me, Irene, I know what's best. It'll be over soon, Irene, and we can forget this ever happened.' Trust me, trust me. Trust me!' Swollen, beetroot-red eyes bulged with unshed tears, but it was her quivering chin taut with dimples that gave her away. She was trying so hard to stay strong.

Don leaned forward to rest his forearms on his knees, his hands open and inviting. She didn't budge. 'It's okay, Irene, you're allowed to be upset. Waterworks are not a sign of weakness and

237

I'm not the enemy.'

'No, it's not okay, Don. It will never be *okay*. I can't trust anyone: not grown-ups, not my mother, and obviously not Lissy. I can't even trust myself. So stay away from me, and leave Lissy alone, because you're only making things harder.' Without chair arms to grab, Irene rose unsteadily, but her glare was far from wavering. 'Lissy's got a chance to go home to a family who loves and wants her. Don't bugger that up, Don. I know what it's like to not have the choice.'

The screen door smacking closed, the way it rebounded — banging twice — added bullet points to Irene's unspoken belief that: one — Don Dawson was the embodiment of all men; and two — all men were bastards.

Irene was wrong on both counts, but was she right about him and Lissy? Would backing off make the situation easier? What if his constant pressuring was affecting Lissy's moods, and not those hormones she had explained to him in snappy sentences a few weeks earlier?

'What don't you get, Don?' she'd shouted. 'Our bodies are changing. Irene and I have to make the perfect place for a baby to grow. The hormones help.'

You, maybe! Don had thought at the time.

21

Calingarry Crossing, 2014

The dark cloud that has kept up with Beth is now stalled directly over the cemetery and spitting spasmodic but plump raindrops at her. A drenching might be good for farmers, but the timing sucks.

Really sucks, Beth muses as she heads towards the domed, red-tiled roof to get her bearings, as Tom had suggested. The circular colonnade of decorative pillars is grand in appearance rather than size. In fact, if this was a park rather than a graveyard, the tiny structure could be mistaken for a compact band rotunda. Its elevated position does indeed provide a 360-degree view of the sizeable cemetery to make the task set out in her mother's simple map ridiculously daunting.

Beth activates the weather radar on her phone, then checks for messages and notifications, but it seems her social life has stalled along with the rain cloud. Only because her agent insists does Beth bother maintaining an online presence, which mostly comprises a neglected Facebook account. Her life isn't interesting enough. Some colleagues do a better job of networking, while maintaining their private lives, but she has no private life to protect, no kids to worry about, and no family to shield. Still, for someone with thousands of so-called Friends and Followers,

Beth's never felt so lonely. She has her work but, as evidenced by the decline in offers, acting won't keep her busy forever. Over tea at Dawson's Run, Tom had mentioned diversification as a survival strategy for families on the land. Perhaps Beth needs to reassess her options so she's prepared for the future, with its drought of auditions and flood of rejections.

With the rain heavier, all Beth can do is wait for the storm to pass, like she waits for her agent to call with news. Maybe she needs a new agent, or no agent. She can start afresh and explore new opportunities, like the partnership she'd mentioned to her mum during that special shopping day.

★ ★ ★

'I only promised to look at the business plan, Mum. Nothing more,' Beth had assured her. But, as the concept had required significant financial input, her mother's advice had been swift and unsurprising.

'Be careful what you promise,' she warned. 'Any partnership is problematic when you don't know the person well.'

'Or even when you do,' Beth muttered.

'I gather you're referring to your idiot ex-husband and the recent sexual harassment allegations?' she said. 'Some men don't understand 'no' means 'no'. Such a small word. The first one every child learns. In my day, good girls did not say 'no', or question their elders. We were to be seen, not heard, and expected to do what we were told. When a grownup says, 'Trust me, I'd never hurt you', we believed them. At least, I did.'

Beth wanted to quiz her mum, if only the woman had stopped for breath, and if only the fitting room they'd been sharing in the high-end fashion store had been big enough for Beth, her mum, and the impassioned speech she launched into.

'Men want to make women feel powerless when we are not, Beth. We're free to make our own choices and carve our own paths. Whatever else you do, avoid those who don't consider strength a positive female trait. Hold tight to your independence. Speaking of tight . . . what do you think of this dress?' she asked, while bending over to reposition both breasts in her bra. 'One other thing, darling,' her mum added. 'Promise me, when you're my age, you will be able to say the life you chose was the one you wanted. Make a decision now to leave nothing undone, and never settle for less when there's more. Always hold out for the right one. Speaking of right, this neckline is all wrong. Let's try the plain cream dress again.'

The woman who changed her hair colour as frequently as she moved houses stood with Beth in front of the dressing-room mirror. At fifty-eight, in only her bra and full briefs, her mum was still beautiful, and still with the glow of a mature bride-to-be, but with the giggle of a girl. Of all the men to win her mother's heart, it had been a squat Italian tradesman with a smile as big as his property portfolio. Irene was finally

241

trusting a man with her heart. Dinner at a fancy restaurant would make it official.

'Do you suppose it's an emerald? I might've dropped a hint.' Irene grinned. 'Maybe I'll take the green for tonight and save the cream dress for the wedding. I'll want everything perfect for the happiest day of my life.'

'*The* happiest? Really?' Beth quipped, as she recovered the green dress from the discarded hook. 'And here I was thinking my birth was up there as the highlight of your life.'

The equally playful retort Beth had expected from her mum didn't eventuate. In its place, in the fitting room filled with a mother's mirth seconds earlier, Beth tried talking her way out of the mood-killing gaffe.

'Don't forget to check the bottom of your champagne glass before downing the dregs. Okay, Mum? Choking on the ring, no matter what colour the stone, will make the night memorable for all the wrong reasons.'

★   ★   ★

Before leaving the house that night, Anton had surprised both women by popping the question. He'd wanted to include Beth.

'After all,' he'd said, 'I get myself a daughter in the bargain, no?'

★   ★   ★

Standing rigid under the small domed roof, rain dripping from its edges, Beth fiddles with the enormous emerald ring sitting skew-whiff on her more slender finger. She squeezes her eyes tight and tells herself those too-few hours it had sat on Irene's chubby wedding finger over dinner with Anton had been the happiest of her mum's life.

'G'day,' a voice says. 'Mind if I join you?'

'Oh, hello! Sure.' She shuffles across to make room for The Rev. 'I'll feel less self-conscious about standing on a stranger's memorial if I have you for company.'

'Don't reckon they'll mind,' he says, flicking the rain from his umbrella before closing it. 'Paying your respects, are you?'

'Not exactly.' Beth tugs the map from the back pocket of her jeans, but the now-damp paper rips. 'Damn!' Her cheeks warm. 'My apologies, Rev. I'm needing to find a specific section in the cemetery, and the map is not the best.'

He leans into Beth for a closer look. 'Hmm, yes, I see your dilemma. Never hopeless, though. In faith we find hope,' he adds, sermon-like. 'And hope is the most universal thing we all need to hang on to, Beth. Hope keeps the living alive.' He studies the paper she's trying to protect. 'Ah, yes, that area with the big X would be the old pauper section.' Misinterpreting Beth's reaction, he explains, 'It is sad that, years ago, people without the money to pay for a proper burial were interred without cost, or at least minimal cost. I can point you in the right direction. Any minister worth one's salt knows his or her way around their local joint. You'll need to find the big linden tree, but . . . '

Beth's hopes plummet. 'But what?'

'With that area boggy at the best of times, and with this rain forecasted to keep up overnight, you'll be needing solid boots. Better still, try waiting until the good Lord sends sun to dry out the paths. It's one thing to take shelter like this; you don't want to go traipsing over the residents and disturbing the ground unnecessarily.'

'No, no, I'd never . . . ' Beth's gaze shifts to her slip-on canvas shoes. 'You're telling me to wait?'

'A day or two,' he says. 'I can guarantee all will be the same here tomorrow, and the next day. Should be all good by Saturday. A big night at the pub,' he adds. 'The annual shindig brings the beach to the bush. People drive for miles to enjoy one night. They forget the hardships and have a laugh. You don't want to miss it.'

'Sounds like fun, but . . . ' Beth shrugs. 'I won't know anyone.' She could add: *And nothing reminds a person of how alone they are better than a party with a room full of strangers.*

'You look like a capable woman, Beth,' The Rev says. 'I reckon staying away from the dance because you don't have a date is pretty much relegated to what my generation calls the good ol' days. I'm surprised Tom hasn't asked you to go with him. I could arrange a lightning bolt to give the lad a kick along.'

'No, please, you're right,' Beth says. 'I am a big girl. I don't need to wait for a man to ask me out.' Her mum would second that.

'Then I'll pray for sunshine,' he says. 'The Lord still listens to me. In fact, He listens to anyone in need of help or guidance. No maps required. Rain's easing. Best dash.' He pops his brolly open and raises it over his head. 'Nice chatting, and if I were you I'd stick around town, if for no other reason than the experience of attending a beach party on the edge of the outback. You might even enjoy yourself. Miracles do happen.'

Beth returns the smile, but her mind is elsewhere, knowing it will take a miracle to get an answer to the question now burning a hole in her brain: *Why the pauper section, Mum?*

22

Dandelion House, 1974

The bang on a wooden post outside the milk bar was like the crack of a starter's pistol. The noise startled a whimper out of little Amber, perched on Cheryl's knee where she sat on an upturned milk crate.

'Never again.' Irene slumped on a second crate she'd kicked alongside Cheryl's. 'I hate the way everyone looks at me.'

'Lower your voice or the whole town will be hearing you.'

'Let them hear about the rude biddy in the bakery. I asked for a loaf of bread, but rather than take one from the shelf she gets this brick from out back.' Irene rapped her knuckles on the loaf. 'Does that sound fresh?'

'It's crusty, and it will toast well.' Cheryl was trying to sound upbeat. 'The inside will be fine.'

'No!' She coughs. 'It won't be *fine*. *Nothing* will be fine ever again.' She coughs deeper and grips her throat. 'The old cow treats Lissy and me like lepers and makes us wait for no good reason while her smart-alec son smirks and makes jokes. It's not fair.'

'She's not lying,' Lissy piped up. 'I hate going in there, too.'

'How about a milkshake each?' Cheryl passed

Amber to Lissy. 'I'll order. Vanilla okay for every-one?'

Lissy nodded and cuddled her new charge with the ginger hair and big smile. Amber's baby talk and antics had been a welcome distraction from Irene's tantrums these last few months.

Cheryl returned quickly and dropped her purse into the bag on the footpath by her feet. 'My advice, girls, is to ignore those nasty people. They're baiting you. But it's a good lesson because the world is not always fair, especially to women.'

'Especially the stupid ones, like me.' Irene's head dropped onto Cheryl's shoulder.

'You're not stupid,' Cheryl said, while patting Irene's back.

'I must be, or I'd have picked Uncle Pete for the creep he was, and said something before it was too late. Before he could tell me, 'Too late to say no, Irene'. I went along, figuring he'd do the same as always, then go, but instead he . . . ' She sniffed and coughed some more. 'I was stupid telling Mum I was pregnant, but I couldn't trust the priest at St Michael's.'

'Why not?' Cheryl asked.

'Because a girl from school went to him for the same help last year. One day Meghan's in class, the next she's gone. The whole family vanished, and when a *For Sale* sign went up on the lawn by the footpath outside her house, that's when Mum said nothing would force *her* out of her home. She said this was my mistake, not hers. Then, when I suggested a doctor could help fix things, she slapped me so hard.' Irene's hand went to her cheek. 'She said I was selfish to take an innocent baby's life and I had to prepare for God's punishment.'

'What punishment?' Cheryl scoffed. 'God loves us all, Irene.'

'Not girls like me. Mum says God's lesson comes with the baby. She says when a bowling ball is squeezing out between my legs and splitting my lady bits, I'll remember to think twice before letting a man touch me. But I-I didn't l-let him. I-I didn't . . . '

'Oh, for heaven's sake!' Cheryl shushed Irene, but no amount of back rubbing stopped the girl's spluttering and coughing. 'Come on, be strong. Getting hysterical is not good for you, or the baby. I want to help, but you have to calm down. Oh, thanks for these, Col. Leave them all there, will you?' Cheryl instructed the store owner. 'Lissy? Take a milkshake and let Amber have a sip, please.' Though a toddler, the child understood and immediately attached her lips to the paper straw poking out of Lissy's tin tumbler. 'We should drink quick and go back to the house,' Cheryl said. 'Wherever this smoke is coming from, it's getting worse.'

Col had stopped to pick up the wire mesh frame holding the *Daily Mirror*'s news headline. 'The wind's not helping,' he said. 'Dawson's Run will have serious damage done before they contain this monster.'

When the straw fell from Lissy's open mouth, Amber latched on again. 'Dawson's Run is in the fire's path?' she asked.

'The Dawson place is the source,' Col replied.

248

'Damn fool has put neighbouring properties at risk when he should've known better than to spot weld in a dry paddock.'

Lissy baulked. 'Don started the fire?'

'No, his brother. Twice the brawn and half the brain of young Don. Old Bruce is a damn fool for favouring tradition over his second son. Not my business, though. After today, there may not be much left of the place to fight over.'

Lissy ached from having Amber's legs attached like a barnacle around her belly. Her back hurt from standing, and now her heart was breaking for Dawson's Run. 'We have to do something.'

'They've got every portable water tanker from around the district on hand, lass. It's hot and dangerous work, but Don's a smart lad. He knows what he's doing, but with Dawson's Run in the bloke's veins he won't walk away easily. Never known a more passionate farmer.'

Lissy was in a panic, the drink in her hand forgotten, until her coughing spasm shook liquid out of the cup and down the front of the tent-like dress she'd chosen specifically for the trip into town.

'Wind shift,' Col said, collecting the fallen Coca Cola A-frame. 'If I were you, ladies, I'd get home and stay inside.'

'But I need to know Don's safe.' Lissy's eyes stung as tears spilled onto her cheeks. Fear and something else had twisted together to form a knot of dread so tight she struggled to breathe. 'I have to help.'

Col stopped partway through the multicoloured strips in the doorway meant to keep flies out. 'Best way is to head to your island, stay inside, and pray for rain. We're due a downpour. The sooner, the better.'

'Col's right,' Cheryl said, taking charge of her now-crying daughter. 'We'll only get in the way. Leave Don to do what he must. We should go.'

★ ★ ★

'What's really bothering you, Irene?' Cheryl asked as she settled Amber in the car beside Lissy. 'This is about more than stale bread, isn't it?'

'It's Mum,' Irene said, her peevishness filling the passenger seat. 'She won't let me talk to Dad on the phone. She says he's never to know about the baby. He thinks I'm staying with one of Mum's old school friends and helping with her newborn. Mum says the news will be the death of him.'

'So dumb,' Lissy grumbled as she slammed the back door closed. She was in no mood for Irene. 'Fires kill people. Not bloody bad news. Right, Cheryl?'

'Not that I've heard, but no mother is dumb, Lissy. We all have different ways of worrying about our children, as you may well discover. Irene's mum was smart enough to send her to Dandelion House,' Cheryl said as she turned the car towards the old punt road.

'Yeah, the most boring place on the planet,' Irene muttered, while flicking the tiny triangle side window open and closed.

'Shut up, Irene, it's not boring.'

'That's your opinion, Lissy. Take off your gooey love goggles and you'll see nothing but weeds, dirt and animal dung. I bet Mum figured that if she sent me some place in the city, I wouldn't go home. I probably wouldn't. Instead, I'm stuck here.'

'That's enough!' Cheryl's uncharacteristic retort shocked Irene silent — Lissy too. 'Your mother is paying money for you to be here, when she could've sent you to a place where they force girls to work off the cost of their so-called care. You really don't want one of those places, Irene. I know what I'm talking about.'

Lissy knew as well. She knew more than anyone realised. She'd heard the same exasperation in Cheryl's voice during a conversation with Doc Wynter. He'd been telling her about a medical conference in Sydney, and it sure didn't sound like he'd enjoyed the trip one bit.

★ ★ ★

'Punitive and authoritarian,' Doc had said, not knowing Lissy was eavesdropping.

Cheryl and Doc had taken their tea to the far end of the veranda to ensure privacy, assuming Lissy would stay in the kitchen with Irene and the remaining hot scones. Instead, she'd filled a plate and headed to her room. With its window ajar, their voices were clear.

'The allocation of duties for unmarried mothers in those city maternity homes is tantamount to slave labour. They take in scared young girls, make them work, and coerce them into signing

251

legal documents stamped 'BFA', without explaining what the letters stand for. Then they segregate unmarried mothers — referred to as 'A-Mothers' (A for 'adoption') — keeping them from other mothers-to-be until the delivery, when their faces are covered, and their babies swiftly removed from the room. The mothers don't hold them, or get told the sex, and this is all under the pretext of a process best for all.

'Worse still,' Doc continued, 'post-delivery and pleading for a pill to take away their pain, unmarried mothers are unaware it's stilboestrol, a medication to dry up the milk supply.'

'How can professionals who are supposed to care for patients be so cruel?' Cheryl was really upset, her voice mere whispered disbelief.

'We're not all bad,' Doc said. 'Gypsy's growing underground of informants is telling us that much, as well as gathering the proof we'll need. Change is coming.'

Cheryl scoffed. 'No parliamentarian will speak out on behalf of unmarried mothers. Such a pathetic boys' club.'

Doc tutted. 'Careful there, you're talking about your father-in-law, and probably your husband if there's truth to the rumours.'

'Exactly,' Cheryl said. 'Which makes me an expert on the inadequacies of our representatives. This isn't the Dark Ages. A mother should have the right to choose.'

'Thanks to Whitlam, and some credit to Gypsy for being so persistent with her lobbying, we have our first female adviser for women's affairs. No-fault divorce legislation is imminent.'

'Big deal! What about the young mothers whose grief is killing them now, Doc?'

'I understand your frustration, Cheryl, and believe me, the symposium was not an easy couple of days. One blasted doctor — and I use the title loosely — admitted to using young mothers as teaching aids. One after the other, students inspect the patient for dilation. He takes up to a dozen young doctors at any one time on his rounds. Girls as young as fifteen are nothing more than lab rats to these men, and I wouldn't put it past others to use their positions of power in other ways.'

'Pregnant, unmarried, and without family support does not allow a woman too many choices, Doc. Facilities are benefitting financially from these girls and their predicament. If not funding for the mothers, government should investigate and provide support services.'

'They've introduced a Supporting Mothers' Benefit,' Doc said. 'However, a single mother is only eligible once deserted, divorced, or if her husband is in prison or a mental hospital.'

'You can't possibly be serious! Can we do something?'

'Yes, Cheryl, we can, and we are. Gypsy's compiling a report, and I'm meeting in private with a federal member; but change is slow and, as you know from personal experience, every girl's situation is different.'

'I just wish I could do more, Doc.'

'You're doing the best thing by covering for Gypsy's absences. Now, Cheryl, I know you won't mention any of what I've said or what we're doing to your husband, or his politically motivated father. Gypsy prefers the town remains none the wiser to her involvement, even though I don't think we'd be achieving nearly as much without her. The groundswell since she hit her straps has been enormous. I also believe that thanks to you helping out, Gypsy is able to focus. Having Willow to think about is making a difference. She wants the child to grow up in a compassionate world. One with opportunities that celebrates difference and doesn't discriminate.'

'Gypsy could make life so much easier for herself,' Cheryl said. 'People in town would respect her if they knew; I'm certain. But she doesn't care what anybody thinks, does she?'

Doc chuckled. 'You're right about Gypsy. History has shown women stoned for less. But what I admire most is how she responds when those who consider themselves without sin cast those stones.'

'I'm not following you,' Cheryl said, sitting again.

'Our Gypsy catches the damn things, doesn't she?' Doc said. 'And rather than throw them back, she collects them. Where do you think Don gets the stones to cobble together those lovely seats?'

Cheryl and Doc both chuckle. 'I do love the way you think, Doc, and you're quite remarkable yourself. I owe you so much.'

'Dearest Cheryl,' he said over the sound of scraping chair legs. 'Your happy face — and a few tomatoes from that vegie patch over there

— are thanks enough for today. But please, remember, if anyone hurts you in any way and you need to talk, you can trust me.'

★ ★ ★

'I can't trust anyone,' Irene said as the punt bumped into the opposite bank. Her whimpering, coughing and complaining hadn't stopped since leaving town. Lissy had tuned out until the river crossing, where Irene's misery rode the punt, clinging to them and dragging the trio down as they reached the other side. 'What if no one wants my baby? Mum said a bastard like mine won't come out right.'

Cheryl draped an arm around Irene's shoulders, guiding her down the punt's ramp and onto the riverbank. 'Okay, so maybe your mother *is* an ignoramus.' She smiles. 'All babies are beautiful, Irene. Some are extra special. I promise you I know what I'm talking about.'

Lissy could ignore Irene by counting her strides, although the uphill walk to Dandelion House was a lot harder than the first day she'd forged up — teeth gritted, suitcase in hand. She'd been so prepared to prove she wasn't used goods and a lost cause. After meeting Irene, Lissy had become even more determined to get through her confinement with dignity. Four and a half months on, Lissy was a different person. No longer a teenager and not quite a mother, she was missing her home, and missing being the youngest daughter whose mum and dad did all the thinking, worrying, and decision-making for her. That was yet one more irrefutable fact to prove that Lissy — a month away from giving birth — wasn't ready to be a parent.

Once on the veranda, Irene sighed and collapsed onto the swing seat next to Lissy where she was catching her breath.

'You're such a great mum, Cheryl,' she announced. 'I wish you'd been mine.'

'All parents care,' Cheryl replied while jiggling Amber on her hip as she paced the veranda. 'Some don't realise how grown-up their children are until something like this happens. They handle the shock differently. You've frightened your mum, Irene. That's all. Once you're back home and she knows you're all right, things will return to normal.'

'Except I'll never have a boyfriend. Who'd want me?'

Cheryl had walked to the front door and stopped with the screen ajar. 'You know you never have to tell anyone. We're allowed to keep our secrets.' She winked; smiled. 'I'll put this one down and get us all some cordial.'

'I'll help,' Lissy said, following close behind.

★　★　★

'Do you have secrets?' Irene asked as Cheryl placed a tray with three glasses and a jug of green cordial on the outside table.

'Of course,' she replied. 'Some secrets are okay to keep forever. Others you'll tell, but only to the right person and when the time's right.'

All three sipped their drinks in silence until

256

Irene said, 'Gypsy's secretive.'

'No, Gypsy keeps to herself,' Cheryl explained. 'There's a difference. A person who takes the time to know her will be rewarded. She has wonderful tales of her time living on the road.'

'I heard Gypsy's mum fell pregnant to a fellow from a circus family,' Lissy added.

'Yes,' Cheryl says. 'And it was common knowledge Maeve's future in-laws were none too happy about her wanting to stop travelling and settle down. Their son was the headline act. One night they arranged to have both him and Maeve drugged, and Maeve transported to a maternity facility, miles away. They told their son she'd stolen a truck and run off with a worker.'

'What happened to Maeve?' Lissy asked.

'She woke up in a different bed, in a room with two dozen other girls, who did factory work until they delivered and their babies were adopted.'

'I don't get it, Cheryl,' Lissy said, intrigued. 'If they forced Maeve to sign adoption papers, how did she and Gypsy end up together? Did her boyfriend find her?'

'Yes, and in the nick of time, but with his parents not forthcoming with the truth, the search went on for months. Seeing him almost shocked poor Maeve into labour.'

'Can shock do that?' Irene butted in, but Lissy shushed her so Cheryl could continue.

'Every innkeeper turned Maeve away. They recognised her tunic as the type unmarried mothers wore in maternity homes back then. While looking for shelter, she collapsed, and Gypsy was born that night — in a tent — after being taken in by the kindly wife of a fight promoter. They stayed on with the boxing troupe, married, then began touring outback Queensland. Although Maeve hated fighting, her husband became a crowd favourite and earned good money. She knew it wouldn't be forever. Just until they could repay the generosity.'

'Did they leave?' Lissy asked.

Cheryl shook her head and said, forlornly, 'A blow to his head forced Maeve to watch the man she loved die.'

'Oh, no, poor Maeve.'

'Yes,' Cheryl said, 'and soon after, she began to fear she and her baby would no longer be welcome to stay on. She had to earn her keep, so she made herself an attraction in the hope women and wives would come to the shows with their husbands. Naturally, the owners loved the idea of increasing attendance, but with news of the bewitching fortune teller soon travelling far and wide, Maeve worried her late husband's parents would be able to find her and Gypsy. They'd be sure to claim she was a crazy person and a fraud and have her put away.'

'What did she do?' Lissy asked.

'The isolation at Dandelion House would protect Gypsy, but first they had to find a way back from the Northern Territory. Not an easy journey, or safe for a woman in those days; harder still with a small child. En route, she met a homeless girl in the family way, and they journeyed together. After arriving, Lilliana had her baby and met a Calingarry Crossing farmer. Maeve stayed on here and continued to support other young girls in the family way.'

'Lilliana stayed in town?' Lissy asked. 'And she lived happily ever after?'

'Forget her,' Irene said, crossly. 'What happened to Maeve?'

Cheryl sighed. 'She was here, alone, chopping wood when a huge splinter pierced an artery in her leg. A lonely, tragic end, because Gypsy had left home several years before. Although very young, she'd gone away with her mother's blessing.'

'She left her mum behind?' Lissy asked.

'Yes. Maeve realised she could hardly champion a woman's right to choose and not let her daughter make her own decisions. Gypsy had wanted to know her grandparents and understand her dad's early life. She left Calingarry Crossing and travelled with the circus until Maeve's death brought her home to carry on her work. Over the years, Dandelion House has helped many girls.

'So you see, Irene, you really are in the best place,' Cheryl said. 'As confusing as this can be, you have time to work out your feelings. Many girls said goodbye to their babies here, but they were ready and well-informed.' Cheryl reached across to hold Irene's hand. 'You did nothing wrong. Your uncle is the bad person. I know you're Catholic, and Reverend Lindeman is a Presbyterian minister, but I trust him. He's a great supporter of Gypsy's work. As for the people in this town? Ignore them, girls. Stay strong, Irene. Be independent, even though some men don't consider strength in a woman a positive trait. But most of all — ' Cheryl paused. ' — make sure you can say the life you chose was the one you wanted. Make a decision to leave nothing undone, and never settle for less when there's more. Gypsy told me the same thing and I've never forgotten.'

'You didn't tell us about the father of Gypsy's baby,' Irene said. 'Where is Willow's dad?'

Cheryl swallowed hard and pressed a hand to her neck. 'My throat tells me we've talked enough. A good dose of honey will help. The smoke must've changed direction again. Let's go inside.' She stood. 'We'll make tea, then toast that old bread until it's golden brown, and add lashings of butter and honey.'

'I'll be in soon.' Lissy continued to stare at the darkening line of grey in the distance. 'How can we have blue sky above and Dawson's Run be in such danger?' She put a hand to her chest and felt the rattle of her breath wheezing along anxious and overworked airways. What must breathing be like for poor Don? He was somewhere under that thick line of grey, and putting his life on the line to save the family property Lissy had expected he'd walk away from.

'He would want us all inside with the windows closed,' Cheryl insisted. 'No sense putting your health, or your baby's, at risk. Come on.'

★   ★   ★

'I'm sad for Gypsy,' Irene said as Cheryl placed piping-hot toast onto their plates. 'Is the reason

Willow's sick because she was too old to be a mother?'

Cheryl hooted. 'Gypsy's not old, and if you ask, she'll tell you she was waiting for the child who would need her the most.'

'That's nice,' Lissy said. 'Willow's so cute, and I like Gypsy. She's big and kooky and colourful, like I imagine her crystal-ball-gazing mum was. Do you reckon she learned how to tell the future too? That would be sort of cool. Reckon I might ask.'

'Where is everyone?' Gypsy's voice boomed, the screen door slammed shut, and she floated like a colourful kite along the hallway towards the kitchen. 'Well, you three are looking like the proverbial cat. Dare I ask about the canary's fate?'

Lissy threw herself against Gypsy's pillow-like bulk, finding comfort in the swirling scent of incense and aromatic oils that permanently wafted around her. 'I'm so sorry about your dad.'

'I see. Well, that answers that question.' Gypsy cast a sideways look at Cheryl, then peeled Lissy away so she could retrieve a teacup and saucer from a cupboard. 'What else have I missed?'

'There's a fire,' Lissy said. 'Have you heard anything?'

Gypsy fiddled with the knob on the transistor radio sitting atop the refrigerator. 'If you tried tuning into the news rather than gossiping, you'd know. They've got their hands full. Rain is what's needed to stop the spread to Cedar Cutters Gorge. Hopefully this letter brings brighter news.' She pulled an envelope from the deep side pocket in her kaftan, thrusting it in Irene's direction.

'A letter for me?'

'Got your name on it,' Gypsy replied, lowering the announcer's scratchy voice. 'Want to share?'

'It's Mum's writing,' Irene said, ripping the envelope and almost the letter itself. 'She didn't mention a letter when we talked, and . . . Oh!' Irene slumped, the notepaper landing with a thud in her lap.

'What?' Lissy asked.

'She says I'm to write another letter to my father and tell him that, although the farm is a long way away from everything, I'd like his permission to stay on because I'm enjoying the responsibility that being a governess brings, and . . . '

'And what?' Lissy urged, her frustration mounting.

'Check this out.' Irene thrust a second sheet of paper at Gypsy. 'She's made up an imaginary family with names and ages for me to memorise, and . . . ' Irene's voice sounded small, broken. 'I don't want to lie to my dad.'

'Oh God! Is that all?' Lissy grumbled. Get over it and *lie*, she wanted to shout.

Instead, while Gypsy and Cheryl comforted Irene, she went to her room to watch the sky and to pray.

★ ★ ★

Even with the window closed, the smell of smoke lingered, along with the milk bar owner's words: 'Don won't walk away from Dawson's Run easily.' Lissy's thoughts shifted to Maeve, who'd had the benefit of seeing into the future. Why hadn't she predicted the knockout blow? She might have saved her husband's life. Instead, she'd sat helpless as he died in her arms.

Lissy didn't need a crystal ball to know Don would be safe, because nothing was allowed to happen to him. Her baby needed a father, and Lissy needed Don. If Lilliana could live happily ever after in Calingarry Crossing with her baby, so could she. Lissy was never more certain of anything.

23

Calingarry Crossing, 2014

Tom steps out the shop door and slams shoulders with Beth.

'Geez, sorry, mate!' he says automatically. 'Then again, not really.' He grins, boyish-like. 'I was thinking about you and, well, here you are. How was the cemetery yesterday?'

Unsure how to answer such a question, Beth simply says, 'Wet?'

'Yes, fabulous, isn't it?' Even with a blue sky, and under the cover of a shop awning, Tom instinctively raises a palm to the sky as if catching the precious drops. 'Barely enough to touch the water tanks yesterday, but we're expecting more later today,' he tells her. 'Glad you ran into me. Saves me tracking you down.'

'Er, you ran into me,' Beth says, eyeing the paper package he's moving from one hand to the other. 'Looks heavy.'

Tom puffs up and slaps the parcel twice. 'Five kilograms of prime barley-fed Dawson's Run beef ribs, born and raised and butchered in honour of my birthday.'

Beth guesses the meat is the reason Wally is behaving, sitting obediently at his master's feet, eyes fixed, hopeful.

'You told me you didn't acknowledge the occasion.'

'This is true, but a weekly roast is definitely a family tradition, and I figured if I say it's a belated birthday lunch you'll come. A cheap date for me because I won't need to buy you dinner.'

'What an invitation!' Beth quips. 'But maybe not today.' She could joke about having developed an allergy to family traditions after those Christmases with Gran, but the parcel looks heavy and Wally is drooling on the toe of Tom's boot. 'I don't want to get in the way of your roast ritual.'

'Are you kidding? Uncle Don will love it. He always cooks way too much for two. Please?' He forces his bottom lip into a boyish pout. 'My uncle wasn't at his best when you met him, but he loves company and I'd sure enjoy having you — over for a meal, I mean.'

Another quick glance at the dog drool has Beth wondering when she last enjoyed ribs. 'Okay, yes, thanks,' she says. 'But I'll need to change first.'

'Sure, as long as it's not too much.' He winks. 'Wally and I can hang around and drive you.'

'I'm certain I can find the way, Tom.'

'Fabulous! Whenever you're ready, then.' He whacks the parcel again. 'Best get me old mate home and in the oven. Come on, Wally.'

As the man and his dog wander down the street, Beth tries to not think about Tom's 'old mate' having been among the big-eyed bunch of curious cattle in the paddock.

★ ★ ★

265

'Welcome back to Dawson's Run.' Tom opens the screen door, fussing awkwardly to relieve Beth of the wine and chocolates, while going in for a welcoming hug. 'Thanks for these. I'll, ah, stick them in this fridge over here. She's a humid one today,' he chats while making room in the small bar fridge for another bottle.

'I thought I heard a car.' Don appears from around the corner of the veranda. He's smiling his crooked smile. 'Nice to see you back,' he tells Beth. 'Come, sit here. You too, Tom, while I put the finishing touches on the meat.'

'I'm more than capable, Unc. I know your secret ingredient. Besides, the cook gets to taste.'

'Exactly,' Don retorts, already on his way to the front door. 'And about that secret recipe . . . I only revealed what I wanted to. That keeps the secret in the secret recipe. Stay out here and entertain your friend.'

Beth waits for Don to be out of earshot before saying, 'He's not wearing his brace?'

'Pressure sores from straps meant to keep the brace firm,' Tom explains, while dragging a seat out from the table and smacking the cushion before Beth sits. 'He'll never complain. Reckons he doesn't want people to remember him as a whining old bugger. In reality, he complains less than anyone. He says we all have two choices — live and make the most of life, or give up and die. He chose life.'

Don reappears with three wineglasses and Tom plucks cork coasters from a stack beside the paper serviettes, folded and in a basket. The table is obviously precious, Beth muses, fingering the varnished surface.

'She's a beauty, isn't she?' Don says. 'Broke my heart to see what fire can do. The most magnificent tree. Blackened but still standing a week later, while others around her succumbed. I thought for sure she was a goner, too, but against all odds she stayed strong and sprouted new growth in spring.' He seems to go somewhere in his mind, the pause uncomfortably long for Beth. 'I used to sit under her shady branches after work. Some days I needed to pause, to breathe, to be grateful.' Don is paused now, his gaze fixed on Beth. 'Sad thing is, just as I'm thinking she might adapt and flourish, lightning struck. As quick as a flash, she was gone. There was nothing I could do.'

'What you've done here is a wonderful tribute,' Beth says. 'It looks beautiful.'

'Even better with food on it,' Tom remarks. 'The roast smells good, Unc.'

'I agree,' Beth says. 'And I feel a bit like a drooling Wally right now.' She smiles and touches the corner of her mouth.

'Here, in case you need it.' Winking, Tom scoots a second serviette across the table. 'Only three settings, Unc? Matt not eating with us?'

'Your son is at an age when friends come before old farts. And I suggest from the slicked-back hair, clean shirt, and overpowering cologne, one or more friends may be of the female variety.'

'A local girl might mean we see more of him.' Tom poured water from a bottle into three plastic tumblers. 'I'm getting used to having an

267

extra pair of hands around the place.'

'He's a good lad, and you're lucky to have him in your life.'

'Luckier still to not have him at the lunch table,' Tom jokes. 'I've seen the way Matt inhales food.'

'You haven't seen me attack a rack of beef ribs yet,' Beth announces.

'Then we'd better dish up.' Don nudges his nephew. 'Give us a hand, Tom.'

* * *

'Here we go! Hope we've done right by the beast,' Don says, his tongs clamped around a good-sized rib. 'Pass your plate over, Elizabeth.'

Beth doesn't correct him. She's too busy blocking the image of her lunch having had legs and the freedom of a Dawson's Run paddock. For a few minutes there's a clinking of cutlery and tongs on stoneware plates, and chatter about tenderness and taste. When the conversation segues into farm talk about feed and agricultural practices, the pair answer Beth's questions between mouthfuls of food.

Don's the first to finish, eating little in Beth's opinion. He's piled more meat and bones into a dish for the two dogs. Excusing himself from the table, he takes the scraps away, returning soon after with the joey pouch hanging around his neck.

Beth lets out a surprised 'Oh!' and pulls out the adjacent chair. To her delight, Don chooses to sit beside her. 'We won't be calling him Little

Joey for too long,' she says.

'Speaking of names . . . ' Don looks at her. 'I may have called you Elizabeth earlier. You said nothing so I assume that's okay?'

'Yes.' She'd heard him use Lissy's name again, too, but Beth had let the slip pass. She's happy to have Don questioning her aloud, rather than with his eyes. He'd been like an audience of one over lunch, scrutinising her every move, looking through her and beyond her. 'On my birth certificate I'm Elizabeth, but I didn't much like the name. Makes me think of The Queen,' she chuckles. 'For a while, at school, I was Lizzy, or variations of the name: Busy Lizzy, Dizzy Lizzy, Tizzy Lizzy. You know how kids are? I didn't care, but Mum hated it, so we found a compromise. We did that a lot. At the next school we used Beth.'

'It suits you,' he replied. 'Elizabeth makes me think of The Queen, too.'

Beth's still laughing over Don's comment when Tom joins them, three mugs in hand.

'Hey, Unc, you're not trying to steal my date, are you?'

Over coffee, Beth listens with interest to Tom's passionate oration on the benefits of barley as fodder. She learns Dawson's Run livestock enjoys daily feeds of five-day-old, hydroponically grown sprouts, which Tom and his uncle produce in the big shed. Don, a self-taught technology whiz, is Captain in the Command Cockpit, but quick to brush off any praise.

'You only have to pick up a book and you'll discover how to do something, if your mind's

269

open to learning,' he says.

Between them, Tom and his uncle have conceptualised both manual and hydraulic farm management systems, developing automated processes with help from engineering companies keen to *enable* farmers like Don. Technology manages routine chores, including monitoring fences and water troughs. Programmable ear-tags monitor the herd, and remote-control drones provide visuals on Don's computer screen to check dams and locate fence crawlers — those cattle that find their way onto the wrong side of the boundary.

'The banquet of barley is way cheaper than bales of Lucerne hay,' Tom tells Beth on the side. 'And grass-fed allows us to hike the price per kilo up at the sale yards.'

'Enough farm talk, Tom. More coffee,' Don announces with a vigour Beth has not seen before. 'You always have been able to talk the leg off a dead cow. Makes me wonder why we pay the butcher.'

Beth can hardly credit their levity on wine. Over lunch the three of them had eked out a single little-bottle. But Tom is extremely jovial, and when he thanks his uncle for the meal by planting a purposely noisy kiss on his head, Don shoves his nephew playfully.

'I suspect you had one too many with lunch.'

'Perhaps not as much as this little one,' Tom says, leaning across the table to scoop something from a half-empty glass before handing it to Beth.

'What is it?' Don asks.

'A ladybug,' she replies, presenting her palm. 'Does two in two days mean double the luck for me? It was my wine glass. What do you think, Don?'

He says nothing, leaving an awkward pause for his nephew to fill.

'Beth was telling me yesterday she had an imaginary friend as a child. A ladybug she named . . . What was it again, Beth? Buggy-what?'

'Buggy-boo.'

Don rises from the table so fast, his right arm pendulums wildly, knocking the empty wine bottle and starting a domino effect, ending with Beth wearing what's left of the wine. While Tom soaks up the spillage with a wad of paper napkins, Don disappears inside the cottage without a word.

'Sorry about that, Beth. I'm not sure what was up with him. He's been reacting to the weirdest stuff lately.'

'No apology needed,' she tells him. 'But you can walk me to my car. I need to get back to the hotel and get these clothes off.'

★ ★ ★

'What?' Beth asks as Tom tugs twice on the car's door handle.

'You locked it? Out here?'

She waves her keys and the remote beeps, lights flashing. 'It's a city-girl thing,' she says, leaning her back against the door, 'and I'm a proud city girl.'

'You reckon? Let me take a closer look.' With one arm braced against the car, Tom holds a

271

finger to her chin, lifting her face until she's drowning in the pools of brown staring back. 'Nope, as expected, you are the most countrified city girl I've ever had the pleasure of meeting.'

His face is so close to Beth's she can count the honey-coloured flecks in his irises. At that moment, with his arm the only thing stopping his body from falling into hers, Beth finds herself falling a little bit in lust.

'I'll take that as a compliment,' she says, ducking under his arm. 'Thanks again, Tom. I enjoyed lunch, and my harem pants enjoyed the wine.'

'Yeah, I'm sorry again about my uncle. Like I said, he's been a bit doddery.'

'I understand,' she says, opening the driver's door. 'Ageing brings with it all kinds of challenges. In fact, Tom, how are you feeling? You are a year older.'

Beth's sass is short-lived when his free hand moves to the back of her neck and pulls her close. 'Then surely I must be due a birthday kiss right about now.'

Kissing him seems the most natural thing, his mouth moulding with hers so exquisitely it's difficult to stop. But she does, pulling away, again ducking under his arm. They are, after all, standing in plain sight of his uncle's house and it's starting to rain.

She opens her palm to the sky. 'I should get going.'

'It's only rain,' he says. 'It'll dry off.'

Beth slips into the driver's seat, closes the door and lowers her window, in the hope Tom leans in and kisses her again. He doesn't disappoint.

'You know, Beth, it's dry in your car and there's this place not far from here. Cedar Cutters Gorge was the spot for necking about twenty-five birthdays ago. I'm sure I remember how that works.'

The roar of the engine starting drowns out Beth's laugh. 'I'm sure you do, and I'm also sure you broke a few hearts. Speaking of broken hearts,' she says, the car at idle, 'your uncle called me Lissy again.'

'Take it as a compliment, Beth. The girl was apparently beautiful and spirited. I'm guessing he sees the same in you. I know I do.' Tom taps the roof twice. 'Take extra care on the dirt in this rain. The bends sneak up on you.'

'You're forgetting my two ladybugs,' she says. 'I have luck on my side. But thank you, Tom Dawson. It's nice to have someone worry about me.'

24

Dandelion House, Summer, 1974

'Where's all this rain come from?' Lissy grumbled. 'And when will it stop? I'll go crazy if I don't get out of this house soon.'

Irene plucked another dish from the soapy water. 'If you ask me, you're already crazy.'

'I *feel* crazy. I've seen so little of Don since the fire. Once in seven whole days.' Lissy sighed and stopped drying the teacup to rub the sweat beads from her forehead with the back of her hand. The humidity was stifling. 'But soon I'll be Mrs Don Dawson, and I can't wait to be married.'

'You really told him yes and meant it?' Irene asked.

'Of course.' Lissy pushed open the window above the sink, using a wooden spoon because her belly no longer let her reach. 'I'm not leading him on.'

Irene looked disbelieving. 'And you won't change your mind again? You're totally happy to stay here, a farmer's wife in a small town, when you've dreamed of being famous? For months I've heard you singing and stomping around your room. And I've seen the way you dance under the willows by yourself. Your imagination is bigger than Calingarry Crossing, Lissy.'

'I'll have you know, Irene,' she said, crossly, 'when I'm doing those things I'm not *dreaming* about being famous. I'm pretending. There is a difference.'

'I'm not trying to be mean,' Irene said. 'You're beautiful. You could do anything you want, *be* anything.'

'I'm going to be a mother.' Lissy splayed the fingers on her left hand, tugging at the gold ring that had slipped on easily a few days ago, but was no longer budging. 'And I'll be a wife.'

Three days ago, Don had visited Dandelion House briefly to show all concerned he was genuinely unscathed. Not so the property. He'd stunk of smoke, and ash stained his skin and his clothes, but when his arms had wrapped around her, squeezing tight, Lissy knew what *right* felt like. She was no longer the giggly girl who'd fallen for the flirtatious picker and cried for her mum. Her desires were different. While the child part of Lissy might *need* her mother, the woman in her *wanted* Don. She'd known for certain when Don had held her, almost crying as he explained how close he'd come to losing everything.

'Not everything,' Lissy had told him. 'You'd still have me, and I want to help. I want to meet your family and I want us to *make* a family. You, me, him.' She'd taken Don's hand then and pressed it against her belly. 'And whoever else comes along after you've made me a farmer's wife, Don Dawson.'

Later that afternoon, showered and in his best corduroy jacket and trousers, Don returned to Dandelion House to escort Lissy to Dawson's Run.

Lissy was yet to break the news to her family so, as soon as this rain stopped, she would get a lift into town and telephone.

'Can I tell Mum you'll be my bridesmaid, Irene?'

'No! Keep wiping.' She pointed at the growing stack of dishes in the draining rack. 'I don't get it, Lissy. You can do anything you want, but you're going to tie yourself to Don Dawson. Why? How do you know there's not some perfectly good bloke — and not so weird — waiting out there to meet you?'

'A good man is better than a good-looking one. Besides, Don isn't weird, Irene.'

'You expect your parents will accept the guy?'

'They can like it or lump it,' Lissy said. 'I figure if I go home and let Mum and Dad fall head over heels in love with the baby first, when Don arrives for the big meet and greet they'll love him for loving me. We'll spend a few weeks with the family before returning to Calingarry Crossing, with their blessing. There's lots to fix and tidy after the fire, so we'll stay on at Dawson's Run for a while, but where we live doesn't matter to me. The idea of building something together is exciting. In a crazy way, the fire and my fear of losing Don was the best thing.'

'And his family is cool about the baby?' Irene asked.

'We surprised them, but they were fine, although his mum and dad are older than I'd pictured. His dad is crook, and his mum looks sort of shrivelled and toasted. When his mum stopped looking at my belly to focus on my face, and Don went out the back to talk with his dad in private, Mrs Dawson asked me all kinds of stuff.'

'And what did you tell her?'

'The truth. That I made a stupid mistake, but I love Don.' Lissy watched Irene silently stack the last of the dried crockery in the cupboard. 'Then, as we were leaving, Mrs Dawson wanted to try this thing. She hung her wedding ring on a string, dangled it over my belly and confirmed it's a boy. Everyone got very excited. I didn't meet the brother or his wife, but Mrs Dawson said having a wedding to plan for, and a new baby, is what Dawson's Run needs. When I explained Mum would be involved in planning the wedding, she was like, 'whatever'. So cool. Nothing like my parents.'

'I guess he'll be here with Gypsy and Willow anytime,' Irene said.

'I hope so,' Lissy replied, turning off the kitchen light. Don was on a rescue mission, collecting Gypsy and Willow, as the bus they'd boarded in Saddleton got bogged after part of the road washed away.

In the living room, the pregnant pair slouched against opposite arms of the sofa, looking like two lazy bookends — legs outstretched and both hands cupping their respective bellies.

'I feel like I could burst,' Lissy said, hand-batting the soft pink pig from the middle of the sofa into Amber's playpen and reigniting a burst of toddler talk.

'Cute, isn't she?' Irene said. 'I'm glad Cheryl's

277

staying tonight. I like her. She cares more than my mum.'

'As if we need a babysitter,' Lissy grumbled. 'In a matter of weeks we're going to be mothers ourselves.'

Irene nodded in agreement. 'I guess we'd hardly be doing anything different if we were on our own. Maybe sneak out to go dancing? Hit the closest nightclub? Imagine us dancing 'The Bump' and 'The Bus Stop' with these bellies?'

Dragging herself to her feet, Irene dopey-danced around the living room to nonsensical lyrics. Lissy joined her and soon a squealing Amber was bobbing up and down on her bottom, her red cheeks bouncing, fat fists pumping the air.

'What on earth . . . ?' Cheryl swept into the room, bundling her little girl into her arms. 'One day you girls will understand the consequences of rousing a child this close to nighty-night time. To bed with you, my little dancing queen. Oh, and Irene, I meant to ask. What was the news from home?'

'News?' she quizzed.

Cheryl looked across at Lissy who'd fallen back onto the sofa. 'You passed on Irene's mail, didn't you?'

Lissy bowed her head, shame burning her cheeks. 'I figured it could wait until tomorrow. Letters from your mum only make you cry, Irene. Sorry. It's in the hall table drawer, but don't ask me to get up.'

'I'll get it!' Cheryl huffed, swinging Amber onto her hip. 'Seriously, Lissy, you will not know what's hit you when you have a child. You'll be doing all the fetching and carrying then, and it won't be to your schedule.'

'I really am sorry, Irene,' Lissy whispered once Cheryl had left the room. 'Can I make it up to you by filling the big claw bath? Mum says a good soak washes away your worries.'

'You know we're not allowed,' Irene replied. 'Big tubs take too much water out of the tank.'

'Der! Open your eyes and ears. The tanks are overflowing. As long as the water's not too hot or too cold, what's the problem?'

'What if it is too hot or too cold?' Irene asked.

Lissy shrugged. 'I dunno. Gypsy says to avoid extreme anything when we're this far along. But a bath? That's so unfair when we're both like great big hippos walking around on exhausted emu legs. A few minutes of weightlessness in a tub can't hurt.'

'Cheryl will hear the water running,' Irene said.

'Not with the rain on this roof and with her room on the far side of the house. She'll tuck in with Amber soon, story time as usual.'

When a knock at the front door startled both women, they hauled themselves up. Visitors to the island were few and late-night arrivals even more rare. They shuffled from the living area, sock feet skating across the kitchen linoleum and into the hallway.

Cheryl made the door before either girl, calling to them over her shoulder, 'It's only Don.'

'I won't come in.'

'Of course you will,' Lissy said as she reached the door. Despite the oilskin, rain had saturated

Don's clothes and his hair dripped water. 'You'll blow away out there.' Lissy took charge of the flyscreen, flinging it wide and poking her head out. Hair whipped her face and her night dress blew up like a billowing tent. 'Where are Gypsy and Willow?'

Don had just shaken the bushman's coat from his shoulders and let it fall in a crumpled heap when Lissy tugged him inside.

'I couldn't get to them in the end,' he said, dripping on the front door mat. 'A landslide over the road has stopped all traffic in and out of Saddleton. On the bright side, had the bus been a few minutes earlier the situation could have been worse. The passengers are uninjured, but with a long wait ahead of them.'

'Poor Willow.' Cheryl hugged her daughter tight. 'She's scared of the thunder.'

'I got through to Hugh Ducker via CB radio,' Don said. 'He's also caught up on the Saddleton side of the mess, but he promised to personally deliver Gypsy and Willow as soon as he could. Until then, I didn't want you ladies to be out here alone and wondering.'

'That's admirable, Don,' Cheryl said. 'But there's no need. I'm prepared to stay overnight in lieu of Gypsy.'

'I don't mind sticking around. I — '

'No, Don,' Cheryl cut in. 'It's late. I'm sure there are things to do at home. How's the clean-up going?'

'To be honest, I'm finding every reason to stay clear of the place.' Don wrapped both arms across his chest. He was saturated, his skin prickled with goose bumps, his cheeks and jaw aquiver. 'Tonight's storm has got nothin' on Dawson's Run. We survived the fire, but there's one almighty explosion brewing. Dad and Michael are like two sticks of dynamite, and Wendy wandering around and whining is like flint on stone. I don't want to be anywhere near when the sparks fly.'

As if driving the point home, a bolt of lightning forked in the sky behind Don.

Lissy prepared for another thunderclap. 'Let Don stay, Cheryl, please.'

'Definitely not. Gypsy would have a conniption.'

Don nodded. 'She would, but better she rant and rave than battle the punt crossing alone with Willow. The current is strong, with logs and debris coming downriver from the old cedar mill. One person won't be able to control the punt, and Hugh won't go near the water, even on a calm day. He still believes the island is cursed and the river swallows up people whole. Gypsy will have her hands full in these conditions and we don't want Willow being unnecessarily scared. Do we, Cheryl?' Don fixed his gaze on her. 'You won't know I'm here, I promise. I'll check the animals are on high ground and secure what I can. Then I'll keep watch for Hugh's truck from the sleepout. There's no missing a burst of those pig-hunting spotlights from there. I can take the punt over and make the crossing with them.'

'Fine, fine,' Cheryl relented. 'But by nine o'clock I want both you ladies in your beds.'

'I'm going now,' Irene mumbled. 'Three's a crowd.'

'Before you do … ' Cheryl tugged the envelope from Amber's grasp. 'Sorry about the chewed corner. I'm off to my room now. I'm on storytelling duty and surprised my audience isn't screaming the house down. Be good. I'm trusting you, Lissy.'

25

That same night

'For goodness' sake, you're freezing. What are you doing?'

The wrinkled slip of a girl shivered in the bath. Only her head, a bulbous belly, and two knobbly knees protruded from the water. Cheryl's heart rate rocketed.

'Leave me alone,' Irene cried. 'My mother's right. It is a demon child. I want it gone.'

'And what makes you think this is the way?' Cheryl tutted. 'Let's get you out. We'll talk.'

Irene offered no help, her body a dead weight. 'There's nothing to talk about. I killed my dad. It's all in the letter.'

Cheryl picked up the paper from the floor. Though soggy in places, the blurry edges of smudged ink couldn't soften the sharpness of a hard-hearted mother:

Are you proud of yourself, Irene? Killing your father? I asked you to do one thing — to tell him a small white lie. Instead, I had to lie for you. When he came home from the pub and said what he'd heard, I confessed to knowing about your made-up stories. I said you were looking for attention and his brother did nothing wrong. The truth, of course, is Pete likes to brag to his drunken mates, is weak, and a sucker for slutty young girls. Your behaviour and the shame it has brought was supposed to stay our secret. I warned you that disappointment would break your father's heart — and you have. You are no daughter of mine and I want nothing to do with you, or your demon child.

Cheryl was aghast. 'What sort of mother writes such a thing?'

'My-my mother,' Irene sobbed. 'R-right there in bl-black and wh-white, but I never said anything to Dad. I-I promised.'

'Calm down, sweetheart, small breaths. It'll be okay.'

'Never, never,' she wailed louder. 'Nothing will ever be okay ever again.'

Managing to coax Irene out of the bath and back into bed, Cheryl waited until the sobs turned to soft snoring. When she returned to her own room, exhausted, a tickertape of thoughts kept her awake: What sort of mother abandons her daughter? What will become of Irene? She'll never manage a baby alone.

'There but for the grace of God, go I,' Cheryl muttered. It was her turn to weep and to wish Gypsy was here with Willow — both safe and snug.

The one person Cheryl wasn't concerned about was Lissy. Girls like her — the pretty, confident ones — always landed on their feet. Not so the men who fell for them, and Cheryl feared for Don's heart. He didn't deserve a broken one. As she closed her eyes, serenaded by the suckling sounds coming from her daughter in the cot, Cheryl made three wishes for the morning: to bring sunshine, the sound of Willow's baby talk to the house, and news of every soldier coming home from Vietnam.

★ ★ ★

The room was still black when a noise forced Cheryl bolt upright, forcing her to fumble about for the bedside lamp. With Amber asleep, sucking on her thumb, her chest rising and falling, Cheryl breathed a sigh of relief and drew on her dressing gown. Hearing muted voices, she padded to the kitchen, but rather than Gypsy and Willow, as she'd thought, a dishevelled Don and Lissy, clad in her flimsy nightdress, stood in the hallway, pin-straight like kangaroos caught in the headlights.

Cheryl tutted. 'I'm very disappointed in you both. I expected better, Don.'

'It's not what you think,' Lissy said. 'He couldn't stay in the sleepout. The roofs leaking everywhere. My room's not much better. But forget us. It's Irene. I heard her cry out and her bed's all wet. It's not a roof leak, Cheryl. Something's really wrong,' Lissy said. 'I was coming to get you.'

A wilted Irene — her flaccid arms a ghostly shade of pale — was propped up with her back against the headboard, chin on her chest.

'Help me, Don,' Cheryl instructed as Doc's training mantra kicked in: *Think slow. Move fast. Triage.* 'Grab her shoulders. I'll lift her legs. Mind her head,' she prompted. 'We'll carry her to Lissy's room. I assume you know the way?'

'I can help,' Lissy said, then raced ahead to position herself on the far side of her bed, arms outstretched.

'No, don't!' But Cheryl's warning came too late. Lissy winced and doubled over. 'Don't strain this late in your pregnancy. Leave the heavy work to me and Don,' Cheryl pleaded. 'You can grab towels and blankets. Don, you'll have to fetch Doc Wynter.'

'No!' Lissy cried, grabbing Don by the arm. 'Why?'

The girl looked genuinely afraid. Or was Lissy's wincing and pinched face pain-related? Cheryl shook her head. She didn't have the mental capacity to think about anything other than Irene.

'Gypsy's not here, Lissy, and I can't manage on my own.'

'Is Irene having the baby?'

'I don't want to wait until she is to get help, Lissy.' Cheryl was confident she could capably monitor and guide the mother-to-be. From her own experience, and having assisted Doc many times, she knew it was the delivering mothers who did most of the work anyway — when all went to plan. 'We need to be prepared.'

★ ★ ★

'Please, Cheryl, no!' Lissy hung like an anchor on Don's arm. 'You heard him say one person

286

alone can't manage in these conditions. The river killed Gypsy's grandparents, it nearly killed me, and this house killed her mother. Hugh's right. The place *is* cursed.'

'We can do without the hysterics, Lissy,' Cheryl said, while training her gaze on the watch's hand ticking each agonising second until she found a pulse and began counting.

'She'll be fine,' Lissy stated. 'It's Irene. She's bunging it on, as usual.'

Cheryl ignored her and looked at Don. 'I can't make you do anything, but you do know this river better than anyone.'

Slowly, Don peeled his arm from Lissy's grasp. 'She's right, Lis, and the punt is strong. I'll find Doc and be back in no time.' They hugged and Don kissed the top of her head. 'Rest. You'll be fine.'

'Yes, she will, Don. It's Irene who needs you now.' Impatient, and with concern growing with every passing minute, Cheryl almost pushed Don to the front door and into his still-damp *Driza-Bone*. 'The second you're back, the two of you can hold hands and never let go. For now, though . . . ' She shoved his hat into his chest. 'Irene needs you to hurry.'

★ ★ ★

While rain lashed the roof and gutters overflowed, Lissy stayed busy locating leaks inside, positioning every tub, saucepan, bucket and empty coffee tin available until, fighting fatigue, she took a turn watching Irene so Cheryl could attend to Amber.

'Is that you, Lissy?' Irene murmured, her eyes flickering open.

'Yes, I'm here. Does it hurt?' The tear that squeezed out of Irene's eyes was answer enough, but she'd gone deathly pale. 'You'll be okay, Irene. I promise.'

'I don't want to be okay, Lissy, and I wish the baby was gone because I can't keep it. I can't be on my own with a baby.'

'But you'll have me and Cheryl and Gypsy,' Lissy said. 'Stay in Calingarry Crossing and we can be here for each other, like we wrote in our letters.'

'Only you'll be a respectable married lady,' Irene croaked out, 'and I'll be a single mother wearing a tin wedding band and living on stale bread and shame.'

'Hey, come on, I'm supposed to be the drama queen!' Lissy tried, but the quip failed to crack a smile on her friend's face.

At that moment, as they held hands, Lissy realised how good a friend Irene had become. They'd started out as two strangers with three things in common: both were teenagers, both were unmarried, and both were about to give birth to their first child. They'd shared more than a few months in a house. They'd shared their hopes and their dreams and made a pact to never tell their secret.

'Lissy?' Irene was saying. 'The baby really is better off in heaven now Dad's there to love it. I want to go home. I need to make it up to Mum. Dad would want that.'

Lissy could hear the words, but she'd run out of ways to console, other than holding Irene's hand. Her back ached terribly in the wooden study chair she'd pulled up to the bed, and every move delivered a stabbing sensation to her leaden pelvis. Heavy with exhaustion, she slid down in the seat, spread her legs wide, and wedged a pillow between her shoulder and the bed frame. If she could just close her eyes for a few . . .

★　★　★

A hand squeeze and a whisper woke Lissy, jerking her body upright in a rush. Lightheaded and groggy, she had to pinch her eyes to stop them stinging from the harsh overhead lighting.

'Did you say something, Irene?'

'Yes,' she said, her voice small. 'Tell Don I'm sorry for making him go for no reason. I'm feeling much better.'

'Good!' Lissy squinted at her watch, disappointed she'd slept. She hadn't wanted to close her eyes until she knew Don was back and safe. Two hours ago, Cheryl had made Lissy a fresh bed in the adjacent room, but not wanting to let go of Irene's hand, she'd made do with the hard chair and a soggy pillow. 'You can apologise to Don yourself any minute now,' she told Irene. 'Soon we'll all be sitting around drinking tea and laughing over you giving us a terrible fright.'

'Until then,' Irene whispered, 'will you keep holding my hand? Please, Lissy, I'm so scared.'

Cheryl could not believe her tired eyes. 'Oh, Lissy, what have you done?'

'Do you suppose Gypsy will be mad about the floor?'

Drag marks over timber were the least of Cheryl's concern. Lissy had managed to manoeuvre a second bed into the room, butting the mattress as close to Irene as the small bedside table between them allowed. The pair were laid out side-by-side, hands clasped where they hung between the beds.

'She wanted me to stay,' Lissy whispered over Irene's snores. 'But I couldn't keep my eyes open and everything's aching so bad. The bed wasn't heavy to move, just awkward. I knew you'd say no if I asked.'

'Oh, Lissy, Lissy.' Cheryl tutted while pressing a palm against the girl's forehead, before checking her pulse. 'Are you feeling all right?'

'Woozy, but I'll be better when Don's back.'

Won't we all! Cheryl delivered a reassuring smile, while inside she silently pleaded. But with God yet to prove he'd heard her previous prayers, she had only herself to believe in.

Cheryl could prepare a delivery room, and she'd assisted in numerous home births when circumstances had called for one, but two deliveries at once on her own put her in uncharted territory. At the faintest shriek of her own child in the playpen down the hall, Cheryl left both girls clinging to each other, but not before hearing Lissy's whisper.

'Hold on, Irene, Don will be here with Doc soon, and in no time we'll be awesome mums, like Cheryl.'

26

Too early even for the birds, Don stood on the bank cursing the wait. At least having to call the punt back from the opposite side meant someone had made it across to Dandelion House during the night while he'd been knocking on doors and rousting his brother from his bed to help dig the truck out of a bog.

Once on the veranda, Don dispensed with his coat and impatiently peeled muddy, rain-soaked socks from both feet. From the entrance hall he could see Doc and Gypsy in the kitchen, both their faces unreadable under the shifting shadows of a pendant light set swinging by the draft of the open door.

'You got here, Doc. How come I missed you?' When Don hadn't found the doctor at his home, he'd tried the pub just before closing. The few remaining patrons had made little sense, with one suggestion starting Don on a wild goose chase to two outlying properties. 'I thought you'd got caught up in the Saddleton roadblock. I worried all the way back how to break the news to Cheryl. How's Irene doing?'

'You've done well.' Doc joined him in the entry hall, his hand landing heavily on Don's shoulder. 'When I got word Don Dawson was desperately trying to track me down, I put two and two together and came here.'

Don shot Gypsy a desperate look. 'I never said

why I was looking for Doc, I swear. Just that someone needed him. I never talk about what happens at this house, like you asked.'

'I know,' she said, coming towards him, dry towel in hand.

What struck Don at that moment was Gypsy's amble. He'd never known the woman to dawdle. Her stride was always purposeful. Often she talked while she walked; too bad if Don didn't keep up. A quick towel-dry of his hair did little to allay the tremble that seemed to have taken over his body since he'd stopped rushing. He'd expected to walk into a hive of activity, but there was no hive, and not a single buzz of busy in Gypsy. Something was wrong. Don needed no more evidence than the hug she was giving him. Her voluminous arms squeezed so tight and landed two generous pats on his back before releasing him.

'Hugh got us to the punt at the same time as Doc,' she told Don. 'But you raised the alarm at the pub. You did your best. That's the important thing to remember.'

Don shook his head. 'No! What's important, Gypsy, is you and Doc got here in time to help and everyone's okay.'

A noise turned Don around and he noticed Cheryl at the far end of the kitchen table in the semi-dark, her face buried in folded arms.

'Is Cheryl crying? Why?' He looked to Gypsy, then Doc, then towards Lissy's room at the end of the bedroom corridor, light ablaze.

'Hold on, son.' Doc's hand on Don's shoulder wasn't nearly robust enough. The world's strongest man could not have held him back.

Don thought Irene looked different without the pout she wore most days, like all the misery had drained out of her. In a second bed, crammed alongside, was Lissy. His Lissy. His sleeping beauty. How either of them managed to sleep under the fluorescent ceiling light, Don didn't know. Gypsy had fitted the tubes several years ago at Doc's suggestion, but all they did tonight was make the small bedroom appear sterile and cold. Hardly a welcoming first look at the world for a baby.

'Lis?' he whispered from the doorway, not wanting his movement to startle her awake.

'Come with me, Don,' Gypsy said. 'I'll make us a cuppa.'

He didn't want a drink. What he wanted was to hold Lissy, but his putrid hands and mud-caked clothes stopped him. Something else stopped him: Gypsy's hand on his elbow. He jerked his arm free of the persuasive tug. He needed to stay.

'I don't want tea,' he said. 'I want to know what's going on. Did Irene have her baby or not? Where is it?'

'We delivered both babies tonight,' Gypsy said. 'Lissy's, too.'

Don wasn't sure what he'd expected to see post-delivery, but not this. 'That's not possible,' he said. 'Lissy wasn't due. Cheryl said so. Besides, I promised I'd be with her when it happened.'

'The girls were together,' Gypsy said as her

hand massaged between his shoulder blades. 'They helped each other, Don. They were very brave.'

'No!' Don shrugged her away and let out a sob. He'd wanted to be with Lissy, to support her, to tell her when to push and to pant and to breathe normally. More than that, he'd wanted to understand the crippling pain as a woman squeezes new life out of her body. He also wanted to know the pain when she squeezed the bejesus out of her husband's hand. He'd craved such a memory so they could laugh over it for years to come and embarrass their son with stories when he turned twenty-one. 'Where's the baby?' he asked. 'Is he okay? Can I see him?'

'Lissy's baby is fine, Don, and while Irene's fine, not all the news is good.'

'So, he's sleeping then? Good.' He tried to rally a smile, to be a man, to be strong, to be fatherly. 'It is a boy, isn't it? I told Lissy it would be. So did Mum.' Don was talking to no one in particular. He was convincing himself all was as it should be.

Poor Irene, he thought, noticing how very pale both girls seemed. Had she been told? Had Lissy? *She'll be so upset.* When he looked down at his wife-to-be, the uncontainable quiver in his chin rattled another sob loose, and tears like rain lashed his cheeks.

'I've got you, Lis,' Don whispered. 'I'll be right here when you wake up. I'm ready, in the way Cheryl's book says I should be.'

Chapter 12 had stated a new mother needs rest, and many modern husbands were choosing to step up and share the responsibility. Don was excited to do his bit, buoyed by the thought of holding the long-awaited bundle of joy. But first he needed to fetch the dry work clothes he kept in the shed. He was so cold, his shiver almost a convulsion. Behind him, Doc and Gypsy murmured, while Don was torn between waking Lissy and letting her sleep. He moved closer, tried to slide a strand of hair from her eyes, but his fingers shook too much. Instead, he traced the line of her neck and shoulder, down over the soft crook of her arm and all the way to the hand resting on top of her belly. It was the same hand he'd held while fumbling with his grandmother's gold signet ring a few days earlier, when Lissy had wept and laughed and told Don he had clumsy hands and a clumsy heart so big she looked forward to tripping over it every day.

★ ★ ★

Don must have fallen asleep in the chair by the bed because the next thing he knew was Lissy's voice urging him to listen.

'Remember those silver linings,' she whispered. 'You need to open your eyes to see them, Don, and open your heart to love again.'

★ ★ ★

After clearing the combination of sleep and dried tears gluing both eyes closed, Don squinted at the brazen sunlight. How was it possible for a new day to begin and look no different to any other?

'Dear, dear Irene,' said the voice outside Lissy's window. It was Gypsy. Don's ears strained to listen. 'I know you're suffering, Irene, and hurting in so many ways. My job now is to help prepare you so you can restart your life. Your body will experience changes over the coming days and weeks, but I'll take every step with you. We'll get you right again, don't worry.'

Don craned his neck until he could identify Irene. Ordinarily seeped in sadness, the morning sun was creating a golden aura to make her appear angelic. She was sitting with her head lowered and making a kind of high-pitched whimpering noise that reminded Don of the Dawson's old farm dog after his dad took her surviving pups away prematurely. Don had cried that day, and he was crying now: for Irene, for Lissy, and for his broken heart.

'We covered breast-feeding not long after you and Lissy arrived, remember?' Gypsy was saying. 'In particular, the use of milk-suppressing drugs, needed in certain situations. We can use them to ease the discomfort in your breasts — which, I'm sorry to say, Irene, gets worse before it goes away. As Doc mentioned, though, the alternative is wet-nursing Lissy's baby. The choice is yours, and I do understand this is a lot to take in, but you have the essential colostrum a newborn needs, and babies are most alert in the first few hours. This is the ideal time, Irene. Lissy and her baby need you to do this.'

A growl grew in Don's gut and he repeatedly barked the word 'No!' while charging down the hallway, flinging the screen door wide. 'You can't

297

do this. You can't. I won't let you.' He stood rigid on the veranda of Dandelion House — a place that had brought so much promise to his mundane life. 'Are you hearing me?' He stared Gypsy down. 'I said no.'

'Don, please — '

'No, it's not right,' he shouted. 'You can't be sitting here giving the baby to Irene. Lissy is . . . she's . . . she's right inside that room.'

Irene's shoulders began to shudder with the sobs she was obviously trying to hold back. After a quiet few words with her, Gypsy stood slowly. At first she looked cross, but her face softened and she offered Don a sad smile.

'I know Lissy's there,' she told him, 'but she's also gone, and this isn't helpful, Don. And this isn't about you. I'm sorry, but you don't get a say.'

What's new? he wanted to shout. Instead, he turned on his heels, knowing Don Dawson was, again, a man without a voice. If he had no claim and no say, he would leave rather than be a witness to the unthinkable. He'd already said sorry and goodbye to Lissy a million times while holding her hand. He wanted no more of this place. In fact, if having the things he loved constantly ripped away was to be Don's destiny, he wanted no more of this life.

27

A Week Later

For seven days, Don endured all seven stages of grief alone in his cottage, in the room he'd painted mint green, and with his rifle close at hand for when he found the courage. On the eighth morning, debating with the devil in the darkened room, a splinter of sunshine broke through the blinds and a whisper sounded.

Find the silver lining, Don.

Weary from lack of food, Don hauled himself up, let the roller blind spring open, and rubbed the disbelief from his eyes. While he'd chosen to battle the blackness alone in a room, outside, days of rain and sunshine had daubed new life over a fire-ravaged Dawson's Run. The specks of green sprouting from once-barren fields, and flourishing over limbs of blackened trees he'd given up for dead, told him the impossible. Life would go on with or without him.

That was when Don decided he, too, would survive, because he was strong and he was needed. His Lissy might be gone, but he had a purpose waiting for him at Dandelion House. Little Lissy was his silver lining.

★ ★ ★

That afternoon, Don was back on the punt, staring across the river at the house atop the hill he'd sprinted up on numerous occasions. But with no Lissy waiting for him, and no blaring pop music to meter out his pace, he trod the well-worn track to the dirgeful drumming of a sad heart.

As he passed the circular garden bed and saw Irene, the beat doubled. When he spotted the baby in her arms, his heart rate trebled. At first, the sight of Irene frantically tucking her boob back inside a pink-striped shirt was a shock, until he recalled Gypsy's wet-nursing discussion. At the time, Don's heart had said it wasn't right, and he'd stormed off like a petulant child. He hadn't intended staying away for so long, but he was back now and ready to have his say. Don Dawson had found his voice and he would be heard.

'Hello, Irene.'

When she looked directly at him, he saw no trace of the teary woman who'd sat on the veranda in a trance-like state listening to Gypsy talk about breastmilk; nor did he see the sullen girl who'd hidden in the shadows for five months. She even smiled at Don, her small nod a silent invitation to sit. The afternoon sun, now low in the sky, might be contributing to Irene's glow, but the aura of contentment clinging to her changing shape was as obvious as the wet circle on her striped shirt. The transformation was remarkable and the confidence kick Don needed, because he was here for a reason. The man who liked to fix things had the perfect repair for both his and Irene's broken hearts.

'Isn't it the obvious thing to do?' Don asked after outlining his proposition.

Irene didn't answer. She'd listened without comment, seemingly content gazing at the bundle in her arms. Only when Don reached out to stroke the baby's cheek did she flinch, and with the sharp turn of one shoulder put her back to him, her grip noticeably tighter.

'Sorry,' he said. 'I'll ask permission next time. I do understand.'

And he did. Her protective response was no different to the old farm dog having had its pups taken prematurely. A week later, Don had found old Bess suckling a litter of kittens in the hay shed. 'Feral, most likely,' his father had said while filling a bucket with water and snatching all six kittens up. It wasn't without a fight, and the infection from the bitch's bite had kept Bruce's hand out of action for weeks.

'I came to see you, Irene,' Don said. 'But it can wait a few days.'

As hard as waiting would be, he might come back more prepared to overcome her objections — of which there would be many he hadn't yet considered. But what Irene did next both surprised and terrified Don in equal measure. She faced him and offered the baby, her lips curling at the corners. Irene was smiling — at him.

'You want a hold of her, don't you?' she asked, then sniggered as Don immediately thrust both hands forward, palms up, as if receiving emergency sandbags to send down the line. 'Not like that, silly. Create a cradle with your arms, like mine. And relax, she won't break.'

Oh, but she might, Don wanted to say. Or he might. His heart was already trying to break through his chest as he realised the preposterousness of hands the size of dinner plates trying to do anything with something so small. As Irene handed the swaddled baby to Don, then began peeling away the thin cotton cover to expose the teeny body bit by bit, memories of Henrietta and her chicks pecked at Don. He saw himself as an excited young boy, sitting cross-legged in the chook shed and peeling the rubbery white membrane back, only to find the baby chicken unmoving and deformed.

'Open your eyes, Don,' Irene said.

He couldn't. When wrapped tight and snug, holding the baby had felt like cradling a bundle of warm laundry. That much he could manage. It was a different matter without the swaddling.

'She's perfect and she's watching you,' Irene was saying. 'Look at her.'

When he eventually opened his eyes and saw the impossibly tiny and terrifyingly frangible infant, Don's fear grew. She was perfect, with ten tiny fingers and ten cute little toes, making his next thought about how to protect her. If he held on too tight he might crush her. But if didn't hold tight enough she might wriggle free and fall out of his arms. But what scared Don more than anything at that moment was a future with her. Or worse, without her.

'Now you need to breathe, Don,' Irene said.

The woman who used to skulk away and lurk in the shadows seemed poised and confident, with her smile suggesting she was enjoying seeing him squirm.

'But I don't want to drop her, or crush her, or hurt her — ever.'

'You're doing fine, and if you think you can manage on your own, I'll make us tea.'

Don nodded. He wasn't ready to give her back. With the baby cradled in his arms he was no different to old Bess. So desperate to nurture and protect he would bite any hand that tried to take her away.

* * *

'Sorry for not coming before now,' he said as Irene placed a tray with two cups and a teapot on the table where once there'd been a record player and a crate of LPs. 'It was selfish of me.'

'We figured you'd surface when you were ready, but everyone was worried,' she told him while pouring both cups. 'Especially when Doc was having trouble finding you.'

Don recalled hearing pounding on both locked doors, but had assumed it to be his brother trying to roust him for work. In the blur of his grief, Don had no interest in seeing Michael, or anyone else, and selfishly he'd given no thought to Irene.

'How's things with your Mum?' he asked gently. 'You've spoken? She knows your baby died?'

Irene shook her head. 'She's not interested in

the truth, Don. But I'm okay,' she said, trying hard to be brave. 'I asked Gypsy and Reverend Lindeman to look after things for me.' From between the pages of the closed book on the table, Irene tugged two sheets of foolscap paper. One page was blank. The other, with its scribbled lines and symbols, was a kind of mud map. 'After explaining where they put her, I went to my room and I drew this, in case. But I don't think I'll ever go there.'

'Maybe in time,' Don said. 'We can go together and set a headstone in place, if you like.'

'No point.' Irene shrugged. 'According to Mum, my baby never existed, and the only person who cares — me — will soon be a long way from here. Yes.' She answered Don's unspoken question. 'I'm allowed home if I apologise to Uncle Pete and pretend my pregnancy never happened.'

'But it did, Irene.' Don immediately regretted the harshness in his voice. He looked down at the baby stirring in his arms and recalled the moment he and Lissy had felt those first kicks. Irene had experienced a life growing inside her, too. How it was possible to pretend otherwise, Don couldn't fathom, but nor would he sit in judgement. That's not why he'd come. 'Irene, your mother need never know there's a small plaque in a country cemetery. All I need is a name and I can — '

'Don't you start, Don. I tried, okay, but I can't.' Irene didn't speak angrily and she wasn't looking at him. Her attention was on her fingers, nails bitten down and picked raw at the cuticles.

'Tried what, Irene?'

'To name my shame. That's all I'd be doing. A name means it existed,' she said. 'And what if I was to one day meet someone with the same name, or hear it on the TV, or read it in a book? I'd be reminded. Doc keeps asking for a name for his register, and Cheryl suggested we name her after a tree. I thought about that.' She was staring at Don, sad eyes welling up. 'Maybe a tree that will grow big and strong because my baby will never get the chance. A sprawling, shady tree with limbs like giant arms.' She smiled at that. 'Something admired for its beauty and with big leaves — maybe heart-shaped — and little flowers, pure white that will fall like snow in summer. That's what I'd want. Only . . . ' She flicked a fresh tear from her cheek and sniffed. 'Before I go home, Don, would you take my map, find a beautiful tree like I described and plant it for me?'

He nodded, and the pair sat without words until Don said, 'I started a headstone for Lissy this morning. I would've kept working but I wanted to see you and, if you agreed, talk to Gypsy.'

Irene blew on her tea before setting the cup on the saucer, her eyes downcast. 'She's been wanting to see you, Don. To tell you.'

'Tell me what?'

'Lissy's gone.'

'Gone where?' Don tensed, enough for the baby to whimper in his arms and to prompt Irene to shift in readiness.

'Her parents made their own funeral arrangements,' she informed him. 'They've taken Lissy home to be buried.'

'They *took* her?' Don closed his eyes,

convinced any second the baby would crumble to nothing in his arms — gone, like Lissy.

'They want no part of this little one,' Irene said.

'But what about the sister? She was going to — '

'Nope, they changed their mind. Lissy's father told Doc straight-up to find a family for the baby. I guess that means we have something in common, sweet-pea.' Irene teased the baby's bottom lip with the tip of her finger. 'Our families don't want us.'

Don's mind reeled. This was his chance.

'I care, Irene, and I'm offering you a choice. You don't have to go home.' When she didn't respond, he added, 'I care what happens to you and the baby. I can look out for you both. You can stay in Calingarry Crossing with me. The three of us can be a family.' Both Don and Irene looked down at the baby's face scrunching up and turning crimson. 'What do you reckon, Little Lissy?' he said. With her mouth open but emitting no sound, she looked like a newborn kitten with its silent mewling at a pitch only a mother can hear.

Could Lissy hear Don? Would she agree? He looked beyond the veranda to the patch of ground where Lissy used to dance, then to the cloudless blue sky above. *I might have lost you forever, Lis, but you've left behind a tiny version of yourself in need of a family. I want to be that family.*

'No!' Irene's shriek startled Don. 'Bloody hell!' She plucked a handkerchief from the cuff

306

of her shirtsleeve and dabbed at the growing wet spot on her boob. 'You interrupted feeding time,' she said, suddenly angry and reaching for the baby. 'I need to finish. You can sit on the steps over there and wait.'

★ ★ ★

Whispered swearing from Irene prompted Don to subtly check her state of dress before turning around fully to observe. Mumbling and mopping puke from her shoulder one minute, the next she was pressing the baby's palm to her lips and pretending to blow raspberries.

'You sure are a big stinker for a tiny thing. A stinky, stinky little bug are you.'

Irene *would* be the perfect mother for Lissy's baby, Don decided there and then. All he had to do was make her believe he would be a good father.

★ ★ ★

'So?' Don dared after a fresh pot of tea and too long a silence. 'You have to agree my proposal makes sense.'

'To you, maybe,' Irene quipped. 'It's hardly the offer a girl dreams of getting from a guy.'

Don shrugged. 'Yeah, sorry. With time on our side I'm sure I could do better, but we need to act now, or risk losing the baby to strangers. And look at you both,' he added, nodding at the baby in Irene's arms. 'She's clearly bonded. You're so natural with her. You were meant to be a mother,

Irene. Is going home and pretending otherwise the right thing — for you?' Don waited. Overwhelming the woman would not work in his favour. 'Why not give it a go? Let's show Doc and Gypsy we are united and prepared to do whatever it takes. They won't say no. Why would they?'

Irene took a deep breath and stood. Leaning over the big blue pram to her left, she settled the baby and flicked a colourful mobile into action. 'I get what you're trying to do,' she said, sitting again but with one hand jiggling the pram's handle. 'I feel so torn. True, I'm not ready to go home, but I won't stay at Dandelion House with all the bad memories.'

'Then stay at Dawson's Run,' Don said, pulling on the reins of his excitement. 'No strings. You'll be free to come and go as you please. Doc can do house visits, and you'll have privacy and all the time you need to work whatever out. You know Lissy would want this,' he added, desperately. 'Remember your pact?'

Irene's hand stalled, the pram stilled, and she looked at Don square on. 'Yes, I made a promise,' she said. 'To Lissy, not you. If I accept your proposal, do you promise to never forget that fact and never ask more of me than our partnership requires?'

Partnership? Had Don used that term? No wonder Irene wasn't jumping for joy at the prospect.

'Partners,' he said, resolutely. 'You and me. And I promise. I do.' Although not the way he'd pictured delivering those two words, they seemed an appropriate conclusion to their *negotiations*.

'I promise to honour and respect you from this day forward.'

After more agonising silence, Irene stood and thrust out a hand for Don to shake. 'Deal,' she said. 'Doc's still inside with Gypsy and Reverend Lindeman. We'd best talk to them before they leave.'

★ ★ ★

'G'day, Don,' Gypsy said. 'I wondered when we'd be seeing you. Join us. Sit down.'

After positioning the pram to one side, he sat nervously beside Irene, feeling small on the opposite side of the enormous kitchen table. The Rev smiled and Doc shoved strewn paperwork into a pile, closed the cover of a leather-bound diary, and folded both hands on top.

'I gather this is about Lissy's baby?' Gypsy continued.

'Yes,' Don replied quickly. 'We don't believe she would want the baby to go to strangers. If not to her real family, then Irene and I thought we could keep her.' He immediately regretted his word choice. The baby sounded like a lost puppy. 'You know what I mean.'

'I see.' Gypsy leaned in and folded her arms on the table. 'Before we talk further, you should know Reverend Lindeman has a church-going couple happy to adopt. They're Catholic,' she added. 'And not too far away — in Saddleton. They'll raise her as their own.'

'And she won't have to carry the stigma children of single mothers suffer,' Doc added. 'The baby will have a true family. The couple can take her anytime.'

'No way,' Irene growled, placing a protective hand on the sleeping baby in the pram. 'No one's *taking* her anywhere. Family guarantees nothing. I've been raised by good church-going parents, and my mother told me to not come home until I was ready to repent for my slutty behaviour and for killing my father with my lies. But that would not be the truth, and isn't lying a sin?' Before Reverend Lindeman could utter a word, she added, 'Raising a child on a lie is also wrong, and Don and I don't intend to forget Lissy or take her place.'

Doc started to speak when Irene said over the top of him, 'Lissy and I promised we'd be there for each other. If she was here holding my baby she'd do the same, but God took mine away and I need to believe this little one is the reason. I want to do this. The baby will always be Lissy's, but I can love her as good as anyone. I think I love her already.'

At that, the baby squawked and Irene reached over to pick her up.

'What about you, Don?' Gypsy asked. 'Do your parents know?'

'My mother was excited about welcoming another baby to Dawson's Run and, as you know, our family can do with some happiness.' Don turned to Doc Wynter. 'Cheryl said you can make it happen. You've connected parents with babies before. That's all we're asking of you now.'

A look passed between the trio opposite and Doc seemed visibly uncomfortable, his thumb nervously leafing the pages of his leather-bound diary.

'Right, well, if you're talking adoption,' he said, 'I'm afraid you and Irene fail to meet the most basic requirements. But, as Cheryl alluded to, I am the delivering doctor and responsible for the lodgement of paperwork. In the past I have matched couples with babies in need of a loving family. Doing so requires certain precautions to protect those in government departments who help me. As such, I'm careful to never leave a paper trail that might raise questions in the future. Or worse, destroy those families later in life. Had you not waited a week before speaking up, Don, what you're asking might be doable and simple. The thing is, I've already advised Lissy's family of the baby's condition — both verbally and in writing with the letter of condolence I sent. They know the baby is healthy and will be adopted, as requested. But . . . ' Doc and Gypsy traded glances and a nod each. 'Irene's age and status means she cannot be a legal guardian. The *only* way I can meet your request would be to record her baby as living, while Lissy's family will go on believing the adoption took place as requested.'

Irene spoke next, surprisingly composed. 'And if they change their minds and want to connect one day?'

'From my one discussion, I sincerely doubt that will ever happen,' Doc said. 'Besides, closed adoption laws in this state protect the children involved. They get a new birth certificate that identifies the adoptive parents only. All other information is sealed. Lissy's family will assume an adoption took place and they'll have no access to details. There won't be an adoption, of course, which means, any way you look at it, what you're asking us to do will require an enormous lie.'

'My mother has been training me well in the lie department,' Irene said, coldly.

'Dear Irene.' Gypsy looked concerned. 'Do you understand what Doc said just now? If he registers you as this baby's mother, it will mean, on paper, your baby never existed.'

Nobody spoke. Nobody breathed, until Irene's head gave the tiniest nod. 'Yes, I understand.'

'And you, Don?' Doc's expression questioned. 'While I admire your devotion to Lissy and to telling her child the truth, I must impress on you there would be grave consequences for us all. Wanting to share your memories is admirable, but it will be many years until the child is old enough to understand the importance of keeping a family secret. You're a good and honest man, Don. How will a lie of this magnitude sit with you?'

'In every other sense it's the right thing to do,' Don replied without hesitation. 'I won't be a legal parent, but Irene will, and I can protect her and the baby. Then, when the time is right, I'll find a way to let her know about the amazing and spirited and clever Lissy; how much I loved her, and that Lissy . . . Sorry.' He coughed, needing water to clear the lump in his throat.

At the sink, Don filled a glass, his focus on the changing light playing with the willow trees at the bottom of the property. With the day almost over, he was again in a battle against time, hoping to change a mind, hoping — for once — someone would hear him and see him as the best man for the job. Don already knew he was worthy because . . .

'. . . Lissy loved me,' he said to the quiet gathering at the table behind him. When a gust of wind ruffled the weeping limbs, Don swore he saw Lissy dancing. Knowing it wasn't possible didn't stop him watching, wishing, hoping. 'I didn't believe I'd ever find someone to love me,' he said. 'I never imagined love at first sight even existed. But it is real. Lissy and I are proof. She's gone now, and I'm left behind to let go. Please, don't make me say goodbye to her baby as well. There's no reason we have to. The parents have turned their backs on their own flesh and blood. What does that tell you?' Don took a deep breath before he turned around to focus on his future at the table. He walked back to stand in silent solidarity with a seated Irene. There wasn't a dry eye in the room, except for the baby with her rosebud mouth tight around Irene's little finger. 'Doc, Gypsy, Reverend Lindeman,' Don said. 'Don't send her to strangers. You all know me. I'm a good person. Let me keep this part of Lissy.' He dropped onto one knee to smile up at Irene. 'Let me look after you both.'

* * *

And so, Always Obliging Irene seemed to slot herself into a life meant for another woman. She

313

moved into the small cottage with Don on his family property and, over time, the pair grew accustomed to the close confines, to each other, and to their new roles.

Having impressed Don by batting away every objection Doc and Gypsy had thrown at them that day, Irene reverted to being the quiet one. But Don understood. Her grief was twice as hard.

28

Dawson's Run, Autumn 1975

With the baby bottles and teats boiling, as per the method in *Chapter 16, Sanitising and Safety*, Don set a timer and stared out his kitchen window. Despite the massive storm three months ago, the Dawson's dusty paddocks were back to crying out for more moisture to wet thirsty roots. If only it was possible to capture tears. Don had cried enough to end the nation's drought.

Even though a baby in the house softened his grief by overlaying bad memories with happier ones, Don knew he'd mourn every loss until his dying breath. With the farm gone to his brother, and with the love of his life replaced by a duty-bound stranger, no one would blame Don for taking that long walk into the paddock, like others before him. Every day he looked for a reason to not die. He found it in the rise and fall of a small, pink chest, and in eyes so bright and beautiful they mended his heart any time a memory gouged it open. Life might not be as he'd planned, but Don was a father, and he thanked Lissy every second of every day for her words in the early hours of that morning.

While neither he nor Irene dwelled on the tragic events — at least, not aloud — Don found the nerve to ask Doc what had gone wrong. Reluctant to discuss patient details, the man explained her death in one heartbreaking sentence.

'Although Lissy presented with no signs what-soever, we faced a common enough complication, with blood loss we weren't prepared for.' Doc sighed. 'Another maternity home, closer to a big hospital, might have made a difference. Then again, Don, sometimes, like love, the strongest turns out to be the most fragile.'

Don walked away, his head shaking at the awful irony. Had Lissy's parents made a different choice and sent her somewhere else, she and Don would not have met. Instead, Dandelion House had brought them together and now it, too, was changing.

★ ★ ★

Gypsy broke the news gently the next time Don saw her. Bizarrely, it was in the milk bar, where she was seated with her daughter in the booth behind two of the town's busiest tongues. She welcomed Don, asked him to sit, and began to explain she could no longer raise Willow in isolation.

'Thank you for all you've done around the place, but it's time,' Gypsy said. 'Being a good role model to a child should be every parent's primary concern. My second priority is keeping up the fight for women's rights. I can't do either job with Dandelion House operating as it is. Willow needs a home of her own, not a boarding house. It's important she's able to foster friendships as she grows older. She needs to be like other children, free to have friends over for slumber parties. More than anything, I want my daughter to have connections to the town, to be accepted.' Then Gypsy sat straight, winked, and raised her voice a notch. 'Closing the doors to Dandelion House will give people less to talk about.' She smiled while pulling the stroller close and passing the crust from her plate, folding Willow's fingers into a fist. 'My hope is we've turned a corner and the appalling treatment of unmarried mothers, and maternity homes in general, will be a thing of the past. I'm hopeful people will be more tolerant and accepting of those who walk different paths, and one day soon women *will* get the understanding, the protection and the support they need. In the meantime, we must all keep making a noise and demanding the government listen. Society would benefit from having more men like Don Dawson,' she said, smiling. 'I'm immensely proud of you. It's time you focused on family, too. You and Irene have a lot more to learn.'

★   ★   ★

He'd known when making his proposition three months ago there would be challenges ahead, and while Don had found his fatherly feet, he remained no closer to figuring out the woman he'd asked into his life. He had no way of knowing what Irene was thinking when she stared dreamily out the window by day, or at night when he caught her lost in thought and gazing at the living room ceiling, the glint of a tear in her eyes. Some cues Don picked up on, but he struggled to know how to provide comfort, or even what affection was appropriate. He didn't want to push or do the wrong thing. He never wanted Irene to fear him or lose trust in him. Whatever their relationship was, it was growing stronger, and with every good day the thread binding them — the precious girl Don called Little Lissy — pulled them closer.

He and Irene relaxed into each other's routines, apologising less for those unintentional transgressions, like the touch of a hand or the brush of an arm when transferring the baby. Neither looked to the other for affection, nor sought intimacy at night. Don wondered if things would one day change. Did he want them to? Was it even right and reasonable to expect more of Irene if his whole heart would never be for her alone? He'd never lie or lead a woman on. Don Dawson was no B & S dance one-nighter, nor itinerant grape picker.

Together, Irene and Don were alone. She was company after a hard day's work, even though his conversation had to compete with the constant click-clack of knitting needles. After the first few months of knitting furiously, a quilting project introduced a different style of needle, and the old Singer sewing machine added a new thrum to his nights. Copious squares of cotton, sorted by colour, occupied one end of the laminate table they sat around each mealtime, where Don's handmade highchair sat proud at the head. Transporting Barbara's old treadle machine from the main homestead to the cottage had been the biggest icebreaker, until Irene said he might as well set it up in the space by the refrigerator because she spent most of her day in the kitchen, or in the adjacent laundry annex.

Don fulfilled every request without complaint, and when fabric swatches finally swallowed what was left of the kitchen table, he built a bigger one from a burnt tree trunk, constructing it on the veranda. The project had taken several weeks from the first saw cut — when he uncovered the majestic ironbark's heart — to the sanding and final coat of lacquer. He'd left the slab's perimeter naturally blackened, which Irene seemed particularly pleased about.

'A bit rough around the edges,' she'd said, her smile soft, genuine. 'A bit like me.'

For Don, the table was both a tribute to the fallen and a reminder of Doc's claim that the strongest can come crashing down without warning. The tree might have remained undiscovered, rotting in a distant paddock. Instead, it had a second chance at life on the newly extended cottage veranda, which was fast becoming Don's favourite place to sit. At dusk, when the weather was to Irene's liking, she joined him, her latest cross-stitch or embroidery in hand. There was, in fact, a difference between cross-stitch and embroidery, Don learned, and on the occasion he'd mentioned a recurring motif in her design, Irene's smile had said she appreciated his noticing.

'Our two favourite things — Lissy's and mine,' she said. 'Ladybugs and dandelions.'

Should he have known that fact about Irene? Maybe he needed to learn more.

Each morning, before leaving the house at sunrise, Don stopped to observe Little Lissy asleep in the mint-green room. On the occasions when she was wide-eyed and gurgling, he'd stop to breathe her in, knowing he wouldn't return until she was tucked into bed that evening. Between snippets of sleep, Don became an expert at bottle feeds, nappy changes, and pacing the floor while hushing cries. He didn't mind. Those moments sustained him as he laboured all day. Some nights he deliberately worked late, usually blaming his brother. The truth was, part of Don preferred Michael's constant complaints about Wendy over a beer in the sheds, to the tight confines of the cottage where a taciturn Irene kept his meal warm on the stove.

One day, without warning, she surprised Don. Maybe she'd sensed his restlessness, or motherhood was softening her, a life with Don no longer deemed dull. She bundled the baby, a thermos and biscuits into the Holden car Don had restored so she could get around town and driven to the cemetery to find Don at work in the gardens. Though flat out refusing to attend services, she enjoyed the harmonious strains of parishioners singing. The weekly picnic became such a happy habit that Don let himself believe their rendezvous was a date. On one of those days, while packing up the picnic, he'd noticed Irene mouthing the words of a hymn while gazing absentmindedly into the far reaches of the cemetery. That was the moment Don had realised the rendezvous was not about him at all, but about the child that never existed.

29

Don could not fault Irene's mothering. She hadn't lied when telling Gypsy she had lots of love to give. What a shame none of it came his way. Instead, the partnership remained platonic and Don gave all his love to Little Lissy. He told himself he didn't need a woman's affection, but that had been the first of many lies he told himself. The first chapter of every parenting book Don ever opened — he'd consumed dozens since meeting Lissy — had begun with the same words: *Parenting is about sacrifice.* Abstinence wasn't easy, but his need was not so strong it pushed him towards services available in the city. Not yet anyway, and never while his Lissy's touch lingered in his memory.

Sacrifices were not a new concept to Don, but rather part and parcel of life on the land. Livestock and crops came before recreation and weekend activities, which meant physically and mentally exhausting farm work too often came before wives and children, although never by choice. The strained relationship Michael and Wendy shared was all the motivation Don needed to try and fit his family into every day. Irene was not yet twenty-one and, despite still quietly grieving her own baby, she carried out her role of nurturer with such devotion. The woman deserved more: more respect, more consideration, more of him at home. So did the adventurous toddler who was bringing new experiences to Don to make every day different.

Slowly, he and Irene were coming together as parents, planning and working as a team. Don desperately wanted to be a good partner and provider, but life on the land continually tested them both. The region had endured more drought than not over the last decade, with tensions as tight as purse strings. A lack of water meant half of Don's feed crop was dead or dying and, with the government's revised irrigation permits insufficient, all that was keeping the rest alive were more sacrifices on his part. They needed a few decent downpours for sure, but good rainfall remained as erratic as Irene's mood. Keen to include her in farm business, one night over dinner he'd tried to explain the difficulties of keeping a crop alive until it took hold.

'With enough attention and TLC, roots do form — eventually,' Don had said, not knowing if he was referring to his crop or to Irene. *Perhaps both?*

Irene avoided outside work. She seemed content inside the house, surrounded by her swatches and monthly subscription magazines. She tended the vegetable garden and fruit trees she'd insisted Don plant, and she was learning to turn everyday food into a feast, often cooking enough to share with the extended family. There were also ample meal disasters, which Don endured — lying convincingly. Everything in Don's life as a parent and partner was demanding a new level of patience and understanding. At least Irene's special knack was with the old Singer, and hairdressing shears kept the Dawsons from presenting in public as hard-up as the drought was keeping them. Don's only wish now was for the weather to change, along with his luck in the bedroom department.

★   ★   ★

Not only did he and Irene now regularly kiss goodbye each morning, her goodnight peck on his cheek, while seated side-by-side on the lounge, had also shifted to mouth-on-mouth. Further intimacy usually stopped there, with Irene announcing a favourite TV show was about to start. There also seemed to be an endless basket of washing to fold or to iron before bed.

When both the TV and the iron broke and they couldn't afford replacements, Don had said a prayer of thanks. Irene, however, took to being busy at bedtime in other ways: a tricky crochet pattern, a stitch count to be kept with her needles, a section of her cross-stitch requiring concentration — and always when Don was desperate to hit the hay. The most excited he saw Irene was when he brought home her monthly McCall's Craft Magazine and the associated materials they couldn't afford. There were worse addictions, Don would tell himself. Unlike Wendy, whose vice filled her wineglass, Irene's filled the house with handiworks and first-place ribbons from the Calingarry Crossing Agricultural Show.

★   ★   ★

Out of the blue, following third birthday cele-brations, Irene asked Don to stop calling the child Little Lissy.

'No abbreviations of any kind.' Full stop. No explanation.

Don didn't argue. They'd fought enough over a name for the birth certificate Doc arranged, with Irene settling on the Anglo version of Elisa-betta. Even though the child couldn't get her tongue around the name Elizabeth, Don agreed the choice was respectful. For Irene, it was a common name, and common was necessary to avoid attention, curiosity or comparisons. Don never liked the formality of 'Elizabeth', though. 'You're my princess, not a queen,' he'd tell his Little Lissy on the quiet.

★ ★ ★

By four, his princess was demanding a nightlight to keep the bogeyman away. After tucking Elizabeth in, Don would join Irene in the bed they'd shared intimately for a year. The shift had coincided with a letter from Lissy's mother to Doc Wynter, explaining changes to her circum-stances and listing questions: Had the formal adoption been swift, or was the child with foster parents? Did she know about her real family? Was a visit possible? Could they write to her?

The enquiries were 'typical and nothing to worry about', Doc had assured an anxious Irene.

Soon after, Irene's affections and attention to Don's needs changed for the better, tempting him to propose marriage. Reverend Lindeman was a very modern man of the cloth and prepared to conduct a wedding for so-called evil sinners. If Irene preferred a low-key ceremony, he would fill out the necessary paperwork. While marriage alone wouldn't change Don's legal status with Elizabeth, being legally bound to Irene as her husband would bring a level of certainty. Though Irene rejected his proposal, insisting any legal change of status might ring alarm bells with the authorities, the letter from Lissy's mum had spooked her into putting more effort into being a wife. Even though he wished her motivations were different, Don didn't object for fear rejection might add to her insecurity and distrust.

Ironically, that letter had brought her to his bed and made them a real family, finally.

One night, as Irene fussed with the contents of her bedside drawer, Don examined the current cross-stitch balancing on her knees. Her own design — intricate and featuring tiny red ladybugs spotted black-included eight lines of verse:

I had a little girl once, a bond that will never sever.
I knew the moment I saw her she'd be a part of me forever.
A teeny tiny wonder, as cute as a bug was she,
Buzzing with all her buggy friends under the lovely linden tree.

He didn't ask her to explain the words. He didn't have to. Some topics would forever be off limits.

Don's parents were another taboo subject. As impressive as Irene was as a mother, Barb and Bruce were elderly and of the old school. They disapproved of Don needlessly taking on the responsibility of another man's child and cohabiting. They'd been happy to welcome Lissy as a wife, but not a woman who didn't love their son, or a child without the Dawson name.

'None of this is natural,' his mother had tisked.

'I'd expect this sort of shenanigans from your no-hoper brother,' Bruce had said. 'Not you, Don.'

Both Dawson boys were turning out to be disappointments, with unhappiness seeping deep into the foundations of the family Don was working hard to bring together after fire almost destroyed them. Cracks formed, deep and permanent, and in November 1979, on Elizabeth's fifth birthday, Don's world crumbled into a million pieces.

30

Dawson's Run, 1979

'Why are you sleeping here, Dadda? I want to ride my horse.'

Feeling more like fifty-eight than twenty-eight, Don lifted his groggy head, rubbed bleary eyes, and smoothed the horseshoe moustache he'd grown two years ago.

'Breakfast first, my princess.'

'I'm eating mine now,' a proud Elizabeth announced.

'Yes, you are.' With the tip of his finger he scooped the dollop of butter and Vegemite from the corner of his daughter's mouth, holding it high. 'Hmm, how about you go into the kitchen and get your old dadda some bread to put his Vegemite on.'

Don hoped Irene's words yesterday had been a bad dream, but the imprint of the sofa's crocheted cover on his left cheek suggested her bombshell had been real and shattering.

'I'm leaving Calingarry Crossing,' she'd announced to his family as Don had flipped hamburger patties on the barbeque.

At least she'd waited until Elizabeth had unwrapped her birthday presents, including the surprise rocking horse. The fifth birthday addition to the backyard mini farm had been designed for an energetic little girl who craved the outdoors and loved to mimic her dadda.

Even before Elizabeth had started walking, she'd explored the far reaches of the veranda, one day learning she fitted under the railing. With the gap quickly wired and the veranda kiddy-proofed, she started following her dadda around the house, four chubby limbs clambering over the boards to keep up. When Don stopped at the back door to drag his boots on, Elizabeth pretended to do the same with her socks. When he grabbed his hat off the hook, she cried for her own. When Don pecked Irene's cheek goodbye, Elizabeth hugged Irene's legs before tottering towards the door expecting to saddle her pretend horse and work all day alongside her dadda.

With Irene struggling to keep tabs on the wandering child, Don eventually fenced the entire yard, and with leftover timber he built the first mini farm component — a simple sandbox. Over the years, Elizabeth's imagination made the simple sandpit so much more. Together, father and daughter worked that pretend paddock and grazed plastic cows. They sowed make-believe seeds in the sandy soil and watered the imaginary crops with magic waterless cans. For her fourth birthday he'd wanted to build a treehouse, but Irene had insisted, 'The child is too small to climb, and treehouses are for boys.'

'Okay,' Don had said and promptly started work on a ground-level structure, calling it a unicorn stable.

By five, Elizabeth knew the difference between an imaginary unicorn and a real horse, and with his nephew pleading with his parents for a pony,

Don talked to Michael about saving up to buy one jointly. Until then, he would give his daughter an Irene-approved pony made from wood, with a golden mane courtesy of scrap fringing found at the bottom of the haberdashery box. The singular moment of joy when Don had unveiled the present yesterday had made those two weeks of working at night worthwhile. His girl had fed and groomed her rocking horse, oblivious to the kerfuffle at the barbeque where Don's patties burned from neglect, eventually catching fire and bringing the party to an end.

He couldn't understand why Irene had chosen her daughter's special day to announce she was leaving. They hadn't yet cut the cake when he'd bid his family goodbye. His parents' piteous smile had been difficult enough, but worse had been watching his brother wrangle an intoxicated wife and a hysterical six-year-old son away before his promised turn on the painted rocking horse.

Irene's announcement at yesterday's party had been bothersome and insensitive, and before Don went anywhere this morning he would tell her so. First, he needed to shock himself awake with a face wash. The shave could wait.

* * *

'I'm sorry,' Irene said the instant Don walked into the kitchen for his Vegemite toast.

He knew the sound of an apology well enough. The words, like Don's life these past five years, lacked authenticity. The fact Irene spoke them

330

while scraping stale fairy bread into a plastic bucket for the chooks was further proof of her disingenuousness. But why he took issue was odd, given his family was founded on an enormous and damaging lie.

'Elizabeth, honey,' Don said. 'Can you take the chooks their breakfast bucket while Mummy and I talk?' Asking the five-year-old to tidy her toys would ignite a tantrum. There was never an argument when the chore involved farm work. 'Come here first.' Don snagged her by the shirt, reeled her back between his knees, and yanked her singlet down and into the elastic waistband on her shorts.

Elizabeth squirmed. 'I can tuck in myself, Dadda.'

'Yes, you're my big girl,' Don said, snatching a quick hug.

Only after the bang of the laundry door, when he saw Elizabeth through the kitchen window, her long, sinewy legs skipping towards the chook yard, did he dare resume the conversation.

'Don't do this now, Irene,' he pleaded. 'Lissy's due to start school.'

Irene turned on her heels and strode out of the kitchen, returning in a huff and driving her disenchantment home with the thud of the laundry basket on the table. 'Her name is Elizabeth.'

Don stared at the mountain of ironing. Should he have done more around the house, bought her gifts, or said yes to the electric sewing machine thingamajig she'd swooned over in the latest magazine?

'The decision to go isn't about me, Don,'

Irene said. 'It's for Elizabeth. Staying here is no longer in the child's best interests. Besides a city school providing more opportunities, you know I'm out of a job. My presence in the barber's shop was supposed to help bring female clientele *in*. Not surprisingly, I had the opposite effect. There's no place for me in this town, and I want to work and support us.'

'But you never had to take a job,' Don said. 'I promised to look after you both and a promise is a promise.'

'Yes, Don, and you made promises to Lissy, but five years ago we were too young and silly to know any better.' Irene plucked a tiny T-shirt top from the basket, smoothing it against her body before folding it. 'Fibbing to an inquisitive child is one thing. Deceiving the town is another. Lying convincingly to people while under the critical eye of your parents who know the truth because, for some idiotic and unfathomable reason, you told them without consulting me, is plain humiliating.' More clean laundry items made their way into piles on the table. 'Your mother already thinks I'm unworthy, Don. She looks down on me and silently scrutinises every word to come out of my mouth, as if testing for honesty. The facade of a happy family isn't enough, and it's not right for Elizabeth. We can't tell her the truth yet, and when we do, you know better than anyone that secrets don't stay a secret forever in small towns. Someone somewhere will figure out what we did, and when they work out the connection, we *will* lose her. Neither of us want that to happen, which is why

I'll go where we aren't known and won't be found. For goodness' sake, Don!' Irene was no longer bothering to fold the laundry items. 'Don't look at me like that. Think about what might happen. Do you want such uncertainty for the child?'

Don crumpled into a kitchen chair, struck dumb by Irene's candidness. So devastated and desperate when Lissy died, he'd convinced himself creating a family unit was best for everyone. But had he been thinking only of himself? While crazy with grief, had he simply expected happiness would miraculously rise from the mess of misery?

Don stared at her. 'Did I coerce you into this life with me, Irene?'

She sighed. 'That's not what I'm saying. I was young and confused and emotional, and with no concept of the future. I'm wiser and getting older by the day. I need to do something with my life.'

Don cursed his selfishness. He hadn't thought beyond what he'd wanted and what he'd considered best for Lissy's baby.

'Irene, please, sit with me.' He reached out, but she wasn't having a bar of him.

'I don't blame you, Don. I made my own decision back then. What you were offering made sense. I thought I'd find purpose and a place to feel safe. I genuinely wanted to look after Lissy's baby. I still do. Never doubt my love for the child. But I can care for her anywhere.'

'Then why not here, where you both belong?'

'I'm not sure where I belong, Don, and I can't live where I'm constantly reminded about what happened; not if I'm to do my best for the child.'

Don smacked the table. 'Her name is Elizabeth, and I'm her father, damn it! I have a voice.'

Irene's busyness slowed, softened. The bluntness in her response did not. 'You're not her father, Don, any more than I'm her mother.'

'Exactly,' he said, not missing a beat. 'Which means we have an equal claim on her. Leave Lissy with me.'

'Claim?' Irene mocked. 'Like you want to stake your claim on that Cedar Cutter's Gorge land? And what do you expect will happen when you're working all day every day? Your parents are too old to be full-time carers of a growing girl, and your sister-in-law likes the bottle too much to be trusted with a child, even her own. Something's not right at your brother's house, and to be honest, Don, you should be worrying more about your own flesh and blood.'

'What are you saying?'

'Check in on your nephew more often,' Irene said. 'Wendy isn't coping and Michael seems oblivious. It's not a good environment for a growing boy. He's here at the cottage so much, Elizabeth asked if I was his mum. As for his tantrum yesterday, it was not about the rocking horse. He didn't want to go home. He wanted to stay here, but I can't, Don. My hands are full enough raising one child and keeping the damn dust out of our dinner and clothes.'

As if to prove her point, Irene shook a small, clean singlet and watched particles travel along the sun's warm rays. Don's anger soared with them, his head and neck prickling with sweat and dread.

'So, this is about my house not being good enough. Maybe if we hadn't filled the linen press with fabrics and yarn, or wasted money on magazine subscriptions . . .'

'Please, Don, how about we both take a deep breath?' Irene mellowed, pausing to glance out the kitchen window. A dreamy Elizabeth was ambling back, an empty bucket swinging in time with whatever ditty she was singing. 'We don't want this to get ugly. You and your brother are very different. You've been wonderful, and Dawson's Run is special to you, but I'll end up like Wendy if I don't leave. Do you want to see me drinking my lonely days away?'

Don's shoulders sagged. 'But I'll never see her if you go.'

'She barely sees you as it is,' Irene said as quick as a flash. 'And neither do I. I'm keeping all three households going because no one else is capable, but your old parents look at me like I'm a gold digger.'

Don tried to laugh. 'What bloody gold? Where?' All he saw through the window's dusty coating was the land he loved dying. 'Don't forget why I'm working such long hours, Irene. I'm busy because I'm saving up for a place of our own. For you. So you can have windows with seals, your fancy tumble dryer, and a modern kitchen with moulded cutlery drawers.'

'No, Don.' Irene made no attempt to stop the tears raining down her cheeks. 'Developing a property is your pipe dream. Mine is developing a girl — one who is very real right now and will not wait for anything. I'm not sure how to make you understand,' she said between sobs. 'I'm not sure I understand myself. It's all too much, but at the same time not enough. Not for me. Not like this. Not anymore. I'm sorry. All this time and I still feel like an interloper.'

Five years of fury beat inside Don, trying to break out, wanting to rage and wreak revenge on anyone and anything. He pressed a hand against his chest to quell the beast.

'Give the folks time, Irene. They need to adjust to the situation.'

'The *situation*!' The word fired like shrapnel, designed to punish Don for another poor choice. 'How I despise the word. Five years is long enough to adjust, Don, and through every one of them you reckoned you'd find the money to hire a farmhand so we might see more of you. I know, I know.' Irene raised her palms at him. 'It's been years of drought and I've got everything I asked for. 'One day soon, Irene, I promise, blah, blah, blah.' But we're not talking about the rain, a craft magazine, or an overlocker, are we, Don? You need more than I can give, and I need more of everything. I'm sorry. I'm sorry for hurting you. I'm sorry you'll miss Elizabeth, but you'll remain special. She'll know how wonderful her Uncle Don was to us both when we needed help.'

'Uncle?' Don spat the word like it was poison. 'I'm Dadda!'

Irene sighed, her tears evaporating with her anger. 'But you're not — not really — and I'd like to avoid raising the girl on more lies than is necessary. I need to prepare her for the truth and, when the time's right, let her choose her own path. Calingarry Crossing isn't the best place. A woman has so few choices here, believe me.' Irene rammed the laundry basket on her hip. 'If you'll excuse me, my decision for the day is whether to fold all this laundry or spend hours ironing clothes no one sees us in because no woman in town thinks enough of *me* to visit.'

Don was tempted to grab Irene's elbow. The conversation was not over. Then he heard Lissy's last words before she slipped away: *I trust you with our girl. Make sure she gets to choose her own path and be supportive of her choices, even though they may not be yours. Promise me.*

'Oh, Lissy, Lissy.' Don raised his face in a mock prayer.

Should he try talking to God for real? There was a first time for everything. He wouldn't ask for much: just one decent bloody rainy season and one beautiful little girl in his life.

★ ★ ★

'Where will you go?' Don asked from the doorway to what was once Irene's room. Open on the unmade single bed was a partly packed suitcase. How long had it been there, rather than on top of the wardrobe? Did he really miss so much?

'I'll be in Saddleton. Mum's allowing us both to stay, but it won't be forever. There's no work there either, no way for me to support us. And no, Don . . . ' Another flash of Irene's palm gagged him. 'You can't be sole supporter. I'll find another job. I *want* a job. My dad once told me a girl can't go wrong with a trade. He reckoned people will always need haircuts. That's my plan, because I want to make a future for the two of us and see Elizabeth grow into an independent woman. She's starting school next year, and I'd like to be settled before then, and earning money so she has stationery and a uniform like the other kids. I don't want her singled out.'

Don slumped against the wall, the repetitive smoothing of his moustache helping reclaim some composure so he could think. 'I heard you tell Lissy you hated your mother. How can being there be better than here? What will you tell her?'

'Nothing,' Irene replied. 'My mother taught me to lie, remember? But forgiveness is a process and it only requires one person taking one small step. If I'm to be a good role model for my daughter, I first have to be a good daughter. Making amends matters and so do family connections.'

'What about my connection? At least if you stay in Saddleton I can be a part of your lives.'

'Really, Don?' Irene huffed. 'You'll magically find spare hours in your week to drive all the way to Valerie's and back again? You might need Elizabeth to show you how to saddle the unicorn.'

'Are we going unicorn riding today, Dadda?' His girl was back in the room, her baby gumboots walking mud, or more likely chook poop, over the floor mat. 'Is that why Mummy's packing a bag?'

'No one is going anywhere today, Elizabeth,' Don said, firmly. 'And, Irene, I promise to tell Michael I need time off. We can talk more. Tomorrow is Sunday. We'll have our regular picnic. You like going there. I know you'll miss those moments.'

★ ★ ★

Before Irene could respond, Michael Dawson's booming voice bounced off the walls of the tiny weatherboard place she'd sweated in over summer and shivered in each winter.

'Hey, little brother, where are you?'

She dabbed both cheeks, stiffened her shoulders and put on her 'everything's fine' face. If only the wood and wire fence Don had erected to keep a growing girl in and the wildlife out was as effective at keeping brothers at bay. Not one Dawson knew how to knock. 'It's a country thing,' Barbara once told Irene. 'It's not like we have anything to hide, do we?'

'What's keeping you?' Michael called. 'You gunna be long, or what?' He stopped in the doorway to the room, flustered and red-faced, his eyes on the suitcase, then on his brother. 'I need you to unload the auger before heading off, and you need to get onto the fencing. This property is not a one-man bloody show. Everyone needs to work.'

When Michael looked directly at Irene before turning on his heel, she had expected Don would stick up for her. Instead, she got a rushed peck to her cheek before Don picked up Elizabeth from the floor where she was playing with her favourite first birthday present: a pyjama bag in the shape of a red and black-spotted ladybug.

Irene sank onto the bed and hugged the small decorator cushion while watching Don cuddle Elizabeth. 'I'm so tired of fulfilling other people's dreams,' she said. 'I'm barely twenty-three years old and I'm living in a dead woman's shadow and raising her child.'

★ ★ ★

As Don closed his eyes to breathe in the sweet scent of innocence, his need to protect consumed him. Hackles bristled and a growl began building deep in his gut.

'*Don't* say things like that, Irene.'

'Why not?' she challenged. 'Have you ever considered what the last five years has been like for me, alone in this house and trying to be a mother?'

'What do you mean, 'trying'? You're a wonderful mother, Irene.'

Another huff. 'Except in the beginning when I had no idea what I was doing and nobody to turn to for help. You all expected me to get over my loss. Instead, I had Elizabeth — a constant reminder of what my own baby would've been like on every birthday. I was desperate for one of you to understand, but there was no talking to your mother, no support from your sister-in-law, and no mothers' group happy to welcome me. I was 'that girl from that house'. I always will be in this town.'

'What about Cheryl?' Don asked. 'She offered help.'

'Yes, and we met in secret a few times, but I didn't want to risk upsetting Jack. Her husband has a temper.' Irene picked up the small silver frame from the dresser, hesitating before returning the photograph and straightening the doily. 'Gypsy would've helped me, but she had her hands full with Willow and, to be honest, I think Elizabeth and I are too painful a reminder of that night. So, you see, Don, I've done right by everyone and fumbled my way through in the hope God wouldn't punish me further. I've done my penance. Let me go.'

After Don lowered Elizabeth and Buggy-boo to the floor, he rose and fixed his eyes on Irene. If they embraced, might she reconsider? Would she take pity on him and change her mind when she felt the life seeping from his body?

'I can do better,' he said. 'We can work this out. Let me make a promise to you this time, Irene. Forget about fixing the evening meal tonight. Michael and I have been butchering. I'll come home in time to put a roast in the oven. I'll set the table outside with candles and we'll watch the sun go down. I'll make it nice. We'll talk. We'll work through this together. We can. Okay?'

With the blast from Michael's car drowning out his final words, Don pecked Irene's cheek and strode away determined to do whatever it took to keep his family together and Irene happy.

341

He'd start by telling his brother where to shove his horn.

★ ★ ★

With Don gone, Irene paused as the soundtrack of her morning played out in the sounds and then the silences of the cottage: the echo of his promise to come home early, the thud of boots on creaky boards, and the slam of the screen door as a final crescendo. Then nothing, the stillness broken only by the hum of a child's sweet singing and the drone of a worn-out refrigerator that kept Irene awake at night.

When sleep finally came, so did the nightmare images of uniformed men bursting into the bedroom to snatch Elizabeth and handcuff Irene. As she did her walk of shame, poked and prodded by her wooden-spoon-wielding mother, townsfolk pointed their fingers and pelted her with stale loaves of bread. Alongside her mother was Uncle Pete spitting vile condemnation: 'Liar!' 'Slut!' 'Father killer!' 'Whore!'

'Baby snatcher!' Lissy would scream after clawing her way out of the ground to join in.

The nightmare was always the same, and always ended with Irene sitting in front of a blank headstone, alone and weeping for her nameless child.

Sobbing now, Irene turned into the bedroom she shared with Don, dropped the half-filled suitcase on the prize-winning patchwork quilt, and wiped beads of brown sweat from her forehead. She glanced at the broken ceiling fan over the bed and then at dust devils dancing over dry paddocks, while in the distance, Don was starting the tractor and setting the hole digger in motion. When the cloud of brown enveloped him, Irene knew what to do. But she had to hurry, before she changed her mind.

Blood surged as she ripped clothes from hangers and scooped personal items from the top of her dresser in one go. No time to be choosey or tidy. What fitted fit. The rest would stay strewn over the bed she'd reluctantly shared with Don. The shift into his room had been at Irene's instigation; an attempt to make the most of her life because she was still young, still attractive, and needing adoration — or so she'd thought. As a lover, Don had been kind, gentle and considerate. But she didn't love him in the way she should — the way he deserved — and doubted she ever could. Had she been honest with him any time he curled behind her in bed and whispered, 'Can we?', he would have known the sensation did nothing but stir shameful memories of her uncle and his sickening reassurances about family love. Despite everything, Irene remained dutiful and rarely rejected Don. She stayed quiet and accepted his soft affection while hating every minute. But the experience had taught her living without intimacy from a man was possible. She had a daughter and they would have a fine life together, the two of them.

'Hey, there!' Irene said when Elizabeth skipped into the room and flopped to the floor with her favourite toy. 'How would you and

343

Buggy-boo like to go on a holiday to the beach?'

Her eyes lit up in the way Lissy's used to do. 'With Dadda?'

'No, darling, the two of us. Won't that be fun? We'll be like best friends on a road trip, but we have to be quick.' Irene scooted her into the mint-green room with its pretty wallpaper borders and lacey curtains that, although washed monthly, never looked clean. Stopping at the hall cupboard to retrieve the parcel secreted behind the linen pile, she crammed the contents into an old duffle bag, along with some shoes. Then, as she swung both doors wide on the small wardrobe, she told her daughter, 'We can only take what will fit in the suitcase. Pick one toy and one book.'

Elizabeth glanced around the room as if stocktaking her little life: the box brimming with Dadda's handmade toys, the crocheted security blanket she'd had from birth, and the ladybug-embroidered pillows and bedcovers. When she stopped at the window overlooking the backyard, no doubt wondering where they would fit her mini farm and rocking horse, Irene considered changing her mind. At the same time, the wind changed and the unmistakable smell of country wafted through the gap in the window and blew dust over the pretty lace curtains.

No, she told herself. Nothing would be different around here unless Don could pull off a miracle, bring rain, and make money grow on trees. While Lissy might have loved Don and enjoyed farm life, she wasn't here. Irene was, and she didn't believe in miracles.

'Elizabeth, help Mummy. Choose your favourite coat, quickly.' Irene delved into the depths of the wardrobe until she found a parka. 'Look! Ladybug red. Pop it on and let's go.' With both the duffle bag and suitcase full, they wore their coats to avoid carrying them. 'Just 'til we get to the car,' Irene said, as Elizabeth tried wriggling free. 'Let's race.'

Weighed down with her own coat and the duffle bag draped over one shoulder, Irene contemplated the suitcase still on the bed. Fifty metres away was the reconditioned Holden, parked in the copse of She-oak trees by the machinery sheds.

'Why you are you crying, Mummy?'

'I'm not crying, sweetheart,' she replied. 'I have something in my eye.'

A quiet country life was not what Irene had pictured for herself. Farming held no interest, while the constant whirr of machinery, and the plumes of powdery dust that seeped inside closed cupboards and under bed covers, had irked her from day one. Today, the billowing cloud engulfing Don would be her friend. With his head down, focused on the clamorous machinery, Irene would be in her car and driving away before he noticed.

'If you want Buggy-boo, you need to hold on tight.' She folded Elizabeth's fingers around the favourite toy. The other tiny hand she clenched in her own, prepared to drag the child if need be. 'Ready, sweet-pea? Last one to the car is a rotten egg.'

They'd barely made the halfway point when

Elizabeth became a dead weight, tugging until the duffle bag slipped off Irene's shoulder. 'Buggy-boo! Buggy-boo!' she cried.

With the suitcase in one hand and her daughter swinging off the other, refusing to walk, Irene's arms ached. Her clothes were sticky under a coat too heavy for the day, the sting of perspiration in her eyes unbearable, and her window of opportunity was closing. Any minute Don would look up. He'd see what she was about to do and try to stop her. Going back for the abandoned ladybug was out of the question.

'Let this be a lesson, Elizabeth,' she said in a whispered shout, while tossing the bags on the back seat. 'If you want something, girl, hold on tight.' She dragged her daughter to the driver's door, pushed Elizabeth across the bench seat, and pinned her by the coat tails to keep her inside the open window.

Having manipulated the stiff gear stick into first and released the handbrake, Irene thought about the choice she was making. When she dared one last look at the man she was leaving behind there was nothing but more dust. Decision made.

31

Calingarry Crossing, 2014

Having waved Beth away, Tom marches towards the cottage to the beat of his exasperation.

'Leave those,' he tells Don, who's busily stacking glasses and dishes one-handed into the specially designed trolley. 'Sit, please. I'd like to talk.'

'We need to tidy up. Then I need to rest.'

'Later,' Tom says, and pushes one of the canvas deckchairs behind his uncle's knees, forcing him to sit. He positions a second chair directly in front and leans forward, peering into Don's eyes. 'What's come over you? I thought you'd be happy I've found a girl I like enough to bring home for a special lunch. But you seem to be, well, I don't know . . . ' Tom's frustration escalates. 'You tell me. What's going on?'

'Sorry, mate,' Don says.

'It's not me who needs the apology, Unc. The other day you had a shot at single mums, which is bloody rude and, frankly, quite odd coming from the man who raised me on his own. I've noticed the way you stare at Beth. Next thing you'll tell me is she's not good enough, or maybe remind me what happened the last time I fell for a city girl. Is that the problem? Or is it Dad's anniversary? You used to get moody this time of year.'

'I used to get drunk,' Don says, his voice flat, worn out. 'Ever since your one-nip ritual put an end to that, *moody* is all I have left.'

Tom leans closer. 'If you remember, Unc, we made the choice together. Later, you thanked me and said, 'drinking away from your problems leaves them behind for others to deal with'.' Tom pauses. 'You know, when I was little, I used to think *I* was your problem.'

'Yes, yes, I know you did, mate.' Don's shoulders sag. 'And I admit I was a wallower for far too long. Dawsons are darn good at it, from memory. But you, Tom, will always be the best thing to have happened. Having you in my life helped me in ways I've never admitted. You've made me happy. You still do, unless you're cross-examining me.'

'Happy is good, Unc.' Tom sits back into the chair. 'Happy means smiling next time you see the woman I fancy, and who I think feels the same about me. I meant to ask her to the beach party until your less-than-graceful exit. I reckon after today she'll be thinking those grumpy-old-man traits are hereditary. Should've seen the way she floored it out of here, like she couldn't wait to get away from the place.'

'Don't say that!' Don's out of the chair before he's muttered the last word. 'And it's time you stopped calling me *Unc*.'

'Why?' Tom's bemused. 'You are my uncle. Had you agreed years ago I would've called you Dad.'

'I'm not your father.'

'Close enough.' Tom shrugs, but he's hurt and

confused, and cross Don has decided to wander away mid-conversation to water the new saplings lined up on the trestle table. Tom joins him at the potting station and grabs a second spray bottle. 'Why the big deal anyway? You did everything a dad would do. You fed me. Watered me. Grew me. You built me a mini farm, for Pete's sake. Which reminds me, Matt's keen to restore the old rocking horse.'

'Should've dismantled the thing years ago,' Don grumbles.

'Why? Do you know how cool I was in school? No other kids had their very own miniature farm.'

The spray bottle lands with a thud and Don squares his shoulders, but all the stance does is exaggerate his lopsidedness. 'There's something I need to tell you, son.'

Son? 'Go on,' Tom says.

Don takes a deep breath in and lets it out in a rush. 'This woman you seem so taken with . . . You know her well.'

Tom's mouth slips into a sly grin. 'I'm working on it.'

'No, I mean you already know her well. You were young. Too young, perhaps, to remember the small girl who lived in this house until her fifth birthday, when she went away.'

Following his uncle back to the table and chairs, Tom picks through the memories of that young boy aching to help his dad outdoors on weekends, but relegated to staying indoors most of the time fetching for his mum.

'I remember the lady who lived here with you,'

Tom says. 'She used to come by the house with food. She was nice. She took me to my first day of school because I couldn't get Mum out of bed.'

The same lovely lady had embroidered the initials T.D. inside the collar of Tom's school uniform, and on the sports-day clothes that always ended up in a messy tangle on the change room floor on Friday afternoons. If she saw him on the way to the school bus collection point, she'd stop to inspect his lunchbox. She sighed a lot and sniffed his sandwiches, poking the bread for freshness. Most days she made him wait outside while she started from scratch. He never told his mum her lunches likely ended up in the chook bucket.

'I liked the lady,' Tom says. 'Her lunches were the best, especially those Anzac biscuits and dried fruit. Wait a minute!' He jolts upright in the seat. 'There was a little girl. With a lisp. Bossy thing who claimed every toy by pointing and saying '*Lithbeth's*'. She was Irene's daughter, right?'

Don shakes his head. 'She was Lissy's daughter.'

'I'm confused. Lissy was the love of your life,' Toms says. 'She and her baby died.'

Don sighed heavily, as if releasing forty years of anguish. 'Lissy died. Her baby lived and spent five years here with me and Irene. The truth is, Tom, I built that mini farm for Elizabeth, one piece for each birthday. I'm sorry. I know you loved it, but the damn thing's been a reminder all these years and I'd rather — '

'Stop!' Tom barks. 'Stop talking, Uncle Don, please. Let me get this straight.' He's up and pacing, running both hands back and forward over his head. When he stops at the corner of the veranda, he cups his skull as if the billion questions banging to get out need holding in. 'Uncle Don, are you telling me the woman I introduced you to as Beth is the same child?' The silence stretches all the way to the tired-looking rocking horse and to the sandbox overgrown with weeds. 'And you're sitting there now apologising for the mini farm not being mine? This is unbelievable. As if the bloody thing matters.'

'Tom, please, come back and — '

'Hang on! Hang on! How can you be sure Beth and Elizabeth are the same woman?'

'At first I wasn't,' Don says. 'For years I've thought I could see Little Lissy in women's faces everywhere. But this time my heart knew. And she mentioned Buggy-boo.'

'I'm still confused, Unc. How does the woman you lived with fit into all this?'

Don looks away, before glancing at Tom. 'I'm thinking we'll need a nip for the rest of the story.'

'You're out of luck,' Tom says, distractedly. 'The bottle is at my place.'

'Under the sink,' Don says with a flick of his head. 'Left-hand side, behind the potato bin.'

★ ★ ★

'Any more confessions?' Tom asks, returning with the secreted whiskey bottle and two glasses.

351

'Pour and I'll talk,' Don says. He launches into the time he worked at Dandelion House where he fell head over heels for a young pregnant woman. 'Both Irene and Lissy gave birth at the house on the same night. I lost Lissy, while Irene lost her baby, but she agreed to move into Dawson's Run to care for the child.' Don downed the whiskey shot and pushed the glass to one side. 'We lived together, both of us committed. I treated the baby as my own, but I'm not the biological father, Tom, so you can get that look off your face. There's no familial connection.'

'Small mercies!' Tom quips. He could do with a second shot. Instead he walks the bottle and both empty glasses to the outdoor kitchen, calling over his shoulder, 'Go on.'

'I see Beth's been well loved,' Don says. 'I see it in her defence of Irene and her reluctance to let go of the ashes. Tells me we made the right choice forty years ago.'

Tom storms back and smacks both palms flat on the table. 'The right choice? For who exactly?'

'Please, calm down and I'll finish.'

Tom straightens, arms folded. 'I'm waiting.'

'Giving birth does not guarantee connection, Tom. That much I know you understand.'

Yes, Tom knew not all mothers sacrificed for their children. As cruel as leaving him with his elderly grandparents and his uncle had been, by walking away, Wendy had given Tom permission to love Don without feeling guilt.

'Elizabeth and Irene had a clear connection from the start,' Don tells him. 'Some bonds are special and I treasure ours, Tom. Please, don't be mad.'

'I'm more than mad, Unc.' He drops into a seat, fearing the worst. 'Exactly, what did you do?'

Don returns the stare, his good eye as fixed as his false one. 'I'm not ashamed, Tom. I made sure Beth had a mother who would love her. A father, too.'

'So you and Irene took her from her real family to play your own version. Like adopting an abandoned puppy from the pound.'

'See? This is exactly why I said nothing all these years, and you can't either. People jump to conclusions rather than ask questions. We didn't *take* anything anyone wanted.'

Tom peers across the table. 'It was legal?'

'Yes and no. The only other option was to let the child go to strangers. Lissy's parents wanted nothing to do with her.'

'That *child* is the woman I think I could fall in love with. I can't believe you're dumping this on me. I'm not sure I even want to talk to you right now.'

'Then talk to Cheryl,' Don says. 'Tell her I sent you. She'll confirm everything.'

Tom flinches. 'The lovely woman who hangs your laundry and cooks casseroles is in on this ruse?'

'You know she used to help Gypsy at the house. Please, son, don't be angry.'

'Don't start calling me 'son' now!'

'Hey, guys, everything okay?' Matt's stopped at the door and Tom wonders how much he's heard. 'I tried calling your mobile, Dad. I checked the feed shed on my way in and the water pump is playing up. It's Thursday, and that means — '

'The pump guy is working in Saddleton. Of course he bloody is.' Tom's groan punctuates the awkward silence.

'We could lose a batch of barley if we don't identify the problem ASAP,' Matt reminds him, needlessly.

Tom bites his lip, pockets his phone and stomps to the rack by the door to grab his hat. The timing could not be better. A pump problem is the distraction he needs until he can come to terms with this bombshell.

'Tom,' his uncle calls out with some urgency. 'What are you going to do?'

He sighs, knowing he'll likely be damned if he tells Beth and damned if he doesn't. 'First, Unc, I'm going to save our income. Then I think I'll steer clear of town and Beth. I need a day or so to think. If she leaves in the meantime, I'll assume it's meant to be.' Tom wipes the sweat off his forehead before he slams the hat on his head. 'There's one thing I do know for certain. One lying, duplicitous bastard has already hurt her. I won't be another one. You raised me to be better.'

32

Still full after Don's delicious beef ribs and roasted potatoes, Beth declines Maggie's offer to reserve a quiet table for dinner. A shower to wash away the wine residue in her lap is her priority, followed by a mid-afternoon nap to stave off the dull ache squeezing her temples.

'There's always tomorrow — Chicken Parma Friday,' Maggie says.

'Sounds great.' Beth smiles. She wants to do nothing tonight except relax with a good book and a happy ending.

The words *relaxed* and *happy* have not been part of her vocabulary for some time, and yet she feels strangely content being in Calingarry Crossing. Though still weighed down by her mother's ashes request, gone is the sense of urgency and the uptight, easily flustered feeling she's been living with since losing Irene. Misery is not easily dealt with, but Beth is finding it difficult to be sad when in Tom's company. Tomorrow, if it's not raining, she'll work off the extra serving of gravy and pumpkin by walking to the cemetery and, should she find the spot, she can be miserable in the task alone. But that's tomorrow. Tonight, Beth's happy dwelling on the delicious lunch and the delightful Tom Dawson.

Despite the uncertain start and abrupt end to the meal, Beth had warmed to the old man who lovingly referred to his nephew as 'chief cook, bottle-washer, and beloved nag'. The moniker reminded Beth of Irene, who would refer to herself as 'chief cook, bottle-washer, and bread-winner'. A proud woman, her mum had rejected handouts and, with very little, made mundane ingredients taste amazing. But Beth's favourite meal was Sunday movie night: a rented VHS from the video store and a sofa picnic with chunky sliced bread Irene insisted they bake themselves, and only one knife between them. Who cared if the Vegemite mixed with the peanut butter? Not the Fallone girls. That's what mates did, and that's what they were. There was never any shortage of fresh white bread in the Fallone home, and from day one Beth's lunchbox always had the freshest sandwich. In fact, the first day of school with her pink Barbie lunchbox was probably Beth's earliest memory.

★ ★ ★

Unlike some mothers at the school gate, Irene had remained upbeat and encouraging while waving Beth into the playground. There was no escorting to the classroom, no fuss, no fanfare. According to Irene's Law, the early cutting of apron strings developed more capable adults, as did calling her by her first name. Beth was told *Irene* was a perfectly reasonable replacement for Mum, but the choice was hers. For Beth, there'd been little discussion required on the topic and she chose *Mum*. That Christmas, to make her point, she'd bought a coffee mug emblazoned with *BEST MUM EVER* in big red letters.

356

Beth's tenth birthday present from Irene had been both practical and built to last. The trendy wheelie suitcase with the hidden handle that slid up and down with the press of a button had Beth feeling very grown up. Were they going on a holiday? Hopefully not to Gran's. Beth hated going to Granny Valerie's at Christmas. With that suitcase came news. Irene had a new job in a different salon; her four-year apprenticeship was over. The day she secured a senior stylist job in a swanky city salon, mother and daughter had celebrated by eating pancakes with lashings of white sugar and lemon juice. Pancakes soon became the treat of choice, with every birthday to follow calling for a crazy concoction.

On her thirteenth, she'd had her first official taste of champagne, followed by pancakes with strawberries sprinkled with sherbet powder and lime juice. High on sugar, they'd cranked up the second-hand stereo and she and Irene had bopped until they dropped to the *Saturday Night Fever* soundtrack on full bore. The next year, when the Reader's Digest album boxes arrived in the mail — featuring instrumental tracks by *Henry Mancini* and *The Boston Pops Orchestra* — Beth put on a show with made-up lyrics. Not only could she sing and dance, her drama teacher sent a note home telling Irene her daughter had 'a look and passion to take her places'.

Over the next few years, Irene's No-Apron-Strings Law prepared Beth for solo trips interstate to attend auditions. Most times she stayed overnight with a forensically vetted family and enjoyed being a part of their noisy lives, if only briefly. The one time she'd baulked about leaving home was on the eve of her first real stage production — Andrew Lloyd-Webber's *Cats*. Ten years on and people still couldn't get enough of those quirky trash-can alley critters. The role meant six months without her mum and Beth hadn't let go of home so easily on that occasion, resulting in an embarrassing send-off scene at the boarding gate. While Irene had remained stoic, it was obvious Beth's tears from the first day of school had been there all the time, waiting to fall.

'Listen to me,' her mum had said while wiping Beth's cheeks. 'You'll never know how strong you can be until you try. For heaven's sake, I was having a baby at your age.'

'Mum, I'm not sure telling your eighteen-year-old daughter such a thing while sending her off to another city for six weeks is a good idea.'

'I say it as a reminder. You're a good girl — and smart,' Irene added. 'I've taught you to know right from wrong, and when something seems too good to be true — '

'It usually is!' Beth finished in her usual sing-song voice.

'Stay strong, sweet-pea,' Irene whispered mid-hug. 'Remember to hold on tight to those dreams. And whatever you do, make your own choices, buy your own drinks, and carry your car keys in your hands.'

'Thanks, but I don't have a car, Mum,' Beth said.

'Yes, sweet-pea, you do. It's waiting in

Melbourne for you at the Taylor house. Mr Taylor will make sure you get practice and Mrs Taylor will come up and visit relatives once your show is over, so you won't have to drive home alone. They've helped me plan everything. So, pass your test first go and get those P plates.'

'Are you for real?' Beth hugged. 'Oh, wait!' She hugged tighter. 'Of course you're for real. You're my mum. The very best a daughter can have.'

★ ★ ★

If only Irene was still alive. Beth wonders what she would make of Tom. What does Beth make of him? Is he too good to be true? Since the divorce, she's dated a few men and mixed in professional circles bursting with charmers, but Tom's different from the slick, trendy entertainment type. Beth hasn't enjoyed the company of such a down-to-earth man for ages — or wanted one to ask for her phone number as much.

And why the heck hasn't he?

Had he asked, Beth might have suggested they swap numbers, which would mean rather than lying in the dark at 8 pm listening to the clink of beer glasses and the echoes of laughter floating up through the floorboards, she might call Tom to kill an hour, chat about goodness-knows-what, and end up with plans to meet him for breakfast or coffee, because . . .

'Because you like him, Beth,' she says. 'Admit it. You. Like. This. Man. And that's okay, Beth Fallone. You. Are. Okay.'

You're doing better than okay, she tells herself. Yes, she's in town because her mum insisted, and no amount of grieving can change what's happened, but sitting around being miserable and whiney is the last thing Beth wants to do. Her mum detested both wallowers and wallflowers.

'What do you reckon, Mum?' Beth speaks to the ceiling. 'Do I take myself to the beach party on Saturday night and have a good time, despite the cafe owner's nudge failing to prompt Tom?'

Maybe the guy isn't into fancy dress parties, Beth muses. Not everyone loves a costume like she does. Beth could easily while away half a day scanning the racks in the op shop next to the pub to find her outfit. Not only might she snap up a bargain, she'll be contributing to the economy of a small town.

'Win-win!' she says, sighing contentedly. 'No wallowing, no wallflowers.'

⋆   ⋆   ⋆

If requesting a woman's phone number flowed easily off Tom's tongue, he could call Beth and arrange to meet. Unfortunately, he gets little practice asking in a town as small as Calingarry Crossing, where he mostly bumps into the people he needs. While the strategy works fine where no urgency exists, Tom needs to see Beth in person. He has to get what he knows out into the open and without shattering her world in the process.

His uncle was spot on about one thing. Beth is

360

struggling to release the ashes, which makes Tom fairly confident she won't be rushing off tomorrow and, hopefully, not before the biggest night on the Calingarry Crossing event calendar. There'll be no avoiding the noisiness of Saturday night's beach party, even with her room located at the far end of the pub. If he doesn't bump into her there, he can throw back a glass of courage and rock up to her room to say g'day.

Or Tom, you can mind your own bloody business, be loyal to the man who's loved you all your life and let sleeping dogs lie. Maybe admit this one's no more a keeper than the last woman you dated for seven months. You haven't known Beth seven days yet.

But why? Why should he have to back away from someone who makes him feel so damn good? He'd been a child when all this happened. He'd played no part in his uncle's decision-making, and there is no shared ancestry. Don wouldn't lie about that. *Would he?*

33

For Tom, the day to himself yesterday had been productive, both physically and mentally. He'd deliberately avoided town, his uncle, and dodged Matt who had earlier witnessed his exasperation via a string of profanities while solving the water pump issue. Soon the lad would be back home with his mates and his mother, and with a new vocabulary courtesy of Tom — another thing for the ex to comment on. At least Matt didn't inherit his mother's aversion to small-town life. Like Tom, his son wears country dust as a badge of honour. The only thing to get the boy squeaky-clean these days is a date, and his knocking off early to put extra effort into dressing suggests he has a hot one for tonight's annual shindig at the pub.

The prospect of bumping into Beth at the beach party has prompted Tom to change his shirt three times, each one ironed to within an inch of its life. According to chatty Lorna at the op shop when he saw her in the cafe, 'the lass with the long legs' had spent considerable time sorting through clothing racks for possible beach party outfits. Tom regrets not asking Beth to go with him, but the issue with his uncle has kept him off-kilter. Even now, with the party already underway, Tom's standing before the mirror, tossing up if going is the best course of action, and unsure if Matt is on the mark suggesting cut-off jeans will be a hit. More likely it's a cheeky son's payback on his poor old dad with the lily-white legs. He considers the thongs Matt had offered, until remembering the broken glass incident at last year's event.

Deciding on socks and sturdy boots, he takes a final look at his ridiculous outfit.

'Daggy, but at least I'll keep all my toes.'

★　★　★

The first sign Tom is late to the party is the level of intoxication, evident in the back-slapping and beer-raising while he weaves through the crowded bar area. He heads for the rear deck where a bandana-wearing DJ has the crowd grooving to The Beach Boys. From amid the throng on the dancefloor, Cait and Sara yell, urging him to join them. While waving a not-on-your-life hand in their direction, he identifies the third dancer. *Beth!*

Great minds, Tom tells himself as he takes in the frayed denim shorts sitting low on her hips, along with a white shirt tied at the front to expose enough skin to make his stomach twitch. Her glossy brown hair is caught in cheeky pigtails, the red peak cap swung sideways to flatten her fringe, and both cheeks have zinc-cream stripes. Keen to get a beer into him first so he might relax, Tom elbows his way to the bar.

When he returns to the dance area, drink in hand, the song changes to a Bollywood number and a flash mob gathers in chaotic lines. The crowd moves in a kaleidoscope of colour, with the more experienced leading the overly enthusiastic in repetitive moves that look simple enough. There is loads of hip action and repeated hand flicks, with one move remarkably similar to twisting imaginary lightbulbs into non-existent ceiling sockets. When the song changes and Beth reaches a hand towards Tom, fingers urging him to join in, he shakes his head and chuckles. She's kind of cute when she's had a few.

★ ★ ★

Beth shimmies over to Tom where he's observing from the sidelines. The wine has done its thing — boosting her confidence and making her feel a little bit sexy. She circles him, stopping behind to rest her chin on his shoulder. He smells good.

'Late again, cowboy? And where's your beach outfit? I'll have you know I've spared no expense on my little number.' She steps in front of him and strikes a pose. '*Ta-dah*! All up it cost a whopping $12.50, not including the zinc cream, which is actually toothpaste. See?' She swipes at the white paste and sucks her finger with more fervour than is possibly appropriate in a public place — not to mention in front of a man she's only known for a few days.

'This shirt *is* my idea of fancy,' Tom says in response to her question. 'By fancy I mean it's been ironed twice in your honour. Can I buy you a drink to make up for my tardiness?'

'I'm impressed with the shirt,' Beth says, pondering the teeny-tiny spinning sensation in her head. 'But the pattern is making me feel woozy.' Her wink is another sure sign Beth's on the way to intoxication, because she can't wink without looking like a deranged Samantha from *Bewitched*. 'Maybe water would be good.'

'Too easy,' Tom says.

He takes her hand and they weave their way to the water station at the far end of the bar, passing surfboards on trestle legs that make interesting tables for the odd cheese platter and bowls of nibbles. Then they head outside to the sand-covered beer garden where a beach volleyball game with a giant inflatable ball is underway.

★   ★   ★

'Let's go over there.' Tom points towards vacant canvas chairs on what's normally the dining deck. 'We can talk without yelling.' Not that he's planning a serious conversation. Tonight's about furthering their connection and having fun. The other stuff can wait.

They settle awkwardly onto striped deck chairs — the lounging variety found on cruise ships. How appropriate, given the sinking feeling Tom's had in his stomach since his uncle's confession.

'I thought you weren't coming,' Beth says. 'Your uncle again?'

'You could say that.' Tom raises his glass. 'Here's to troublesome uncles.'

★   ★   ★

With the chairs uncomfortable and impractical for her short shorts, Beth does her best to

365

wriggle around until she's partially facing Tom.

'So,' she says. 'Out with it. I want the truth. All of it.'

'I-I beg your pardon?'

Beth laughs, hard. 'Don't look so petrified. I'm asking why a woman in town hasn't yet grabbed you for herself. Fear of commitment? Your appalling taste in shirts?'

'Oh, um, yeah, I suppose the problem could be my shirts, or the online profile and hashtags.'

Beth's hand mutes her laugh. 'You have an online profile with hashtags?'

'Why not? If the word *hashtag* was important enough to be added to the Oxford English Dictionary this year, I figured them worth a shot. What do you think about this profile? *Down-to-earth country guy in charming small town: hashtag One-Cafe-Town, hashtag Must-Love-Country-Life, hashtag Beware-Bulldust.*'

Beth's unsure if she should be smiling but, as usual around Tom, she can't help herself. 'You put those hashtags on a dating app profile?'

'No, but if I had before meeting my wife, I wouldn't have made it past first base with her and we would've saved ourselves a lot of angst. Except for Matt.'

'Not sure online profiles are meant to be honest,' Beth says. 'That may be your first blunder.'

'You mean make everything up and repeat past mistakes?' Tom shakes his head. 'No way! The best policy has to be honesty.'

His reply is sobering for Beth. 'You're right,' she says. 'Honesty is my number one, which is why you won't find me online.'

366

'After honesty comes compatibility and connection,' Tom adds, 'and even though my ex wasn't really into cowboys, I fell head-over-heels.' He explains they met at a two-week training course on the Gold Coast. 'Hydroponics for Barley Production. Riveting stuff.' He laughs, then clarifies she was not an attendee but working with the hotel conference team. 'On the last day she told me I had a sexy cowboy swagger and my arse looked good in denim.'

'That's honest.' Beth grins. 'How did you react?'

'Like any bloke in the same situation,' Tom says. 'I asked her out on a date, which she accepted on the condition I wore jeans and my hat. Not a hard thing to do for a small-town bloke, and a woman who's easy to please can't be all bad. She arrived at the pub in shiny cowgirl boots and with a brand-new Akubra. Next thing, she's telling me she wants to run away to the country and live on a farm. We made eight years, during which time I discovered she didn't run to the country to be with me. She ran away from a crappy life in the city and thought the country worth a shot. I was a mess for a long time after she left.' Tom swigs more water. 'There's been one other semi-serious relationship, but she had a problem with me sharing so much of my time with Don. After her, I threw myself into farm work and haven't let myself fall the same way again.'

'No swipe-rights?' Beth asks, keeping the conversation light.

'I'm not on a dating app.' Tom smiles. 'I was joking. Will from the cafe is at me to set up the profile for real, but I'm resisting. Waiting for desperate status.'

'Ha! Well, when you do, and if you want my advice — not that I'm an expert,' Beth adds. 'Rethink those hashtags.'

'I'm open to suggestions,' Tom says.

Beth taps a finger to her chin and grins. 'How about *hashtag I-Can-Dance?*'

Tom's shoulders stiffen. 'Me? Dance? Sure! Nothing choreographed or fancy,' he adds, 'but I can move my feet without breaking my partner's toes, and my arse does look good in denim. How can I go wrong?'

'Show me.'

'My arse?' he asks.

'No,' Beth giggles, 'your dance moves. Sitting in this chair is killing me.' She extends her hand. 'Come on, help me up and let's boogie.'

They make it to the dance floor at a song change. With the track from *Dirty Dancing* not a fast one, nor the slow kind to bring two bodies together, the moment is awkward, making Tom's steps self-conscious and stilted.

'I checked out your Facebook page yesterday,' he confessed. 'Dancing with a ridgey-didge dancer is making me nervous. Not sure what my hands should be doing with this beat.'

'When in doubt . . . ' Without dropping her gaze, Beth draws one of his arms around her waist, doing the same with the other. 'That's nice.'

His expression quizzes. 'Slow dancing? To this?'

'Slow is good.' She closes her eyes, savouring

the moment. It's been a long time since a man held her in his arms to dance — no rehearsals, no routines, no rules.

Just sway, Beth.

★   ★   ★

Tom wants to move closer, hold tighter, breathe her in, but it's not possible with half the local cricket team currently sledging him from the sidelines.

Part way through the tune, perhaps sensing Tom's unease, Beth lifts her cheek from his shoulder. 'Would you prefer to sit this one out?'

'No, I'm good,' he assures her. 'As long as you understand I draw the line at Patrick Swayze lifts.'

Rather than laugh, Beth kind of purrs and nuzzles his neck. 'Mm, now there's a man with the moves and a nice butt.'

Tom takes a deliberate step back, grips both her shoulders and stares Beth down. 'Is that so? You want moves, eh? I'll give you moves. Gangway everyone,' he shouts.

A space opens up on the dancefloor as Tom removes both boots. Then, without breaking eye contact with her, he moonwalks away before turning around to moonwalk back. While a cheer and calls for more erupt, Tom grins and makes a point of lifting Beth's dropped jaw with his index finger. Then, crossing four fingers to form a hashtag, he says, '*Hashtag Yes-He-Can-Dance.* Only now he really needs to top up with something other than water, and see a man about a dog, as they say.' Tom raises the back of her hand to his lips and kisses it. 'You stay and dance your heart out. Sara and Cait clearly want you back by the look of that, and I rather enjoyed watching you earlier.'

★ ★ ★

As fun as bopping with the girls has been, including their sexy bump-and-grind disco reprise from the eighties, and the botched *Nutbush City Limits*, Beth's head pounds from the DJ's heavy-handed bass. When she spies Tom watching her from amid a raucous bunch of blokes wearing lifesaver red-and-yellow, she frowns and cups her hands over both ears. Almost immediately he takes the cue, nodding his apologies to his mates before wrestling her from Sara and Caitlin, who grab an arm each in protest.

Beth and Tom are both still laughing when they stop in the foyer, at the bottom of the pub's staircase. When their laughter fades and he's failed to make a move on her, she kisses him, but it's brief and lacks the promise of their previous kiss.

'Is something wrong?' Beth asks, wondering if she's possibly looking haggard in the harsh lighting.

'Yes, actually,' he says, 'I'm, um, well, before I, ah . . . You need to know something, Beth.' A half-dozen drunks burst through the door to her left and disappear through the door to the right.

'What is it?' she asks when the foyer is clear.

'Well, you see, I'm a bloke who prefers to be out in the open. Tonight's been great, but . . . '

'You want to be out in the open?' she repeats. 'Okay, sure. Sorry.' She giggles, feeling foolish. She's totally misread everything. 'Let's go outside, then!' She grabs Tom's hand, but he doesn't budge.

'No, Beth, I mean I prefer to be open and honest. You are amazing and beautiful and totally unexpected. The thing is — '

Beth stops Tom mid-sentence with a finger against his lips. 'Look,' she says, blushing. 'Obviously I respect your honesty, and I admit my comprehension is not the best after a few wines, but if you want honesty from *me*, Tom . . . I didn't expect someone like you either. Shh!' she says. 'Let me finish. I'm forty years old — soon to be forty-one — and getting older by the minute standing here. I've been so angry and confused and lost — until tonight, with you. I feel like the old me, and I've enjoyed a much-needed good time. While I can appreciate the sweet country gentleman thing, we both know I won't be sleeping until this music stops. So unless you're dumping me because I'm not your type, or unless a woman is breaking some small-town protocol by asking a guy up to her room, I'd really enjoy some quiet and some company. Your company,' she qualifies. 'There is a good selection of teabags upstairs, if it helps you decide. If not . . . ' Beth shrugs, waits, but Tom suddenly seems overly interested in the floor, his pause stretching out until it's embarrassingly long. She's about to admit defeat and say goodnight when his hand tightens around hers.

'Teabags, eh?' He looks up, grinning. 'Say no more. *Hashtag Great-Company, Loves-Tea.*'

Unsurprisingly, they skip the tea station at the top of the stairs and continue along the hallway hand-in-hand. Beth's ridiculously nervous all of a sudden. She can't turn her mind off Tom's earlier story about a destructive fire on Dawson's Run when, barely a toddler, he'd been determined to one day become a fireman. In her slightly inebriated and highly charged state, Beth is now visualising a grown-up Tom in yellow firemen's pants and braces, his bare, beat-worthy chest and biceps slick with sweat and smeared with ash. There is no stopping to sip hot tea in Beth's fantasy version. They are just two hot bodies jumping each other the second the door to her room closes. The pair take turns to strip their clothes away, not bothering to fold the bedcover back, and they're into it — the sex wild, the orgasm crazy.

Oh, Beth, it has been a long time! To curb her grin, she bites her bottom lip. Then she slips the barrel key into the lock on her door, shoving it open. Sadly, the room isn't a movie set and Tom isn't a fireman. He's a gentleman who she's wishing wasn't so well-mannered.

'A penny?' Tom asks after shutting the door behind them and taking both her hands in his, pulling her close.

She has to look up slightly to meet his gaze and the spark in his eyes ignites another giggle.

'Not for a million bucks will I tell you what I was thinking,' she says. 'Some secrets are best left as secrets. Don't you reckon? I suppose you could try kissing it out of me.'

That's one hell of an invitation. If only Tom could stop thinking with his head. Is she right about secrets? Or is he a fool for not telling her before tonight? Then again, he hadn't expected to find himself in her room, their bodies already fused, the outcome inevitable if he doesn't stop kissing her.

'Beth!' he says, breathless. 'I need to tell you . . .'

'Shh!' she replies, her lips caressing his ear before working their way back to his mouth, pausing briefly as both hands tangle with his hair. 'There's only three words I need to hear from you, Tom Dawson, and one of them had better be 'condom'.'

Barely breaking from her kiss — his words a whisper — he slips a hand into the back pocket of his shorts, mumbling, *'Hashtag He-Has-Condom'*.

Giggling, and becoming increasingly impatient with Tom's buttons, Beth slides both hands underneath and reefs his shirt over his head, flinging the fluoro floral number to the floor. She does the same with her own shirt, stripping down to the white lace bra, before kissing Tom again.

Bloody hell! What's a bloke to do? Maybe if Tom closes his eyes and imagines anyone but Beth, he might block the raging battle that isn't going away. *To tell or not to tell?*

'Beth, oh Beth, I really wish I could — '

'Oh, believe me,' she interrupts. 'I'm wishing the same, so please stop talking, Tom Dawson, and take me to bed.'

They fall onto the mattress, a tangle of limbs and lust and longing. They kiss, make love, talk, laugh and make love again. Only after the last crate of stubby bottles hits the recycle bin somewhere outside do they fall asleep in each other's arms.

★　★　★

Awake after less than three hours' proper shut-eye, Tom curses his internal country alarm clock. He wants to stay, if only to watch Beth sleep, but farm work dictates his days and he'd promised his son time off. There's no way he can call and explain, 'I've met a girl, son, and we've spent the night bonking our brains out. You need to cover for your old man.' That's never going to happen.

When he leans close, kissing Beth's nose, she stirs but doesn't fully wake. 'Stay in bed. It's early. We'll meet up this afternoon.'

'Yes, please,' she mumbles.

Tom can't help but smile. He hasn't felt so freaking fabulous in ages. If only he didn't have such a heavy secret weighing him down. The sooner he shares what he knows the better. And he will. After last night, there's no doubting their connection, or his feelings. How to tell without hurting her is the question. As much as he doesn't want to end what's barely started, he won't deny Beth the truth, like his uncle has done. Don's intentions forty years ago had been good, his proposition the result of love. Perhaps, in time, Beth will see it that way.

'You're not leaving town today, are you?' he whispers. 'You'll be here? I'll see you later?' She nods, her head still on the pillow. 'Good, we need to talk.' When Beth attempts to wake herself, Tom kisses her again. 'Shh! Not now. Don't open your eyes. Later.' He shifts a strand of hair cemented in the smeared toothpaste stripe still on her cheek. 'Besides, if you thought this shirt of mine was bright last night, it'll give you retina damage in daylight.'

34

Beth hears the door close. She has no regrets about last night. She hadn't over-indulged on alcohol or made an idiot of herself by giggling or crying too much. After making love, and with her head resting on Tom's chest, they'd fallen into an easy conversation about where they both were in their lives. It was the practical stuff she'd never discussed in her twenties when curled up with a hot guy. The last thing on their minds back then had been mundane life choices, but Tom seemed to care about a lot of things, and with a rare intensity. The man was sweet and attentive and he'd been oh, so gentle with her. Beth hopes she hadn't talked too much about her ex, or the depth of sadness she'd experienced after Richard's betrayal. She had cried a little when mentioning the baby. Tom shed several tears, too. Then they laughed, agreed crying after hot sex was totally uncool, and promptly made love again.

Beth throws back the bedcovers, keen to tackle the day, which means trying one more time to connect with her grandmother. Not even a grumpy Valerie can knock Beth off her happy perch. Due to catching the old lady off guard last visit, Beth considers calling ahead to inform the office. Maybe they can prepare Valerie for a day out. They can drive back to Calingarry Crossing and reminisce over a pub lunch before Valerie helps carry out Irene's final wish. As a mother, she would want to be included, and as Beth's grandmother she'd want to be supportive. To re-establish the connection Irene surely meant by this final wish, it appears Beth will need to make all the moves to ensure it happens.

She puts on the cat dress she'd packed for the occasion, one of Irene's favourite handmade creations. The outfit is so called not only because the fabric has kittens playing with balls of yellow and blue wool, but because the dress has enjoyed nine lives. Being wrap-around style, it survived every wardrobe clean-out from each relocation because it had adjusted to Beth's every growth spurt. While some items were not so lucky, the bust-enhancing, waist-whittling, hip-reducing little number with the cats lived to see another two-plus decades.

'A very lucky dress!' Beth says, securing the ties in a bow at the back. 'And lucky, lucky me!' She giggles and falls back on the bed that still smells of sex. Even without the fireman's outfit, Tom's love-making had been the perfect blend of sizzle and slow burn. 'Almost too good to be true, Mum, and maybe even a keeper.'

Tempted to stay on the bed and satisfy herself while imagining Tom, movement in the next room startles her straight. *Oh, my!* What if The Rev had heard them last night? Could he be the reason Tom had left so early?

★ ★ ★

Being a Sunday, and with the nursing facility having a chapel, Beth expects to find Valerie in

377

her church clothes. Instead, her grandmother is in a nightdress topped with a blue cardigan. The TV is on.

'Hi Gran, did the office tell you I was coming? I called ahead.' The box Beth left the other day remains on the floor, untouched. 'You haven't had time to go through this yet? I thought you might find a keepsake or two. We could go through it together, if you like.'

'I want nothing of your mother's,' she announces over the sound of a church choir in full voice.

Beth's bright, sunny world clouds over. Not to be brushed off, however, she seizes the TV remote and lowers the volume.

'Gran, I wish I knew why you and Mum never got on. She and I were so close.'

'I suppose you think the fault is mine. Your mother liked to cast the blame on anyone but herself.'

'I'm not blaming, Gran. How can I when I don't understand what went wrong?'

'Until you have a child, Bethy, you can never understand.'

Beth opens her mouth to speak, but a gasp is all she manages. Is her grandmother meaning to be cruel, or does she not remember the day Beth rang from the hospital because she thought Valerie would want to know her great-granddaughter was with the angels?

Beth folds into the visitor's seat and stares hard at the sunken woman melded into the old armchair. 'I *had* a baby. Remember, Gran? I gave her your middle name — Grace.'

Beth had given birth like any other mother; except she'd known from the onset of her induced labour the baby would not live long enough or open her eyes to see Beth and understand she was her mother.

'Yes, it must have been awful for you, Beth, dear, but God makes these things happen for a reason.'

'What are you talking about, Gran? What possible reason would your precious God have?'

'Not my place to say.' Valerie huffs like the tired old dragon Beth always saw, her fire extinguished long ago. 'After the truth killed your grandfather I didn't want to interfere with your lives. Your mother wanted the same. Five years on and she's begging to come back home with you. A few months later she up and leaves. Not sure why we had to endure all those Christmases that followed. There wasn't a religious bone in Irene's body.'

Beth had been too young to remember living in Saddleton. She remembers enough about the annual Christmas trip to know Valerie was not one of those huggy grandmothers who baked treats and pinched cheeks. All Beth got at Christmas was silence, a Sunny Boy iceblock, and a bag of chips to keep her quiet while Sunday church services played on ABC TV. Mostly bored out of her brain, Beth either nattered with her imaginary friend, or pretended her grandmother's cat, Kitty, genuinely enjoyed being stalked from one sunny spot in the garden to another. Sometimes Beth would sit cross-legged at her grandmother's feet and untangle balls of knitting wool under Kitty's watchful eye.

After a Christmas lunch comprising cold meat and coleslaw — because it was too hot for anything baked — Valerie would break out a tin of store-bought pudding, stick a few silver five-cent pieces in Beth's serving, and slosh cold custard from a carton on top. More silence followed in the afternoon while Beth colour-sorted her gran's button collection into disused tobacco tins and Irene flicked the pages of tatty *Woman's Day* magazines.

Finally, and without Gran breaking the seal on the shortbread biscuit tin they always brought with them, there would be a stilted goodbye on the front porch. Gran never bothered waiting to wave them off. Kitty, however, did stay as they drove away, no doubt to make sure young Beth was gone for good.

'Why weren't we like other families, Gran?' Beth asks, finally.

'Because we weren't. Your mother made sure of that.'

'How?'

'By letting herself get pregnant.'

Herself? Ordinarily Beth would consider such an antiquated viewpoint amusing, but her mother needed defending.

'Mum told me about my biological father,' she said, sitting up straight and proud, despite the unforgiving plastic of the chair. 'An Italian boy. A grape-picker who was backpacking around the country.'

'Backpacker be buggered!' Valerie harrumphs. 'Your mother was a born liar and well-practised at pulling the wool over everyone's eyes. You got your acting ability from her, I suspect.'

Beth is cross now — at her gran for badmouthing Irene, and with herself for thinking the morning's euphoria would survive a visit with Valerie.

'Look, I'm not sure what you mean by acting ability, Gran, but I can say with certainty that Mum didn't get *herself* pregnant. Perhaps you've forgotten it takes two to tango.'

The slap of Valerie's hand on the chair arm startles Beth, slapping away whatever's left of her smug smile.

'I've forgotten nothing, my dear girl. Including how your mother's promiscuous behaviour literally broke her father's heart. So don't you dare lecture me about right from wrong. God is my saviour, and if your mother had been open to Him she would never have brought such shame to us all.'

'What a terrible thing to say, Gran.'

'Do not judge me, girl. You are too like your mother.' Spittle rains from the corners of Valerie's mouth, landing on the sky-blue nightgown to speckle it navy. 'Young people think they can do what they want, consequences be damned. Then, when God says no to granting you a child — no doubt for good reason — you denounce Him and question Him rather than embrace His decision. Then you have the hide to ignore Him and find other ways to have your bastards. Building babies in test tubes is unnatural, and so was your mother letting her father's brother into her bed.'

Beth almost gags on the mouthful of air

rushing into her lungs. She can't speak. She can barely breathe.

'Ah, see, not so high and mighty now, Bethy. You want to know why God made it so hard for you to conceive, and when you went behind His back He took your baby away? It's because God knows better.' Valerie's body stiffens, the grip on the chair arms bleaching her bony fingers white. 'How else was He to dry up those incestuous genes you're carrying, courtesy of your mother? Better to be gone, is what I say.'

Beth stands, staggers back into the bed and clutches her shoulder bag to her belly. 'I don't know what you're talking about, but I agree it's better I'm gone, Gran, and as far away as possible. I'm not sure why I bothered. Rest assured, I won't make the same mistake ever again.'

Beth almost knocks a resident off her walker as she dashes along the corridor and out the door. She's desperate to breathe in air not tainted by Valerie's abhorrent beliefs and despicable lies.

35

Dementia! Beth convinces herself on the return drive. Her Gran is regressing, reliving a traumatic event from her childhood, her addled mind struggling to make sense of a memory. Only last year the government established the Royal Commission into child sexual abuse, and already the talk surrounding churches has been damning. If an adult abused Gran as a girl it might explain the wooden hugs, her indifference, and today's outrageous outburst.

Why, then, hadn't Beth shed a single tear on the drive back? Shouldn't she be upset for Gran? Did Irene know? Is that why she'd tried so hard all those years to keep the connection? Beth wants to be mad, but all she feels is sad, and a little guilty. She's not been a very good grand-daughter. How can she stay mad at a confused old lady who has suffered terribly at the hands of adults she once trusted?

Beth's own confusion is mounting as her car idles at the familiar four-way intersection. How did she get here? A few days ago, she had sat at this same crossroad hoping Dandelion House Retreat was a place to take the edge off. Thanks to Tom, it was in a way because, since that first visit to the island, he's made Beth laugh the way she used to laugh with her mum. If she's being honest, he's also made her realise finding love might be possible. If only she could open her

383

heart and trust a man.

They can't all be liars and cheaters.

Perhaps the memory of last night is the reason Beth isn't collapsed in a crying heap and damning her gran to hell. She checks her phone, hoping for a message from Tom, but remembers he doesn't have her number. She contemplates driving out to Dawson's Run to find him, but fears bumping into his uncle. She also doesn't want to come on too strong after being so forthright last night: inviting Tom up, taking the lead, asking about condoms. Beth decides to park up somewhere and delay her return to the pub until dusk when the place will be busier and she can slip upstairs unnoticed. In the meantime, she'll find a spot to watch the water and try to chill out. Maybe scroll through the book library on her phone and find beautiful words to block out Valerie's ugly ones.

★   ★   ★

She parks with the car facing the Calingarry River and lowers the windows for air, but it's soon too hot, even under the tree. Drawn by the punt's billowing windsock suggesting cool breezes await, she boards and settles on the wooden bench abutting the metal railing with its chipped paint and rusting joints. Easing off both ballet flats, she swivels her bum and lays back, legs outstretched. With one arm protecting her eyes, the other rests on the concave of her belly.

In the hope the hypnotic lapping of waves against the hull sends her to sleep, she mutters a mindfulness chant for good measure. Rather than soothe, however, resentment festers. A river is so self-assured. It has direction and purpose. It knows where it's headed. If only Beth could be as certain about her future. If only she could turn back time and do things over. If only she could stop saying 'if only'! She's sounding more like her mother every day.

Eyes still closed, she breathes deep — in (one, two), out (one, two) — until the river running beneath carries her consciousness away.

★ ★ ★

A shudder, combined with an engine ticking over, stirs Beth awake. The punt's moving, leaving the riverbank and her car behind.

'Oh, no, no, no!'

Dopey from sleep, and madly searching for the stop button, she notices a person on the opposite bank waving.

'Hello there!' The woman in long beige shorts and a red top calls out over the groan of the punt's ramp coming to rest.

'I'm so sorry,' Beth gushes. 'I was enjoying the sun, and the next thing I know . . . Here I am.' She pauses to take in the dirt patches on knobbly knees and the garden trowel dangling from the woman's hand. 'Did you call the punt over?'

'No,' the woman answers. 'I'm told there's a short circuit in the wiring, but some days I swear the thing has a mind of its own. Did you want to see the house?'

'I have already, sort of. I was here the other

day. Tom Dawson was kind enough to bring me over for a sticky beak. The place is intriguing.'

'Yes, and we get tourists from time to time wanting to look around. A few years ago we conducted tours, but interest eventually died off. Secretly . . .' The woman leans in to whisper as if people might hear. ' . . . I'm glad.'

'I'm not really a tourist,' Beth says. 'But I read your website.'

'I only volunteer here,' the woman offers, smiling. 'The children keep me young, plus I get to pass on my love of gardening and instil the joy of eating what we grow. I'm Cheryl.' Her eyes narrow. 'You look familiar. Have I seen you around Calingarry Crossing?'

The woman shields her eyes, despite the large-brimmed sunhat doing a fine job. The sunny yellow colour and red scarf is one Beth has seen before, on the laundry woman Tom pointed out at Dawson's Run. The one who'd once married the biggest moron in town, if she remembers correctly.

'Guess I have one of those faces.' Beth shrugs, hoping the woman isn't on the verge of recognising her. People can be curious, but she's not interested in talking about the job today. 'I've been in town a short while and the other day I was a bit lost.' *Oh, how true!* she muses. 'Then Tom found me, sort of.'

Cheryl steps back. 'You're Elizabeth? Your mother died? Oh my God!' Without warning, she grabs Beth in a hug, her arms squeezing suffocatingly tight. When she pulls away, she's dabbing her face with a gardening glove. 'Forgive me. It's just . . . ' As the woman stands back, inspecting Beth at arms'-length, she has the open-mouthed, wide-eyed, dirt-smeared face of a child. Beth has an inexplicable urge to thumb the grime away, but the grown woman seems embarrassed enough, her cheeks fast becoming as red as her hat scarf. 'My, it's hot for this time of the year! Let's go up to the house. I'll pop the kettle on. Please,' she says again as if anticipating Beth's refusal. 'I'm all done here.'

Beth nods. How can she say no? The woman's pleading with her and offering tea. There might even be more hugs involved. Cheryl's embrace, though unexpected, had been quite lovely and exactly what Beth was needing.

'Let me drag your cart up.' Beth takes charge of the garden trolley and the pair trek uphill under the canopy of cool, green Liquidambar leaves that are starting to turn.

'Come in, come in,' she says, when they make the veranda. 'Don't worry about your shoes.'

In the kitchen, Cheryl's mood shifts to welcoming and inquisitive, but behind her questioning is a guardedness Beth's seen before. It's what she calls *The Recognition Effect*. It often happens when a person unexpectedly meets someone famous in their everyday life. Beth wouldn't have thought her face too recognisable, as she's no Cate Blanchett or Lisa McCune, but an avid theatre buff — musical or otherwise — might pick her. Perhaps Cheryl has seen her in a television ad. Commercial jobs, combined with corporate video projects and, more recently, narrating audio books, keeps the money coming in.

'The kids will be done with Tiffany's lesson soon. Then it's story time, when I do a reading,' Cheryl explains. 'I'd love for you to stay.' There is a nervous energy to her voice and in the way she fusses with whatever's at hand.

Definitely The Recognition Effect, Beth muses before telling Cheryl, 'Sure, okay. I like a good story, but I don't want to be in the way, or put you to any trouble.'

'Oh, Elizabeth,' Cheryl says, almost dreamily. 'Having you here is no bother. Never.'

Beth notices the woman's hands shaking. 'Let me help.' She relives her of the cling-wrapped scones and a Tupperware container of cookies, placing them on the kitchen table. 'Story time sounds like fun. Mum and I would regularly pick a book and take turns reading. I used to put on voices. Must have got my love of acting from her.'

'From your mother?' Cheryl says. 'Of course, you would have. You've achieved so much. I saw you in Cats years ago. Drove to Melbourne especially.'

Wow, Beth thinks, the woman really is a fan.

'Clean hands,' she tells the first lot of youngsters to barge into the kitchen. 'Quick! Quick! We have a very famous actor joining us today. Who wants to pick a book?'

★ ★ ★

With the storytelling over and the children back in teacher Tiffany's care, it's time for Beth to leave. As much as she might like to stay and play Peter Pan forever — pretending nothing else exists — life as a grownup is waiting on the mainland.

'Thanks again, Cheryl. No dinner needed tonight after those scones. They are seriously the best.'

'Award-winning,' the woman announces. '1974, '75 and '76 Calingarry Crossing Show.'

'You were on a roll. Why stop entering?'

Cheryl's smile stays small on her lips, vanishing altogether from her eyes. 'I, too, was lost for a long time, until I found my . . . What is it young ones say? My mojo?' Her smile widens. 'Baking helped. Speaking of food, take these with you.' She slips two buttered scones into a paper bag she retrieves from a drawer. When she places them in Beth's outstretched palm and curls her fingers over, Cheryl's hand stays wrapped tight. 'I'm glad the punt had a mind of its own today. Meeting you, sharing this time together, means more than you know.'

'Oh, that's very kind, Cheryl, and you seriously have some fabulous little actors in your group. I might see one or two on stage, or on the big screen one day.'

'A nice idea, but a romantic ambition for most of these children,' Cheryl says, as she hooks her arm and they stroll the hallway. 'After their time here they'll return to their isolated rural properties with no access to basic support or services, much less the help needed to fulfil fanciful dreams. Singing and dancing aren't practical pursuits for most, even in a small town like Calingarry Crossing. You were luckier than many, Elizabeth.'

'Excuse me?'

Cheryl apologises as they head off the veranda

389

and down the three stone steps, passing the circular garden bed. 'What I mean — *Beth* — is city kids rarely realise how lucky they are.'

'I suppose you're right. Thanks again, Cheryl. I can only hope the punt is working or you might be stuck with me.' When Cheryl doesn't react, Beth adds, 'I heard they used to call this place the House of Wishes.' She crouches in a patch of dandelion flowers to pluck a blow ball. 'I might make one on my way out.'

'I've made the same one every day for forty years,' Cheryl says, as the sun brings tears to her eyes. 'And now I know wishes come true. Goodbye, dear girl, and condolences on your mum. She's done a wonderful job with you — just wonderful.'

'I think so,' Beth manages to say, despite her quivering bottom lip and a perplexing reluctance to leave.

'Stay strong.' Cheryl hugs her one last time. 'And whatever you do, make sure the life you choose is the one you want. Make a decision to leave nothing undone, Beth, and never settle for less when there's more.'

★ ★ ★

Back in her hotel room with a tumbler and a bottle of wine on the bedside table, Beth reflects on her time with Cheryl. How is it possible to feel a stronger connection to a stranger than to her own grandmother? Cheryl's parting comment reminded her of Irene. While denying she was a feminist, her mum fostered independence

390

and relished a motherly self-reliance lecture.

'Didn't you, Mum?' Beth rolls off the bed to retrieve the purple gift bag from the dressing table, removing the A4 envelope she'd collected from Angela. 'What's this Calingarry Crossing thing really about? You haven't sent me here for Valerie. And what's so special you kept it locked in a box and hidden under blankets, rather than with your important papers?'

Today's Dandelion House detour, and story time with Cheryl and the children, has bolstered Beth. Irene did do a great job raising her. Beth is also back in the saddle and feeling less vulnerable than she had a week ago. But is she strong enough for this? She scans the unaddressed envelopes tinged yellow with age and spread over the bedcover. Then, with a deep breath, she closes her eyes and chooses one.

A birthday card. Covered in red sparkles. *Damn!*

After stopping to rinse her hands free of glitter, Beth nicks along the hall to grab a hot drink from the beverage station. Tea and scones in her room, followed by a wine chaser, is exactly what the doctor ordered for dinner. Back on her bed, she puts the mug on the nightstand and, with more care, removes the contents from a second envelope. The glitter-free card is an old-world, die-cut design outlining a purple umbrella. The brolly's owner — a pretty girl wearing a flounced bonnet — has a flower-filled basket hanging from her other hand. A small yellow dog with a red bow to match its dangling tongue sits obediently at the girl's black Mary

Jane shoes worn with white, lace-trimmed socks. The embossing is beautiful, the pastel colours pretty, and while the card isn't a keepsake and addressed to Irene — as Beth had expected — the handwriting inside closely resembles her mother's constrained cursive. The inscription reads: *To my darling, Linden.*

'Who's Linden?'

Beth picks more envelopes, barely acknowledging the front message and going straight to the inscription. The more cards she opens, the faster her hands move, the harder her heart bangs inside her chest.

Choose. Open. Read. *Heartbeat.* Discard. Choose. Repeat.

Some cards have giant numbers on the front, including a big number 10 putting glitter over everything she touches. Beth no longer cares about the green specks when she reads the inside: *To my sweet-pea, on your tenth birthday, love Mummy.*

Mummy? Tenth? Sweet-pea? 'What the . . . ?' Beth wipes a cheek. It's wet. Probably glittered green now. She grabs another card:

Happy sweet sixteen. I wish I could see you.

Seventeen: *So grown up.*

Eighteen: *Congratulations. Love you forever.*

Choose. Open. Read. *Heartbeat.* Discard. Choose. Repeat.

★ ★ ★

Finally, Beth sits back amid the array of greeting cards with one name going around and around

392

in her head: *Linden*.

Two wines down and a perfectly reasonable explanation settles in Beth's mind. She had, or has, a sibling — a girl most likely named Linden who Irene clearly never forgot and was, maybe, too embarrassed to mention. But is she older or younger? Irene wasn't yet eighteen when she fell pregnant with Beth. Had she aborted a second baby, conceived too soon after the first? It happens. Probably more so back then when there'd been so little education and support for women. Therapy and coping strategies help mothers deal with loss. Was that behind the cards? Part of Beth's treatment had been writing a letter to her dead baby. Adoption might've been another solution to an unwanted pregnancy, and that might warrant the same coping strategy for a grieving mother. Is that a likely explanation for the lifetime of birthday cards?

Why hadn't Gran, while spewing her disgust, mentioned a second pregnancy? Had the old lady confused Beth with Linden? Is Linden the victim of abuse and alive, living with another family? Does she live in Calingarry Crossing? Is she here now?

36

Tom tries keeping his voice to a whisper as he raps on Beth's door. 'Maggie said you were up here. Why won't you answer? You're scaring me, Beth. At least say something.'

'Tom, I'm packing.'

'Packing for what?' he asks, cautiously, his mouth almost pressed to the door.

'I'm leaving. I have to get away. I'm sorry.'

With those three sentences painfully familiar, Tom flattens both palms against the door, followed by his forehead. He closes his eyes and grits his teeth until his jaw aches.

'Please, Beth, I can tell by your voice you're upset. Driving isn't a good idea. I'm not going until you let me in.'

Creaking floorboards offer hope until the door flies open and Beth's face — a shade of fury mixed with frustration and despair — stares back. Tom's almost afraid to ask.

'What's happened?' He holds out both arms and she surrenders, rag-doll-like. 'Beth, what is it? How can I help?' He steers her to the bed, eases her into a seated position, but she does nothing, her arms dead weights by her side. 'Tell me what you need.'

'You can't help me, Tom.'

God! She sounds broken. 'Try me,' he says.

When she looks up, her eyes have been rubbed raw. 'I need to know why Gran was so mean, and who Linden is. After that, explain how I can feel so alone at my age.'

'One thing at a time, Beth,' Tom says. 'What happened with your gran?'

'Oh, Tom, you had to be there. She said the most horrible things about Mum and me, but don't ask. What she said is too awful to repeat.'

'Nothing can change the way I feel about you, Beth, so out with it.' Tom's arm tightens around her shoulder and she nuzzles his neck, crying and telling him about the visit with Valerie.

Every. Shocking. Word.

★　★　★

'I understand dementia screws with memories,' Beth says. 'But what if I'm wrong? What if Mum was sexually abused by an uncle? Such trauma would explain her distrust of men, and some of her attitudes.' Beth runs a hand over the card-littered quilt. 'I can tell myself Gran's confused and she's mixed me up with whoever Linden is. But, Tom, it's me who's confused. So, I'm leaving. There must be answers in Mum's personal papers at home. I need to take a more thorough look and I need the familiarity of my apartment. There are no answers here, so it's no good sitting around conjuring up questions. But if Gran is right, if what she said about me is — '

'Shh, shh! Don't go there, Beth. She's not right.'

Beth clamps down on the urge to keep crying, and to lean on the man whose arms feel far too persuasive. Instead, she's up and attempting to re-pack her suitcase.

'I'm not sure why she'd say such a thing, Tom, but I can't think here. I don't want to think. I need my normal, but until then I can lose myself in a character. I know I can do that much,' she says. 'I'll take any part on offer. I don't care. And when the season ends, I'll find another role.' Beth slams her makeup bag on the bed. 'At this point, I need to be anyone but me.'

'There's nothing wrong with you, Beth. Please, don't go. I want to talk to you, but I need you to be calm.'

'And carry on as if nothing's happened?' She shoves the suitcase.

'Soon it'll be too dark to be on the road and you've been drinking.'

'You're not my mother, Tom,' she snaps.

'No,' Tom says, calmly, 'but the next kangaroo might not be so lucky.'

'I'm fine, and the walls in this place are way too thin.'

'Well, if you won't stay at the pub, Beth, let me drive you out to Dawson's Run for the night. I'll stay with Don and you'll have an entire house to yourself.'

'I don't need to be by myself, Tom, I need to be busy and doing something that has purpose.' Beth can only hope her agent, Eunice, doesn't let her down. Instinctively, she checks her phone for messages. Nothing.

'What if you took over caring for Little Joey?' Tom says. 'The little guy is growing fast. He'll soon be a handful for Don.'

She inhales, exhaling loudly, waiting a few

beats before speaking. 'A joey can't help me, Tom. I appreciate your efforts, but the final straw at this point would be me bottle-feeding and comforting a tiny baby *anything*.' Beth resists the gentle tug on her arm. 'Don't stop me, please. It's a long drive back to Sydney and I'd rather be off country roads before dark.' She scoops the cards on the bed into a pile before slipping them back into the same yellow A4 envelope. 'Maybe I'm wrong for being hard on Gran. What if she's the only one being honest? My mother has evidently kept secrets. But we all do, don't we?' She pauses to look at Tom. He's standing beside the bed, head bowed, hands shoved into his pockets. 'We keep things from the people we love. My husband did, and there's stuff I never told Mum about my life because I didn't think she needed to know every detail. But is not telling the same as a lie?'

★ ★ ★

Tom's certain his gulp is a sonic boom in the little room. She's asking *him* about truth? *Bloody hell!* He has to tell her. He will tell her when she's not rushing off, and in the daylight, drip-fed, with lots of hugs.

Beth dumps her handbag on top of the suitcase, ferreting inside, most likely for her car keys. The thought sickens Tom. His loyalty to Don and his concern for Beth is tearing him in two.

'I'm not sure when a secret turns into a lie, Tom,' Beth says. 'I know my husband was a master at both. And don't get me started on producers who lie every time they say I'd be perfect for a part, thinking women over forty will fall at their feet to get a role. Not me. There was only one role I was prepared to do anything for.'

'And what was it?' At this point, Tom's prepared to say anything to stall her, to give himself time, to change her mind. 'Did you get it?'

'Motherhood, and no.' She slouches on the edge of the bed, her shoulders stooped, both hands pressed childlike between her thighs. 'I wanted a baby more than anything. A child to raise and nurture and guide. You're so lucky to have Matt. It's verging on too late for me.' She shakes her head and sighs. 'We like to think we choose our destiny. All I know is, I'm so busy blaming Gran, when maybe our omniscient God does make our choices.'

Tom slips beside her on the bed to massage Beth's neck and shoulders. 'For sure, life can be a shit,' he says, 'but my uncle taught me something when I was young. He used to sit me down and tell me to find silver linings in the bad things, and to be grateful for the good.'

Beth winces, her censure swift and sharp. 'Grateful? Have you heard anything I've said, Tom?'

He grabs her hand before she can move away, pinning it to his lap. 'Yes. Every word. Now you listen to what I have to say without making any judgements or decisions. Once I've said it, you'll know everything I do. No more secrets.'

She's propped on the edge of the bed, like a

kangaroo stills on the side of the road — wary of whatever is hurtling towards her, but with no appreciation of the devastating force behind it.

'Go ahead,' she urges.

Tom keeps his gaze on her hand in his. 'I've been trying to figure out how to say this.'

She places her other hand on top, sandwiching his, her voice deliberately soft. 'Say what, Tom?'

He begins slowly. 'There's more to Dandelion House than I told you the other day. I think I mentioned the place was for unmarried mothers, which is how I know you can't be what your gran's suggesting. There is no incest. Your father was a picker working the grape harvest.'

'Thanks for trying.' Beth pats Tom's thigh and leaves him sitting on the bed. 'But according to Gran, Mum fabricated the picker story. Guess I know why!'

'It is true,' he says. 'The Italian is definitely your biological father, but . . . '

Beth freezes in front of the dresser mirror, watching Tom in the reflection, her dress skewiff and her face a crumpled mess of confusion. 'What are you telling me, Tom?'

'Irene is not your birth mother. She raised you as her own, and for the first five years you lived with Don in his cottage on Dawson's Run.'

Beth tilts her head, her stare a mix of fear and curiosity, her voice small. 'What did you say?'

'The day Irene took you away, Don had his accident. He never saw you again.'

When Beth falls back against the dressing table, a vase with tired lavender stems hits the floor. Tom braces, expecting it to break, but the vessel is stronger than it looks and stays intact. He can't say the same for Beth.

'I'm sorry to be the one to tell you,' he says. 'Perhaps it's how things were meant to be, so I can be here for you.'

Beth's head snaps up. 'Meant to be? You mean like fate? Are you going to suggest I find one of your stupid silver linings, Tom? Because if what you're saying is true, there isn't one. There isn't.'

'If not fate, Beth, something brought you back,' he says. 'It has to explain our connection.'

'What does, Tom? I'm not keeping up. What connection?' She thrusts her open hand, palm out, in his direction. 'I don't *have* connections. I have no one.'

'You do. We have a connection. We've met before, Beth.' Except for the dramatic rise and fall of her chest, she is unmoving, her stare fixed on the fallen vase. 'You lived in the cottage on Dawson's Run.'

When Beth looks up, silent tears are streaming down her cheeks. 'Just. Stop. Do *not* say another word.' She inches towards the door as if Tom's a monster to be feared, and for a moment he wonders if she'll bolt. Instead, her body crumples and slides down the door to the floor. She draws her legs to her chest and clasps her head to her knees, rocking. 'I can't deal with this. I've lost too much already. I lost my mother — the mother I've known for forty years. Irene!'

Even though every fibre of his being needs to hold her as she weeps, Tom stays put. He's angry with himself. The timing is all wrong. He should've encouraged her to stay in town and better picked the moment.

Just when he's thinking Beth will never stop crying, her head jerks up, her eyes piercing.

'You are very well informed and pretty damn cool about this, Tom. Exactly how long have you known?'

Another gulp echoes in the silence. There it is, the look that says a man has betrayed her — again.

'Thursday,' he confesses. 'After the roast. I would've preferred not telling you on top of everything you're dealing with, and I selfishly didn't want you to go until we'd given this — us — a chance to develop into something more. But with you so intent on leaving tonight, I —'

'And if I was staying?' The incredulousness in her tone wounds him. 'How long would you have waited, lying to me any time the subject of mothers came up? Not such a great foundation for a relationship, Tom, and not what I consider a connection. More than anything now, I want to go back to the city and to my old life. There is comfort in the familiar and I need to keep achieving — professionally, at least. I owe Mum. I owe everything to her. Irene is the only mother I've known.'

'If you owe her anything, Beth, surely it's to be happy.'

'Yes, Tom, and you also deserve happiness, which means not falling for another woman who so easily runs back to the city. And I am going.' She springs to her feet, grabs the purple gift bag with her mother's ashes and puts it by her suitcase. 'I have a life to figure out.'

'I told you, Beth, I've already fallen. I don't want you to walk away from us like this. I know better than anyone we all have our tipping point. As strong and as capable as you are, I want to be here for you. I want to take care of you when you need someone, Beth. And when you don't — when you need space — I want to give you that, too.'

'I-I don't know what else to say to you, Tom. Sorry. I can't deal with us right now.'

'What are you going do about your mother's ashes? She sent you here for a reason.'

'And I can't bring myself to leave her behind. Not here. Not after this.'

Tom speaks calmly. 'You know keeping her ashes isn't the answer.'

'Oh? What is?' Beth's knuckles squeeze white where her fingers touch her hips. 'You seem to be the knower of all things, Tom.'

'Let's take five, eh?' He raises both hands in surrender. 'They say that in your business when a break is called for, right?' He waits for her nod. He waits a little longer until her shoulders fall and her breathing softens. 'I *am* falling in love with you, Beth.' He raises another hand to mute her. 'And I will let you go for now, but I'll track you down. For that reason, it would help if I had your number.'

'I know where to find you, Tom, but . . . ' She pauses. 'In my biz we also say 'that's a wrap', and as great as it's been, the ensemble members go their separate ways. I wish things could be different for us.'

'Right!' Tom curses under his breath, knowing

he's made a complete balls-up. He understands she needs time, but it hurts. 'Gotcha!' he says. 'Looks like I'm done. Any bloke, even one as thick as me, will eventually take the hint. The messenger does always get shot.' He stops, picks up a stray envelope that's fallen to the floor and tosses it towards the bed as if he doesn't care. The slam-dunk into her open handbag makes him laugh out loud. 'I guess you win some and you lose some,' he says, looking at Beth one more time.

If he could be certain her tears were in any way for him and what might have been, Tom might keep fighting and insist on a message when she arrives safely in the city. At least he could capture her number on his phone.

He brushes his hands together before folding his arms. 'I guess it really is a wrap. It has been a short but a great season, Beth.'

Tom needs all his strength to pass her on his way to the door without stopping to hold her in his arms one more time. But he knows what he must do. He's been here before. He has no choice but to say goodbye to the woman he's fallen for — hard.

★ ★ ★

Beth closes the door and scans the pokey room, knowing she doesn't belong in Calingarry Crossing any more than Irene's ashes. One day she'll work out what to do with those. For now, while she's still unpacking everything Tom told her, she knows he's right about one thing. It is too late and too risky to leave.

As she collapses on the bed and surrenders her head to the pillow, the phone beeps. A text from her agent: *Voice-over gig. Actor needed to bring authenticity to role. Perfect for you. Best, Eunice.*

Beth doesn't reply. Whoever she is after Calingarry Crossing, she cannot pull off a job requiring honesty and authenticity.

37

Despite the early hour, Beth doesn't stop at the nurses' station, or register as directed by the big red sign. She's not the least bit interested in being compliant, polite or respectful of privacy.

When she finds Valerie's door closed and the *Do Not Disturb* in place, Beth mutters *too bad* before barging inside. Her grandmother is wide awake and appears neither sickly nor fragile. On the contrary, she looks quite *disturbable* and more like the grandmother Beth remembers — unyielding and distant. The other adjective that has eluded Beth all these years, the one to describe her grandmother's coolness towards her, comes to Beth in that moment. *Disgusted*. If Tom's admission is true — and he has no reason to lie — the greatest irony is that her gran's disgust and distance all these years has been for nothing. Irene adopted an unwanted baby and Beth can't wait to set Gran straight.

'Oh, hello, dear, I thought you'd be back in the big smoke by now.' Valerie discards her crossword book and pen. 'Come for the box, I s'ppose. Good, I almost tripped over the damn thing.'

Nauseated by the scent of sad, old person, Beth takes a deep breath to clear a path to the speech she'd rehearsed on the drive over.

'You've made a terrible mistake, Gran,' she starts. 'By rejecting Mum and condemning her for betraying God's law, you missed out on so much. Most of all, you missed out on knowing me. I so wanted a grandmother, like all my friends. One who loved me and spoilt me with treats and hugs. One who let me love her back. I desperately wanted a big family — any family — but you didn't want me. You're the disappointment, Valerie, whereas Mum ... ' Beth sighs. 'She gave so much of herself. I got lucky with Irene. She wanted me and she played her part beautifully. She was there for me and she loved me when nobody else did. And I loved her — always and no matter what. That stands true today, Gran. Even more having learned the truth.'

'What truth? What nonsense are you talking about, Bethy? Sit down and let the bee in your bonnet settle.'

'I won't be staying, because I know what Mum did and didn't do. The only *mistake* she made was wasting our Christmases with you. Mum protected me from the apathy and ignorance that tries to tell single mothers and their children they're evil and not good enough.'

'Your mother was wicked,' Valerie growls. 'I'm looking at the proof.'

Beth doesn't know how but she keeps herself together. 'No, you're not seeing any such thing, Gran, because Irene chose to never divulge the truth. Your acceptance was so important to her, I think maybe she wanted to tell, and that's what staying connected has been about. But Mum wasn't wicked. She was a child who made the mistake of trusting adults. Adults who should've been protecting her and encouraging her to speak up. She needed to be believed, not shamed.'

'Your mother needed very little encouragement. Case in point.' Valerie simpers.

Beth has run out of the rage that had fuelled her drive to Saddleton. It's hard to detest an old woman who's dead inside. One thing is for certain: Beth's not ready to grow old, and she sure as hell won't end up grumpy with regrets.

'You missed so much, Gran, while I missed out on nothing. I feel sorry for you.' Beth's about to turn on her heels. 'I'm going and I won't ever be back, but I will leave you with this. Listen carefully because I *do* know the truth. You, Valerie, are not my real grandmother. But . . . ' She stops, breathes, eyes narrowing. 'If your precious God came down and gave me the choice — be the devil-child born of incestuous sperm, or biologically related to you, Gran — I'd pick the devil.' Beth stretches out the dramatic pause, partly to make Valerie squirm, and partly because it's a struggle to be this person, this scornful woman filled with derision and anger. Knowing she can't ever be like Valerie gives Beth the control and confidence she needs to deliver her final message.

'Irene is not my biological mother. She adopted me after her baby died. But she will always be Mum, and I thank her for raising me and making me the strong, capable woman you see before you. And whoever Linden is, she's bloody lucky to have avoided knowing you because, as it turns out, I am not the demon child, nor related to you. You see, Gran, I'm not sure whose blood flows through my veins, which means all these years you've been disgusted by the wrong grandchild. Here.' Beth tosses the hand mirror from the dresser onto Valerie's bed. 'Take a good look at yourself.'

With nothing left to say and no time to say it, she picks up the unopened box of her mother's things and leaves without looking back.

38

Beth refuses to cry while fighting to fit the extra box in the hatchback she'd haphazardly filled with her belongings. Only when she notices the unopened envelope in her handbag do tears threaten. With shaking hands, she lifts the flap and slips another card out. It's illustrated with a cottage and picket fence, a tiny key — the silver paint cracked and peeling — tied to one corner with a yellow ribbon, and the words:

YOUR KEY TO THE DOOR.
HAPPY 21ST.

The handwritten message inside rocks Beth: *Although you are lost, you are forever at home in my heart. I'll come to you one day and we'll be together again.*
The sob she's holding back has enough pressure to break Beth, but she has to keep it together, get on the road, and get far away from this place. As she slams the boot and rams the loose card back inside her handbag, there's no ignoring her guilt. Irene wants her remaining ashes to be spread in Calingarry Crossing, and a good daughter would respect her mother's wish. She is in town, and it isn't a lot to ask.

★ ★ ★

409

The flash of sunlight reflecting off the red-domed rotunda she'd sheltered under only days earlier is sharp. Beth flinches and looks to the ground, at the cloud shadows drifting slowly by. Only when they pass does she ask herself why she's taken so long to figure out the domed centrepiece of the cemetery is likely the circle in her mum's diagram. She rotates the paper every which way to line up other marks. The map has four corners and presumably so does the Calingarry Crossing Cemetery.

'Needing guidance?' The old minister startles her.

'Oh, hello, Rev, I didn't hear you coming.'

'Perhaps you weren't listening, Beth,' he says with a twinkle in his eyes. 'Those shoulders of yours appear to be carrying the weight of the world. Why don't you come here and sit for a bit?'

'I don't have time.'

'You do.' He eases himself onto a bench made from a slab of cement supported by rocks cobbled together. 'Come on.' When she doesn't move, he pats the space beside him. 'It's solid and more comfortable than it looks. I assume you haven't yet found what you're searching for?' He nods to indicate the map in Beth's hands.

'Actually, Rev, I've discovered too much, making me more confused than ever.' She points to the childish squiggle on the map. 'And I may have been reading this wrong. I wondered about this.' She taps to a spot on the map. 'All the lines are drawn with what looks like ordinary blue biro. They are faint — old-looking — except for

410

this loopy circle surrounding the faded X. It's a different pen. Added later, I'm thinking. This could this be a tree. You mentioned the pauper's section, and I'm wondering if there's a big tree in the vicinity, or if . . . ' Beth's excitement dwindles and she sighs, slouches. 'Never mind.'

'I reckon you're on the right track,' he says.

'You do?'

'Sure. Knowing which way is up is the first rule in understanding. As for the tree, I can suggest a man who knows every inch of this place. A keen gardener, he planted most of what you can see. All manner of species. I'm sure he'll be happy to point them out.'

'Thanks, but I don't need a botanical tour. I need someone to tell me I've got the right spot. Only then can I let my mother go and try to make sense of what's left. Once I've spread her ashes, I'll be done.'

'Is that so?' The Rev asks with a tilt of his head. 'You do have a choice. If it's not the right time, you can postpone.'

'There's no decision-making required,' Beth says, adamant. 'Mum seems to have made them all for me. What I should and shouldn't know, I mean.' She breathes deliberately in through her nose, exasperation pushing her breath out in a huff. 'My being here is about Mum's wish to have her ashes scattered. That's all.'

The Rev ferrets in his trouser side pocket. 'Let me get this straight, Beth. Once you've found this mysterious spot, you plan to blindly carry out the request and go back to your life without knowing the most important thing. The *why*

411

behind your mother's wish.'

'I don't have to know why.' Beth watches The Rev eking out strands of tobacco along a cigarette paper.

'If you weren't interested in the why, Beth, you would have found the spot, spread those ashes, and been on your way days ago. The fact you're still here tells me you won't be satisfied unless you understand the reason.'

'No,' she says with a vehement shake of her head. 'I don't want to learn anything else. I don't want to think. I don't want to ask questions.'

'Yes, yes, you do. The word 'why' is among the first words to come out of a child's mouth.'

Beth looks down at her tan ballet flats, now putrid from traipsing over dirt tracks. 'You're right. I was one of those annoying kids and Mum's answer was always the same: 'Because' she'd tell me. Only behind that single word, my mum hid a million little secrets.'

'Well, tell me this, Beth,' The Rev says before licking the paper and rolling it between his thumb and fingers, 'when you take on an acting role, do you not delve into the character to know who they are and what they want? To do a story justice, you take time to understand the character's motivations.'

'Yes, but this isn't a movie or a play, Rev. It isn't fiction. This is my life.' Tears she thought were dried up spill onto both cheeks. 'And it's a lie. I-I don't know who I am. My mother's not my mother and my father is God knows where. Sorry, but if that's not enough, there may be another child, named Linden. I know more than

412

I knew a week ago, Rev. I'm told Mum — Irene — stayed at Dandelion House, but as for what's true . . . ' She shrugs. 'I'm lost.'

'I've found you, Beth, and we can take one step at a time to figure this out.'

She smiles at the kindly man. 'The trouble is, Rev, I'm not sure I want to know.'

'You will, in time,' he says. 'Your generation fought for decades to have access to information and to fight for the right to choose. Women have taken the baton from people like Gypsy and they're fighting for justice and equality today with the same passion. You do want the truth, Beth, and you only have to ask. Start by asking Don Dawson. Whatever you're hoping to find, he can help.'

She gives in and slumps to the bench beside The Rev, wondering how the old minister knows so much.

'I know all this,' he tells her, 'because I've been around a long time. I got to know the women who stayed at Dandelion House, and two special girls forty years ago stand out. While opposites, the pair shared a strong bond. Had events played out differently, once they left Dandelion House they would have stayed firm friends for life. I had a soft spot for Irene and Lissy.'

Beth hopes the heart beating triple its normal rate is not as obvious to The Rev as it feels against her ribcage. 'You can tell me about both girls?' She's already giddy with too many possibilities. 'What I mean is, I can't imagine what it must've been like back then for unmarried mothers.'

413

'Then and now,' he says. 'There'll never be total acceptance, but I'm gladdened every day common sense prevails, and grateful for those who fought to change the law regarding abortion and forced adoption. Not an easy path or choice, but strong women — and there were many, including young Irene — led the way for change.'

Beth stiffens. 'Irene did?'

He nods. 'Some babies, like hers, were not meant to be in this world, and while she could've wiped that traumatic period from her life and gone home, she chose a difficult path, less taken at the time. She lived up to a promise and chose to be a single mother in the seventies. She chose this knowing there would be struggles and she would be disowned, but once she'd held Lissy's baby, she knew she would be a better mother than any stranger. She had a purpose and a reason for getting on with her life.'

'Irene told you that?' Beth asks.

'She didn't have to,' he says. 'I saw it. Irene needed saving and to know real love. So did you. And because Lissy couldn't raise you, Irene became your mother.'

Beth's mouth drops open. She's too stunned to comprehend the swarm of questions, like wasps sticking her brain. Questions like: *Why did Lissy not want me?*

Instead, she asks The Rev: 'What was Lissy like?'

'I can tell you her struggles and her home life were very different to Irene's. Don fell madly in love and offered her security with him.' The Rev stashes the small tobacco tin to his pocket. 'But

Lissy was young and, while determined to keep you and love you, she was very torn.'

'Love?' Beth's struggle to repeat the word sounds like a harrumph. 'How is abandoning your child 'love'?'

'See? You are curious. You want answers.' The Rev smiles, stands, drawing a deep breath as he lights his cigarette. Then, doffing his hat, he says, 'Go see Don Dawson, Beth. He can help you.'

39

As Beth hoped, Tom's car is not at the cottage, but the man of the moment is seated on the veranda. Is it her imagination, or are both Don and his dog on alert as Beth's car draws to a stop? As she pauses at the bottom of the steps, he seems neither surprised nor annoyed, beckoning Beth to join him at the table. He doesn't need to speak. His mien suggests he knows why she's come.

'I hope my turning up unannounced is okay?' she says.

'You've come to me for the truth, and I'm glad,' he replies. 'Would you like tea?'

The scraping of chair legs disturbs Lazy Bones, moving the dog to his water bowl by the door.

'I'd like to get straight to the point,' she tells Don.

'An admirable quality,' he says. 'No sense over-complicating things with small talk. Never been too good at it myself. Ask and I'll answer.'

Beth is immediately struck dumb, clawing her mind for questions, until she spies the twenty-first birthday card shoved in the side pocket of her handbag. Linden seems like as good a place as any to start.

'I need to know about her,' she says. 'I'm having trouble keeping track of the threads, but I assume Linden is Irene's baby. Then there's

Lissy,' Beth adds. 'I believe I might also need to know about her.'

Don pulls his chair close enough that if he was to lean forward he'd be able to reach her hands where they grip her knees. Beth can tell he wants to.

'You're here, my sweet Little Lissy.' He smiles. 'I've waited decades for the chance to tell you about your mother. It's been a relentless and exhausting task keeping these memories.'

★　★　★

Beth seems to have cried from Don's first word, until the end of his sad, sad story. There's no doubting the validity. He's answered too many questions Beth hadn't known to ask. Most importantly, her birth mother did not give her away. Lissy was excited to be a mother and a wife, and her last thought before slipping away had been of her baby's future.

'Irene was very different,' Don explains. 'She was a frightened teenager wanting an ordinary life back at home with the father she loved, and who loved her. Within hours of discovering he'd died, Irene went into labour, but the baby she didn't know she wanted until that moment was, sadly, incapable of life outside the womb.'

Beth can't help but flash back to the loss of her own baby. Irene had been a rock during that period. She'd comforted Beth morning and night, and thought to secure the hospital bracelet, and arrange photos and plaster keepsakes when Beth couldn't think at all. Still numb with grief, Beth had leaned on Irene to deal with the funeral directors, to secure a plot in a lawn cemetery and a headstone. Then, on the day of the funeral, she'd almost carried Beth into the tiny room in the crematorium. How had Irene been so in control? *How?* Beth makes a mental note of yet another unanswerable question and tunes back into Don's storytelling.

'Back then, it wasn't the children who weren't wanted,' he tells her. 'Mothers weren't wanted because they were unmarried. They brought shame. Despite her mother's rejection and her own grief, Irene committed to loving and nurturing you,' he says. 'She made you the wonderful woman you are, but she didn't do it alone, Elizabeth. For five years, I was with you.'

When Don pauses and his face drains of colour, Beth stands and offers to get water or tea — anything to keep him talking. He declines both, telling her he needs to purge himself of the past before he can stomach any part of the present.

'I saw Lissy in your eyes forty years ago as I cradled you, and I see her in you now, standing there, looking to me for answers.' He pats the chair and Beth sits again. 'You've had a lifetime of lies, Elizabeth, which was never my intention; nor Irene's at the start. I'll not add more, not when you've come for the truth.'

Beth can only nod and try to keep breathing — slow and steady.

'Dear Elizabeth,' Don starts, 'letting you think the bond with Irene was so instant she immediately stopped grieving, would be wrong.

418

She was young and without loving support. She'd endured a terrible loss.'

Beth nods. That much she can understand. 'You also lost, Don.'

'Yes, but Irene's past complicated things for her. She grappled with motherhood more than I knew, but she fell in love with you, Beth. Just not with me, so I lost you both.'

'And Lissy's parents? You said they had a change of heart before the birth, suggesting the sister raise me. Why would you not revisit that option when Lissy died? I might've been reunited with family.'

'Ah, yes, if only I could make you appreciate all that happened back then. The decision to have Irene wet nurse was best for you. No one predicted the girl who never wanted to be a mother would form such a strong attachment so quickly. One day I got this crazy, desperate idea, and when I saw her with you I was convinced it would work. Had we chosen another path and gone to Lissy's parents, they would have cut Irene and me out of your life. The father had made no bones about his feelings. But I must take full responsibility.' He stopped to clear his throat. 'I pleaded with Gypsy and Doc to let you stay, to let me keep a part of Lissy close. It's no excuse, but I hope it helps you to know Lissy had agreed to marry me.' He looks down at his right hand resting on his knee, the thumb twirling a gold signet ring on his arthritic little finger. 'This belonged to my grandmother. Lissy was planning to tell everyone about us after the birth, but that morning, when she knew what

419

was happening, she made me promise to keep you safe. I tried.'

★ ★ ★

Wet-faced and wavering from Don's candour, Beth excuses herself, needing space. She heads inside the house, needing to splash her face with water in the bathroom at the end of the hallway. As she passes the mint-green room, she slips inside. The meaning behind Irene's poem is now painfully clear, the last line finally making sense: *Under the lovely linden tree.*

Rushing back to the veranda, she grabs the phone out of her handbag on the table where Don has placed two glasses of water.

'Something that can't wait?' he asks.

'*The linden tree.*' Beth reads directly from the internet search results. '*Asymmetrically stunning and deciduous. The healing properties found within its bark, and the heart-shaped leaves and white flowers in summer, makes this ornamental tree one of the most beautiful and . . . and admired.*' She sniffs and looks up from the phone to Don. 'The tree reference in this map. It's a linden tree. Right? Irene's baby is buried underneath. But you already know that, Don. You planted the tree.'

The tiniest nod, a blink of recognition, a moment of silence.

'Let's walk,' he says, moving before Beth can object.

Without his foot brace, traversing the veranda is slow, his gait exaggerated. He manages the stairs at the back of the house one at a time, and when on the stone path, cracked and weed-infested, Beth instinctively moves to Don's left side, prepared to support his good arm. The lanky man looks down with the smile of a proud father, until the path steepens and he stops.

'Do you remember the rocking horse, Elizabeth?'

Beth's gaze follows his fmger to the coral tree. 'I think maybe I do.'

'Go,' he prompts. 'Take a look. I don't do well without a path these days.'

Beth does as she's told and stands amid the mini-farm's weather-beaten workmanship contemplating what she's learned. Who does the truth make her? If not Elizabeth Fallone, who is she? As for what she can do next, that answer is not a difficult one. Don can show her the spot in the cemetery, and finally a mother can be with the baby she'd carried, lost, and never forgotten. Then, in the same way Irene needs reuniting with her baby, Beth needs to connect with Lissy.

'I recognise that look,' Don says when Beth returns to him. 'The look of a woman who's decided and won't be stopped.'

'You saw the same in my mum? In Lissy?' she clarifies.

His smile is answer enough, but it fades. 'And in Irene the morning she left Dawson's Run with you. Seems I'm fated to be surrounded by strong, determined females.' Don sighs and they wander back to the veranda and to the table where they sit. This time close to each other.

'Oh, Elizabeth, how I wish you'd had the

chance to know your mother.' He leans back against the chair, his memory in the shape of a crooked smile. 'If Lissy could see you, she'd be so proud.'

'*Irene* was proud,' Beth says purposefully.

'And her love unconditional,' Don adds. 'I watched her give all she had to you in those early years. How, with a mother like Valerie, she learned to love, I'm not sure.'

'What do you know of Valerie?' Beth asks.

'Only her effect on Irene. She wasn't a loving parent.' Don pauses. 'If I'm to be entirely honest, Irene suffered abuse in all forms for years. As a result, she distrusted most people, especially adults. I nicknamed her The Quiet One, not realising all she was locking inside. Initially, motherhood terrified her — she expected to fail — but within no time she was terrified of *not* being your mother and determined to give you a better childhood. You taught her to love, Elizabeth, but she lived in fear of Lissy's family claiming you back.'

Beth's curious. 'How did she take another woman's baby and it be legal? I've seen my birth certificate.'

'Gypsy let it be so, and the local doctor had the authority to register births and deaths and adoptions accordingly.'

'He fiddled the books?' Beth asks.

'Doc could seal the truth using the closed adoption laws of the day. The parents had requested Lissy's body be returned to the place of her birth for burial and the baby rehomed.'

'Rehomed?' Beth's voice almost fails her.

'They acknowledged their daughter's death while disowning her flesh and blood?'

Don nods. 'Lissy's father was a domineering husband, and the man mistakenly put his community standing and reputation before everything. Having Lissy's sister raise you as her own was a solution he'd agreed to *only* while Lissy was alive.'

'And her death meant they no longer needed to acknowledge her illegitimate child.' Beth's voice hardens. 'They could wash the stain away and pretend I never existed. My God!' She reaches out to take Don's hand and somehow finds a smile. 'Sounds like your decision to keep me was best after all. They don't sound much like family to me.'

'Hear me out, Elizabeth,' Don says. 'If I'm to tell the whole truth, there was another option. A couple who wanted to adopt. Reverend Lindeman knew them. Good people, apparently.'

Beth baulks, sits back. 'Maggie's dad was in on this?'

'When needed, he would support Dandelion House by finding loving homes for unwanted babies, while Doc completed the official records. But in your case, Doc had already informed Lissy's parents of their granddaughter's birth. That complicated things.'

'Complicated how?'

'What had transpired meant he could officially register only one birth — yours to Irene. At the same time he verbally advised Lissy's father you were, as requested, in loving care, your adoption details sealed. We had to cover our tracks.'

423

'I see,' Beth says, watching shame lick his cheeks ruddy.

'We removed all existence of Irene's baby, and Gypsy buried her in Calingarry Crossing cemetery. From then on, Irene and I were your family.'

My family. Beth lets the words tumble around her head. She's designed her whole life around one parent, one mother. Irene had been Beth's moral compass. She'd taught her right from wrong and supported every decision, encouraging her to chase her dreams. How might those choices have been different under the guidance of her real mother had Lissy lived and married Don? What would life have looked like in a small country town that didn't support the arts? What would Beth be, if not a performer?

With the endless scenarios both exhausting and unsettling, Beth's thoughts rewind to the day she met Don. He'd picked her straightaway. He'd called her Lissy. Did she look like her mother? Or had he seen Little Lissy, who he'd guided through those formative years? If only Beth could remember *him*.

'Dear Elizabeth.' Don leans forward to hold her hands. 'What happened with Lissy and Irene, the way it happened, affected everyone associated with Dandelion House. Irene's baby wasn't the first loss, but the place thrived on more happy endings than tragic ones. It was never again a facility for unmarried mothers. Gypsy closed the doors after your birth and eventually withdrew. Assumptions were made, and poor Cheryl suffered. Not that anyone in town knew the facts.'

Beth's eyes bug open. 'Cheryl? The same woman who volunteers at Dandelion House? I met her only yesterday. She's lovely.'

'She is indeed.' Don smiles, his hand tightening. 'And you met forty years ago. Cheryl helped deliver you.'

'Oh!' Beth lets out a small laugh. 'Well, I guess that explains a few things about our meeting.' She stares hard at Don. 'You said Cheryl suffered. How?'

'If anyone in town knew what went on behind closed doors, they never said. Such was the power of the Bailey name. I wanted her to leave Jack, but she remained loyal, coping the only way she could. She came out the other side — with a little help.'

'Why stay?'

'There were lots of reasons. Times were different back then and walking away was harder for women,' Don tells her. 'Mostly she stayed out of love for her daughter, Amber. Family was everything to Cheryl. Still is.'

'And my real family never looked for me?'

Don releases her hands, sits back and says, 'Once. You were around three years old. A letter arrived at Dandelion House. It was after Lissy's father died. But, please know this,' he says, pleadingly. 'Irene and I always intended telling you the truth once you were old enough to understand.' Don reaches for the water, sips twice. 'But Doc's visit, and the letter from Lissy's mother, was a reminder of the risk. A risk we brought about by asking him and Gypsy to play God on paper. The arrangement was a lie.'

'What did Doc tell you my family wanted?' Beth asks.

'I recall the occasion almost verbatim. He'd stood ashen-faced on this veranda and told Irene that Lissy's mother and sister wanted to connect. I recall he reassured us then, but I still asked him outright, for Irene's sake: 'Can they take her from us?'

Doc said he planned to write back and explain the law prevented adoption details being shared and to reassure them the child was in a safe and loving environment. In addition, he would tell them the adoptive parents had been advised of the biological grandmother's wish to connect, but any decision regarding contact remained with them.

'After the visit, Irene's distrust of people worsened,' Don adds. 'Even though I reminded her she was listed as the biological mother, she'd convinced herself they could prove she'd lied and God would again see her punished, just as he'd punished her baby. For two years, she grew suspicious of everyone, even me. I blamed myself for her leaving. I thought I'd driven her away from Dawson's Run, but all those years it was the worry of losing you.'

Beth holds up a hand to pause Don, to let his words sink in. 'So, when Irene took me, why didn't you go after her?'

'The day she left, this happened to me. Even after all the surgeries and rehab, what use would I have been? I was half a man who could barely feed himself. How would I protect you? In addition to that, my accident made the news, and Lissy's family lived not so far away from here that a farming accident of such significance would not have reached them. Questions might be asked about a wife who ran off with a child, and I couldn't draw attention to Irene. I chose instead to let you both go. But I mourned your loss every day, Elizabeth, like any parent would, and it was a grief so profound and lasting. I never gave up hope. I got on with the life I'd been handed, and I stayed busy and focused on doing what I could to help my brother.'

'Tom told me about Michael,' Beth says.

'Yes, poor Mike. My accident was the last straw. I think he knew, if he'd let me stay and work things out that morning when he arrived and saw Irene packing . . . ' Don lets the sentence dwindle and he shrugs. 'No matter. What is, is. Mike asked me to keep an eye on young Tom, and Wendy didn't argue the toss. I'm glad she took off. That boy deserved better and he sure as heck helped fill the void in my life. But nothing stopped me wishing you back to me, my beautiful Little Lissy.' Don smiles. 'And here you are. I'm being selfish but . . . I'm glad you know. No more lies.'

Beth leans forward and clasps Don's hands between hers. Raising them to her lips, she whispers, 'Thank you.' For what, she's not sure.

For a long time they sit and stare at each other's red and watery eyes, until Beth asks Don, 'Assuming Lissy still has family, will you help me find them?' She waits for him to nod. The movement is small, unconvincing and not encouraging. 'Lissy's full name might be a good start,' she says, hopeful.

'I'm sorry, Elizabeth, I was never privy to any letters or documentation, and Gypsy had a first-name-only policy. Some girls didn't even use their real name,' Don explains. 'Gypsy reckoned anonymity protected the girls and their families. Doc kept names in a journal, but he's long gone. If Lissy did mention her last name to me, and I'm sure she would've, it's been forty years. They were different times — simpler — and I'm afraid my only interest in names was making hers Mrs Dawson.' He pauses, his gaze shifting. It seems he's genuinely trying to recall. 'I'm sure I would've asked all the regular questions had our relationship been a conventional one. As it was, we had so much to learn about each other in such a short time and some details weren't important. I know she carved the letters L and A in the trunk of a willow tree very early on in her stay. She claimed her initials were a sign she was destined for Hollywood.' Don smiled. 'Lissy danced to her own tune in more ways than one, but her voice was incredible — powerful, but angelic.'

'Really?' A half laugh, half sob escapes from Beth's lips. 'What sort of songs did she sing?'

'Lissy loved all sorts of music — everything from Motown to musicals. She loved Judy Garland, and on trips into town she'd sing *We're Off to See the Wizard* and *Somewhere Over the Rainbow*.' Don looks skyward as if hoping to see one. 'I'm sorry, Beth, this isn't helpful.'

'Oh, but it is, Don.' He'd given her something she didn't know she needed. A tiny piece of the puzzle; the reason a tone-deaf Irene had paid for singing and dance lessons they couldn't afford.

'Despite her father insisting on the name Monica, Lissy used her name — short for Elisabetta,' Don adds. 'It's why Irene called you Elizabeth, to honour your birth mother. The vineyard was near Stanthorpe and Lissy had a sister who went to Italy to marry.' Don turns serious. 'Of course, I'll do everything I can to help. I'll ask Cheryl what she remembers and let her know the time has come.'

'The time?' Beth quizzes. 'What time?'

Don looks at the floor before meeting Beth's gaze. 'She and I are the only ones still alive to face the legal consequences, once the truth is out.'

'Oh, I see.' Beth fidgets in her seat, unsure what to say or do or think. Maybe the news hasn't properly sunk in. Or perhaps it's too much to digest on top of everything else. 'I have lot to process, Don.'

'You do, yes. Forgiveness is also a process. I once heard Irene say that in relation to her mother.'

'And Mum always was right.' Beth smiles, knowing there will be a time to find forgiveness. 'Irene loved a lecture. She used to tell me to get my priorities right. That's what I need to do now. Stanthorpe's in Queensland, isn't it?' she asks Don while launching her phone's map app.

With the town only two hours from Calingarry Crossing and nine hours from Sydney, the decision is made for her. Another quick search locates Stanthorpe Cemetery and Beth activates the audible driving directions before grabbing her handbag.

Don stands with her. 'You're going now?'

'If they took Lissy home, she'll be buried in a cemetery there. I can't be this close and not go to her. It's my first step while I figure out the rest. If I leave now, I'll be at the cemetery before dark. Will you come with me, Don?'

With an almost violent shake of his head he says, 'Lissy's always been right here.' He presses one of Beth's hands to his chest where his heart beats. 'And while her memory has been a great source of comfort for me these last forty years, another woman deserves my loyalty. If I was to visit any grave and say anything, it would be to Irene to tell her how amazing she is, and to say thank you for being a wonderful mother and doing such an amazing job.'

There's an awkward few seconds before Beth pecks his cheek. 'You'll get that chance with Irene, Don. I promise. Right now I have to find Lissy. You understand, don't you? She . . . She was my mum.' Beth doesn't bother wiping away the fresh bout of tears. 'Please tell Tom goodbye for me.'

'Will you wait a minute?' Don asks, already headed into the house. 'I need to do something before I see you off.'

His urgency has Beth worried. Is he planning to call his nephew? Tom could be as close as the main homestead.

Keen to avoid another confrontation, where he insists she not drive into the night, Beth starts towards the car. By the time Don has caught up

430

she's already in the driver's seat.

'I'm sorry.' Guilt makes her grimace. 'I really need to make a start.'

'I want you to have this. Take it. It's yours.'

When he tosses a plastic shopping bag across the steering wheel and onto the passenger seat, something red, black and furry partially falls out. Beth's tempted to investigate, but every second she delays is a second of safe driving conditions lost.

'I'm returning something precious to its original owner,' Don explains. 'And I want to give you this. Open your hand.' He lets a silver necklace drop into Beth's palm. 'It was Lissy's pendant, but Irene refused to let you wear a religious medallion. I was keeping it safe until you were older. It's yours now.' He curls her fingers tight around the keepsake. 'There's a ladybug keyring in the bag as well. Lissy won the prize at our annual fair. What a day!' The memory ignites a spark in his eyes. 'One of the most memorable of my life. As is today, dear Elizabeth, for very different reasons. Drive safely.' With a tap on the roof he adds, 'And thank you for coming to me, for giving me the opportunity. I've wanted this more than you'll ever know. Go do what you need to do.'

As her car rattles over the gravel and corrugations, and Don's lanky frame grows smaller in the rear-view mirror, Beth tastes new tears at the corners of her mouth. On the passenger seat, a limp ladybug toy — red with fluffy black spots — shakes its way out of the plastic shopping bag to prompt a memory.

Through the dusty plume at the rear of Beth's car comes the crystal-clear image. She's a young girl, screaming for her beloved Buggy-boo abandoned on the ground, and crying out for the man she'd called Dadda.

Beth slams her foot on the brake, fumbling with the blasted seatbelt until she's free of the car and running towards her dadda's out-stretched arm. She wraps both her arms around his shoulders and he hugs back so tight Beth can barely breathe.

'I'm sorry for leaving you then,' she cries. 'And I'm sorry for going now. Please understand, Don, I have to do this. But I'll see you again. I promise you haven't lost me this time.'

40

Beth takes a break from driving to beg the owner of the closing cafe in Tenterfield for a takeaway coffee, and to stock up on paper serviettes. The wad of rough tissue paper on a nose rubbed raw has made her long for Tom and his soft cotton handkerchiefs. In the car, she tries playing music and belting out tunes, but with every kilometre to click over, a different emotion consumes her. Howling one minute, the next she's throttling the steering wheel and screaming obscenities at the road.

Other times, she feels numb and assumes it's the same sort of shock that's supposed to protect the grieving, to prevent them from being overwhelmed by every emotion, all at once. At one point Beth checks the rear-view mirror and sees a smile. *A smile?* She touches a hand to her lips as if not quite believing her eyes. What part of Don's life-altering disclosure is smile-worthy? And yet there it is, looking back at her from the mirror.

★ ★ ★

At the Stanthorpe cemetery, with no Queensland-based results from her *Aussie Graves Online* name search, Beth's only option is exploring the array of headstones on foot, hoping there's only one Elisabetta. The question is, what does she do

433

if she finds her? Sit for an hour, two hours, three? How much time can make up for forty lost years with the woman who had carried her for nine months? Should Beth have brought flowers? What kind had her birth mother liked? Irene considered fresh flowers a waste.

After an hour squinting at faint inscriptions in the fuzzy haze of last light, Beth drops to her haunches, mentally and physically spent. About to abandon her search for the day, she notices a tiny grave to her left has a pair of knitted booties and several toys, including a small, weather-beaten teddy folded over on itself. Unkempt, the offerings greying, Beth stops to reposition the toys and straighten the stuffed bear.

'You're not forgotten, little one, and you're not alone,' she whispers. 'Find Grace and say hello from me.' As she steps back, eyes stinging from the cold, an icy chill reaches her bones through the thin shirt that has Beth craving warmth, alcohol and a comfy bed.

Preferring a room with an en suite to a pub stay, she heads south with Tenterfield in mind. Passing through Ballandean, some twenty kilometres from the border into New South Wales, a flash of grey bounds in front of the car's headlights, forcing Beth to steer onto the verge. As her ears echo with the mechanic's dire warning about big bucks colliding with small cars, she finds herself in a stare-off with an enormous kangaroo.

'Not another one. You stupid, stupid animal. Don't you know who I am? Beth Fallone, roo killer!' Not even a flash of high beam and a toot of her horn shifts the animal. 'What do you want?' she screams. '*Argh!*'

Muttering a few more profanities and checking all's clear over her shoulder, Beth shoves the car in reverse gear to steer around the mulish marsupial. Her initial manoeuvre puts a signpost in the path of her headlights, the reflective arrows pointing in all directions to a dozen wineries. Estate names are faded, a few taped over to indicate they are no longer open to the public, but one is a B&B sign. To the right is a larger signboard with the same B&B inviting weary and wine-soaked travellers to: 'Take a break, enjoy a bite, recover in a comfortable bed'.

Perfect. Beth is weary, and with luck they'll sell her a bucket of recovery wine to take to bed. She can stay the night and return to the cemetery in the morning.

'Good idea. Thanks,' she says, scanning the darkness. But the kangaroo is gone.

★　★　★

The strobe effect of moonlight through the avenue of towering pencil pines plays havoc with Beth's headache. At the end of the long driveway is a floodlit courtyard with a fountain and a choc-a-block car park to one side. The place looks busy. Hopeful of a vacancy, she grabs her bag from the passenger seat and gets out.

'Hello!' A woman approaches. She's small, but spritely for her age and squinting over half glasses to avoid the glare of the fountain's floodlight.

'Sorry to arrive in the dark,' Beth says. 'I was hoping you'd have a vacancy.'

'Of course. Follow me to reception. Until our new paving is in place we must use the old cellar-door entrance.'

Beth keeps up as the woman ducks through a small opening in a larger roller door. The pungent, fruity smell is immediately nauseating and the blackness disorienting, until her vision adjusts and a wall of wine barrels stacked four high come into focus. One and a straw will do, she tells herself while following the woman right, then left, then right again. Beth wants to worry for the old lady negotiating the warren, stepping up, around and under obstacles, but it's obvious she's walked this path many times before.

When they emerge from the dim passageway, stepping into a room with wall-to-wall glass, a gust of garlic coming from the kitchen reminds Beth she hasn't eaten all day. Ordinarily, she would enjoy a nice pasta dish for dinner, but with life far from normal, she'll settle for a bag of crisps and a drink in her room.

'I've got this, Nonna. Hello and welcome to Armenti's. You'd like a room?'

'Yes, please,' Beth says, slipping the credit card from inside her phone cover. 'Just for one. Just me.'

The tall, thin woman wearing all black, a knot of blonde hair on top of her head, walks Beth the short distance to a reception desk where she processes the credit card before handing over a key and a map.

'Do you have bags?' the woman asks. 'We have

a golf cart. I can drive you and your luggage to the lodge.'

'I packed light,' Beth says. Unless the girl's referring to emotional baggage, in which case she'll be requiring a forklift. 'And the walk will do me good,' she adds.

'Follow the blue-lit bollards to the lodge.' Beth is told. 'And no need to book for dinner. Menu details are on a board in the common area. Come on up any time before eight.'

Locating the lodge was not difficult. After dropping her bag, Beth splashes her face with water, sprays a liberal amount of perfume, and throws on the first warm top she puts her hands on before heading back up to the restaurant. A quick bite before bed.

* * *

'Welcome!' The face smiling at Beth is definitely related — older than the one that checked her in, but not as aged as the woman who guided her through the labyrinth. 'A table for one?'

'Yes, I am alone.'

The woman's smile fades and Beth realises she is again on the verge of tears.

'Oh my gosh!' She swipes at her cheeks. 'Sorry. The ravioli special would be great. And a giant glass of wine will also help. It's been a big day, week, month, year.'

The woman offers a kind smile. 'I'll pop you at a table at the back and bring you a drink, but you might like to use the bathroom first. The door is behind you.' She touches Beth's shoulder, fingering the sweater's exposed seam. 'You're all inside out and back to front.'

'Oh,' Beth kind of chuckles — the sound strange, even to her, 'you have no idea.'

★ ★ ★

After eating too much, drinking too fast and still too wired to go to her room, she's up and examining the wall with its gallery of pictures depicting early winemaking processes and workers.

'Ah, the all-important pictorial history,' a voice says behind Beth. She turns to see the middle-aged woman who'd served her earlier. 'Every family vineyard has at least one brag wall. This is mine. I am Rosa.'

'I'm Beth,' she replies. 'You own this place, Rosa?'

'Yes. This is me, here, in Italy on my wedding day.' She points to the small metal plate pinned to the frame and engraved with the names *Rosa and Marco*. 'Forty-two years ago, in Valle d'Aosta — Italy's northern alps.'

Beth wonders if that might explain the fair complexion. 'You must feel quite at home here. I think someone forget to tell Stanthorpe it's not winter yet.'

Raucous laughter coming from the banquet table on the closed-in deck takes Rosa's attention. 'I apologise for the noise. My daughter, Connie, has come home to help with the vintage and she's catching up with friends for a belated thirtieth.'

'She doesn't live here with you?' Beth asks.

'No, her dream from the time she could walk was to dance,' Rosa says. 'I wished she'd been interested in the business, but it is more important a woman makes her own decisions. I grew to learn this too late in life,' she says with some melancholy. 'Only the good history should repeat itself, yes?'

'You'd like to hand over to the next generation?' Beth asks.

'Of course, I get weary, but I am my own boss.' Rosa smiles, then shrugs. 'I have no plans to leave here, but I hope my grandchildren will one day take over.'

Walking away would be difficult, Beth thinks. The vistas are spectacular from every window. Sunrise and sunset must be incredible. 'But surely, Rosa, you have places you want to visit, things to do and . . . Argh, sorry!' she gushes. 'Your choices are none of my business. It's just . . . I grew up with a single mum who gave her good years to putting family — me — first, which meant she found love too late.'

'Of course, mothers make such sacrifices. Italian ones remind their children daily.' Rosa's laugh fades quickly as she moves to the next photo. 'Connie wanted to follow in her great-grandmother's footsteps. This is her.' A mostly sepia photograph shows a serenely beautiful woman with lips and cheeks tinged red to match the embellishment in her hair. 'My grandmother was a prima ballerina in the *Corpo di ballo del Teatro alla Scala*.'

Beth is familiar with Milano's La Scala Ballet theatre — the oldest and most renowned dance company in the world. 'Would you liked to have danced also, Rosa?'

'Me?' Her head shakes. 'My father was, how do you say . . . ? Not very progressive. After my brother died very young, the responsibility fell on me to produce male heirs. I was given to the third son of a family known to my grandparents. They lived in the same village. Marco was older, but he knew the wine business and was well-off. Sadly, I never grew to love him as both families had hoped.'

Beth is shocked at the thought of someone being forced into an arranged marriage but says nothing.

'Tradition,' Rosa explains anyway, 'and an old-fashioned father, although I'm sure I should not be boring you with my family stories.'

'Actually, someone else's family story is exactly what I need,' Beth says. 'Drinking alone isn't fun and I do intend drinking more tonight. The wine is lovely and I may have mentioned it's been a difficult time. Your family story is a nice distraction from mine.'

Rosa scans the empty dining area exaggeratedly. 'You are my only paying guest and to be honest, as much as I love having Connie home, she and her friends do make me feel old. I would enjoy talking with someone a little closer to my era.'

'Good,' Beth says, her attention back on the gallery. 'Maybe tell me about this chap. Such a happy face.'

Rosa shares a memory of her brother, before shifting to the cordoned-off winemaking memorabilia on display in one corner.

'You were the only girl, Rosa?'

The woman hesitates. 'No, not always. Let me get us *both* more wine, eh?'

Beth nods, then occupies herself studying the relics on display and the feature wall filled with memories.

When Rosa returns, she shares more tales about the vineyard: the crippling early picking and pruning processes, the shifts in industry trends over the decades, and the quality varietals that make Ballendean's cool-climate wines so unique. While the pair enjoy another very smooth wine, their conversation doesn't touch on the matter of siblings again.

★ ★ ★

The birthday gathering is dwindling, with the last of the hangers-on in a huddle of hugs and kisses. Before long, the birthday girl with the duck-like dancer's gait glides across the room: upright carriage, extended neck and carefully turned-out feet. Years of plies and sweat at the barre are rarely left behind when a ballerina leaves the dance studio or stage.

'Great night, Mama, you're the best.' While Rosa wraps an arm around her daughter's waist, Connie kind of hangs off her mother's shoulder, grinning a little drunkenly at Beth. 'Hi, I'm Connie. I checked you in. Hope we weren't too rowdy.'

'Birthdays are meant to be noisy,' Beth says, raising her empty glass. 'Many happy returns.'

'I'll get more wine and toast with you. I

441

opened a bottle before everyone bailed on me. Even Nonna nicked off early.'

'You know Nonna enjoys her quiet time with her dessert wine in the evening.'

'Yeah, well, I have wine crying out to be drunk and the fire outside has got life in it still.'

Rosa seems uncomfortable with the idea. Beth thinks it's perfect: the fireplace, the company, and the wine. She's only had three smallish glasses. 'One more can't hurt.'

After bringing a water jug and glasses to the coffee table, Rosa sits demurely at one end of the L-shaped chaise sofa, while Connie sits cross-legged on one of several scattered ottomans, hugging a cushion to her chest. Beth's happy cradling her wine, watching the fire's flames flicker, and savouring the whole body and mind release, courtesy of the warming red. As the trio chat, Beth learns the property is no longer a working winery. Corporate conferences and special events are more profitable, with the small amount of grapes grown under contract to a well-known label.

'Such is the quality and reputation of Armenti's grapes and processes,' Connie explains. 'Workers harvest the grapes and we feed the workers, because one thing is for sure, those pickers know how to have a good time after a hard day among the vines. When they're done, they appreciate Mama's homemade treats. Harvest used to be my favourite time of year. Not my nonna's,' she adds with a finger-wag. 'No, no, no! Nonna avoids pickers like the plague, tolerating 'those terrible transients' and casting all pickers as black-hearted womanisers that we are to 'feed, *but to never fall for*'. Right, Mama?'

Though Rosa has fallen quiet, the snippets of conversation Beth has harvested so far confirms life on the family vineyard hasn't been as romantic as it sounds, and Rosa chose single motherhood when the man she married turned out too similar to her father.

'Dad *and* granddad hid their abuse under the word 'tradition',' Connie announces with more wild air quotes. 'Bloody bullies is what they were. They wouldn't get away with treating their wives like that these days.'

'Remember, Constance,' Rosa says, 'we would not be here and so fortunate if not for those who worked the vineyard before us.'

Connie scoffs. 'Fortunate?' Her face pinches and she waggles another warning finger at Beth. ' 'You are a fortunate woman. A visitor allowed to stay in my house, but you will do things my way — blah, blah, blah!' That was my father's — and my grandfather's — idea of 'fortunate'.' The birthday girl guzzles the dregs of another glass.

Sensing Rosa's awkwardness, Beth changes subjects, asking Connie about her dancing.

'Three kids ago I was pretty good.'

'Three? How nice.'

'Some days.' She grins. 'Better if I could talk hubby into moving back to the country, closer to Mama. I'd prefer she sell this place and come stay with us, but there's no budging her. Unfortunately, Craig likes his personal space and reckons he's allergic to grapes, which means he

443

so should not have married an Italian vintner's daughter whose family lives on wine and hugs.' Connie laughs and dangles the wine bottle mid-air. 'More?'

Rosa declines, while Beth quickly calculates a reasonable comatose state of slumber is probably two more drinks away. She drains the dregs before stretching for the bottle and resting the neck on the rim of her glass that's refusing to stay still.

'Are you married, Beth?' Connie's eyes interrogate. 'Got kids?'

'Divorced. Cheated on.' She raises her full glass in a kind of toast and glugs another mouthful. 'The marriage lasted ten years, my baby lasted ten minutes.'

Uh-oh! Did she say that out loud? Two sets of blinking eyes suggest the tell-all stage of intoxication has sneaked up on her.

'Well, bugger that!' Connie hoists herself out of the seat, heads to the birthday table and returns with another bottle.

Rosa sticks to water. Beth eyes the jug, knowing she should do the same.

'Something tells me I know you,' Connie says. 'Should I? Are you a dancer, Beth? You're built like one. Mama tells me I take after my aunt. I have her build. She wanted to be a dancer.'

Rosa slides closer to Beth, a motherly hand stroking her back. 'Connie, I think you need to slow down. Our guest need not know our entire history.'

'I'm sorry, I — ' Beth chokes out the apology.

'What is it, dear?' Rosa asks.

'I-I think it's just wonderful Connie knows who she takes after. I don't know anything. I never knew my dad and, after forty years, I don't know my mum.'

As if she hasn't already embarrassed herself enough, Beth is sobbing, her cheeks awash with tears spilling over to trickle towards her cleavage.

Rosa takes her wine, placing it on the coffee table. 'Connie, refill the water jug, please.'

'Oh, God!' Beth leans forward, lowering her head to her knees. 'As you can probably tell, my top wasn't the only thing upside down and inside out when I arrived tonight. Thank you,' she says, grateful for Rosa's soothing hand rub on her back. 'My life has turned on its head and there is no quick fix. No fixing me at all. My life is in a million pieces. I can't go back to who I was, and I don't know who I am to move forward. I'm not sure how I'm feeling, except . . . ' The only word at that moment is 'abandoned'.

When Connie returns, Beth is explaining her mother's car accident, the strange request to spread half her ashes, and twenty-one handwritten birthday cards to a child named Linden. ' . . . who I only found out about after Mum died,' she adds, sitting straight again. 'Not that Mum was my real mother, or so I was told twenty-four hours ago. I have a gazillion questions and no chance of any answers. I know she grew up on a vineyard, so I came to Stanthorpe because I believe she's buried here somewhere.'

When Rosa's back rub slows, almost to a stop, Beth turns in her direction. The woman's gaze is exploring the landscape of her face, every frown line and freckle under scrutiny.

'That's why I drove up here, thinking the least I could do is find her, but it got dark and cold and then a kangaroo appeared. The next thing . . .'

Rosa's hand drops away. 'Who told you about your mother?' she asks.

'Someone I scarcely know.' Beth shrugs drunkenly. 'And yet I believe him. It's my weakness — believing everything a man tells me. So, here I am, the guest from hell and a blubbering mess making an idiot of myself with total strangers.'

Remembering the stash of paper serviettes from her cafe stop, Beth digs a hand into her jeans pocket and pulls out the forgotten pendant at the same time. How easily she might have lost something so precious. She loops the chain over her head and lifts the medallion towards Rosa.

'I was given this today. It's all I have of my birth mother. I'm not sure of the significance because religion didn't factor into my childhood. Maybe you can tell me if the saint depicted is significant.'

As Beth holds the medallion face up, Rosa is quick to offer an explanation. 'Of course. This is one I am very familiar with. Saint Monica is 'the patroness of mothers, women suffering difficult marriages, and of those anxious for their children'. We Armenti women know her too well.' Mother and daughter share smiles and the dreary mood Beth's responsible for lifts, fleetingly.

Something's wrong. Rosa's smile is too short-lived, her pause palpable, sobering Beth. Even Connie, now perched on the other side of her mother to examine the necklace, seems concerned.

'Dear one.' Rosa looks up. 'I know this pendant.'

'Yes, Mama,' Connie says. 'Nonna has one the same.'

'Yes,' Rosa agrees. 'To replace the one she put in my sister's safekeeping four decades ago. This is the same St Monica. The engraving on the back — though worn and difficult to make out — is her name. Here.'

Connie and Beth butt heads trying to see. When Beth sits back, holding her forehead, she sees Rosa is crying silent tears.

'You say this came from your mother's possessions, Beth? Your mother who died and is buried in Stanthorpe Cemetery?'

Beth's nod is almost as indecipherable as her whimpered one-word reply. 'Why?'

'Because, dearest, there's something you need to know. Someone you need to meet.'

★ ★ ★

The kitchen lights flick off, followed by the dining room, leaving the area where the trio sits on the veranda illuminated by decorative lanterns, fairy lights strung across overhead rafters, and a dwindling fire.

'Sorry to put you in the dark, ladies,' the chef says. 'You were so quiet out here I thought everyone was gone. I'm off home. See ya!'

Home! Beth blinks away a fresh bout of happy tears.

447

'When did you know?' she asks, having found her voice after hearing Rosa's story.

The woman's smile is yet to wane. 'My heart has been telling me all night you were no stranger, but I didn't want to listen. I was too afraid of disappointment. I have looked for Elisabetta's features in so many faces, desperate to find her in one — to find *you*. And now you have found *us*. How is this possible after so long?'

'Who cares how?' Connie pipes up. 'My Aunt Lissy is your mum? That is so freaking cool.'

Rosa huffs a laugh. 'Oh, how Papa hated the name Lissy. But she'd insisted it was less *woggy* than Elisabetta. Fitting in and being Aussie had been so important to my little sister. She was all 'Mum' and 'Dad' and Vegemite.' Rosa has yet to release Beth's hands from her lap. Not that she minds. 'I came back from Italy and we tried to find you,' she continues, 'to bring you home to us, but we heard you were adopted and happy. We had no rights and no access to information back then. But now . . . Ahh, Beth, how could I not see the resemblance straightaway?'

'How come Nonna didn't see?' Connie says.

'Perhaps it is the sadness your expression carries.' Rosa wipes the pad of her thumb under Beth's eyes. One, then the other. 'Our Lissy was always such a happy girl.'

Connie's sitting forward, her earlier signs of intoxication gone. 'We have to tell Nonna.'

'We do.' Rosa stands, glancing at her wristwatch. 'And it's not too late. Benetta phones her brother in Italy this time every week.

448

Besides, I can't keep the news until morning. I won't sleep and she will never forgive me.'

'Wait, please.' Shocked sober, Beth tries standing, ignoring Connie's helping hand. The giddiness, she decides, is not from too much wine, but from too much truth, and way too fast. 'I'm sorry, Rosa, I don't mean to be rude but . . . How do I know what you're telling me is true?'

'See for yourself.' Connie says, urging Beth to follow her into the dining room. 'Show her, Mama.'

The pair direct Beth to a set of ten wall photos Rosa had not covered earlier.

'This is my Aunt Lissy.' Connie points.

The word 'Mum' forms in Beth's mouth but nothing comes. She's crying too hard for words, praying she isn't in her little lodge room already in a dream-like drunken stupor. Part of Beth wants to pull back, to pause, to look at the facts and make certain Rosa's not mistaken. Assumptions too quickly formed can end in heartache. She and Valerie are proof. Instead, Beth is blindly following Connie and Rosa through the same maze of wine barrels, back into the car park and towards a hedge hiding a small, standalone cottage, lights ablaze. Even if Beth wanted to turn back or run to her car, Rosa's hands hold hers too tightly to try.

'Come in, Rosa,' the old lady replies. 'Is something wrong?'

'No, Mama, something's finally right.'

The older woman doesn't get up. She pushes her glasses along her nose and squints through the glare of the overhead reading lamp. 'What is all this fuss that can't wait until morning? Who else have you got there? Connie? Turn on the big light and turn down the heat, dear.'

Connie does as she's told, leaving Beth exposed and in the spotlight — one she'd never imagined being in.

'See who's come home, Mama,' Rosa says. 'This is Beth.'

Beth's heart plummets when the woman's head shakes and a gnarly index finger wags back and forth, as Connie had done earlier.

'No, no, this cannot be true.'

'Please,' Beth manages, slipping the necklace over her head as she moves closer. 'Look at this. It belonged to my mother.' Beth crouches, almost falling in front of the armchair as she extends her open palm.

When the old lady's trembling finger flips the medallion over, the silence is so profound Beth's certain she can hear all four hearts beating.

When Benetta does speak, her voice is a whisper. 'How I prayed to God,' she says. 'Night and day I begged Him to return my baby girl and the child our foolishness and my weakness lost to us. And now it is you — home at last. My girls! Let me hold you.'

All three generations cling to Beth and to each other, their tears and laughter meshing together.

Connie's the first to break away from the embrace, heading for the small kitchenette. 'We need your Vin Santo stash, Nonna? We need to toast.'

Rosa pulls her daughter into line. 'It's late. We

need to let Mama rest.'

'Rest?' Benetta scoffs. 'I will not be sleeping. I do not trust myself to sleep for fear I'll wake up from the dream. How else do I believe our Elisabetta's girl is here with us?'

'I am real,' Beth says. She's back on her haunches and taking Benetta's hand in hers, pressing the palm to her cheek. 'And I've grown up with so much love,' she adds. 'I learned the truth about my birth mother — about Lissy — only recently, which makes how I found you an unbelievably short story.'

'And a long one for those of us who have been waiting a lifetime to find you,' Benetta says.

They hug again, and for a woman of her vintage, Benetta's embrace is fierce.

'You really wanted me?' Beth asks.

Benetta sits tall and puts Beth at arm's length, the old lady's bright eyes taking in every feature. 'Every beat of my heart has wished you to me,' she says. 'Had I got my way, Elisabetta would never have left home in her condition. Together, we would have found a way. Not until after my husband's death was I free to make my own decisions. I wrote to the doctor who worked with Dandelion House, explaining our situation had changed. You would have been three years old. The reply let us know you were in loving hands, so we reluctantly moved on, but we never stopped hoping to one day find you, or you us. It was for this reason Rosa endures. Despite an unhappy marriage, she did not walk away from this place.' Benetta urges her daughter to move closer and they hold hands. 'Knowing you were

451

out there gave her the strength to stay. Then she managed what I could not. Rosa stood up to her husband. Refusing to leave or sell the vineyard after he left, she changed the business into a model she could manage without a man. I am so proud.'

Beth looks up at a wet-faced Rosa.

'I'm proud of Mama, too.' Once again, Connie drapes herself around her mother's shoulders. 'She believed staying was the right thing, and that one of these days Lissy's child would know to come home to us. She waited. We've all waited, Beth.'

'And here you are,' Benetta says. 'A tiny piece of my Elisabetta. But we are to call you Beth?'

'My mum . . . ' Beth falters. 'Irene insisted on the name Elizabeth out of respect.'

'Elizabeth. How wonderful!'

'Yes, she was.' Tears Beth thought she'd run out of flow freely and without shame. 'One day I'll tell you all about her.'

'Yes, yes, you must.' Benetta smiles.

'For now I should let you sleep,' Beth suggests as the tiny Swiss Cuckoo clock on the wall chirps.

'We should do many things,' Benetta says, 'but I want to be selfish and keep you here for myself. You will have so many questions and more to learn, and Rosa will be best to share stories about your mother. She and Lissy were close before my husband sent her to Italy. So, so young and unprepared for life with a man too like her father. I found some comfort knowing Elisabetta's predicament had, in a sad way, spared her from suffering the same fate. But I wonder,' the old lady says, 'in wishing for a better life, had I wished her away from us forever?'

'You will all have questions,' Beth says, looking around the room. 'And I can tell you this. There is a man who can answer all yours about Lissy's time at Dandelion House. His name is Don Dawson, and he lives in a New South Wales town not too far from here.'

'Ah, Don,' Benetta says. 'The man who won my Elisabetta's heart. She spoke of him often over the phone. I would love to meet him and tell him thank you for loving my girl.'

'He really did.' Beth smiles. 'And I reckon he needs to meet you too, Benetta.'

41

Cliché or not, there is no better way to describe the last seven days for Beth than a rollercoaster ride. She's experienced incredible highs she never wants to end. Then, without warning, she would find herself free-falling into impossibly dark places in her mind. The breathtakingly unbelievable lows remain a struggle, with the task of understanding who she is both rousing and draining.

Still trying to grasp a future without Irene, Beth is now grieving the birth mother she will never know, with people she's never met before. Up and down, around and around. The speed with which information is being shared, and the rush of discovering how alike she and Lissy are, is pushing Beth to places in her head she's never been before. As incredible as stumbling upon Armenti's has been, Beth's quest for the truth is far from over.

A mindboggling search lies ahead, with one crucial thing to find. Herself. But how, when Beth Fallone no longer exists? That person is gone. Without Lissy as a guide, life is like a giant jigsaw without the picture on the lid to help, and with only half the pieces. How can she ever be whole again?

Why is it Beth thinks of Don at that moment? Is it because he, too, was broken and, in his words, left to live as half a man?

If there is a skerrick of silver lining in all this, it's having three generations of strong Armenti females supporting Beth, their tears and laughter meshing together over days of self-discovery. Mostly, she's been a silent observer around the raucous dinner table, or a sobbing mess in front of home movies. By day, she's devoured photo albums showing her birth mother as a teenage girl with a huge smile and a dramatic pose for the camera. How surreal to know the face captured by a lens was, for a moment in time, real. Elisabetta was real and she was Beth's mother. She might have made mistakes, but she had a life and dreams. She'd wished for love and she'd found it with Don. And she'd given birth to a healthy baby. A strong baby, Beth reminds herself when she feels overwhelmed. Even with Beth's dark hair and olive complexion — courtesy of the picker no one dared mention in front of Benetta — the resemblance to Lissy is unmistakable, which makes Beth wonder . . . How was it she never blurted the question so many attention-seeking children asked of their parents?

'Did you adopt me?'

Had she asked, how might Irene have answered? Mother and daughter might have been the centre of each other's world, but they were different in many ways. Irene had preferred lists and plans, while Beth loved improv. Their differences continue to sneak up on Beth. Things like not fitting the same way her friends fitted together with their mothers. Occasionally she had joked with

Irene about certain traits and peculiarities: Irene's skin was pasty without makeup, her hair thin and mousy when not chemically permed and teased out, while Beth's complexion was envied by those who had to spend hours in a solarium for the same result. Beth was also slim and supple like a dancer, while Irene's portly but ample proportions had appealed to Anton.

One day, while commenting on their dissimilar appearance, Irene had said, 'We don't have to be the Bobbsey Twins, Beth. My job is to be a good mother. I'm doing that.' The rebuke had sounded defensive, the term 'job' sitting uncomfortably with Beth. Even Richard had once said of his mother-in-law, 'Irene is *the* most adaptable and obliging woman. She slots herself into every role she takes on. I wish the actors I worked with were as agreeable.' Irene had been a paint-by-numbers nurturer, never deviating, everything in order, and definitely no going outside the lines. There was a time when Beth had longed to mess up the photo frames that stood in order of height, but she didn't ruffle her mum. Other than the occasional disagreement, they had lived quiet lives without conflict.

While Beth knows she'll love Irene forever, what's important as she gets to know the Armenti women, is ensuring they get to know Irene; because she was, like the coffee mug confirmed thirty years ago: BEST MUM EVER.

Whatever else Beth discovers about her birth mother, or herself — and there'll be heaps in the coming days, weeks, months — she knows her resilience and drive comes from both nurture and nature. Beth Armenti-Fallone's DNA makes her capable of anything, and she'll be needing every scrap of courage as she claws her way through the rubble in search of salvageable pieces of her past. That's after she scours the disappointment, digs through the resentment and betrayal, and finds understanding and self-acceptance amid the mire. Eventually there will be healing, but not yet.

Again she thinks about Don. Like him, Beth has a lot more falling down to do before she learns to walk into a new life. Without Irene — the best-ever *picker-upperer* — Rosa is keeping watch. It is what family does.

* * *

Showered and refreshed after a seventh night of surprisingly solid sleep, Beth's looking across the sprawling vineyard and picturing young Lissy among the vines when Rosa sidles up behind.

'I can still picture Lissy among these vines with her sheep,' she says, stopping to inspect a leaf. 'But I cannot imagine your shock, Beth. We at least knew of your existence. We spoke often of Lissy — and you. We never stopped hoping, but . . . ' Rosa shakes her head. 'I can't know how you must be feeling.'

'To be honest, I'm still reeling,' Beth says. 'I keep thinking of questions. Little things, like was Lissy a huggy person? Irene was a great mum, but our hugs were . . . Well, they never felt like I imagined hugs should feel. That's until I got to a boarding gate and, as much as she pushed me into going away, she always hung on, kind of desperate-like. It was weird. I blamed my grandmother for the lack of affection we displayed as a family.'

'Well, our Lissy definitely loved hugs.' Rosa wraps her arm around Beth's shoulder, squeezing tight. 'I can't believe we're letting you go tomorrow. There's still so much to share.'

'A break will give us all time to regroup and think up a whole batch of new questions.' Beth pats her tummy. 'Besides, I need to slow down on the pasta and wine.'

'We should head back,' Rosa says. 'The cold hits hard and fast in this part of the country, especially once the sun drops away. But before you leave us tomorrow, Beth, Benetta is insisting on an Armenti brunch. The family tradition involves friends and food and all hands-on deck. As an Armenti, you'll be required in the morning. Unless you inherited Lissy's knack for getting out of kitchen chores in favour of vineyard work.'

* * *

Beth arrives at the designated time of 9 am to find the three generations of Armenti women already at work over stovetops and work boards.

'Chop, chop!' Rosa instructs, indicating a board piled with sprigs of basil and lemon thyme.

'Drink!' Connie tells Beth as she pours Prosecco into a glass flute.

'*Saluté!*' says Benetta, as they form a circle to clink glasses.

The music selection is varied to meet with the

458

multi-generational workforce, of which Beth quickly feels an integral part, impressing Benetta with Irene's secret quick-rise bread recipe.

The grazing plate is festive-looking, every colour represented in the layers of tissue-thin prosciutto, chunks of cheese, and with small dishes containing olives, balsamic oil, pickled eggplant and beetroot. When Dean Martin's *That's Amore* plays and the quartet's voices blend in perfect harmony, Connie takes extra delight belting out the line about having had too much wine. When the song ends on a big, combined '*That's amore!*', the women all down tools to comfort a crying Beth.

* * *

Beth's stomach is full, the car bursting, and she has a second suitcase bulging with new clothes — the result of a shopping trip into Stanthorpe for the essentials needed to cover her unexpected stay. There's also the hand-me-downs from an afternoon session with her cousin, Connie. Like teenagers, they'd sorted through hangers and drawers, trying on dresses and shirts. Connie not only had a dancer's figure similar to Beth's, they had the most in common, and spent hours talking while strolling the vineyard and making plans that excited Beth in ways she would never have imagined a week ago. Sometimes, while chatting to Rosa, Beth had closed her eyes. She'd wanted to imagine Lissy. The sisters sounded apparently so alike, Benetta had admitted to doing the same many, many times. As for

Norma, she is the adoring grandmother with warm hugs that mould to Beth, who tells waggish tales, and makes yummy homemade treats.

Several Tupperware containers now sit on the back seat of Beth's car, engine idling. It's time, and her aunt is the first to step forward from the milling crowd of family and new friends, her hug intense.

'I knew you'd come home one day.'

'Thank you for waiting so I could find you, Rosa.'

'See ya soon, cuz,' Connie says with a peck to Beth's cheek and a whisper, 'Tell me as soon as you know. I can't wait to break the news to everyone.'

'Will do.' When Beth tries returning her cousin's wink, the trio laugh at her failed attempt. Yet another Lissy trait.

She turns to face Benetta. Beautiful, courageous Benetta who'd tolerated a bully for the sake of her family. Then, the second she could, she tried to find the missing piece that would complete their lives.

'I can't believe I have an actual Norma.' Beth smiles. 'I'll be back for more hugs soon, Benetta. We have so much more to share.'

'Next time you must show us your photos, and maybe you have a box of special pieces to bring. Things to help us get to know Irene.'

Beth beams. 'When we have more time. I have a whole box of Mum's things to show you. Thank you.'

The pair reaches the driver's door and as Beth climbs in, Benetta reaches for the ignition, fondling the small black and red ladybug charm on the keyring.

'Oh, that,' Beth comments. 'I'm told it was Lissy's. Not quite as significant as Saint Monica.'

'Or perhaps it is,' Benetta says, seriously. 'In Italy, the ladybug has the nickname *commaruccia*, which translates to 'little midwives' because it's said the ladybug brings children.'

If only it was so easy, Beth thinks. Instead, she blows Benetta a kiss out the window and says, 'I guess it has. It brought me to you.' Blowing another kiss out the window, she waves and shouts, 'Love you all.'

★ ★ ★

An hour down the road, after pulling herself together, Beth makes a phone call.

'Eunice, it's me.'

'You sound spritely. Thought you'd dropped off the face of the earth, honey. How's tricks?'

'Complicated,' says Beth. 'I'm calling to let you know I'll be back in Sydney, but not for long, so until further notice, hold off on finding me work.'

Eunice doesn't ask for details. She's an agent who doesn't get any more involved with her clients than she needs to.

'Before you go, honey, I had a call from a fellow very eager to get in touch with you. It was last week. Sorry, you know it's a crazy time of year. His name is . . . Hang on, I have it somewhere.' There's a shuffling-paper sound, the occasional profanity, and a thud. 'Right, here we

461

go. Tom Dawson. When he told me it was personal, but he didn't have your number, well, I thought he sounded kind of dodgy. I said I'd shoot you a message. I'll send it now. Take care, honey, and keep in touch.'

Within seconds of her hanging up, a message beeps.

So, who is Tom Dawson? Delish or dodgy?

42

Dawson's Run, One Week Later

Tom is tired. Tired of checking for text messages that never come, and tired of calling by the cemetery so often the local clergyman stopped him in the street one day to comment on his regular attendance.

'I thought only ghosts haunted graveyards, mate,' he'd said.

The same clergyman — progressive and passionate about growing the one remaining Uniting Church — had whistled his way into town a year ago. While Tom warmed to the bloke and his quirky approach to preaching, not all his parishioners considered Monty Python's *Always Look on the Bright Side of Life* an appropriate song choice. But they also know they're lucky to still have a church. Many in towns elsewhere, of all denomination, are being sold to help fund The National Redress Scheme for victims of child sexual abuse. Not that any such scandal had touched Calingarry Crossing.

Every time Tom passes the *For Sale* sign on the old church he wonders what might become of the historic building. What could reasonably stand in its place that would be good for the community?

'What do you reckon, Wally?' He pats the dog sitting in the passenger seat. 'I love you, mate, but that face is a sorry substitute for Beth's. And we really need to do something about your farting and your breath because we're stuck with each other, mate. Come on, let's go home.'

Arriving at Dawon's Run, prepared to attack the stack of jobs he's let pile up, Tom finds his uncle at the computer doing a task he had neglected.

'What's with the long faces?' Don asks, looking from Tom to Wally and back to Tom. 'I'll make us a cuppa, eh?'

★ ★ ★

After sprinkling liver treats at his feet for both dogs, Don shifts the plate of fruitcake out of the sun and comments on the decades of wear and tear. 'Could do with a new coat of lacquer.'

Tom scoffs. 'If only protecting a human heart was as easy.'

Don observes his nephew's hunched and disheartened appearance. Like a petulant child, he's currently finger-drawing the shape of infinity in the dusty surface, over and over.

'Patience, Tom. The girl's got things to work out.'

He tantrum taps the table. 'Yeah, well, I'm bloody not waiting until I'm a distant memory. I've already contacted her agent, but I'm prepared to go to Sydney and camp in her waiting room for as long as it takes to find Beth.'

'You won't find her in Sydney,' Don says.

'Really?' Tom's huff is heavy with sarcasm. 'Well, if you know so bloody much, Uncle Don, where the hell *will* I find her?'

Despite his efforts not to, Don smiles. 'Behind you. If I'm not mistaken, her car is heading up our access road.'

★   ★   ★

Tom whizzes around, squinting into the sun now low on the horizon. When he turns back towards Don, his uncle is heading inside, the screen door slamming shut.

'Tom! Tom, I met them.' Beth's out of the car and running before his brain can confirm if she's real. 'I have a family.'

He's barely made it down the veranda steps when Beth leaps into his arms, her legs wrapping around his hips. He's spinning — at least his head is. How could he have missed the woman this much? They kiss — multiple, quick and random pecks to each other's lips, cheeks and forehead — until Beth jumps down and pulls away, excitement firing from every perfect pore on her body.

'I have stacks to tell you, Tom. And I have photos. Where's Don?' Concern edges her voice. 'Is he all right? Is he here?'

'I think he's giving us space to say hello.' Tom holds her at arms-length, giving her the once-over. 'So, hello! I'm so glad to see you.'

★   ★   ★

Beth can't stay still. She springs onto her toes and cups Tom's face. 'Hello, yourself.' She kisses him on the mouth, soft but brief. There's too much to say. 'I'm sorry it took Eunice so long to pass on your number. I should have called you when I got to Sydney, but there was so much to figure out. I also wanted to see you and tell you.'

'Tell me what, Beth?'

She beams. 'Everything, but most importantly, I am definitely not running away. I'm running to something because it feels right. *You* feel right, Tom Dawson.' The other news, she won't know herself for a few weeks. 'And I can tell you this,' she adds. 'I am so lucky to have had two mothers. They were so different, yet so alike. Both had their rights stripped and their freedom to choose denied by unfair laws, and by their own families. It's because of Irene and Lissy, and so many like them, I get to choose my destiny. And so . . . ' She stiffens and lifts the determined chin Benetta said was Lissy's. 'As of now, Tom Dawson, I'm taking control and making changes. No amount of resentment will alter the past, but I can take charge of my future.'

'Sounds like a big job.' Tom grins. It's the same one Beth fell in love with that first night in the pub. 'Sure hope you can squeeze a cuppa in at the same time. Come on,' he says.

'I do have a big decision, that's true,' she says, stopping before the veranda. 'Two big ones, actually. In a few weeks there may be more. Told you I've got a lot to think about.'

'Do I factor into one of those?' he asks. 'And when are you going to let me in on them?'

'You do, and as soon as I can,' she says. 'As soon as I work out who I am. I've played so many roles. It's time I stopped and played me. I may never know everything, but I do know Irene's map was my way back to the past. All I need now is a map to help find my future.' She props on the first step, turning to look down at Tom. 'And a big, strong, map-reading man to read it for me. What do you reckon?'

43

Four Months Later

Beth has returned to Stanthorpe several times, finally visiting the cemetery where, four decades earlier, Elisabetta Armenti's body had been laid to rest with barely an inscription. Aldo Armenti had snatched the spirited girl who was at home with dirt beneath her feet — who was choosing a life in the country and love over duty — and elaborately entombed her.

In contrast to Stanthorpe's manicured lawns and gardens, is the bare earth and broken headstones in the corner of Calingarry Crossing's dilapidated cemetery. At least, it was rundown until the working bee. What immense joy Beth had derived from watching the team comprising Tom, Don, and Will boss each other around. *Poor Tom!* Beth chuckles at the memory.

While dozens of townsfolk had pitched in, it was Cheryl's persistence that saw a full military service for the returned remains of a *Fromelles* soldier. As well as the local lad, the ceremony acknowledged all who had lost their lives to war and were yet to find their way home. It was quite a sight for Calingarry Crossing with not a dry eye as multiple generations of the soldier's family stepped forward, forming a circle of linked hands.

★ ★ ★

With the importance of family and connection on Beth's mind, she slips out from under the covers before sunrise — out of a bed, a room, and a house that's starting to feel a lot like home. She grabs her phone, clicks the *Message* icon and attaches the ultrasound image before tapping out the news: *Dear Eunice. Found a role. Busy for the next 18 years — at least!*

In the bathroom, she stands side-on to the mirror, the shirt tail pinned under her chin, her hands emphasising her belly.

'I guess, little one, if a condom couldn't stop you from becoming you, you're going to make it into the world and be strong. Besides,' she says, 'there are too many people waiting to say hello. They are family, and we are loved.'

44

Under the Linden Tree

'Good morning!' She's surprised and a tad curious to find Don polishing a newly set headstone in the furthest corner of the cemetery. 'Looks like we both wet the bed. What's all this about?'

'Tom helped me,' he explains. 'It's for Irene's baby. Better late than never.'

'But the grave has stayed unmarked for so many years, Don. Why now?'

He drops the cloth in a bucket by his feet. 'When I offered forty years ago, Irene told me she considered headstones morbid reminders.' He huffs. 'I admit, not a great start for a relationship, given I was a monumental stonemason. Of course, there was more to it.' His gaze drops to the headstone. 'Now Irene is at peace, the truth out, I can do this. Every baby, no matter its age or circumstances, deserves to be recognised and immortalised. They need a respectful farewell.'

'Mothers as well,' Beth says, holding out the purple gift bag. 'I think I've run out of excuses.'

Don looks up, nods. 'I'll give you some privacy.'

'No, please, I want you to stay. Let's do this together. But first, let me see your work.'

On the ground, shaded by thick limbs bearing heart-shaped leaves, is a marble headstone with the words to Irene's poem: *Under The Linden Tree*.

Beth tears up. 'Oh, wow! That's perfect, Don.'

'Not perfect, and I might have been a better stonemason before my accident, but a promise is a promise. I did have help from a certain nephew who has picked up a few of my talents and better traits over the years.'

'Tom has a lot of your good traits, Don, and it's a beautiful epitaph.'

Beth no longer hurts, knowing the rhyme recited to her each night while Irene tucked the bedsheets snug as a bug, had been a grieving mother's homage to a lost child.

'I made a plaque for Lissy,' Don says. 'As a centrepiece to the fragrant memorial garden I'm planning. Yellow daisies and freesias. I know she'd like it, but I'm unsure how to approach the subject with Benetta.'

'Oh, Don, you one hundred percent don't have to worry. Getting to know you is bringing Benetta and Rosa that all-important closure. They'd wanted so much more for Lissy. Benetta said she could never bring herself to visit the Stanthorpe grave. Your gesture will mean the world to her.'

'And about your closure?' Don nods at the purple gift bag. 'Shall we do it together?'

'Together.' Beth nods. 'Always.'

Even with only one working arm, Don's return hug is tight — desperately tight and trembling, as though he's holding back. Had Irene's hugs been a sign she was holding back? Had Beth stopped during any one of them to ask if everything was okay, might Irene have told the truth?

'Are you okay, Don?' When Beth pulls away to

ask, his hand stays firm and fatherly on her shoulder.

'I do want you to know something, Beth,' he says. 'It's a kind of odd thing to be saying here, in the middle of a cemetery, but, well . . . I am alive!' He smiles. 'I died in so many ways in that paddock forty years ago. Then I died over and over again with each passing year when you didn't come back. I had Tom and he made me keep going, but you, Beth, have brought life back into a worn-out old bugger. You've made me whole again. I love you, my Little Lissy. Let's do this together — for Irene.'

★   ★   ★

Finally, Irene's ashes are scattered beneath the linden tree with the tiny soul whose spirit has dwelled in the dust for four decades — waiting. Beth is about to crush and dispose of the dreaded purple gift bag when she remembers the ethereal woman from the funeral home. What was her name? *Jesamiah something-or-other?* She must be due a lovely bunch of flowers for starting Beth on this journey. Hopefully, she'll also be able to answer a few questions. Like how did she come by the note containing her mother's last wishes?

Beth searches the base of the bag, finding a business card that's blank on both sides. 'That's weird.'

'What have you lost?' Don asks.

'Um, I need to check the backseat of my car for something. Won't be a sec.'

With the early sun momentarily hidden behind cotton-wool-like clouds, lined silver, Beth finds herself drawn to the circular monument that had provided protection from the rain. It sits centre-stage on the grassy knoll, its domed roof gilded by the glow of early light.

'You've done well, Beth.' The voice startles her.

'Oh, hi, Rev! I've been meaning to drop by the pub to say hello, but, well, it's been a crazy time and I haven't been feeling the best, so . . . ' He nods as if he knows, which isn't possible. This is one family secret Beth's keeping from the town — for now. 'I really appreciated out chats, Rev. They helped.'

'We aim to please. I know Calingarry Crossing will be all the better for having you around. Both of you,' he adds with a wink. 'Children keep small towns young and vibrant.'

Beth groans on the inside, the huff to follow more a sign of her resignation than irritation. 'Okay, Rev, so the small-town grapevine is working overtime, but I can't stop. I'll see you around.'

'I'll be here, Beth. You need only look up anytime you want to chat.'

'Up?'

Hardly! Beth wants to add. She's wanted nothing to do with God after seeing how Valerie's warped beliefs ruined relationships. At the same time, she feels lucky. She looks down at the ladybug on the car keys in her hand — Benetta's *little midwives*. She's about to share that bit of trivia with The Rev, but he's gone. She's alone under the memorial with its brass plates set over a mosaic floor pattern so crazy and colourful it reminds her of a kid's kaleidoscope. Pausing to thank the rotunda's so-called residents for the shelter, she starts with the largest plaque at the centre, encircled by smooth pebbles and coloured glass.

> *Georgie & Jessie — forever together,*
> *on earth and in heaven.*
> *George Huckenstead*
> *Jesamiah Huckenstead*
> *Died together — 1938*
> *Forever one.*

'Huckenstead?' Beth moves to the outer section of the tiles where plaques are laid side by side. She reads all three: 'Beloved parents to Maeve. Grandparents to Gypsy. Great-grandparents to Willow.'

'Talking to yourself, Beth?' Tom's body presses against her back.

'Don't do that here!' She slaps the arms he's wrapped around her shoulders from behind and tries to pull away. 'It's Georgie and Jessie, from Dandelion House.'

'So?' Tom swivels her in the circle of his embrace. He looks bemused. 'They started the town and set aside this space for the cemetery. Guess they deserved to snaffle the prime spot. What are you doing here? I woke up and you were gone. Then I noticed the purple bag wasn't on the bedroom mantelpiece, as usual. Are you okay?'

'I am now.' She kisses him, her arms tightening around his hips. 'Remember that first day on the punt when you told me about Georgie and Jessie?' She waits for Tom's nod. 'I once met a Jesamiah Huckenstead. She's the reason I came to Calingarry Crossing.'

Tom peers over her shoulder at the central brass plate. He shrugs. 'Not this one, you didn't.'

'Obviously not, but . . . Oh, forget it. My baby brain has clearly set in already.'

'Let me get you home,' he says. 'You can put your feet up while I make breakfast.'

'Lucky me,' she says, smiling. 'I've gone from having no one to worry about me, to a life with two amazing men to fuss.' She turns her back to lean into him and shifts Tom's hands until they're cupping her belly. 'And who knows if two men will turn into three?'

45

Dawson's Run, Three Months On

The setting sun casts a peach glow over the furthest reaches of Dawson's Run. Beth is home and soon the house will be filled with family.

'Can you believe we made the tender closing date by a day, and the church is ours? One minute I'm shaking my head at how quickly Connie and I pulled this off, and the next I'm reminding myself it's taken us a lifetime to get here.'

'What's amazing for me,' Tom says, 'is seeing you and Connie together, like you've known each other for ever.'

'Like best friends.' Beth smiles, remembering the day she'd called her cousin to share the news. The church was theirs, the drama and dance studio a reality. 'Mum — both of them,' Beth clarifies, 'would be happy.'

'I think so, too,' announces Don, joining them. 'All I can say is thank goodness you came along, Beth. I didn't think Tom would ever finish this homestead's renovations. All the old place was missing was a happy family to fill its rooms.' Don raises his beer and clinks water glasses with Beth and Tom. 'To mothers!'

'And to fathers,' Beth adds. 'I so wish I remembered my time here with you, Don.'

'You were only five when you went away, but

here's to Irene and her map for sending you back.'

'Come on, my beautiful baby brain.' Tom lovingly nudges Beth into gear. 'You can put your feet up and rest before your visitors arrive.'

'Before my *family* arrives,' she corrects. 'And I don't want to rest. Sit with me?'

From where Beth and Tom cosy-up in the veranda's corner they can see Matt loading his ute, preparing to start the foundations of a relocated and revamped mini-farm.

'Is Matt taller than he was yesterday?'

Tom laughs. 'Probably. The fact he grew into new boots every year made mail-order Christmas presents easy.' When Beth says nothing, Tom cranes his neck to look at her, probably checking for tears. His finger stops on her cheek. 'Are you thinking about your mum's Christmas box?'

'I am. When Angela asked me over to see the contents for myself, I never imagined the Christmas label written on that old box to be anything other than decorations. I remember Irene was always knitting or crocheting something. But to have made a new jumper to size, gift-wrapping one every Christmas and hiding it away . . .'

'I wonder why she stopped at twenty-one?' Tom says.

Beth sighs. 'You can add that to the list of questions without answers.'

'At least you-know-who will find one extra present under the tree each Christmas.' Tom's finger spirals out from Beth's navel. 'And we'll make sure he or she knows Grandma Irene was

477

the knitting nana. Come on, mother-to-be, time to make a move.' Tom's shrill whistle gets Matt's attention. 'Time to wash up, Matt,' he calls. 'You can get back to your project tomorrow.'

'You must've been like him when you were young,' Beth says as she straightens and stretches.

'You mean hard-working and handsome?'

'Ha! If you say so.' She cups Tom's face, peering deep into his eyes. 'Part of me wishes I remembered us as kids.'

'Me too. You might've played Doctors and Nurses with me.' Tom grins, until her elbow jabs his ribs. 'Ouch!'

'And I would've let you ride my horse,' she says. 'I do like that we were mates for a while.'

'Friends before lovers. No better foundation,' Tom says. 'I rather like the idea of fate bringing us back together.'

'Fate? Silver linings?' Beth shakes her head. 'I assume if you're into all that stuff, you wouldn't baulk at the name Destiny?'

'If it's a boy I might have a problem.' Tom grins. 'I, on the other hand, was thinking Patience might be suitable for a girl.'

Beth flattens a hand to her belly. 'And I'm reminded every day how patient and understanding you are. I got lucky with you, Tom Dawson.'

'Lucky? Now, there's a great boy's name. Lucky Dawson.' He moves swiftly to avoid another jab to his ribs. 'Seriously, Beth, I know you've had a lot going on, and still do. I don't mind waiting my turn, and there's no rush to get officially hitched, as long as it stays on the To-Do List and I get to be Dad.'

'No argument there,' Beth assures him. 'You are Dad, but I'm grateful I can avoid the stigma of being an unmarried mother, and that I get to choose what I want and when. Although it remains to be seen how many people want to tut-tut about me getting myself pregnant in my forties.'

Tom's eyes narrow with thought. 'Um, you didn't get yourself pregnant. You had help, remember?'

'Ah, yes, I forgot. An out-of-date condom.'

'Yes, well,' Tom colours, 'I wasn't going through them at a rate of knots. Surely I get bonus points for that?'

'You get bonus points for lots of reasons, Tom Dawson.' Beth laughs, but she's pensive.

The mother-daughter bond Beth never thought she'd experience, will go some way towards her understanding the challenge her two mums faced — challenges hard for Beth to fathom as a forty-one-year-old mother-to-be. So many young girls were forced into a secret world of shame. Others made spur-of-the-moment, life-changing decisions — their hearts irreparably broken and so many lives ruined with regret.

Now Dandelion House has let go of its last secret, Beth hopes the truth will give Gypsy the respect she deserves. The woman with a heart of gold had been so much more than Calingarry Crossing's crazy lady.

Gypsy might have been in Irene's and Lissy's lives for a mere blink in time, but when needed she was the mother they screamed for at the height of their pain; the friend they cried with at the depth of their despair, and when it came to making a choice, Gypsy had granted their wishes. In the case of little Linden, when a distraught, young Irene couldn't find the courage, Gypsy had visited a forgotten part of the cemetery and wept for her.

Valerie would be remembered, but for different reasons. With Beth still listed as Next of Kin with the nursing home, a note had arrived advising she was sole beneficiary of Valerie's estate and to contact Saddleton Solicitors. The money was put to good use, along with a contribution from Rosa, after Armenti's was snapped up by the neighbouring vineyard for an extraordinary price. Following the sale, Benetta settled into a retirement village — starting a wine appreciation club — and Cheryl and Rosa booked cabins on an over-fifty-five-singles cruise around the Pacific.

Beth's phone beeps out a message. Connie and Rosa are an hour away.

'An hour!' Beth wants to squeal.

★　★　★

'Do you credit fate with making Connie a dance teacher?' Beth asks Tom, as they ferry bowls of food from the ute to Don's veranda.

'And soon-to-be proud part-owner of the Lissy Linden School of Dance and Drama,' he says. 'Not that this town needs any more drama. What do you reckon, Unc?'

Don sets an orange juice on the table in front of Cheryl. 'I reckon these flowers don't need any more arranging, that's for sure. Drink your juice, Cheryl, and stop fussing. You've done enough.

The place is looking better than it ever has.'

'You've both been amazing,' Beth says, on her way to Don. But she stops short of a hug, bracing herself with a hand on his good arm and grunting an *'Ooomph!'* before taking Don's hand and pressing it against her belly. 'That was a big one.'

'Popcorn?' Don asks.

'Or stone skipping.' She grins, then straightens up to plant a peck on his cheek. 'I'm so thankful for the stories about you and Lissy,' she says. 'But mostly for being so strong and living on. You've been there for Tom, and you're here for me today.'

'For you and Popcorn,' Don says. 'Every day until my last breath, my darling Little Lissy.'

'Look! There!' Tom announces.

Don, Cheryl, Beth and Tom gaze across the fields of Dawson's Run, towards the hills that herald the start of town. There's a welcome dust cloud on the horizon and it brings with it a new beginning.

Christmas in Calingarry Crossing will be big and busy, and Don's huge outdoor table will come alive, surrounded by happy noise. While not all connected by blood, they are more family than ever because they had a choice and they chose each other.

Acknowledgements

2019 — what a year you've been! The J and I swam with sharks, towed Myrtle the Turtle across The Great Australian Bight, and zip lined over the Daintree rainforest. But our greatest achievement has to be this book, even though I suffered from self-doubt throughout the entire process. That's when The J would remind me turtles only get somewhere when they take a risk and stick their necks out. And so Wild Myrtle Press was born, and the lonely self-publishing process was punctuated by some special people:

Sharyn Rees and Janine Kimberly, whose wonderfully serendipitous catchups and chats about 'sprequals' kept me on track.

Awesome authors, Kathryn Ledson (my caped crusader) and Di Blacklock, whose editing scissors trimmed and tidied my early, unwieldy manuscript. (Any mistakes are obviously mine.) Also, Pamela Cook (I'll be seeing you at the *OMG-We-Did-It Awards* with Lana Peherczyk **(Pe-her-check)**.

Jenny and Terry Harris: I did it! I wrote monumental stonemasonry (and Wally) into a novel.

My 'silver lining pals', Shannon Garner, Marie Barrett and Michelle Gobbels: the love and positive energy you both bring to our world helps us and Wild Myrtle Press stick our necks out.

And to you, my lovely readers, for buying

my books, for sharing your love of reading with others, and for inspiring me to keep telling my kind of small-town stories.

We do hope that you have enjoyed reading this large print book.

Did you know that all of our titles are available for purchase?

We publish a wide range of high quality large print books including:
Romances, Mysteries, Classics
General Fiction
Non Fiction and Westerns

Special interest titles available in large print are:
The Little Oxford Dictionary
Music Book
Song Book
Hymn Book
Service Book

Also available from us courtesy of Oxford University Press:
Young Readers' Dictionary
(large print edition)
Young Readers' Thesaurus
(large print edition)

For further information or a free brochure, please contact us at:
Ulverscroft Large Print Books Ltd.,
The Green, Bradgate Road, Anstey,
Leicester, LE7 7FU, England.
Tel: (00 44) 0116 236 4325
Fax: (00 44) 0116 234 0205

SMALL MERCIES

Richard Anderson

After enduring months of extreme drought on their modest freehold, farming couple Dimple and Ruthie face uncertain times on more than one front. Ruthie receives the news every woman dreads. Meanwhile, Wally Oliver, a wealthy landowner, appears on the local radio station warning small farmers that they are doomed, and the sooner they leave the land to large operators like him, the better. Bracing for a fight on all fronts, Dimple and Ruthie decide to take a road trip to confront Oliver. Along the way, not only is their resolve tested, but their relationship as well. Desperate not to dwell on the past but to face up to the future, Dimple and Ruthie make a crucial decision they soon regret. And when the storm clouds finally roll in across the land they love, there's more than rain to contend with.

THERE WAS STILL LOVE

Favel Parrett

Prague, 1938: Eva flies down the street. A man steps out suddenly. Eva runs into him and hits the pavement hard. His anger slaps her, but his hate will change all, as war forces so many lives into small brown suitcases . . . Prague, 1980: Young Ludek is free. And he sees everything. The world can go to hell for all he cares, because Babi is waiting for him in the warm flat. She IS his whole world . . . Melbourne, 1980: Mala Liska's grandma holds her hand as they climb the stairs to their third-floor flat. Here, Mana and Bill have made a life for themselves and their granddaughter. A life imbued with the spirit of Prague and the loved ones left behind. Because there is still love, no matter what.

A YEAR AT HOTEL GONDOLA

Nicky Pellegrino

Kat Black has never lived a quiet life. She's an adventurer: a food writer travelling the world visiting far-flung places and eating unusual things. Now she's about to embark on her biggest adventure yet — a relationship. She has fallen in love with an Italian man and is moving to Venice for a year to help him run his guesthouse, Hotel Gondola, where she hopes to put down some roots for the first time in years. Kat will write all about her adventure: the food she eats, the recipes she collects, the people she meets, and the man she doesn't know all that well but is going to make a life with. But as Kat ought to know by now, the thing about adventures is that they never go the way you expect them to . . .

CHANGE OF SEASON

Anna Jacobs

Rosalind and her husband Paul move from Australia to England due to his job with a multinational company. But Paul is called away to deal with a crisis in Hong Kong, and Rosalind is left to settle in a new country on her own. One by one her three grown children need help, and there is only Rosalind available, because as usual Paul puts his job first. When she finds out that her husband has been unfaithful for years, it appears to be the final blow to their marriage, especially as she has met another man. Rosalind's confidence grows as she wins acclaim as an embroidery artist and comes into an inheritance. Will her loyalty keep her with her husband, or will Paul get more than he'd bargained for with the new independent Rosalind?